This story contains depictions of domestic abuse outside of the primary relationship, including one nonconsensual sex scene.

HIS RELUCTANT COWBOY

A.M. ARTHUR

carina
press

carina
press®

Recycling programs
for this product may
not exist in your area.

ISBN-13: 978-1-335-44868-2

His Reluctant Cowboy

For questions and comments about the quality of this book, please contact us at CustomerService@Harlequin.com.

Carina Press
22 Adelaide St. West, 41st Floor
Toronto, Ontario M5H 4E3, Canada
www.CarinaPress.com

Printed in U.S.A.

HIS RELUCTANT COWBOY

Chapter One

Two things became incredibly clear to Michael Pearce as he regained consciousness: first, his left cheek was stuck to the faux leather cushion of his living room's sofa, probably from drool; and second, he was clutching a half-chewed rawhide close to his chest like a safety blanket.

The first thing kind of made sense. In the two weeks since Kenny had left him and taken their dog, Rosco, with him, Michael didn't always sleep in their bedroom. At first, it had hurt too much to sleep in their room, which had still smelled like Kenny's cologne. Now Michael was just used to the couch. But he usually remembered a pillow and blanket. What had he done last night to fall flat on his face?

Oh yeah. The finalized divorce papers had shown up. The booze came out. Michael had gone out and found company, fucked his sorrows away, and then drunk more before passing out in the living room.

Classy. Real classy, asshole.

He peeled his face off the couch cushion and attempted to sit up. His stomach sloshed dangerously, and he contemplated whether the bathroom or the kitchen sink was closer. Fortunately, last night's booze fest stayed put for now. He stared at the rawhide and more bits of last night came back to him. Stumbling home wasted. Tripping and falling on the expensive Persian rug, kind of hoping he barfed all over it because Kenny had picked it out and Michael had never liked it. Seeing the rawhide under the couch. Missing his dog so much he'd started bawling.

Apparently, he'd crawled onto the couch and cried himself to sleep with the rawhide in his hands. Definitely not his finest moment. Oh well. Not as if it was the least dignified thing he'd ever done in his forty-one years on earth. He and Kenny had hosted some insane parties in this house over the years, but that was all over now. Most of Michael's friends here in Austin had been Kenny's friends first, and they'd all taken Kenny's side during the separation.

Didn't matter that Michael's creativity and experience had made them their fortune. Money they spent lavishly on this fucking house and their fucking friends. Money Michael no longer had access to, thanks to his idiot, in-love self not paying attention to the contract he'd signed with Kenny when their app first took off. A contract that cut Michael out of the profits if their partnership ever dissolved.

Which it had, about a month ago, when he caught Kenny cheating on him. For as much as Michael had loved Kenny once, and for as amazing as it had been being rich after growing up on a failing ranch, Michael missed his dog the most.

He put the rawhide on a side table and stood, his target the bathroom and a nice hot shower to wash last night's funk off his skin. He also kind of had to pee and his mouth tasted like ass—and not in the good way—so his toothbrush was a priority. Naturally, his cell phone rang somewhere in the house.

Michael always thought of not answering a call—or at least looking at the number—as leaving work unfinished, so he abandoned the bathroom trip in favor of searching out his phone. He found it on the floor of the kitchen. County Hospital, with a Texas exchange. His old home county.

With a wiggle of dread in his gut, Michael answered. "Hello?"

"Is this Michael Pearce?" a feminine voice asked.

"Yes, it is."

"Mr. Pearce, my name is Susan, and I'm a patient advocate at Claire County Hospital. I have you listed as Elmer Pearce's emergency contact."

Oh God, the old man's kicked it. "Yes, I'm his son. Is he dead?"

"No, he's stable at the moment. Mr. Pearce, your father had a stroke early this morning. He was found by a neighbor and rushed to our emergency room, where we were able to stabilize him. He's been briefly conscious, but we still don't know the extent of the damage from the stroke."

Michael stared at a pretentious portrait he'd never liked, but Kenny had insisted they buy. Honestly, for a flaming gay man, Kenny had the worst taste in home decor, but Michael had indulged him. Why hadn't he taken the damned painting and left Rosco?

"Mr. Pearce?"

"What? Sorry."

"I understand this can be upsetting news." She rattled off a few things Michael's hungover brain couldn't make a lot of sense of, until she got to: "He has some paralysis on his right side, so he will need help at home once he's discharged. At least for a little while."

His gut clenched and he moved closer to the kitchen sink. "Paralysis?"

"It's not uncommon with stroke victims, but as I said before, it's early hours and we're still assessing him. He can, of course, receive visitors. I can give you the address if—"

"No, I grew up there, I know where it is. I'm, um, in Austin, so it'll be a while before I can get up there."

"Of course. He'll likely be out of the ER and in a room by the time you arrive, so you can ask at the main desk."

"Thanks, I guess."

He ended the call and put his phone on the counter, brain whirling with too many things he needed to do. Pack a bag. Figure out how to get there. Flying into Amarillo was obviously faster, but by the time he found a flight with enough time to get through TSA, he'd probably be just as well off driving the eight or so hours to his home county. He'd have his own car, instead of driving around in his father's dusty old truck.

A dusty old truck Michael had tried to replace more than once over the years, but Elmer wouldn't take his money. And not because the money had come from a gay dating app. Elmer was just too proud to accept financial help from anyone, even his own estranged son. So he made his metal folk art and clung to a huge piece of land he really didn't need, out of stubbornness and spite. And Michael had stayed in Austin, living the life he thought he wanted to live.

Until everything had come crashing down.

Michael gazed around the huge chrome and white

kitchen and no longer saw himself in it. Having and spending money was wonderful when you were used to being poor, like he'd grown up back in Weston. Having a refrigerator that talked to him seemed like the best thing in the world. Every new gadget, every great invention was scattered around this house. A house Kenny had abandoned for another man with even more money and an even bigger house.

Michael hadn't wanted to contest the divorce. Between the cheating he could prove and the intellectual property theft he couldn't, Michael simply wanted things over as quickly and cleanly as possible, so they'd filed no fault and let their lawyers divide up their (shockingly meager) assets. Michael got the house and half their joint account, which hadn't amounted to much in the way of cash after the mortgage, car payment, and lawyer fees. And with the way Kenny had fucked him over on the business side of things, his personal account wasn't going up anytime soon. Not until he sold the house.

Maybe a week or two back home in Weston, taking care of his father for a while, was what he needed to clear his head and stop cuddling with a dog's rawhide toy. Take a break from the life he thought he wanted and get his priorities back in order. His only real issue, though, was money. Until the house sold, he had a couple of hundred in his personal account to last him. It would get him to Weston, though. And stretch further there than here in the city.

If worse came to worst, he could get a job. A regular, working-class job and forget his lavish, rich man lifestyle for a while. Figure out who he wanted to be in this new chapter of his life. Maybe even rebuild his relationship with his father. If such a thing was possible.

After a quick shower, two rounds of puking, a piece of dry toast, and throwing a bunch of clothes and toiletries into three suitcases, Michael packed up his Audi and hit the road. He'd left a handful of sentimental items behind, including a bottle of one-hundred-year-old Scotch given to him as a gift two Christmases ago, but once the house sold he'd either be back in Austin for good, or he'd fly down to clear things out. Whatever. He'd think about it later.

All he could think about right now was his dad. A man he hadn't seen in twenty years and rarely spoke to, but still loved and admired for his tenacity. His ability to live life as he saw fit, no matter what others thought of him. Growing up, Michael had tried not to care how others perceived him, but that had led to a lot of bullying in high school for being gay. He'd wanted to be accepted and wasn't, so he'd fled to a big city as soon as possible. Made a lot of money. Made a lot of friends.

Friends who'd dumped his ass the moment he lost both Kenny and the fame and notoriety that came with their app's success.

Assholes.

With two ginger ales from a local convenience store and a box of saltine crackers, Michael hit the highway and drove north. He drove past exit signs, trucker plazas, dry land, green foliage, hills and flatlands, and all manner of things. One pit stop when the ginger ale needed to be released, and he tempted his still-queasy stomach with a plain hamburger that stayed down.

Hangovers were the worst any day, but on a day spent driving? Ugh.

Signs for Amarillo began popping up, and on the outskirts, Michael took the exit toward the county hospital and Weston itself. His eyes were sandy, his back hurt, and all he wanted was a nap, but he got his tired ass to the hospital around five that evening. Parked. A lady at the front desk told him where to go.

It was a small hospital and he found Elmer's room pretty easily. The first bed was empty, but Elmer snored away in the second. The wires and leads disturbed him less than seeing the way his dad had aged in the last two decades. More wrinkles on his face, more gray in his hair. Michael's heart ached for his dad and for himself, because they'd both lost so much. And that loss had separated them for a long, long time.

Existing together with that pain had been too hard, too stifling. Separation had been for the best—or so he thought.

Seeing Elmer again in person shifted something inside of him. Even if they never forgave each other for the awful things they'd both said that last, fateful night, Michael would make sure his dad got through this. He'd come out of it the same independent, stubborn old man he used to be, period.

Michael would do everything he possibly could to make sure that happened.

Josiah Sheridan unlocked the front door of the house, heart galloping in his chest, even though his was the only car in the driveway. More than once over the last year or so, Seamus had parked his car elsewhere in order to surprise Josiah, usually when Seamus thought Josiah had done something wrong and needed a lesson. But Josiah had been on his best behavior these last few months; he'd been careful ever since the big blowup the night Brand Woods was stabbed.

As the county sheriff, Seamus McBride couldn't have just walked away without stepping in, no matter how much he disliked the Woods family. Even though Josiah was a CNA and had an ingrained need to help people in trouble, Seamus hadn't liked him meddling.

He'd shown Josiah how much the next day.

But Brand was alive, recovered, and apparently living with one of the other hands on his family's cattle ranch. Josiah was secretly happy for the pair and wished them all the best. Openly, he pretended to dislike their "chosen lifestyle" as much as Seamus did, because that's the lie they told the world. Even though Seamus had been regularly—and not always permissibly—fucking Josiah for nearly two years now, Seamus was firmly planted within the "gay is evil" Sunday crowd.

Some days Josiah longed for the freedom to simply be himself, but he had nowhere else to go and no money to get there.

He went down the hallway to the guest room he still kept his things in for appearances' sake and changed from his scrubs to shorts and a T-shirt. Seamus didn't like him sitting around the house in his scrubs. "They make me think of sick people," he'd often said, "and I don't need that after a long shift."

Josiah didn't particularly need most of Seamus's shit after a long day at work, either, but Seamus was bigger, stronger, and knew where to hit so Josiah didn't have visible bruises. It was safer to keep his snark and complaints to himself. After a quick glance into their bedroom, the bathroom, and the tiny closet of a room Seamus used as an office, Josiah relaxed a bit. No Seamus.

As the sheriff, Seamus's hours were sometimes all over the place, since he was always on call for emergencies, which worked well with Josiah's own flexible work hours. Today had been his last day tending to Mrs. Wellington, who was being moved into a nursing home as they spoke. Her family had decided it was best for her final few months of care, since she was dying from cervical cancer and had signed a DNR.

Josiah eyeballed the cabinet where Seamus kept his favorite liquors, tempted to take a shot of whiskey in Mrs. Wellington's honor. He cared about all his patients, but the end-of-life ones got to him the most. He was simply glad she had a lot of family around to support her in her final days and weeks.

Not like me. If I was dying tomorrow, no one would be there.

Those thoughts didn't hurt like they used to. He'd simply adapted to being isolated and lonely, and to putting up a front for his clients so they didn't see how desperate he was to get out. To get away and start over. To be someone else, anyone else for a little while. To know what it felt like to be truly wanted and loved.

He hadn't felt like that since Andy. A lifetime ago.

Unwilling to wander down that particular stretch of memory lane right now, Josiah checked on the slow cooker meal he'd prepped that morning. He'd mastered those kinds of foods so there was always a hot meal waiting for Seamus, even if he got home before Josiah. It saved bruises later. The food looked undisturbed, so Seamus hadn't been home recently, and it was already close to seven. Josiah scooped out a bowl of meat and potatoes, and he ate alone at the kitchen table in the silent house. Silent save the faint tick of the kitchen's wall clock. For as lonely as he was most days, even with someone else in the house, Josiah treasured these quiet moments alone.

He ate his dinner, then put his bowl and fork in the dishwasher. Drank a glass of water, even though he really wanted one of Seamus's beers. Eyeballed the liquor cabinet once more before going into the bathroom to shower and clean himself out. Seamus was erratic in when he wanted sex, but he was also, well, anal about cleanliness, and it was easier to stay ready than to worry about Seamus using the enema shower attachment on him.

After getting squeaky clean inside and out, he checked his phone. A text from his boss about a possible new client, a stroke patient who'd be in hospital for a few more days but who might need extra care family couldn't provide. Josiah texted back that he was interested, especially now that his schedule was open. Seamus frequently said that Josiah didn't have to work, but Josiah loved what he did. He needed the distance and distraction from the nightmare of his home life too much to give up his career. And he refused to be wholly dependent on Seamus if he ever hoped to escape.

For now, he was stuck here and it was no one's fault but his own.

With nothing left to distract himself, Josiah settled in the living room and kept streaming an Australian medical show that had aired over a decade ago. He couldn't even remember how he'd stumbled onto it, but he'd been intrigued by a show in a setting where patients just…received care. No worries about insurance or bankruptcy or co-pays. Plus, the accents were sexy as hell, even on the female characters.

He was about to learn the diagnosis for one particularly tricky patient when tires crunched the gravel outside. Lights flashed in the windows before shutting off. Dread tightened Josiah's stomach. Seamus was home. He paused his show and fled for the kitchen, got a bowl and fork, and he was scooping food into it when Seamus strode inside.

Once upon a time, Josiah had considered Seamus handsome. Now his smiles always seemed sinister, his touches one small squeeze from painful. To the residents of this county, he was a hero and the man in charge of keeping them safe. To Josiah, he was a walking time bomb.

"Smells good," Seamus said. "You eat?"

"A little while ago. I wasn't sure when you'd be home."

"Okay." He calmly put his service weapon in the lockbox he kept inside one of the cabinets, every motion smooth and without malice. As if he was in an actual good mood for a change. "Give me a beer."

Josiah deposited both the bowl of food and a chilled, open beer on the table at the same time as Seamus sat to eat his dinner. A very late dinner, but Josiah wasn't going to mention it. He hovered nearby, unsure if Seamus wanted company or to be left alone. Some nights he simply couldn't read the man or his intentions. Not in the last few months. Not since the stabbing. It was almost as if Brand Woods openly living his life in a gay relationship was personally offensive to Seamus.

Or it made him feel trapped in his own environment. Josiah had been out of the closet for years before Seamus shoved him back inside and slammed the door. Locked it. And he wanted to get back out again, but deep down he knew that wouldn't happen while he lived here. While he let Seamus…use him. Seamus had to come to terms with his own sexuality and stop hiding. But Josiah had a funny feeling that was never going to happen.

Right now, they shared the same closet and it was slowly suffocating him.

A stifling closet was, most days, better than the street, though.

"Do you need salt or pepper?" Josiah asked after Seamus took his first bite of dinner. Seamus preferred to season his own food, so Josiah was sparse in adding too much of either when he cooked. Having to chew on a mouthful of black pepper for thirty seconds because he'd accidentally overspiced a steak was an experience he would never, ever forget.

"No, it's good," Seamus replied. "Get yourself a drink."

That was not a question, so Josiah fetched himself a glass of water to sip while Seamus ate. "I might have a lead on a new job coming up. Elmer Pearce had a stroke early this morning, and he'll likely need home care for a while. Hayes asked if I'd be interested."

"And you said yes."

Again, not a question. "I did. I've met Mr. Pearce, and now that Mrs. Wellington is going into a nursing home, my schedule is clear. I'd like to take the job."

"Nights or days?"

"I'm not sure. Everything happened today, and Hayes is coordinating with a social worker. Apparently, Mr. Pearce has a son who is coming into town but I don't know how long he'll stay."

Seamus forked a bite of meat. "Okay. Keep me informed."

"I will." The low-key reaction surprised Josiah and lowered his alertness level a few degrees. "How was your day?"

"It was a day. Broke up a brawl over at the Roost this afternoon, which is why I'm so late. Ramie insisted she hadn't overserved either of them, so they probably just got into it over a woman. Got 'em both cooling off in lockup overnight."

Ramie was one of the main bartenders at the Red Roost, and she knew better than to overserve her guests. A night in the drunk tank would probably do those two brawling idiots a world of good. "At least no one was stabbed this time." As soon as the statement slipped out, Josiah regretted the reminder of that night.

Seamus didn't seem angry, though. He simply kept eating, paying more attention to his phone than to Josiah, so Josiah sipped his water and watched his "roommate" eat. He wasn't sure what to call Seamus anymore. *Roommate* was real to the rest of the world. *Lover* had been right for a very brief period of time before Josiah realized Seamus didn't actually love him. Seamus used him for his own needs, Josiah's needs be damned. Once in a while, Seamus was sweet and doting like a proper boyfriend, but it never lasted.

I'm an object, something to use, and I need to get out before he destroys me. But I have nowhere else to go.

No family, no real friends to rely on. He'd kept up a very casual text friendship with Hugo Turner ever since Brand was stabbed, but that was it. He was isolated here, exactly how Seamus liked him. Existing without really living.

"If Elmer ends up needing care," Josiah hedged, "do you mind if I take the job?"

"No, I like the man. And it's not too far from home. I can think of worse people to care for."

Josiah swallowed back a comment about judging who deserved health care based on their background or whatever and sipped his water. No sense in provoking a fight, especially when Seamus seemed to be in a good mood. "Do you want coffee? I can make a pot."

"Coffee sounds great. Make enough for yourself."

He wasn't a huge fan, especially this late at night, but Josiah did as asked. He waited by the brewing pot while Seamus continued eating, and he had two mugs on the table by the time Seamus's bowl was empty. "Do you want more?" Josiah asked.

"No, that's fine."

Josiah exchanged the bowl and fork for the mug of coffee, still slightly unnerved by how calm Seamus was tonight. No yelling, no blustering, no demands. He reminded Josiah of the man he'd first met two years ago. The man he thought he was renting a room from. Nothing like the man he eventually turned into. The man Josiah both cared about and feared.

"Sit," Seamus said. "Drink your coffee."

The quiet demands sent Josiah into autopilot. After putting Seamus's bowl and fork in the dishwasher, he sat across from him with his own mug of black coffee. Josiah used to prefer sweet drinks with syrups and whipped cream to black coffee, but Seamus had disabused him of that habit quickly. *Cheap* and *simple* were two of Seamus's favorite words.

Didn't matter that he had both of their incomes at his disposal.

"Do you want a toothpick?" Josiah asked.

"Sure." Seamus was busy reading something on his

phone, so Josiah took his time getting a toothpick from the box in the cabinet. Walking back to the table with it. Placing the toothpick next to Seamus's coffee mug. Sitting in the chair opposite Seamus at the round table.

Josiah sipped at his coffee while Seamus drank his, did something on his phone and picked at his teeth. Familiar things, sure, but it was all almost too easy. Too quiet. Josiah was braced for an explosion of some kind.

An explosion that never happened. After finishing his coffee, Seamus quietly went into the living room to watch TV. Josiah cleaned up their mugs, wiped down the table, put all leftovers away, including a portion for Seamus to take for lunch tomorrow, and then set the dishwasher to run. After thirty seconds of talking himself into it, Josiah followed Seamus into the living room.

Some science fiction movie they'd seen before was playing on the television, which relaxed Josiah even more. Old favorites meant Seamus was in a good mood, unlikely to lash out or demand anything from Josiah tonight. When Seamus raised his arm and beckoned Josiah to join him, Josiah did, settling on the couch next to his...*boyfriend*? *Roommate?* He never knew what word to apply to Seamus.

Whatever the label, they existed together in peace that night.

Precious, fleeting peace Josiah clung to for as long as possible.

Chapter Two

Michael didn't pull into the driveway of his childhood home until after ten that night, and his entire body hurt from so much sitting and driving in one single day. Not to mention the still-lingering remnants of last night's binge. Dad hadn't woken up for the hour or so Michael had visited before a nurse politely asked him to leave, and that was okay. He'd probably do better seeing and talking to Dad after a good night's sleep.

The property had become almost twice as cluttered in the twenty years since Michael had last seen it. More metal artwork along the fence line, more iron sculptures in the yard of various animals and a few abstract things he couldn't begin to name. The fifth wheel was still parked in the side yard, lights off and probably empty of tenants, since the only other vehicle there was Dad's trusty old 1955 Ford truck with Elmer Fudd painted on the hood.

Michael had several bags with him, but the only one he grabbed was his overnight nylon bag for now. He still had a key, but the sagging, ancient two-story home wasn't locked. The paramedics who'd scooped Dad up and run probably hadn't thought to bother. Not that burglary was a high crime out here in the middle of nowhere. While Weston and Daisy probably had their fair share of drug addicts looking for something to steal, there wasn't a pawnshop within thirty miles to hock their shit.

He let himself into the cluttered living room, not surprised to see previously empty spaces filled with boxes of metal and spare parts and all kinds of things Michael didn't have the energy to identify tonight. A half-finished puzzle of a tranquil lake scene took up most of the dining room table. The wedding photo of Dad and Mom still hung on the wall, the frame dusty and glass filmy from age. Dad had never been the best housekeeper, but the state of the place made his nose twitch and skin crawl, especially after living with Kenny and his OCD about cleanliness.

Whatever, that was a problem for tomorrow.

Michael chugged down a glass of water from the kitchen spigot, forever grateful they had their own well, then took a second glass upstairs with him. Every single step creaked with age, and one groaned so loud he half expected his foot to fall through. The place had seriously fallen into disrepair since Michael had last been here, and it was likely to collapse if Dad didn't do something.

Again, another problem for tomorrow. Or maybe next week, depending on Dad's condition and recovery expectations. A stroke was a big fucking deal.

His old bedroom was still a mix of Michael's own things and other crap Dad had added to it in the form of sculptures and boxes of more clutter. The bed was only slightly musty so Dad had to have been changing the sheets every once in a while, and there wasn't too much dust on surfaces. The Green Day and Foo Fighters posters were still on the walls, probably brittle enough to crumble if Michael dared take them down. He'd grown up in this room, had his first girl-kiss in this room, and realized he was very much gay in this room.

Let a much older family friend who'd had too much to drink take his virginity in this room. At least he could take comfort knowing that pervy old bastard had died of pancreatic cancer a few years ago.

Michael shoved those thoughts away, opened a window for some fresh air, and got ready for bed. His entire body and soul were exhausted after being dumped, going on a bender, and losing his dog, and now he had to figure out how to care for his dad for an unknown length of time, all while selling his overly expensive home back in Austin. More thoughts for tomorrow.

He changed his clothes, brushed his teeth, drank more water, and finally settled in his lumpy, somewhat stale bed, but when he shut off the light, it was too fucking quiet. Not a cricket, not a fan whirring, not even passing traffic. So he downloaded a noise machine app on his phone and set it to Play. The constant, soothing sound helped ease him into sleep for a little while, only to wake to the jarring noise of someone pounding on something downstairs.

He leaped from the bed, chilled by the cool air trickling in from the open window, and hauled ass downstairs, vaguely aware the sun was starting to rise. Disoriented and a little concerned, he grabbed what looked like part of a jack handle and held it by his side like a baseball bat as he approached the front door. Peeked around the pleated sunflower-pattern curtains his mother had sewn a lifetime ago.

A tall man in a sheriff's uniform and a belt too tight

around the middle stood there, sunglasses on but hat in his hands. Waiting. No flashing lights on the car, which eased Michael's apprehension a fraction and he put his weapon down. Unlocked and opened the door. "Can I help you?"

"Sorry to disturb the house so early," the man said, "but I was passing by and happened to see your vehicle. I'm Sheriff Seamus McBride."

"Michael Pearce. Can I do something for you, Sheriff?"

"I take it you're related to Elmer Pearce?"

"Yes, he's my father. I got the call yesterday about his stroke and drove up from Austin. I didn't realize staying at my father's house was suspicious."

McBride's eyebrow twitched. "Under normal circumstances, no, but your father had a burglary a few months ago. I was simply trying to watch out for the property while he's in hospital."

Even though Michael's irritation was rising, he didn't want to pick a fight with a sheriff. "I appreciate the attention, sir. I'm in town for the foreseeable future, so you're likely to see my car out and about. I'll be figuring out my father's future care."

"Good, good. Helps to have family around when you're ill."

"Yes, it does. And may I ask about the burglary issue? My dad and I aren't very close and this is the first I'm hearing about it."

"An issue with an ex-con, who is rightly back in prison. Stole something from your father to set up an innocent man, but the property has been returned. Nothing to do with what's going on now. And again, sorry to disturb you. Welcome back to Weston, Mr.

Pearce." McBride put his hat on, tipped it politely, and headed back to his car.

Michael waited until the man left the property before closing the door and locking it. Growing up, they'd never locked the front door. Not once, even when going away for a few days to a cattle or feed show a day's drive away. But someone had broken in recently, and Michael wasn't going to risk his safety or Dad's property.

He set the old coffeepot to brew while he took a fast shower. The upstairs bathroom had a claw-foot tub with an awkward shower attachment and plastic shower liners that hung on an oval ceiling ring and clung to his skin if he let too much steam rise in the small room. Fast was best.

Since visiting hours didn't start until ten and he wasn't keen on the box of wheat biscuit cereal in Dad's cupboard, Michael poured his coffee into the first travel mug he could find, then headed to Weston's only diner for breakfast, drinking his coffee along the way to try and wake up. He got a seat at the counter, since most of the booths were taken, and ordered more coffee from a young blonde named Shelby.

"Don't know your face, honey," Shelby said as she poured piping hot coffee into the same brown ceramic mug every diner in the country seemed to favor. "Passing through?"

"Something like that. Visiting family for a while." He pointed at the oversize menu of breakfast items. "Anything you recommend?"

Her smile brightened. "You can't go wrong with Donnie's classic breakfast platter. Two eggs, two sausage patties, home fries, and toast."

Donnie wasn't in the diner's name, so that had to be the current cook. "Sounds fine. I'll take the eggs scrambled, whites only. And can I swap the sausage for some sort of fruit cup?"

Shelby scribbled on her notepad. "We can do that. I'll put the order in for you."

"Thank you, miss." Michael hated being a fussy eater sometimes but he wasn't going to eat crap just because he was back in the sticks again. Especially now that he was single for the first time since graduating college. Not that he was on the hunt but it was a lot easier to gain weight than to lose it, especially after forty.

No, that was Kenny talking, whispering in his ear about looking his best at all times. He could eat what he wanted, damn it.

He sipped his black coffee and studied the specials board above the counter, his only other view straight ahead into the busy kitchen. He'd heard too many stories from friends in food service over the years to truly want to see how his food was being prepared; all he wanted was to eat it. This morning's visit from Sheriff McBride still bothered him and he couldn't put his finger on exactly why. On one hand, he appreciated the sheriff taking care with the property of the locals; on the other hand, it was a little creepy. Did he act that way every time a neighbor had a guest?

The food arrived fast and after slathering his home fries and eggs with ketchup, Michael tore into his breakfast, hungrier than he thought for some decent home-style cooking. Shelby refilled his coffee twice. Considering how busy the place was, she was on top of things with every customer at the counter, and even a few at tables and booths. Something about her seemed vaguely familiar but he couldn't put his finger on why. She was way too young to have gone to school with him.

He was finishing his last piece of toast and orange marmalade when a young man strode into the place with an upset blonde girl in his arms, maybe five years old. The man went right to the counter where Shelby was wiping her hands on a towel and handed the girl over. "I'm so sorry to drop her off early, baby," the young man said, "but Hugo's got some kinda food poisoning, Brand is out at a meeting with a possible new vendor for the beef, and I need to get to work."

Shelby bounced the little girl on her hip, her expression clearly unhappy with this turn of events, and Michael tried not to stare. "It's fine. My shift ends in an hour anyway. Susie can play in the office for a while."

"Thank you, you're the best. Love you both." He kissed Shelby and Susie on the forehead before turning and leaving as quickly as he'd come.

"They have got to get more help at that ranch," another waitress said to Shelby as she came by with a tray of food to deliver to tables.

"They're trying," Shelby replied.

"What ranch?" Michael asked without thinking.

"Woods Ranch. It's my husband's family's place, and they've been having trouble keeping a full staff for about a year now. Men come and go, but it's hard to find really qualified rustlers right now."

"Sorry to hear that." Now he realized why Shelby and the young man who'd delivered Susie were familiar. For a long time after their falling-out, Dad had sent Michael clippings about local goings-on in Weston and nearby towns, and he'd gotten the marriage announcement for Remington and Shelby Woods, complete with a photo. Woods Ranch was one of the largest in the county, and when Michael was a child, it had employed quite a lot of workers. But ranching was getting more and more competitive, as was the labor market. Michael had grown up on a ranch, and even though theirs had failed, he knew the life.

I need a job until I sell the house. What if...?

He guzzled down the rest of his coffee instead of speaking up. While yes, he did need some kind of job for now, his first priority was checking on Dad and assessing what sort of help he'd need at home going forward. Michael could be there during the night, but he might need to hire someone to be there while Michael was working. And to hire someone required income. They might be able to survive on just Dad's social security and whatever retirement he had saved up, but Michael couldn't mentally survive spending all day and night with his father. He'd go insane from boredom.

He could compromise with outside help, and he imagined a hospital social worker would be around sometime today to talk with them about it. If Dad listened to anything Michael had to say. They hadn't had an in-person conversation in twenty-odd years and rarely spoke on the phone. Even though Michael sent him new puzzles every Christmas and birthday, they didn't have a relationship anymore. Not since Mom died.

Michael dropped a twenty on the counter for his food and tip, and he left the diner, intent on his car and the long day ahead of him.

Dad was awake when Michael walked into his room about thirty minutes later, his hands empty of gifts, flowers or treats, because he honestly wasn't sure what his father might want. For sure, Dad would have scoffed at flowers, but somehow arriving empty-handed made Michael feel like a misbehaving ten-year-old again, rather than the sort-of-successful forty-one-year-old man he was now.

Dad blinked at him over the remnants of his breakfast, his left hand resting on the rolling tray table near a plastic spoon. He'd dribbled a bit of something down his chin, and Michael sent a silent "what the fuck?" to the staff for letting a stroke patient try to feed himself with his nondominant hand. Even if it was what looked like runny oatmeal and juice.

"Hey, Dad," Michael said. "You, uh…hi." He'd wanted to say he looked good, but that was a terrible lie. Dad was pale. His right cheek and the skin around his eye seemed to droop, and he stared at Michael like he didn't quite recognize him. "I got in last night before visiting hours ended but you were asleep."

Dad said something, his speech a bit slurred, and it took Michael a moment to process the words as "Sleeping a lot. Tired."

"Yeah, I bet. You talk to your doctor about the prognosis?"

After a long minute of Dad staring at him, he managed, "More tests. Physical therapy. Leg's numb."

"That sounds about right. The physical therapy. I, um, I'm staying at the house, if that's okay with you. Seemed easier than that old motel out by Daisy or somewhere in Amarillo."

"That's fine. Staying awhile?"

"Planned to, yeah. I broke up with Kenny. Gonna put the house on the market. Start over."

Dad's expression flickered in an odd way. "Never good enough. For you. Dog?"

Michael's eyes stung. "Bastard took the dog."

"Sorry."

Now wasn't the time to tell his father that Kenny had taken more than just the dog and left Michael with only the house and his car. They could talk about money later. "Do you need anything?"

"Visit?" He tilted his head at one of the visitor chairs.

"Yeah. Yeah, I can do that for a while, Dad."

With a little help from Michael, Dad turned on the mounted TV and they found a morning game show to watch. For the first time in nearly two decades, Michael watched and joked about a TV show with his father, and for a little while, all the old hurts seemed to slip away.

Not forever, but awhile.

Josiah studied his reflection in the bathroom mirror, making sure his scrubs covered any possible sign of last night's rough sex with Seamus. Seamus was good about avoiding obvious signs of anything physical going on in Josiah's private life, but sometimes the aches made Josiah wonder if his physical pain was as obvious to others as it was to himself.

So far, so good.

He finger-combed his damp hair into an acceptable style. Josiah was normally a nighttime bather, preferring to wash the day's funk off before going to bed, but Seamus had woken him up this morning by shoving his dick inside Josiah before he was fully awake, and Josiah had needed to clean up. He was meeting a new client's family member today, so cleanliness and a good, positive attitude were a must.

Didn't matter he was dying a little more inside every day as long as his clients got the best care possible.

He readjusted his thin, gold-framed glasses, disliking how they looked, but he didn't have a choice right now. One of his contacts had ripped yesterday, and he wasn't in the mood to beg Seamus for money to replace them. Josiah worked freelance, rather than being employed by an agency, so he paid his insurance out of pocket, and vision was expensive. It also didn't cover a lot of his degenerative vision issues, so his glasses would have to suffice for now.

"You meet new clients every day," he told his reflection in the firmest tone he could manage. "Chin up, you've got this."

Yes, he had this. Seamus had already left for work, so Josiah used the peaceful quiet to sip tea and reread his client's file. Elmer Pearce, sixty-six, widowed, recent stroke. Partial right-side paralysis. Basic care needs plus physical therapy exercises every day. Adult son staying with him but was looking for employment. He studied the medical information he'd been sent with his client's approval. Elmer wouldn't be coming home until tomorrow, but they still had things to arrange, including a medical bed until Elmer got some mobility back. His meeting with the son, Michael, was scheduled for ten o'clock at the house.

A house Josiah had driven past hundreds of times. It sat right off the state road that led from Weston out to Daisy, and it was only about a few miles from the county sheriff's office. Even if Josiah had only seen it once, he would have remembered the place with its long fence and yard full of folk art made from all kinds of scrap metal and junk. No one could pass a place like that and forget about it after.

Even though Elmer lived alone, it reminded Josiah of a real home. Not that he'd ever had such a thing in all of his twenty-eight years.

Josiah locked up and drove out to Elmer's house. Elmer's pickup was in the long dirt driveway, as well as a nice four-door sedan. Texas plates, so the son had either gotten a rental or he still lived in the state. Josiah had only spoken to him briefly last night to set up this meeting, so he didn't know much about the man beyond his name and that he was in Weston for an undetermined length of time.

He grabbed a folder with his basic credentials, work history and references, as well as rates, and got out of the car. The home's front door opened before Josiah even reached the porch, and he tried not to stare too hard at the man behind the screen door. Tall, maybe six-four if he was an inch, with a frame both muscular and lean, like a wrestler or swimmer. Dark brown hair swept up in a sort-of side part. Square jaw, intense stare, rigid posture that made Josiah's skin prickle with the need to cower.

He didn't cower, though, despite this man being exactly the height and build of people Josiah preferred to avoid being alone with at all costs. Josiah strode across the porch and plastered a smile on his face. "Michael Pearce, I presume?"

"Yes," he replied in a gentler voice than Josiah remembered from their phone call. "You're Josiah Sheridan?"

"I am. It never feels right to say 'pleased to meet you,' given the circumstances, but thank you for your time today."

"Sure, please come in." Michael pushed the screen door open wide enough for Josiah to step inside.

The former farmhouse was familiar in its shape and floor plan. Josiah had been inside plenty since he began his career as an in-home caregiver. Stairs straight ahead, rooms off to both sides. Everything boxy with low archways and scuffed wood floors that creaked with every step. Decor that was at least three decades old, if not older, but somehow still charming.

Michael led him into a cluttered living room. "Can I get you something to drink? I've got coffee in the pot still."

"A glass of water would be nice, thank you."

"Sure. One minute." Michael disappeared into the next room.

Josiah took the brief moment to study the living room and its dimensions. His client would need an electric bed for at least the first few months of his recovery and this room seemed large enough to fit one, if they moved a few pieces of furniture around. A bedroom would be more private, but most clients benefited from being in an active part of the house so they could have more human contact.

The one thing he didn't see many of in this living room, unlike many other homes he'd been in, were family photos. One dusty picture of a man and woman on their wedding day that he assumed was Elmer and his late wife, but that was it. No photos of Michael, or Michael and his parents. Only a few completed, framed puzzles and some metal things he assumed were some of Elmer's folk art. One kind of resembled a horse if he tilted his head just so.

"Here you go."

Josiah released an undignified yelp at the sound of Michael's voice nearby. He hadn't heard the man approach, and he hated the way he flinched and took a step backward. Michael's calm smile flickered briefly, one hand outstretched with a plastic cup of water. His other hand held a coffee mug, which meant a slap wasn't coming for Josiah acting like a paranoid idiot.

"Sorry, man," Michael said softly. "I didn't mean to startle you."

"It's okay, I got lost in thought." He accepted the cup of water and sipped to wet his suddenly dry throat. "Thank you."

"Sure. Please, have a seat. Anywhere you want's fine." Michael took a wooden rocking chair that creaked ominously under his weight, then blew over his steaming mug of coffee. "I feel like I've been living on coffee for the last twenty-four hours."

"That can happen during a crisis." Josiah perched on the edge of a faded floral sofa and put his folders down so he could clutch his cup with both hands. "Sometimes our bodies run on instinct, finding what fuel we can wherever we can. I'm not here to judge you, Mr. Pearce, only to discuss your father's care going forward."

"Call me Michael, please. The only time anyone ever called me Mr. Pearce was during investor meetings a lifetime ago."

"Investors for your work?"

"Yeah." Michael grimaced. "Work I'm very much not doing anymore."

Unsure by the man's inflection if that was a good thing or a bad thing, Josiah steered their conversation back to relevant matters. "I appreciate you being here to help with your father's arrangements. It's always good to have another family member around to coordinate posthospital care, especially the kind your father will need." He handed a folder over to Michael. "This is my résumé, relevant work experience, as well as referrals from several past clients and their families."

"Thank you." Michael put the folder on a side table without glancing at it.

Josiah wasn't sure how to take that, as this was an interview. Was he wasting his time with this job or what?

"I need someone with flexible hours to start, until I find a job around here and know my work schedule. Once I have that, we can figure out a routine that works."

"I don't have any other clients at the moment, Mister— Michael, so I can definitely work with you on my hours. I am a certified nursing assistant, so I am qualified to care for your father's medical needs, as well as bathing, home exercises, and being a general companion while you're away."

"If you're a CNA, why don't you work at the hospital?"

Michael seemed more curious than suspicious, and it was a common question, so Josiah didn't take any offense. He quite liked the firm yet quiet tenor of Michael's voice. The older man was very pleasant to talk to. "I tried but I prefer having a more personal connection with my patients that you don't always get in a hospital setting. Working directly with clients and their families helps me get to know them and their intimate needs."

It makes me feel like I'm part of a family for a little while.

"That makes sense," Michael replied. "I was never great at making connections with clients, but Kenny excelled at it. Probably why we were such great business partners." His calm smile faded briefly.

Josiah surprised himself when his curiosity won out over self-preservation and he blurted, "What business are you in? If you don't mind me asking."

"Technology. Got in at just the right time with smartphone apps, and I got out a bit sooner than I planned, but such is life." An odd kind of grief shadowed Michael's eyes, suggesting this was not a pretty portion of Memory Lane to tread down.

"I'm impressed by folks who work in tech. I can barely operate the calendar app on my phone some days."

Michael's expression went distant. "At least you make a difference with people's lives." He looked so young for a moment, so vulnerable that Josiah wanted to do something to comfort him, but they weren't friends. Michael was a client and this was a business relationship.

Time to bring the conversation back to business.

Josiah picked up a notepad and pen. "Now, does

your father have health insurance, or will you be handling his care through a hospice service?"

Michael blinked hard several times. His back straightened and his demeanor shifted back to a man who was all business. And like that, they got to work on the best care possible for Elmer Pearce's long-term recovery.

Chapter Three

Michael and Josiah chatted for close to two hours about Dad and everything relevant to his future care, and Michael found himself enjoying the younger man's company. He couldn't guess his age, and he'd barely glanced at the résumé folder, so he didn't know Josiah's graduation dates, but he'd guess Josiah was about a decade younger than him.

Josiah was cute in a plain way Michael couldn't really describe. Average height and slender, with reddish-brown hair that seemed to resist being tamed by a hairbrush or product, and a pair of gold-rimmed glasses that made him look like a science fair geek desperate to win first prize. But he also had an aura of fatigue and grief that intrigued Michael. Josiah gave all the right answers to Michael's questions and knew a hell of a lot about stroke patients, so Michael had no qualms with his qualifications.

No, something about Josiah Sheridan was haunted. And Michael wanted to know more.

"It's after one already," Michael said once they'd finalized a delivery time for Dad's bed tomorrow with the service providing it. "Can I buy you lunch? I'd offer to make something, but I'm not much of a cook and the fridge is pretty bare bones."

Josiah stared at him as if he'd spoken in a foreign language before shaking himself out of it. "Um, no, thank you. I've got some calls to make so we're ready for tomorrow."

"You sure? It'll only take an hour." Michael didn't understand why he wanted to remain in Josiah's company. He simply…liked the younger man and felt at ease in his presence. And the way Josiah picked at the band of his wristwatch—so few people his age seemed to wear actual watches anymore—was sort of adorable.

"I'm sure, but thank you again. My, um, I should, ah, get home and finish this up."

Michael glanced at Josiah's left hand but didn't see a ring. Neither of them had spoken about anything too personal, including relationship statuses. But this was also a business relationship, employer and employee, not a friendship. At least, not yet. He'd like to be Josiah's friend, even if they only saw each other at the start and end of a workday. After being away from Weston for half his life, Michael could use a friend or two here.

"Rain check, then," Michael said.

"Sure." Josiah's hesitant smile as he gathered up his papers didn't give Michael the impression he truly meant it. Had he heard through the gossip chain that Michael was gay, and he didn't approve? Michael had openly flaunted his sexuality around town in the months leading up to his departure, not giving a shit what anyone thought anymore, so longtime residents knew.

Whatever. If Josiah turned out to be a homophobe, Michael would deal with it. Not like he was putting down roots in Weston for the long term. He was here to lick his own wounds over the Kenny/Rosco debacle, get his father back on his feet, and figure out a new direction for his life. Nothing else.

He walked Josiah to the door and caught a faint whiff of something sweet and clean, like soap or shampoo. Definitely not cologne. He liked it. Its simplicity fit with what he knew of Josiah so far.

"So the delivery company will set up the bed for you," Josiah said once he'd stepped out onto the porch. "You just need to have the space cleared for them."

"Right, I'll figure that out tonight. Do you want to go to the hospital and meet my father before he comes home?"

"Mr. Pearce and I have interacted a few times, so he knows who I am. But I can be here when he's discharged and you bring him home, so the three of us can have a conversation together about my role in his care."

"That sounds fine. I think the doctor said if not tomorrow, then the day after. It'll give me a little time to go job hunting, too."

"Are you looking for any work in particular?" Josiah pushed his glasses higher up his nose. "I don't know of any computer work, but I can ask around."

"I was actually thinking of applying up at Woods Ranch." Now that the words were out of his mouth, Michael couldn't take them back. Submitting his résumé wouldn't take very long, and considering the long gap in any sort of ranch work, he might not even get a call back. "This place was a working ranch when I was younger, so I know the life. It's hard work for not-great pay, but it beats…well, probably whatever menial jobs are available here or in Daisy. Or elsewhere, but I don't want a long commute if I can help it."

And now he was babbling.

Josiah smiled. "I don't know the Woods family well, but they seemed like a close-knit, accepting group of people."

"Yeah, I'd heard a bit about some incident with Brand Woods and his stepbrother?"

"Not Brand's stepbrother. His boyfriend Hugo's stepbrother. A few months ago out at the Roost. But he's okay now."

"The stepbrother?"

"No, Brand." Josiah's cheeks pinked up and he let out an adorable bark of nervous laughter. "I am really screwing this up. No, a few months ago Hugo's stepbrother got drunk and attacked Hugo, but Hugo's boyfriend, Brand, got in the middle of things, and Brand was stabbed but he's fine now." He looked sideways, as if consulting an imaginary encyclopedia of events, then nodded. "Yes, that's right."

"Wow. I mean, I'm glad Brand is okay." From gossip, Michael knew that the oldest Woods heir, Colt, was openly gay and married to a man, and now the next son was also with a man? It definitely raised Michael's chances of being hired and lowered the odds of taking shit for being open about his sexuality. Michael had no wish to ever be shoved back into the closet, not for any reason.

"He is," Josiah said. "From what I hear, he's done a lot to modernize Woods Ranch and keep them running in the black. I think you'd be a good fit there."

"Why?" Michael hadn't meant to sound confrontational, but Josiah had known him for less than three hours. It irked him when people made snap judgments about him, and he also hated the way Josiah hunched his shoulders and directed his response to the porch floor.

"You seem genuine, Michael. And from my few interactions with Brand and his parents, they seem to thrive off genuine people. I meant no offense."

"None taken." He purposely gentled his tone. "You seem like a pretty genuine person, too. I think we'll get along really well going forward."

"Thank you. I look forward to working with your father. If you'll excuse me." Josiah practically bolted off the porch and down to a dusty two-door sedan. The kind of car you bought to get you to places, rather than for looks or status.

Michael waited on the porch until Josiah backed out of the wide driveway and disappeared down the long country road, heading for his next destination. He shut the door, the house suddenly too big and empty now that he was alone in it again. Josiah had filled in those odd gaps with his smile and wide, haunted eyes, and with his clean, soap scent. Without those things, it was just a house.

A big, lonely house.

No longer hungry for lunch, he snacked on the last of some stale potato chips and bits of turkey lunch meat while contemplating the hospital bed. If Dad's recovery went well, they'd only need it for a few weeks. If it didn't, they might need it a whole lot longer. And since the best spot to care for Dad was in the living room—hello, access to the biggest TV with cable and to the kitchen—Michael spent a lot of time rearranging the furniture. A coffee table there, a love seat over there, things went around and around for a while, until he created a good space for the bed, while retaining one sofa for himself, Josiah, and any company to sit on.

Not that he assumed Dad would get a lot of company, but stranger things had happened. Maybe he'd adopted a few friends in his old age who'd drop by once in a while. For as much as Michael still cared about his dad deep down inside, he knew nothing about the man's life right now. On one level, it hurt, but on another level, it was exactly what Michael had wanted: distance. Distance to deal with his grief so it didn't turn into something darker that destroyed his relationship with his father completely. Distance and the chance to create a new life separate from his dad and this place with all its bad memories.

And that new life had done nothing but screw him in the ass. Figuratively and financially. Often literally, because while Kenny liked to get fucked on occasion, Michael very much liked to bottom. And Kenny always had a high sex drive.

Probably too high, since Kenny had cheated on Michael more times than he cared to remember in the last few years. But Michael wasn't angry about that anymore. He needed to focus on the present, not the past. And in the present, he was stupidly hungry and really wanted a drink. After checking all of Dad's old hiding spots and not finding a speck of liquor in the house—only a few cans of beer in the fridge—Michael grabbed his keys and left.

Instead of back to the diner, he went to the Roost, a not-too-divey dive bar on the outskirts of town. It wasn't quite dinnertime but the place already had a lot of tables taken. Michael sat himself at the bar near a pretty, petite woman with a curvy figure and black hair. She came right over with a laminated menu.

"Get you started with something to drink?" she asked in tone of voice that almost dared him to order anything from her. "Usually I know everyone who comes in here, but you're new."

He loved her bluntness immediately. "Technically, I'm old. Used to live around here until I was about twenty. Back for a while, and I'll start with your best cocktail."

"The place's best cocktail's probably the Moscow Mule."

"I asked for *your* best. What do you make the best?"

She grinned, then went to work, dropping a sugar cube into a short glass, two dashes of bitters, and then whiskey. She stirred until the sugar dissolved and added an orange twist, which impressed the hell out of Michael. Too many bartenders made an Old Fashioned by shaking it or muddling the fruit.

The flavor was perfection.

"Start a tab?" she asked.

"Definitely. I'm Michael, by the way."

"Ramie. Nice to meet you."

"That's a pretty name. It has to be short for something."

"It is." With a wink, she moved on to another customer at the bar.

Amused by her and hoping he'd made a friend, Michael perused the menu. Mostly burgers, with a few sandwiches and appetizers thrown in. Not a single salad or healthy option, but whatever. He didn't need to impress anyone with his abs right now. When Ramie breezed past him again, he ordered the Woodland Burger, which was the only one on the menu made with certified local organic beef. Might as well support the locals while he was around, even if it wasn't exactly in his budget.

He listened to the basic country music piping over the sound system while he sipped his drink and thumbed through his various social media accounts on his phone. He'd unfriended and unfollowed a lot of people after his breakup with Kenny, but he still followed different celebrities and news outlets. No reason not to keep abreast of the world, even when he felt like he'd walked into a completely different world here in Weston. A world where nothing mattered beyond town limits, and the wider issues didn't really reach.

Unlike life in a big city like Austin.

When Ramie delivered his burger and fries, she said, "So I never did get nosy and ask why you came back to Weston."

"No, you didn't."

Her lips twisted into a smirk. "So why did you come back to Weston? We're not exactly known for our fun touristy stuff. We don't have a single postcard about this town."

"My father had a stroke yesterday morning, and I'm in town to help him out."

"Elmer Pearce is your father? I'm sorry."

He quirked an eyebrow.

"Not sorry that he's your father," she continued. "I mean, I'm sorry about the stroke. I don't know him well, but I've seen his work. He's got a very interesting imagination. I'm not originally from Weston, so his yard was very eye-catching when I first moved here."

"Yeah, he's eclectic, for sure. Do you have ketchup?"

Ramie produced a glass bottle, then moved down the bar to help someone, giving Michael a moment to try his burger. Perfect medium, nicely seasoned, basic toppings, but still half the price of a similar burger he'd have gotten at a nice place in Austin. He glanced around the Roost while he ate, so he didn't get grease on his phone. Some of the tables held couples, some single folks, but a few had clusters of young people. Seemed odd for so early in the day, barely five o'clock, but he had no clue about the social scene for young people here anymore. And sometimes it took Michael a moment to realize he wasn't in the "young people" category anymore at forty-one. He certainly wasn't old by any means.

Some days he felt that way, though. Old and worn, like a used-up sneaker that needed to be pitched before the sole fell off.

He was about halfway through his meal when the front door opening let in a blast of sunlight, followed by Ramie saying, "Hey, Woods, you're in a bit early for a drink."

Michael pivoted on his stool. A tall blond man in a brown jacket and boots stepped inside and headed right for the bar. He leaned right over it and kissed Ramie's cheek, and Michael would bet his last penny that this was Brand Woods.

"I need one after today," Woods said. "Beer, please."

Ramie poured him one in a tall glass, and Michael tried not to be obvious about his eavesdropping. If this really was Brand, then he could be Michael's future boss. If Michael applied. Ranching wasn't really his thing anymore, but until the damned house sold, Michael needed cash.

"What's got you all tied up in honda knots?" Ramie asked as she delivered the beer to Brand.

"The new vendor for our organic beef I had to see today," Brand said after taking a long gulp of his beer. "Frank Archer over at the Grove Point CSA."

Michael wasn't familiar with the man's name or that particular CSA, so it had probably popped up in the twenty or so years since he'd last been in Weston. Curious, he shoved a fry into his mouth and kept listening. Maybe eavesdropping was rude, but Brand was only one stool down and not speaking too softly.

"Ouch," Ramie said. "How'd that go?"

"The whole meeting was shockingly professional, considering Frank's kid tried to kill my boyfriend."

Surprise jolted down Michael's spine. This had to be the story Josiah had told him about Hugo and his stepbrother and the stabbing a few months ago. Just thinking Josiah's name made him smile, and he kind of wanted to text Josiah about what he was hearing. But they weren't friends, not really.

Not yet.

"Well, good on you for keeping your temper," Ramie said. "Did you get the contract?"

"I did. Frank agreed to sell ground beef and a few steak cuts in their store. If things go well, he'll add the ground beef to one of the monthly membership boxes. It's still local, but it's the expansion we're looking for."

"That's great news. You've worked so hard on the transition from regular beef to organic, grass-fed, and this is a fantastic new step, especially with how popular Grove Point has gotten this last year or so."

"Yeah. It's definitely a deal with the devil, but I'll do anything I can to keep the ranch going."

"I know you will. Be back." She moved on to help a customer. The place was starting to get busier as it inched into the dinnertime hour, and Michael spotted two new waitresses out on the floor, tending to patrons.

Michael was pretty full from his supper and had tipped back the last of his second Old Fashioned, so he figured why the hell not and slid onto the vacant stool between himself and Brand. "You're Brand Woods," he said in his friendliest-without-flirting tone.

Brand met his gaze, expression both wary and curious. "I am. You seem familiar but I can't remember when we've met."

"Michael Pearce. Elmer's my father. I was a few years older than your brother Colt."

"Right." Brand held out his hand and gave Michael's a firm shake. "You resemble your father. Don't think I've seen you around since I was a teenager."

"Because I haven't been. But I'm sure you heard about my dad's stroke. I came back to town to help him out for a while."

"I'm sure he appreciates that. Elmer's a good man." Something flickered in Brand's eyes. "Welcome back to town, Michael."

"Thanks." He swallowed his pride and said the words before he chickened out. "Listen, this morning I overheard your brother Remington at the diner, and he said your ranch was a bit short-staffed right now. I haven't been in the life in about two decades, but I do know ranching and cattle, and I need a job."

For someone who'd been independently wealthy for nearly half his life, admitting those final four words hurt his pride like a stab to the face. But those words were also very true. He'd come to Weston to help his father, not become a financial burden, especially with the slow housing market in Austin. Plus, Michael couldn't afford to patronize the diner three times a day, so the house needed groceries.

"I've got very vague memories of Elmer having cattle when I was small," Brand said. "Same with a lot of folks around the county. We've got a link on our website for employment. Upload your résumé and I'm sure my dad will give you a call. We're getting by, but it never hurts to have that extra pair of hands, especially with Dad slowing down. He really shouldn't be out rustling as often as he is."

"I'll do that, thank you."

"Out of curiosity, what have you been doin' since you left Weston?"

"Got into technology. Lived without regrets for a long time until I realized bad choices always come back to haunt us. Just need to start over."

"I hear you. Like I said, submit that résumé, and I'm sure we'll talk again soon, Michael."

"Thanks." Taking that as the polite dismissal it was, Michael eased back to his own stool and finished his burger. Still good, even if a bit cold now. The fries he left behind, along with a decent tip for Ramie to close out his tab. Another Old Fashioned wouldn't have gone amiss, but he did need to drive and a DUI on his second night in town was a bad look, especially on someone who needed a job.

He did swing by the small general store for a few groceries and snacks, mostly sandwich things and pretzels, plus a box of his favorite chocolate chip cookies. The junk food was stuff Kenny used to pick on him about, because of the high sugar and salt content, but Michael didn't care about his opinion anymore. He was going to fucking eat what made him happy. No more food shaming from his boyfriend/partner, who thought a glass of water and three cigarettes was a balanced breakfast. No more being what other people expected him to be.

I'm starting over. I'll find out who Michael Pearce really is. One way or another.

Chapter Four

Josiah scraped the now-shredded chicken breast off his cutting board and back into the slow cooker, savoring a deep inhale of the yummy but simple white bean chicken chili he'd set that morning before his meeting with Michael Pearce. This recipe was one of Seamus's favorites and it was so easy, with just a few ingredients. Josiah preferred the hot green chilies to the mild ones, but he made it this way to appease Seamus. He still wasn't entirely sure how Seamus felt about him taking on the Elmer Pearce job, so he wanted to tread with caution. Butter up his roommate.

Seamus had texted he'd be home by six for supper, so Josiah carefully arranged bowls of extra toppings for the white chili, like tortilla chips, sour cream, and shredded cheese. And he had a chilled beer ready for Seamus after he'd come inside and locked his sidearm away. Seamus took a long pull from the can, then belched loudly.

"Smells good," Seamus said. "I'm starving."

"Then please, let's sit and eat."

Josiah served them both portions of chili, grateful when Seamus immediately began to eat, rather than harangue him with questions about today's meeting. Pleased by the brief respite, Josiah focused on flavoring the slightly bland chili with loads of sour cream and cheese.

"You meet Michael Pearce today?" Seamus asked after a few minutes of silent eating.

It seemed an odd question when Seamus knew that meeting a new client had been part of his day's plans. Except... "How do you know Michael's name?"

"Met him early this morning. Was passin' by the Pearce house and saw a strange car. After the burglary incident this summer, figured it was a good idea to see who was staying at his house while old Elmer's in the hospital."

"Oh. Right. Of course. And yes, I met with Michael this afternoon. He's in town to help get Elmer back on his feet."

"So he told me." Seamus gazed at him over a big spoon loaded with chili and toppings. "He's good-looking, too."

"Is he?" Josiah tried to play dumb, because Michael was the tall, muscular type that he'd lusted after during his nursing training but had always been too scared to speak to, much less attempt to pursue, terrified he'd flirt with the wrong kind of guy. But Michael had been so patient with Josiah today, like the Seamus Josiah had first moved in with two years ago.

Seamus watched him a beat before shoveling that dripping spoon into his mouth and chewing.

"Michael is looking for daytime work," Josiah pressed on, hoping to keep Seamus's temper on an even keel with simple information. "That way I'll work similar hours as you and be home in the evenings the way you like it."

"Good. I know you like to keep busy, especially when

I'm not home, but I need you here, Jo-jo." *Here when I need my dick sucked* hung off that statement.

"And I like being here for you. How about a back rub after you're done eating?"

"Sounds good. Very good."

Josiah didn't eat much more after that, his stomach pulled tight with nerves. He couldn't get a good read on Seamus's mood, so whatever happened after the massage could either be moderately pleasant, or unbearably painful.

It ended up being somewhere in between. After giving Seamus his toothpick and cleaning up dinner, Josiah followed him into the bedroom. Seamus stripped down and stretched out, and then made a spinning gesture with his index finger, so Josiah stripped, too.

Josiah did his best to put his "housemate" to sleep with the hardest massage he could manage, working knots of tension out of Seamus's neck and shoulders for what felt like forever. Seamus even let out a soft, content snore at one point.

Hoping Seamus had nodded off, Josiah slid to the side of the bed and wiped his hands on a towel. Strong arms grabbed him by the waist and dumped him onto his stomach. Seamus crouched over him and immediately began to thrust his hard cock against Josiah's crease, moving harder and faster with each passing moment. "Don't forget who this ass belongs to," Seamus said in his ear. "It's mine."

"Yours," he whispered.

Seamus rubbed off until he came, his release coating Josiah's back in sticky ropes that squished between his skin and Seamus's belly. Seamus rubbed his cock all around in the mess before settling on top of him, squashing Josiah uncomfortably against the mattress.

The breathing in his ear slowly evened out. Positive he'd be trapped here for a while, Josiah closed his eyes and remembered Michael's kind, patient smile.

And that smile followed him into a shallow, restless sleep.

Michael did not expect to have an interview with Brand and Wayne Woods at ten o'clock the next morning. But, since Dad wasn't coming home until tomorrow, Michael had the free time and drove to the Woods Ranch with a few minutes to spare. They had a vast, sprawling acreage that included a lot of grassland, a few dry gulches, and two herds of cattle. The regular heads had maybe one slaughter left, if Michael's casual head count was correct, because the family was transitioning over to fully grass-fed, organic beef.

He didn't see the larger herd as he parked, so they were probably grazing far out on the land, filling their bellies and keeping the grass height down. Growing up, Dad had hated mowing the lawn, calling it a waste of time and manpower, so he'd bought a few goats to do the work for him. And it had been fine until the goats started eating the side of the house and garage. Dad had sold them to another farmer one county over.

After that, Michael stopped naming anything that lived on their farm, even the two mutts they'd still had around when Michael left town.

His eyes burned, and damn it, he was not going to cry again about Rosco right before a job interview.

Wayne Woods greeted him by the main house with a firm handshake, and instead of going into the house, they walked over to a smaller building between it and the barn. From what Michael remembered, it had been a bunkhouse for hands once upon a time, but when they walked in, the place looked more like someone's living room/kitchen. The door to the left was shut, but the one to the right stood half-open, and Wayne went that way.

Three sets of bunk beds still stood against the walls, but Brand sat behind a wide desk smack in the middle of it. His office as ranch foreman, Michael suspected. He was proved right when Brand shook his hand, then asked him to sit in one of the two wooden chairs across from the desk. Wayne took the other.

"It's nice to see you again, Michael," Brand began, "I have to say that web app development isn't something we're really looking for in a hand, but your experience might be useful as we go forward and expand our brand of organic beef."

"I can do any sort of software work you need, of course," Michael replied. "That's not even a problem, but I'm most interested in full-time work. I haven't been on a horse in twenty years but I remember how to tack and ride, and I know how to herd cattle. I'm here to help my dad get better, but I also need something to do with my time."

And the paycheck is a perk, too.

"Understandable," Wayne said. "I've known Elmer most of my life and he's a good man. I remember when you barely came up to my hip, son, and I'll always do what I can to help out a neighbor. Seeing as your skills are a bit rusty, we can offer you a trial period of employment. Say, four weeks?"

"I'd appreciate that very much. Thank you." Josiah's tentative smile flashed in his mind. "And I don't mean to be a pain in the ass before I'm even hired, but I'd do really good with a regular schedule, because I've hired an in-home nurse to care for Dad while I'm not there, and I need to coordinate his schedule."

"I think we can work with you," Brand replied. "Days usually start at eight thirty and end at five. Our guys are pretty flexible, so if certain days work best for you and your caregiver, I can schedule you those days." His lips twitched. "As long as you survive the trial period."

"I'll do my best not to disappoint. And I'd love to take a crack at revamping your online presence, if that's something you're really interested in. I always had a knack for coding and computers but…things didn't work out. Got into business with the wrong person. I regret some of my choices but I've also learned from them."

"We all have, Michael. Regretted and learned." Brand's hand drifted across the front of his shirt to rest over his abdomen—probably the place where he was stabbed a few months ago.

Not likely a memory Brand wanted to revisit today.

"If I'm not being too nosy," Wayne said, "do you have your caregiver lined up, or do you need help?"

"A social worker at the hospital already has someone lined up, and we chatted for a while yesterday. Josiah Sheridan."

Wayne glanced briefly at Brand. "I know the boy a bit. He helped save Brand's life the night Hugo's sociopath stepbrother attacked them."

"Oh." Josiah had told him about that incident, but he hadn't mentioned he'd been there. "Well, I'm glad he was there to help. I think my dad will like him a lot, and he seems very focused on his work. A lot of glowing recommendations from previous clients and families." Michael had taken a few minutes last night to actually read the papers Josiah had given him, and it was all solid stuff.

"Josiah would argue he's no hero and was just in the right place at the right time," Brand said. "We tried to invite him and his roommate over for supper to thank them, but they turned us down."

"They?" Josiah hadn't mentioned a roommate, but his living arrangement wasn't Michael's business as long as Josiah showed up and did his work.

"Yeah, he's been living with Sheriff McBride almost since he got to town two years ago."

"Sheriff had a spare room," Wayne added, "and there's probably no safer place to live than with the county sheriff."

Brand's expression flickered, as if he disagreed with something his father had said. Now didn't seem like the time to bring it up, though. Their conversation switched back to the ranch. Brand talked him through the standards for the organic beef, and then led him over to the barn for a tour. It had a break room with a table, microwave, and fridge. The ladder to the hayloft was opposite it. Michael met the horses he'd be riding, saw the tack and feed rooms, and by the time they'd finished, a man on horseback was approaching from one of the fields, two dogs loping along beside him.

One dog, a scarred German shepherd, took off in their direction and went straight for Brand, who scratched the big dog on his head. "This is Brutus," Brand said. "The best dog we've got."

Brutus sniffed in Michael's general direction but didn't posture or growl.

The cowboy slowed and climbed off his horse. The other dog stuck close, some kind of gray and brown mutt. "Howdy," the stranger said. He was probably close to Michael's age, with the tanned skin of a man used to working outdoors. "Jackson Sumner. This here is Dog."

His dog's name is Dog? Okay. "Michael Pearce."

"We're bringing Michael in on a trial basis," Wayne said. "Four weeks to get his sea legs back under him, so to speak."

"Welcome to the team." Jackson pulled off a leather work glove, then stuck his hand out to shake. Had a nice, firm grip.

"Thank you," Michael replied. "When do you need me to start?"

"You said your dad's coming home tomorrow," Brand said, "so you'll need to get him settled and let him meet Josiah. How about the day after? Thursday. Unless you'd rather start the first full week on Monday."

"No, Thursday is fine. I appreciate it. Coming up here from Austin was a last-minute thing, and while I packed for an extended stay, I didn't exactly plan for anything. I'm grateful I don't have to spend a lot of time job hunting."

"I don't blame you. Ranching is hard work, and it's getting even harder to find qualified people. We had to hire temps to get us through calving season last spring. But that's boring business stuff you don't need to worry about. If you've got ideas on improving our website and online presence, though, I'm all ears."

Michael checked the time on his phone. Still had two

hours before the bed was being delivered, so he brought
the Woods Ranch website up. "Well, the first thing I
noticed is that it isn't very mobile friendly, but that's
an easy fix."

Brand waved him forward, and they headed back
to his office to continue their chat.

Josiah was looking forward to meeting Michael and
Elmer at the Pearce house on Wednesday a lot more
than he probably should—not only because Josiah
needed to keep busy and this meeting meant a new
job, but he'd spent a lot of time thinking about Michael.
Michael's patient smile and sharp eyes and rumbling
laughter. Things that made Josiah feel a touch safer
around a near stranger when men of Michael's height
and size usually made Josiah nervous. He wasn't as
thick around the middle as Seamus and didn't carry
himself in a way that suggested everyone else was beneath him, a bug to be smashed. Michael was muscular in a way that would serve him well on a ranch, but
he also stooped his shoulders a lot and walked with
less confidence. As if a much smaller, more timid man
lived inside that big body.

It made Josiah intensely curious about what the man
had left behind in Austin.

Josiah was early, so he sat in his car with the windows
down. It was still warm for September, but not awful,
and he enjoyed the fresh air. He gazed around at the
different metal sculptures in Elmer's yard, things he'd
only ever seen while driving by, but now he had time to
really study them. A tall dinosaur made out of bicycle
parts; a bench that looked like it might have been part
of a car's front fender; all kinds of silhouettes cut out

of some sort of flat metal, including one he was pretty sure was of Elmer Fudd.

The charm of the yard woke up the little boy inside Josiah, who hadn't been out to play in far too long. The one who used to have an imagination, hopes, and dreams. Dreams that had died with his parents and left him on the streets for a long damned time. But Josiah had fought his way back, fought his way to college and nursing school, and he was here now. Maybe he wasn't happy with Seamus anymore, but he had a stable place to live and a job he loved. Helping others the way no one had helped him.

Except Andy.

Josiah closed his eyes and leaned his head back, allowing memories of those two years with Andy to filter back through his mind. Despite their financial struggles, they had loved and supported each other, cried on each other's shoulder, and stood together against any obstacle. Until Andy faced an obstacle he couldn't overcome, leaving Josiah alone again.

He pushed those final, hardest months away and focused on the great times they'd shared, until a car horn startled him awake. Michael was parked next to him, alone in his car, and Josiah was confused for the ten seconds it took for him to notice the ambulance behind Michael. Duh. If Elmer was having as much difficulty with his right side as his chart said, then bringing him home like that made the most sense. And it was possible Michael would have to think about installing a ramp over part of the porch steps, in case Elmer needed the frequent use of a wheelchair to get around.

Thoughts for another day. Today was about settling Elmer in and getting to know the older man a bit better.

Josiah wanted to know the likes and dislikes and hobbies of his patients, so he could actively engage them, rather than just sit around waiting for them to need a bedpan or their lunch.

Josiah climbed out and met Michael in front of their cars, while the ambulance drivers saw to their patient. "How is Mr. Pearce this morning?" Josiah asked.

"Grumpy and ready to be home," Michael replied with a snort. "The bed came yesterday, along with one of those rolling tray thingies, and a portable toilet. Not sure if he'll be able to use that right away, but it's handy to have once he starts getting his mobility back."

If he got it back. Stroke patients were unpredictable, but Josiah planned to do everything he could to keep Elmer's limbs exercised and his spirits up. Mental motivation and belief in recovery was hugely important, especially with older folks who might be ready to give up and let go.

"Oh, I got the job at Woods Ranch," Michael added while the two paramedics pulled their burdened gurney out of the back of the ambulance. "Trial basis for four weeks, and I start tomorrow."

"That's great news. Congratulations. And tomorrow is fine. Like I said before, I don't have any other clients right now, so my time is your time."

"Awesome. I start at eight thirty, so if you could be here around eight? I don't know if Elmer will be up or if you'll have to make his breakfast."

"None of that is a problem."

"Cool, thank you." Michael flashed him a smile that made Josiah's belly wobble in a weird way, then trotted up onto the porch so he could unlock the door.

Josiah hung back during the brief production of bringing a grumpy Elmer into the living room and transferring him to the adjustable bed, which was set up facing the room's large television. A sofa had been awkwardly jammed into the space, too, but Josiah wasn't going to criticize Michael's spatial awareness skills. As long as Josiah had a place to sit near his client, he wasn't going to complain.

Once Elmer was comfortably installed in the bed, the paramedics left. Elmer was no longer on IV fluids or medications, and Michael had texted Josiah earlier that he'd purchased some reusable cups with lids and straws for the first few weeks to make drinking easier. He spotted a box of baby wipes near the portable toilet, plus other sanitary supplies tucked out of the way. In his experience, one of the hardest things to come to terms with for any weakened client was bathroom habits. So many hated the idea of bedpans or even portable toilets, and especially the idea of a near stranger wiping their ass, and it took a lot of patience to develop a routine.

"Mr. Pearce," Josiah said when it was just the three of them. "We've met briefly a few times, but I'm Josiah Sheridan. Michael hired me to be your caregiver during the day while he's working. It's nice to officially meet you."

"I remember you," Elmer said, giving Josiah a squinty stare. "Founder's Day Picnic last year. You tripped and spilled your drink on Sheriff McBride. Funny thing at the time."

It had been funny in its own way, until later that night when Seamus took his humiliation out on Josiah. "That was me. I promise not to drop any drinks on you, though. I'm not usually so clumsy."

"Sure, son, sure. Got nothing against you, so I guess we'll get along okay. You seem a nice fellow."

"Thank you. Michael has seen my résumé, but if you have any questions, feel free to ask them. I've been a caregiver professionally for about five years now, which may not seem like a lot of experience to some, but it's been both challenging and rewarding. I like helping families get through a crisis."

"Don't always get through it, though."

"That's true, and those situations are always tragic, Mr. Pearce. But according to your doctors, you are in an excellent position to regain a lot of your previous mobility and independence. As much as I don't like being out of work, I prefer when my clients succeed and say 'you're fired' versus needing long-term care." Most of the long-term care cases, like Mrs. Wellington, ended up in nursing homes or in-patient hospice facilities.

"You're honest, young buck. I like that. Keep being honest with me, and we'll get along just fine."

"Deal, sir."

"Meh, just call me Elmer. No need to be all formal, since you're gonna be wiping my ass for a while."

Josiah chuckled, amused by the older man's forthright nature. "Elmer, then."

"And if my son is done being the silent, rude type, maybe he can get us something to drink. I'll take a beer."

"You will not," Michael said from his spot across the room, one shoulder braced against a built-in bookshelf. "I bought orange juice, all-natural fruit punch, and nonsweet green tea. Or there's water."

Elmer grunted. "Tea. No soda?"

"Tea." Michael turned his attention to Josiah and smiled. "For you?"

"I'll help you," Josiah replied. "I need to learn your kitchen anyway, since I'll at least be making Elmer lunch on the days I'm here."

"Good point."

He followed Michael through a wide archway into a moderately sized kitchen with outdated appliances and a faded linoleum floor. A small table with three chairs took up space by another door leading into what looked like a mudroom/laundry room. Everything was clean, though, compared to the cluttered living room.

"Cups and plates are in this cupboard," Michael said as he reached into an upper cabinet, and Josiah held back a flinch at the sudden arm movement. "Utensils are in these two drawers, flatware on top and other stuff beneath it. We've got snacks in those cupboards, but there's also a pantry in the mudroom over there." Michael pointed while he poured green tea from a bottle into a lidded cup.

A bottle similar to the one Seamus had hurled against the kitchen wall a few weeks ago, after coming home and finding only half a glass worth of his favorite iced tea/lemonade combo to drink. A warm one was in the pantry, but Seamus hated pouring warm drinks over ice. It diluted them too fast according to him, and he'd already had a long day.

Josiah had spent a long night cleaning the wall and floor of both liquid and glass shards, and he'd nicked his palm. That cut had seemed to take forever to heal, because it was on his right hand, and it was difficult to roll a bedbound patient over with only one hand. Josiah hadn't complained, though, because he'd forgotten to chill the new bottle.

A shadow moved and Josiah took a full step backward, head ducking in case a fist lashed out, and his hip smashed into something hard. He stifled his yelp, though, and only let out a pained grunt of surprise.

"Hey, sorry." Michael stood in front of him, both hands straight out by his sides, his expression an odd mix of confused and concerned. "You okay?"

"Yes, I got lost in thought. I'm sorry." Josiah rubbed his sore hip, a hot blush creeping up his neck at acting like a fool in front of a new client's family. "Did you ask me something?"

"Just what you wanted to drink." His steady gaze held Josiah's for a long moment, seeming to both ask what was wrong and offer support for everything unspoken in Josiah's own expression.

One fucking bottle shouldn't have him this spooked. "Water is fine for now, thank you."

"Ice?"

"Please."

Michael produced a gallon jug of store-bought water from the fridge, ice from a container in the freezer, and poured Josiah his glass. Handed it over with his newly familiar, charming smile. Their fingers brushed briefly as Josiah accepted his drink, and the brief contact sent a tiny wiggle of warmth through Josiah's hand. Warmth he'd probably imagined.

"Help yourself to whatever's in the fridge or pantry while you're here," Michael said, his intent gaze never breaking from Josiah's. *"Mi casa es su casa."*

"It's my house!" Elmer shouted from the living room.

Josiah laughed. "I guess sound carries pretty well downstairs."

"He's always had an eerie sense of hearing," Michael replied. "Made sneaking out of the house as a teenager problematic, but it probably also kept me out of a lot of trouble. I had a pretty strong rebellious streak."

"I can believe that." Josiah sipped his water, mostly for something to do besides stare at the man in front of him.

"How about you? Any fun stories of wild, rebellious teen years?"

His joy at the fun conversation dimmed. "No. I was too busy surviving to rebel against much of anything." The fact that he'd said so much in only a few brief words spoke volumes to the innate trust he had in Michael. But this wasn't about being Michael's friend; today was about becoming Elmer's. "Um, thank you for the water."

He returned to the living room with Elmer's iced tea, which Elmer deliberately gulped like he hadn't had a cold drink all day. Josiah ignored the display and showed Elmer how to adjust the bed with the controller, which someone had originally placed on the right side of the bed. Elmer's weak side. After Josiah fixed it and Elmer was comfortable, Josiah perched on the foot of the bed and asked, "Do you have any questions for me?"

"You datin' anyone?" Elmer asked.

Josiah's brain stuttered for a few seconds. Technically? No, he and Seamus were living together and fucking, but he'd never call what they did dating. But was he technically single? "I'm not sure why that's relevant to your care, but no, I'm not dating at the moment."

"Just curious. You're a good-looking fella. Didn't know if there'd be someone around distracting you on your phone or whatever."

"No. I may get the occasional text from my roommate, but I will never be too distracted to see to your care, Mr. Pe—Elmer. While I'm here, you are my top priority."

"Good to know. You don't mind workin' with my son, do you?"

Michael rolled his eyes, a gesture Josiah only saw because of his position. Elmer couldn't see him. "Why would I?" Josiah asked. He had an idea what the question referred to but couldn't make himself say it first.

"'Cuz the boy's as queer as a three-dollar bill and always has been. Sometimes makes folks uncomfortable. Don't want anyone around who'd shame him for being who he is."

Josiah's lips parted, and he glanced at Michael in time to see his surprise shift back into an expression of familiar patience. "Elmer, I have absolutely no problem with Michael being gay. He's shown himself to a be a very kind, considerate person, and that's what's important. It doesn't matter to me who he dates."

"Good. Boy, where are you?"

Michael moved from his spot by the kitchen archway and stood near the TV, in Elmer's line of sight. "Right here, Dad."

Elmer pointed at Josiah. "You be nice to this one. I like him."

"I have no intention of being anything less than nice

to Josiah, I promise. I like him, too. Might have found someone able to put up with your grumpy ass."

"Hmph."

Josiah smiled, amused by the banter between father and son, aware the pair had a decades-long separation to work through. Hopefully, with enough time and patience, they would come out better on the other side.

Chapter Five

After his first full day at the ranch, Michael was pretty sure that his four-days-a-week workouts at a paid gym was kid's play compared to how sore and abused his body felt, and all he'd done was work around the barn. Then again, mucking horse stalls and hauling around bags of feed wasn't the same as squats or running on a treadmill. Very different muscle groups were used, and he was pretty sure his arms might fall off on the drive home.

Dad had still been fast asleep when Josiah arrived that morning with a small lunch box and thermos of coffee. Michael had been relieved to see him on the porch, bright-eyed and smiling, ready to start his first day at a new job, too. Even though handing Dad a bottle to piss in last night around eleven and then emptying and cleaning it in the bathroom weren't the most humiliating things he'd ever done, Michael had a terrible bedside manner. He was not, nor had he ever been, the caregiving sort.

Meanwhile, caregiving oozed off Josiah in very pleasant waves.

They'd chatted a bit before Michael had to leave, trusting Josiah to handle breakfast and Dad's morning medication, plus a daily sponge bath. Michael definitely didn't need to be around to witness the bath part. So much of this entire situation was outside of his comfort zone and hinted as to just how selfish he'd been in his pursuit of fame and fortune. Cutting out this part of his life until an emergency forced him back into it. But he was here now and doing his best.

He'd arrived at Woods Ranch on time to meet Hugo Turner, Brand's boyfriend. The younger guy had a sweet earnestness about him that was also tempered by world-weariness that Michael understood all too well. The only current employee he hadn't met yet was Alan Denning, who'd been out in pasture with the herd yesterday and was off today. Everyone seemed to rotate duties, and Brand kept a schedule clipboard in the break room so everyone knew what to do. Michael hadn't been surprised at being stuck on barn duty, but his body definitely resented it by the end of the day.

All he really wanted, as he trudged up the porch steps, was a long soak in his old, multijet hot tub, but that hot tub was back in Austin. All he had here was the modified stand-up shower in the downstairs bathroom, or the claw-foot tub upstairs. The shower had a jet, the tub a chance to sit and soak.

I need a fucking drink or five.

He'd gone back to the cowboy life reluctantly, because it seemed the lesser of various evils, but now he wasn't so sure.

He let himself into the house, not surprised to see Dad snoozing in his bed and Josiah watching some sort of reality show rerun. Something about storage bin auctions, so Dad had probably requested it before dozing off. Dad used to attend storage bin auctions when Michael was younger, but they had to travel a long way and his father rarely won anything, so after a while Dad stuck to salvage. That gave him the raw materials he preferred working with and he was even paid to haul the stuff away.

"Hey," Josiah said softly, his smile making Michael's heart trill in an unusual way. "How was your first day?"

"Painful. I feel like the football in a sudden death overtime game against high school rivals with a grudge."

"That's vivid." Josiah glanced at a still-snoring Dad, then stood and walked over to where Michael stood in the entryway. "If you have a tub, a long soak in Epsom salts can do wonders for sore muscles."

"Too bad I don't have someone to rub my shoulders." The comment slipped out before Michael could censor himself, and he realized too late how flirty and inappropriate it was. "Sorry."

Josiah shrugged, seeming unoffended. "I can recommend a good massage pillow for use at night. I can't imagine the work will get any easier."

Okay, so maybe he hadn't blown this or made Josiah uncomfortable with the slipup. "I'll look online later. God knows I'm not used to this sort of physical labor."

"I suppose software designers aren't used to hauling around wheelbarrows full of horse manure."

"Definitely not. Anyway, how did the day go here?"

"Not bad." Josiah retreated closer to the couch and crossed his arms, and Michael disliked their new distance. "Elmer ate most of his breakfast oatmeal and some cut fruit. Soup and crackers for lunch, plus his juice. He had a bit of trouble swallowing some of his pills, but he does well taking them with pudding cups."

"We have pudding cups?"

"I found a pack in the back of the pantry. We can try the sugar-free kind, if you prefer, or buy something with a similar texture he'll like, such as yogurt."

"Don't give me none of that froufrou, nondairy vegan yogurt mess," Dad said, his eyes barely open, but voice as sharp as ever. "I want plain old shit for a plain old man. Pudding is fine for those damn pills."

Michael resisted the urge to roll his eyes, curious how long Dad had pretended to be napping. "Fine, I'll get you more pudding until your swallowing gets better."

Dad grunted.

"I was referring to regular yogurt," Josiah said to Dad. "Plain, strawberry, coffee-flavored—there are all kinds."

Dad stared at Josiah for a few seconds before grunting and grabbing the remote with his left hand. He increased the volume on the storage bin show and seemed to ignore them. Fine with Michael. They'd had a tense time last night, both trying to move forward with their new situation without either admitting to past wrongdoings.

Not that Michael believed he'd done anything wrong in the past, especially not by leaving home and his dad behind. He'd been protecting his own happiness and sanity by getting the hell out of Weston.

"Sounds like we'll be good with pudding," Josiah said, just loudly enough to be heard over the television. "I can swing by the general store once I'm off and pick up some more. I'm not sure what prepared options they have, but I know how to make it from a box."

"You don't have to do that, I can just—" He stopped before saying he'd just do a home delivery order, because he had no idea if any of the phone app places delivered groceries in Weston. Probably not, and if they did, the fees would be outrageous. Living in a big city for so long had certainly spoiled him with certain things. "I can pay you back for your time and the groceries, of course."

"It's fine. Pudding isn't that expensive. Oh, I found some chicken in the fridge and put it in the oven with a can of cream of mushroom soup. It should be done in about thirty more minutes. Your father should be okay to eat that if you cut the chicken up into small pieces and use the sauce as a gravy."

Michael sniffed the air and picked up the faintest scents of cooking food. "That sounds great—thank you for prepping it."

"I'm used to quick and simple oven or slow cooker meals. It's never a problem." Josiah's gaze flickered, as if something bad had raced through his mind and disappeared just as fast. "Um, if there's nothing else, then I'll see you tomorrow morning."

"You can stay for dinner." The words slipped out before Michael thought twice, but he didn't take them back. He enjoyed Josiah's company and wasn't looking forward to another dinner with his dad full of small talk and awkward silences.

Josiah's sweet smile didn't match his disappointing words. "I can't. I have a previous engagement. But thank you."

"Another time?"

"We'll see." He turned and gathered up the few things he'd brought with him that morning. "See you tomorrow, Elmer. Don't give Michael too hard a time tonight, okay? And if either of you have any questions, feel free to call me."

"Eh, go get some sleep," Dad replied. "You look like you could use it."

"Gee, thanks so much." Josiah smiled, but it didn't reach his eyes. "Take care, Elmer. Michael."

"Thanks for everything." Michael held the front door open for Josiah, sad to see him leaving and also grateful for a bit of time to decompress from his own day. If Dad was busy watching TV, maybe Michael could escape upstairs for a long, hot bath to soothe his aching muscles. He watched Josiah ease into his compact car, back out of the driveway, and disappear down the long country road to wherever he lived.

"Don't let the damned bugs inside," Dad grumped. "It's hell to smack 'em with only one good arm."

"Sorry." He shut the screen door, noting the chain at the top was coming loose. He'd need to fix that before a strong wind whipped it right out of the frame. "So you and Josiah had an okay first day?"

"He's a good kid. Smart as a whip. I like him."

"Great." Michael turned from the door, grateful for the cool evening breeze filtering in through the open windows. As much as he longed for his fully air-conditioned home in Austin, he could appreciate the fresh air a lot more now. He remembered so many evenings sitting out on the front porch with Mom's lemonade, watching the occasional car pass on the road and talking about their days.

Michael used to love telling his parents about school and Little League and all the other activities that kept him busy as their ranch failed and their lives fell apart bit by bit. Things that kept him away from the vast acreage Dad had never managed to parcel out and sell, no matter the money offered by developers. Those evenings on the porch, with the sun setting to the left and the moon rising to the right, were precious to him because they'd stopped completely after Mom died.

Maybe one day he and Dad would sit outside on the porch again and talk about their days, but it would be a long time from now. A long, long time.

Dad was focused on the television again, so Michael went into the kitchen. Found the bottle of vodka he'd put in an upper cupboard yesterday and poured himself some over ice, while he checked on the chicken. A note on the counter from Josiah said it should be done around six. Just enough time to cook up some instant potatoes from a box. Not exactly gourmet, but Michael was also a big fan of subscription meal kits, takeout, and delivery, so when he had to cook he liked shortcuts. And mashed potatoes were soft enough for Dad to swallow without a lot of difficulty.

Once the potatoes were done and the meat thermometer in the chicken pleased him, Michael fixed two plates. He cut Dad's meat as small as he dared without tempting the man's wrath, then carried the tray into the living room. Dad insisted on trying to feed himself with his left hand. Michael ate slowly, watching Dad most of the time in case he spilled. But his left arm wasn't used to guiding utensils to his mouth, and after his third try, the potatoes missed and slid down Dad's chin.

Michael reached out with a paper napkin, only to get his hand smacked away by Dad with a terse, "I can clean up after myself, boy." Annoyed at the rebuff when he was only trying to help, Michael gave him the napkin.

The rest of dinner was a test of Michael's patience,

and sometimes he couldn't tell if Dad was being difficult on purpose, or if he was truly struggling. But the
man's pride didn't let him accept help from Michael
tonight, unlike dinner last night when he'd practically
fed Dad his entire bowl of pureed vegetable soup without a single complaint. What the hell had changed?

After the fifth spill, Michael put his own fork down,
temper sparking. "That's it. If you don't let me feed
you, then I'm buying you a big old bib tomorrow.
You're ruining your fucking shirt, Dad."

"Fine." Dad shoved the spoon at him, and Michael
didn't catch the thing before it pinged to the floor.

Biting back anger and frustration, Michael picked up
the spoon, took it into the kitchen, dropped it into the
sink, and returned with a new one. He plunked down,
scooped up a bit of everything—chicken, gravy and
potatoes—and held it out. "Say 'ah.'"

If someone's face could flip the bird, Dad's did. Then
he opened wide, and Michael put the food inside. Dinner was pretty tense and quiet after that, and Michael
wasn't sure why. Okay, so feeding his father like he
was an infant wasn't anything he'd ever expected to do
in his lifetime, but this was what Dad needed. It was
what Michael, as his only child, was willing to do so
his father could regain his strength and independence.
So why was Dad being such a stubborn son of a bitch
about it all?

Instead of engaging, Michael slowly fed Dad until
he was full, then gave him his evening meds with the
rest of the pudding cup from lunch. Once he'd cleaned
everything up, he nuked his own plate and finished eating. Dad focused wholly on the television program, so

Michael tuned him out. If this was how things were going to play out, then so be it.

With Dad's attention elsewhere, Michael stored the leftover chicken and washed the dishes, kind of wishing the house had a dishwasher to simplify life, but it didn't. Dad had always refused to get one, even after Mom died and he complained about having to handwash the dishes every meal. Well, until Michael got sick of hearing about it and volunteered for dish duty so Dad could disappear into his workshop faster and leave Michael the hell alone for a few hours. The kitchen was as tidy as it was going to get, so Michael went upstairs. They didn't have any Epsom salts, so he ran a tub of hot water and soaked in it for a while, allowing the heat to soothe sore muscles.

As he luxuriated in the soak, his mind wandered back to today's brief interactions with Josiah. His gentle smile and quiet calm, and the sad things that always seemed to linger in his eyes. He seemed like a man desperate to be happy but resigned to simply existing, and that bothered Michael. Michael had only known him for a handful of hours so far, but he liked Josiah. Probably more than was prudent.

Josiah was also nothing like the guys Michael was usually attracted to. Like so many others, Kenny had been brash and assertive, perfectly comfortable in his own skin, and wickedly funny. Josiah was none of those things (so far) but something about him intrigued Michael. Made him want to be Josiah's friend, which, even if Josiah had been into him, was all they'd ever be now that Michael was his boss. Michael needed to focus on his new job, selling his house, and deciding where to go from there.

Because once Dad was back on his feet and able to survive without constant supervision, Michael was out of there. Out of the house, out of Weston, and maybe this time, completely out of Texas.

It was beyond time to reinvent himself somewhere new.

Josiah had texted Seamus a few times during his day, mostly because Seamus liked updates when Josiah had a new client. He wasn't sure if it was protectiveness, paranoia, or a combination of the two, so Josiah did as asked to ensure Seamus's calm side when he got home. Seamus knew tonight was leftovers night, because they needed to clean out the fridge before things spoiled and Josiah abhorred throwing away food. He'd spent too damned many nights sleeping hungry to ever waste things if he could help it.

Leftovers weren't Seamus's favorite thing for supper, but after Josiah explained it all in great detail, he'd actually acquiesced and accepted Josiah's side of an argument. Those moments were rare, but also treasured for their scarcity.

His phone pinged right as Josiah pulled into the driveway.

Seamus: Got a call. Might be a late night. Don't wait up.

Josiah's stomach tightened. As the county sheriff it wasn't unusual for Seamus to get a late call he needed to respond to, or a crime he needed to be present for, but they'd been happening more and more frequently these last few months. Sometimes he worried it wasn't really work—he didn't have the nerve to call up the county office and make sure Seamus had actually been called out—or simply Seamus not wanting to go home.

Possibly Seamus being out with someone else, socially or romantically.

For all that Josiah longed for the tender moments of their first few months together, he didn't dare go out and find other comfort. He was too terrified of Seamus finding out and what he would do in response. Josiah also didn't have the courage or means to leave the man and find someone else. Someone who didn't treat Josiah like an object he owned and could play with whenever and however he wanted.

Josiah also wasn't sure he needed better than what he had now. He had a roof over his head, a car that worked, and food in his belly—things he hadn't had for so long as a young person, and he'd never take them for granted now. No matter what the cost to his physical and mental health.

With Seamus out late, Josiah made himself a mixed plate of leftovers, glad to clear two small dishes from the refrigerator. One might have been slightly off, but living on the street for nearly a decade had given Josiah a cast-iron stomach, and he'd probably have to eat rancid, moldy raw meat to get sick.

He ate alone in the little home's screened-in back porch, enjoying the quiet evening. The yard was fenced in, and he'd often imagined a dog or two romping around in the grass, chasing bugs and sticks and entertaining him and Seamus. But Seamus was very anti-pet, so Josiah had nothing. No siblings, no kids, no pets, no one to shower his attention on besides his clients and their families.

Michael's exhausted smile flashed in his mind, and

Josiah grinned at the back fence as he ate. He enjoyed talking to Michael, who seemed as uncomfortable in Elmer's house as a nun in a strip club, and it was both endearing and strange. Michael had grown up there, after all. But he'd also spent half of his life away, living in a big city far from this simple country life.

A country life Josiah sometimes longed to escape from, but where would he go? And with what money?

No, dreams were for dreamers, and he'd long ago forgotten how to dream under the crush of real life and survival. Making it one meal to the next, one night safe to the next. No one was going to swoop in like a conquering hero and whisk Josiah away to a happy life somewhere far from here. Those thoughts were fantasies for children, not for grown-ass adults who knew better.

Survival mattered.

Dreams did not.

Chapter Six

Michael's first full week working at Woods Ranch improved by miles after his first two days. A lot of old riding and roping skills came back to him, and while he still struggled a bit with driving the herd from one pasture to another without the help of Brutus and Dog, he found himself enjoying the work. He was outside in the brilliant autumn sunshine, he liked all his coworkers, and he no longer went home sore and achy and in need of a soak.

All wins in his book.

His favorite, and most unexpected, thing was how easy and open Brand and Hugo were about their relationship, considering how conservative their county was in general. It gave Michael the courage to talk more openly about his own sexuality and some of the years of his misspent youth. The only thing he didn't expand on ever was his reasons for leaving Austin. Kenny and Rosco were still too raw.

Especially Rosco. But Dog reminded Michael a bit of Rosco in her temperament, and Jackson didn't seem to mind sharing his pet's attention with the other hands.

Dad's recovery seemed to be going well. He had nothing but praise for Josiah when the young nurse left for the night, and Michael began to anticipate their brief interactions twice a day, five days a week. Simple good mornings and heartier goodbyes. Hearing about Dad's exercises. Dad still had some issues with swallowing, and that was something that would either improve or carry on for the rest of his life.

Only time would tell about pretty much everything, and Michael had time to kill. His Realtor in Austin had no real bites on the house yet, but Michael refused to lower the asking price this soon. If he simply wanted to off-load it, he could drop it by a few hundred grand, but it was all Michael had. No trademarked app, no contracts, no royalties, nothing but that damned house. If this was his only legacy for fifteen years of work, Michael wanted to squeeze out every penny he could, so he could figure out what came next. Beyond working the ranch and caring for his dad.

What was his next big dream?

No idea, and since he didn't have the money to dream right now, Michael worked his ass off and stuck to the real world.

On his second Thursday in town, to celebrate one full week of Michael being a Woods Ranch employee, Brand and Hugo insisted on taking Michael out for a drink. After a quick call to Josiah, who insisted he could stay an extra hour, Michael agreed to the drink. He met the pair at the Roost. Ramie called out a greeting to their trio from behind the bar. Brand led them to a table in the back and a perky young waitress with frizzy red hair came over to take their order.

"Pitcher of Bud," Brand said, "and how about a platter of nachos, too?"

"Sounds good," Michael replied. He'd worked his

ass off this past week and deserved to splurge some of his hard-earned money on beer and junk food.

Their waitress brought three cold glasses and a pitcher of beer to the table with a promise that the nachos would be out shortly. Brand poured them all beer and they toasted Michael's first week. Michael was more of a cocktail guy nowadays, but he appreciated the simplicity of a cold, yeasty beer with coworkers. So different from the fancy, expensive drinks he and his old friends would order at the best hotel restaurants or clubs, simply to seem sophisticated and show off their money.

It all seemed so stupid now. None of those friends had called in the last few weeks. None of those relationships had been real. Not even his partnership with Kenny. That had been the biggest lie of all.

No more relationships. Not for a long while.

Maybe once he got his shit together, got Dad on his feet, and figured out where he wanted to land, he'd adopt a new dog.

Maybe.

A few townies gave their trio odd looks, but Michael was used to them, and he had a gut feeling Brand and Hugo had gotten used to them, too, as—he assumed— the only openly gay couple in Weston. But Michael had been in more than one brawl as a teen, and he wasn't about to take any disrespect from closed-minded idiots.

"So you don't talk about yourself much at work," Hugo said, once they'd each sipped their beers. "All I know about you is you live in Austin and develop apps. And you seem to really like PB&J sandwiches for lunch."

Michael chuckled. "They're easy lunch food. I'm not

much of a cook and never have been, so my kitchen motto is KISS."

"Kiss?"

"Keep it simple, stupid."

"Oh." Hugo laughed. "Makes sense. I'm not much of a cook, either. I mostly survive on sandwiches, leftovers from Rose's kitchen, or whatever Brand manages to whip up at our place." Rose was Brand's mother, and Michael vaguely recalled the woman entering a lot of baking competitions at both the county fair and Founder's Day Picnic. And winning ribbons.

"Sounds like my basic diet right now," Michael replied. "Protein bar for breakfast, sandwich for lunch, and whatever Josiah throws in the oven for dinner. Except for my days off, but we usually have leftovers to get by on."

"Is Josiah a good cook? We text a bit here and there, but I don't really know him all that well."

"Sure, he's a simple cook but the food is always great. Dad really enjoys it, too. I'm sure after living alone for so long, he's probably grateful to have someone else cooking for him for a change."

"No doubt," Brand said, adding to the conversation for the first time. "Your old man's good people but I bet he gets lonely puttering around on that property alone. I'm a little surprised he hasn't rented out his fifth wheel again yet, just for the company."

Michael wiped a bit of condensation off the side of his glass. "He's probably still a little gun-shy after the whole robbery incident this summer." Before Hugo could bristle, Michael added, "And he knows you didn't do it, and that Buck is back in prison, but things like that can spook a person." He couldn't believe he was defending his dad to other people but there they were.

A few months ago, Dad had come home to find a collection of vintage coins missing, and he'd called the sheriff. McBride had found the coins in the trailer Hugo had been renting from Dad, which was situated on his property. While Hugo insisted he hadn't taken them—who would be stupid enough to steal and keep the goods on the same property as the theft?—Dad had asked Hugo to move out. In a surprising plot twist, Hugo's crazy stepbrother had stolen the coins and put them in Hugo's trailer to frame Hugo and destroy his life. And it had almost worked.

But the Woods clan had rallied behind Hugo, Buck Archer eventually confessed to planting the coins, and Hugo was officially exonerated. It hadn't completely fixed Hugo's tarnished reputation, but it had been a start. All gossip courtesy of one night when Dad couldn't sleep or stop yakking.

"It's understandable," Hugo said. "Elmer being spooked about renting again. Plus, it isn't as if there's a plethora of folks moving to Weston looking for a place to stay."

"Good point." Michael had briefly entertained thoughts of moving into the fifth wheel himself, but until Dad was up and mobile again, he needed to stay close. And that meant in the house, sleeping in his old bedroom. Another grizzled old-timer passed their table and tossed them a sour look. "I guess it can't be easy. Being out around here."

Brand grunted. "It's not, but folks know better than to mess with us now."

"Yeah? Sounds like a story."

"Short story."

"But a good one," Hugo added. "After the coin thing with Elmer, Brand and I came out here for a drink. Three guys got in our faces. We kicked their asses inside, and then again later in the parking lot, because those knuckleheads needed the same lesson twice."

"It was definitely a night," Brand said with a smirk. "Things aren't as uptight as when I was a teen and Colt left in order to be himself, but we also don't go courting trouble. Helps that we're growing a reputation for amazing organic beef."

"True story." Hugo clinked the lip of his glass to Brand's.

The nachos arrived, delivered by Ramie herself. "You boys aren't gonna start any trouble in the bar tonight, are you?" she asked as she set down appetizer plates.

"Not on purpose, sweetheart," Brand replied. "We just came out to celebrate Michael's first week at the ranch."

"Uh-huh. You celebrating Jackson's first week ended in a brawl with two broken tables and a lot of beer on the floor."

"Really?" Hugo perked up. "How do I not know this story?"

Brand sipped his beer while Ramie headed back to the bar.

"Why on earth did you and Jackson get into a bar fight?" Michael asked. The quiet cowboy was the very definition of cool, calm, and collected. It was difficult to imagine him throwing a punch in any direction.

"Someone gave him shit about his hair," Brand replied.

"His hair?"

"Yeah, when he first started working for us, he wore it long. And not like mullet long, or anything, but in a ponytail, maybe to just below his shoulder blades. Used to say it honored his ancestors, but I never asked about his ancestry. First night we came out together, he got some racist shit thrown in his face, but Jackson took them down fast. No one messed with him after that, but he still cut his hair short about a week later. Hasn't worn it long again in the couple years he's been here."

"Huh." Jackson had the kind of tan skin and rugged appearance that could lend itself to any variety of ethnicities, from Indigenous to South American, and Michael wasn't the guy to ask that kind of personal shit. It did pique his interest in the man, though.

Michael grabbed a tortilla chip laden with seasoned beef, cheese sauce, pico, and lettuce, and he took a big bite. The slightest kick of jalapeno warmed the back of his throat, so he chased the bite with a second, nearly naked chip and a swig of beer. Delicious. They forwent conversation in favor of devouring the nachos. Hugo went up to the bar and came back with a small bowl of Ranch dressing, which he dunked some of his chips into.

Weird but whatever.

His cell rang, and Michael's pulse jumped, worried it was Josiah with an emergency. But the name on the screen made his stomach twist up tight and regret all that cheese. Kenny Wilde.

He stared at the phone, thumb hovering over the screen, unsure if he was going to hit the red or green button. Deny or accept. Part of him still missed Kenny and wanted to hear his voice again, especially now. Part of him despised the man and all his manipulations.

The former won, and he accepted the call. "Yeah?"

"Hey, babe, I'm glad you picked up," Kenny's syrupy-sweet voice said, all charm and kindness. The kind of voice that'd soothe you right into a nap and then stab you in the back the second your guard dropped.

"What do you want?"

"I wanted to see how you are. I heard about your dad through the grapevine. I'm so sorry he's sick."

Michael angled away from the table and the curious gazes of his two companions. "He's getting better. I'm coping. Happy?"

"You sound upset. And what is that noise?"

"I'm in a bar with a few friends. And if I'm upset, it's because you dumped me, stole my trademark, took most of my money and my dog, and I'm now living at home with my dad like a college dropout. Care to fuck off, Kenny?"

"Hey, Mikey, don't be like that, I'm calling because I still care about you. Fifteen years of feelings don't go away overnight."

"Yeah, I'm sure it took at least two nights of fucking someone else for your feelings for me to go away." And because he couldn't help himself, Michael asked, "How's Rosco?"

"Who? Oh, um, fine."

The tremor in Kenny's voice made Michael sit up straighter. "What is it? Is he sick?" That question got his tablemates' attention but Michael ignored them. "How is he?"

"Look, Alistair didn't like Rosco, so we had to re-home him."

"What?!" Michael stood so fast he nearly knocked his chair over backward. Uncaring, he stalked to a less crowded corner of the bar, fury briefly blinding him, and he nearly walked into a wall. "Why the fuck did you rehome him? All you had to do was fucking call me, Kenny. He's my dog!"

"He was my dog. I bought him—"

"With money you got from my fucking app!"

"Before we got married, which did not make him community property, and irregardless of—"

"That's not a word and you know it. Where is my dog?"

"I didn't call to talk about the dog, Mikey, I called about your dad, and to see how you were doing."

"I was fine until you called, asshole. Look, I didn't go after you for anything that went down between us. I rolled over and took it, but I will not take this. I want to know where he is and that he's safe, or else."

"Or else what?" All traces of concern in Kenny's voice were gone, replaced by a familiar haughtiness Michael despised. "I know the house hasn't sold, so you don't have the money to sue me. Have fun at home."

"Where's Rosco?"

"He's fine."

"Kenny—"

Kenny hung up.

Michael barely resisted the urge to fling his cell across the room. While doing so might feel good for about twenty seconds, all he'd end up with was the expense of buying another one, and it wasn't his phone's fault his ex was a giant douche. Rosco was with someone else, God knew who, and Kenny didn't seem to give a shit as long as his new boyfriend was happy.

"Dude, I'd ask if you're okay," Brand said from behind, "but something is clearly wrong. Half the bar could hear you yelling."

"Sorry." Michael turned, not surprised to see people at several tables look briskly away. "Not a good call."

"What's going on? Can I help?"

"Probably not. When my ex left a few weeks ago, he took our dog with him. Now he tells me his newest boyfriend doesn't like dogs, so they rehomed him." Hot tears sparked behind Michael's eyes but he blinked them back. "Fucker gave away my best friend."

"Shit, I'm sorry." Brand's face reddened. "I almost lost Brutus to a wild animal this past spring so I can imagine how you feel. Our dogs aren't just animals."

"No, they aren't. Fuck." Michael stalked back to their table and chugged the last of his beer, then poured himself a second glass. He wasn't about to get hammered, but he needed something to take the edge off his temper. If he had a clue where Kenny was right now, he'd have hunted the guy down and given him a very in-person piece of his mind.

And then he'd go get his fucking dog back—right?

Being stuck here, eight hours away, was a convenient excuse to roll over instead of solving the problem head-on. Just like he'd rolled over on the divorce agreement instead of fighting.

Brand whispered something to Hugo, whose expression went from angry to sympathetic in the space of a few seconds. "That's so fucked up," Hugo said.

"I feel like the bastard is doing all this just to hurt me and I don't know why," Michael replied. "All I ever did was love and support him, and all he's done this last month is take from me. And even after everything he's done, I never really hated him until this moment." He gulped from his beer, but after so many years of high-end cocktails, the low alcohol content wasn't doing much for him.

"You gonna need a ride home, man?" Brand asked.

"No, I'll be fine. I haven't been able to get drunk on beer since I was eighteen." He shoved a few more nachos into his mouth for good measure, this time not caring that they were a little extra spicy. He'd pop some antacids when he got back to Dad's house. "I appreciate the gesture, guys, but I don't think I'm going to be good company tonight."

"Completely understandable. You need the day off tomorrow to take care of personal business?"

As much as Michael loved the idea of going back to Austin to hunt Kenny and Rosco down, he had no idea how to go about doing it. None of his old friends were likely to tell him where Kenny was, not even the ones who'd loved Rosco, too. Unless Kenny had given Rosco to one of those former friends. He hoped so. Kenny might be a self-centered prick, but he'd never been deliberately cruel to an animal. Only people.

"No, I'm fine to work tomorrow," Michael said. "Honestly, I think I need the distraction, and I know Josiah likes to keep a consistent schedule."

"I take it that's going well?" Brand asked. "Josiah and your father?"

"Yes, they seem to get along great. Dad has no complaints. He's got a checkup on Monday, so we'll see what his progress is, but Josiah is consistent with his physical therapy."

"Glad to hear it."

Michael tried to put some cash down to tip their waitress, but Brand waved him off with a friendly smile. It had been a long damned time, almost too long, since Michael had done something this simple. Beer and nachos with buddies. No ulterior motives. He'd missed this more than he could express, so he shook Brand's and Hugo's hands, and then left.

He texted Josiah that he was on his way home on the walk to his car. The sports car was a tad out of place in a parking lot full of pickups, dusty sedans, and a few motorcycles. Maybe he should trade it in for something cheaper after all. Something better on gas, better on the backroads, and that would give him a little bit of cash in his pocket. He'd look online later and see what was available locally. No sense in wasting gas driving all the way to Amarillo if he could avoid it.

Josiah was lingering by the front door when Michael walked up onto the porch, and he started talking before Michael even opened the screen door. "I'm so sorry, but I really need to leave, Michael. I forgot I had agreed to meet someone and I'm late, but I couldn't leave your father alone."

"Hey, no, it's fine. My fault." The wide-eyed, red-faced way Josiah bounced on the balls of his feet tempered Michael's initial annoyance at Josiah not remembering this meeting when Michael first called about staying late.

"I told him he could go," Dad shouted from his bed. "Not gonna keel over dead if I'm alone for thirty minutes."

"I know, but I agreed to do a job," Josiah replied. "We didn't have any issues, but if you have questions, text me, okay?"

"Sure," Michael said. "Go do your thing. Sorry about making you late."

"It's fine, and thank you." Josiah practically ran to his car.

Michael stood on the other side of the screen door and watched Josiah drive away, as was becoming his habit. Most days Josiah lingered for a few minutes, seeming to enjoy their brief chats as much as Michael did. Today, he'd be lucky if he didn't get a ticket on the way home—then again, it probably helped having the sheriff as a roommate.

"You have a beer for me?" Dad asked when Michael turned away from the door. He had a game show on TV but wasn't watching it.

"Sure, beer and nachos." Michael went into the kitchen for a glass of water to wet his slightly parched mouth, then returned to the living room. Stretched out on the couch to watch TV for a while. "Did Josiah mention what he was late for?"

"No, just got real spooked when he realized he'd forgotten whatever it was. I told him to leave, that you'd be home soon, but he refused to go. Stubborn Okie."

"He told you he's from Oklahoma?"

"Yep, we talked a bit about Tulsa. Says he lived there a long time before he moved to Texas for nursing school."

That was the most personal information Michael had learned about the young nurse since they met. Then again, he and Josiah never had much time to get personal. One of these nights soon, he needed to ask Josiah to stay for dinner with them so Michael could get to know him better. They didn't have to be best friends, but Michael still wanted to have some sort of friendship with Josiah.

He really wanted that to happen.

"What is wishful thinking?" Dad asked.

"Huh?" Michael blinked dumbly at his father. "What?"

Dad pointed at the television. "That question for the clue. Wishful thinking is the answer."

"Oh. Right." Duh. His dad wasn't a mind reader. "So, um, do you want to watch a movie after this is over?"

"Sure. See if you can find an old Western or something. Gene Autry or Alan Ladd, maybe."

"I'll see what I can find." One of Michael's fondest childhood memories was of watching those old Westerns with both his parents. They'd make big bowls of air-popped popcorn, and sometimes Michael even got a cola to drink as a treat. Mom and Dad loved those movies to bits, because they romanticized the life of ranchers and cowboys, and for a little boy like Michael, it had helped smooth the edges of the rough life it really was.

Especially after the rough life took Mom from them both.

While Dad finished watching his game show, Michael used his phone to find a good movie Dad's cable would allow them to stream. Once he found one he thought Dad might like, Michael went into the kitchen to make popcorn.

Chapter Seven

Michael stood by the front door the next morning, lunch bag in hand, waiting impatiently for Josiah to arrive for work. He wasn't impatient because he was late (a quick call to Brand or Wayne would give him extra time), but because Josiah was always early. He was supposed to start his shift at eight-fifteen, and he always arrived by eight-ten. It was already eight-sixteen, so Michael was antsy and unsure why.

Dad was still fast asleep. He didn't usually wake up until around nine or nine thirty, especially with all the downstairs curtains drawn, which gave Josiah time to settle in before starting breakfast. It was a small grace that gave Michael about an hour of silence in the morning with the television off to drink coffee, have some toast, and get ready for a long day at Woods Ranch.

Long days that were less hot and sweaty as they inched deeper into autumn. Ranching still wasn't his dream occupation, but he was starting to remember what he used to love about horseback riding and wide-open spaces. It made him wonder what better use he could get out of Dad's vast acreage, other than places for snakes, mice, and other vermin to nest all year long in the tall grass.

Thoughts for another day.

Josiah pulled into the driveway at eight-nineteen, and Michael's entire body jerked to attention. He shot a quick text to Brand that he might be a few minutes late getting to work while Josiah grabbed his own cloth bag and…limped? Yeah, he limped his way to the front porch, favoring his left leg a bit, but Michael didn't see a cast or other obvious sign of injury.

"You okay?" Michael asked quietly as he opened the screen door for Josiah.

"Yeah, I'm so sorry I'm running behind. I had a hard time getting up this morning." Josiah's entire body seemed to stiffen as he entered the house, as if not wanting to show weakness in front of Michael. "I didn't mean to make you late."

"It's okay. What happened? Did you hurt yourself?"

Josiah wobbled slightly, and Michael reached out to steady him. The immediate way Josiah flinched and took a step back raised Michael's hackles.

"It was so stupid," Josiah replied, his smile coming across less sheepish and more distressed. "I slipped in the bathroom last night and hit my ribs on the edge of the sink. Didn't break anything but it hurt. I had a hard time sleeping."

Alarm sent adrenaline through Michael's entire body. "Shit, man, did you go to the hospital for X-rays or anything?"

"No, like I said, nothing was broken. Just some bruises and embarrassment." Josiah wouldn't look him in the eye, though, and that worried Michael on an instinctive level. "I really am okay."

"Are you fine to deal with Dad today? Because I can call out if you can't roll him over and shit. Stuff."

"I'll be fine, Michael. Promise. A couple more ibuprofen and I'll be right as rainbows. Or rain, or whatever that expression is."

"Okay." He watched Josiah limp around the dark living room, uncertain about leaving when everything inside him wanted to stay. "Um, there's some coffee still in the pot if you want it. A few sausages in the fridge for breakfast that I cooked up but didn't eat. If Dad's not too grumpy, you can probably crumble one into his scrambled eggs."

Josiah's smile almost convinced Michael that everything was, in fact, okay. Almost. "Thanks. I'm on top of it, I promise. If I have any issues, I will call you. I'll never endanger my patients because of my pride."

"Okay." He glanced at Dad, who was still fast asleep. "See you around five thirty, Josiah."

"You will."

He still hated leaving, and Michael couldn't explain to himself exactly why. But he did, climbing into his car with his lunch and disliking it the entire time as he drove away from the house. His mood must have been all over his face when he parked by the Woods barn and got out. Jackson and Hugo were standing outside chatting, and they both shut up to stare at him.

"You okay, bud?" Jackson asked.

"Huh?" Michael stared at the guy, suddenly aware he had his hat in his hand and his lunch was still on the front passenger seat. He reached inside for the paper bag he'd reused all week. "Yeah, just a weird morning. Sorry."

"Everything okay with your father?"

"Sure, he's fine." With no way to explain the odd vibes he'd gotten from Josiah, Michael strode into the barn and the break room to put his lunch in the fridge.

Unfortunately, he put his hat in the fridge and almost whacked himself upside the head with his lunch. Even worse, Jackson and Hugo both saw it happen.

"Michael, what's going on?" Hugo asked. "Is this about the call you got last night? You know we'll listen if you need to vent. Or if you need help."

"I don't need help." Annoyed at himself, Michael shoved the paper bag into the fridge and put his hat on, even though he was indoors. "Sorry, just having a bad morning. I didn't mean to bring it with me to work."

"Hey, we all have bad days," Jackson said. "If you tell anyone I said this I'll deny it, but even I'm not perfect."

Michael snorted. "I'm so far from perfect we're on different planets. I'm so oblivious to real life sometimes that I couldn't even tell when my ex-boyfriend was cheating on me again." That had slipped out without permission, but he didn't bother backpedaling. Neither Jackson nor Hugo looked scandalized or too surprised, and Michael wasn't sure how to take that.

"Again? Is that recent?" Hugo asked. "Like this morning recent?"

"I found out a few weeks ago when he dumped me, moved out, and took our dog."

Jackson made an angry, growly noise. As if sensing his owner's distress, Dog loped into the room and bumped her head against Jackson's thigh. Jackson squatted to hug his dog, and it made Michael's heart ache for Rosco.

"I'm sorry that happened," Hugo said. "Especially losing your dog. Doesn't sound like the boyfriend was such a big loss, but I know how devastated Brand would have been this spring if Brutus hadn't survived that animal attack. Our pets are our family as much as people are."

"Yeah. Thanks." Michael ran his hand down Dog's back. "Things have been going down for a couple of weeks. A lot of it is why I was able to pick up and move here after Dad's stroke. All I really left behind was an empty house I'm trying to sell."

"So you aren't going back to Austin when your dad gets better?"

"I don't know, and that's the god's honest truth. Austin's got a lot of bad memories now. The one thing I knew when I packed up and drove here was that I needed a change. Can't say as being a cowboy again was what I dreamed for my life, but this is where I am. I'm grateful for this job and that my dad is alive and getting better." Dog licked his fingers and Michael rubbed behind her soft ears. "I don't know if I want to go back or not, just that I need something else right now. Something more real than the life I used to have."

"Totally get that," Jackson said. "We're all here for a reason, man, and they're our own reasons." That particular comment raised Michael's curiosity about his coworker but now wasn't the time or place to ask. Maybe one night he'd ask Jackson out for a beer so they could chat. Get to know each other. God knew Michael needed friends up here.

"Well, being out here on the land is about as real as things get," Hugo said. "I moved back here for a fresh start and I got it. Rustling cattle probably isn't your dream job after working in tech for so long, but it's honest, hard work. Raising beef so folks can feed their families. Wind power so we can be a little bit kinder to the environment."

"I do appreciate the work," Michael replied, still absently stroking Dog's head and neck. "And the chance to start over. Have my midlife crisis in a safe place."

Hugo laughed. "Great, you're already having one? Does that mean Brand is only a few years from his own midlife crisis? Yay, me. What about you, Jackson?"

Jackson smiled and rolled his shoulders. "Had mine a while ago. Why do you think I ended up here?"

"No idea, because you won't tell me."

"Nope."

The exchange only amped up Michael's curiosity about Jackson, but if the guy was this tight-lipped over his past, Michael was unlikely to ever get that story. Sometimes the past needed to stay in the past. Like Kenny. He really ought to block the asshole's number, but right now Kenny was his only lead to Rosco. And if Kenny couldn't be damned to keep him because of a new lover, then Michael very much wanted his dog back.

"There are definitely worse places to have a crisis," Michael said. "But we're probably all inching close to starting our days late and should get to work."

"Good point," Hugo replied. "Work now, gossip later."

"Dating the boss doesn't have extra perks?" Jackson asked.

"I don't like to press my luck. I get a paycheck just like the rest of you guys."

"And you love your boyfriend too much to take advantage?"

"Exactly."

Today's schedule had Michael and Jackson out riding the fence line, watching the herd, and checking for any repairs or lost cattle. Dog followed along at a steady gait, and Michael enjoyed the chance to be out in the open lands of the ranch, distanced from the things that still niggled at the back of his mind, like Josiah that morning. Something was off and a small part of Michael worried it had something to do with last night.

They returned to the barn around lunchtime. Brand surprised them all by bringing half a pan of hot lasagna out from the main house, leftovers from last night's supper. Apparently, Rose had planned the meal before she realized Brand and Hugo wouldn't be home to help eat it, so they got the treat today. The spicy scent appealed to Michael way more than his simple sandwich, even though a gut full of pasta would make him want to take a nap right afterward.

Brand served up big slabs on paper plates. Michael had just fetched his soda from the fridge when his cell began blaring the theme for *The Munsters*, which he'd programmed for Dad's house line years ago. Weird. The phone was in reach of Dad's hospital bed, but there was no reason for Dad to be calling him. The one time Josiah had called during work hours with a question, he'd done so on his own cell phone.

Curious and slightly alarmed, Michael answered, "Hello?"

"Good, you picked up," Dad said, sounding somewhat out of breath. "Something ain't right with Josiah. I think you need to come home."

"What?" He put his soda can on the table a little too hard, only vaguely aware of the other three men in the small break room staring at him. "What's wrong?"

"Not quite sure. He went into the kitchen to get lunch started and then I heard heavy breathing. Pretty sure he's sitting on the floor now, 'cuz I can kinda see his feet from here, but he won't answer when I yell."

"Okay, I'm coming home. Just… I don't know, keep trying to talk to him."

"I can do that."

Michael ended the call. "Brand—"

"Go," Brand said. "You can tell me later."

"Thanks." He bolted outside to his car, glad he'd gotten in the habit of leaving his keys on the driver's seat, because it was one less thing to worry about finding. He tried not to speed too fast down the lane from the ranch to the state road. Dad had sounded safe enough, but something was definitely wrong with Josiah, and Michael needed to get there so he could fix it.

He couldn't fix a problem over the phone. It needed to be right in front of him. The great thing about computers and programming was his innate understanding of numbers. Michael didn't have that same understanding when it came to people. His people skills often boiled down to "talk them into it even if they aren't interested" and "don't let them cry in front of me—I can't handle tears."

He slammed to a stop in the driveway behind Dad's pickup and next to Josiah's car, barely noticing the dust his wheels kicked up. He tore through the yard and up onto the porch and, if he hadn't taken a split second to remember the loose chain, might have yanked the screen door right off the house.

Dad stared at him from his bed, the frame adjusted so he sat completely upright, legs slightly bent, his expression a mix of confusion and annoyance. Josiah sat on the couch, bent at the waist, face resting on his hands, which were braced on his knees. It seemed like progress, since

Dad said Josiah had been sitting on the kitchen floor before, so he'd at least gotten up and moved.

"Josiah?" Michael asked.

Josiah's entire body flinched in a way Michael didn't like.

"Hasn't said much," Dad said. "He's moving around, though, so I guess he didn't have a stroke like I did."

Michael didn't have the wherewithal to laugh or even snort at the terrible joke. He circled the couch and sat next to Josiah, watching the younger man carefully. No obvious sign of injury beyond the very faint trembling in his arms and shoulders. "Josiah? Are you hurt?"

Josiah shook his head without looking up. Muttered something Michael couldn't make out.

Despite his concern, Michael turned to Dad. "Are you okay?"

"Hungry for lunch," Dad replied with a half smile that took the edge off his grumpy tone. "Take care of the kid, first. I'll live."

You'd better, you old bastard.

Michael eased onto the couch, leaving about a foot of space between himself and Josiah, who still hadn't looked up. "Okay, guy, I need you to talk to me. What's going on?" When Josiah didn't say anything, a tiny bit of temper peeked through. "I left my own job to come back here because something's wrong. Tell me what happened."

"I'm really sorry," Josiah said to his hands and lap. "You can dock me the whole day's pay if you have to. I'm sorry."

"Hey, don't worry about pay right now. What happened?" The last thing he needed was someone unreliable looking after his disabled father, but everything in Michael insisted this wasn't incompetence. This was something else.

Josiah looked up. His cheeks and eyes were red, but he wasn't crying or breaking down. He looked miserable, though, and that spoke to all of Michael's protective instincts. "I'm so sorry you had to leave work, Michael. I, um, think it was a panic attack. That's why I collapsed."

Alarm jolted down Michael's spine. "Do you have those a lot?"

"No. Not really." He ran both hands through his thick, messy hair. "I might need a new place to live soon, and after hurting myself this morning, things just snowballed in my head, and I kind of lost it."

"I thought you hurt your ribs last night."

Something a lot like guilt flashed in Josiah's expressive dark eyes. Eyes not blocked at all by his glasses. "Right, last night. Please, can I have like ten minutes in the bathroom to breathe, and then I promise I can keep working. I didn't mean to make you doubt me."

"Hey, I'm not doubting you. You've been great, but we all have bad days. We all get sick or have, you know, moments." Something else Josiah said made it through, and Michael's heart skipped. "You're losing your place with the sheriff?"

Josiah coughed and hunched even deeper into himself. "It's complicated, but yeah, I think so."

"Okay, well that's something we can fix pretty damned easy."

"You can't."

"Sure, I can." Michael lightly tapped Josiah's knee. "Hey? We've got a trailer right out in the yard that no one's renting or living in. Even if your roommate kicked you out today, you wouldn't have to sleep in your car. Shit, we could probably work out a deal on rent in exchange for you helping Dad."

Josiah blinked at him several times, his eyes wet now. "Really?"

"Of course." He glanced over at Dad, whose quiet calm betrayed a hint of anger. But not anger at Michael or his offer to Josiah; he knew his father better than that, despite their estrangement. Dad helped people, and they both knew something wasn't right in this situation. "Look, man, you've been good with my dad and if you've got some problems we can help you work through them."

"I, um, don't know for sure what my circumstances are right now, but I appreciate the offers of help from you both." He popped his glasses back on. "I just really need a few minutes to collect myself, and then I am fine to keep working."

As much as Michael wanted to demand Josiah relax for the rest of the day, he also recognized stubborn people when their minds were made up. "One question first."

His eyes narrowed. "Okay."

"When did you last eat?"

Josiah frowned.

"It's been hours for me, that's for sure," Dad said when no one else spoke. "How about we all three have a good lunch before anything else happens? We don't even have to talk, let's just all eat something."

"Spoken like a true Pearce," Michael said. "If we like anything, it's food. You'd think we were Italian or something, but we're not. Hell, I don't even know what we are."

"You got some Irish in you, boy. Probably why we can all hold our liquor."

Michael laughed, and even Josiah's lips twitched. "How about we do a fridge clean-out? Josiah, you do what you need to do, and I'll see about lunch for us all."

"Okay." Josiah stood and headed directly for the downstairs bathroom.

As soon as the door clicked shut, Michael went to stand by Dad's bed. "I need you to be honest with me, old man, and tell me if you're still comfortable with him being your caretaker while I'm at work."

"I am." Dad didn't hesitate for a second. "He's a good kid, and I think he's just hitting a rough patch. And I'm on board with him living in the trailer for a while if that's what he needs. We don't talk about a lot of personal stuff, but I like him. He, uh, he's a good listener, especially when an old man starts to ramble about his life."

Michael wanted to say he'd listen to Dad ramble in the evenings, but they rarely had any serious conversations. The past, especially, was still too painful. Maybe, though, they could make some new, less painful memories now. "Well, I'll go figure out lunch. And I need to call Brand. Let him know I'm coming back in a bit."

"You do that."

In the kitchen, Michael made the call.

"Hey, is everything okay at home?" Brand asked. Wind blew over the microphone, so he was outside somewhere on the ranch.

"Yeah, we're all okay. Josiah is having a minor personal crisis, but I think it'll be fine. He just…" It wasn't really Michael's gossip to spread, so he stayed vague.

"He needed some reassurance. I'll be back in about an hour."

"You can take the afternoon if you think you need it, Michael."

"I appreciate that." He also got the feeling Josiah wouldn't like Michael hovering or treating him like a fragile flower that would crumble at any moment. "But we're good here. I'll be back."

"See you then. And if there's anything my family can do for whatever's going on, let me know."

"I will, boss. See you in a bit."

Michael set about pulling various containers out of the fridge and arranging them on the counter. They had bits and bobs of different lunch and dinner meals from the last few days, and while nothing really made sense, they had a lot to choose from. He put a plate together for Dad and stuck it in the microwave to reheat.

By the time he had the food and a drink on Dad's rolling table, Josiah returned from the bathroom. His face was red and his bangs damp, suggesting he'd washed his face. He immediately took over helping Dad with his fork. Learning how to eat hot food left-handed wasn't something Michael ever wanted to try, thank you very much.

"If you want to eat, I can do this," Michael said gently.

"It's fine. I'll eat when Elmer is finished," Josiah replied, his tone more clipped than before. "You eat. You've got to get back to work."

Michael glanced at Dad, who shrugged with his eyebrows while trying to spear a piece of pasta. Okay then. With orders to eat, Michael scraped out the last of the leftover noodle bake, some steamed vegetables,

and a final scoop of mashed potatoes. Heated them up
and ate alone at the kitchen counter, not wanting to dis-
rupt whatever lunchtime routine Dad and Josiah had
created. Afternoon news still droned on in the background, because no one had changed the TV channel,
and Michael blocked it out. He couldn't deal with the
real world right now.

He ate slowly and still had a few bites left when Josiah came in with Dad's plate. Josiah rinsed and washed
everything, then placed them in the dish drainer to dry.
He made his own plate and popped it into the microwave, but seemed to make a point about rinsing and
washing empty bowls, before nuking his own lunch.
The guy didn't have to impress Michael; Dad liked Josiah and that worked for Michael.

For now.

"You never answered me before," Michael whispered once Josiah took his steaming plate out of the
microwave.

Josiah put his plate on the counter and sat with a
stool between them, so stiff Michael half expected the
guy to snap a limb or something. "About what?"

"When was the last time you ate?"

Several long seconds passed. "Yesterday at lunch.
I didn't want to eat your father's food for dinner last
night, and when I got home…dinner was over."

"Because of that thing you were late for?"

"Pretty much. And I don't want to talk about it. I
appreciate the lead on a place to stay, but we aren't
friends, Mr. Pearce."

Ouch. "Okay. I don't wanna pry into your personal
life. Just to offer help if you need it. As a friend. I've
taken a few licks recently, so I know how it feels to strug-

gle. And how it feels to chafe when it comes to asking for help."

Josiah poked at the food on his plate for several long moments before looking up. Meeting Michael's eyes. "The last time I accepted help from someone, it cost a lot more than I expected it to."

The heartbreak in Josiah's voice made every protective instinct inside Michael sit up and take notice, and he barely resisted the urge to hug the younger man. "All I'm asking for and offering back is friendship, Josiah, I promise. I know how it feels to have some take and then break your trust. And I won't do that to you."

"I believe you." He speared a piece of broccoli but didn't eat it. "Thank you."

"You're welcome. And if you are losing your place and need help moving your stuff, let me know. I'm off tomorrow, and Brand is great about time off."

"I'll let you know when I know for sure. Last night was probably just a stupid fight, but it helps knowing I have a place to go if I need it."

Last night. The same time Josiah had hurt his ribs. After being late for something. Maybe Michael was being overly suspicious, but everything about this felt wrong. And he made a silent promise to get to the bottom of what was going on with Josiah's "roommate." One way or another.

Chapter Eight

Michael didn't make it eight feet into the Woods Ranch barn before Jackson's slightly broader frame nudged him away from a stall door and against the wall. He'd only known the guy for a week and didn't completely trust him, but Michael also didn't feel threatened by the gesture, or he'd have probably hauled off and shoved Jackson onto his ass.

"I'm gonna ask you something, friend, and I need you to be honest with me," Jackson said.

"Ask," Michael said right away, curious.

"Is Josiah Sheridan in a safe place right now?"

The question threw him for a few seconds, and Michael stuttered finding his words. "I…yes? I mean, he's perfectly safe in my house. My dad's house. All I can say is Josiah thinks he might be losing his spot rooming with Sheriff McBride, but Dad and I offered him the trailer in the yard. He's safe as far as I know. Why?"

Jackson grunted. Looked over both shoulders, but other than some of the horses they were alone. "I'm just being cautious. I knew someone once who was in a bad place, downplayed how serious it was, and things got bad. Really bad. Don't wanna see that happen again to someone else I know."

"I get that on a different level. I wasn't physically in a bad place, but I put my heart and trust in someone who blew both up. I'll keep an eye on Josiah and whatever's going on with him."

"Okay. I'll hold you to that."

"Please do." Jackson's intensity over this surprised him a little, but Michael also appreciated knowing Josiah had more people in his corner than he probably realized. "Thanks, Jackson."

"Sure. You and your dad take care of each other."

"We will."

After helping Jackson muck a few horse stalls, Michael walked over to the bunkhouse for a prescheduled meeting with Brand and Wayne on rebranding the Woods Ranch website and beef, especially for local venues like the Founder's Day Picnic and farmers markets. Even though the bunkhouse was technically where Brand and Hugo lived, both men said to just knock hard and come on inside. Felt odd to Michael, but he did.

The door to Brand's office stood wide-open, so Michael stopped just outside it. Brand was on his cell and he waved Michael inside. Finished up his call while Michael sat in a chair opposite the desk, much like he had the day he was hired. Being in an office space surrounded by bunk beds was a little weird, but whatever. The situation worked for the men who lived here and that was good enough for Michael.

"Hey, everything okay at home?" Brand asked.

"So far so good. Might have a new tenant for the trailer soon."

"This about Josiah's personal crisis?"

"Yeah. I don't wanna spread his personal business around, though, you know?"

"Sure, I totally understand. But if you or he needs any extra help, please reach out. I don't know Josiah well myself, but Hugo considers him a friend, and I help out friends."

"Thank you. I mean it. Your family is, well, you're giving me a chance on the ranch, and I appreciate knowing we've got some backup here."

"Of course. I've always liked your dad, and you have worked your ass off since I hired you. You just keep proving I'm a really good judge of people's character."

Michael laughed. "I'll do that. Now, the ranch branding?"

"Yeah, drag that chair around. Let's see what we've got."

As much as Michael enjoyed being outdoors and working with his hands, he smiled as he settled in to work with his very favorite thing: numbers and codes.

Josiah spent his afternoon cleaning every inch of the Pearce home's downstairs, because he couldn't sit still. Since he'd had so few spaces of his own, he'd learned to keep them neat and tidy. Messes and crumbs enticed roaches and bugs, and he didn't want that, especially in a place where he didn't live. He got a few curious looks from Elmer, but his patient mostly watched TV and ignored Josiah's manic dusting, polishing, window washing, and sweeping of every surface he could safely reach.

He needed a step stool for one spot around the living room's big stone fireplace and chimney, though.

If Elmer wondered, he didn't ask, and Josiah silently

thanked the elderly man for his discretion. Josiah just needed to stay busy right now, damn it, so his brain didn't focus too much on last night and this morning. On his bruises and sore ribs and very real fear that when he went home tonight, he'd find his stuff in the driveway. Or worse, in the garbage cans.

One night. One time he'd been late and forgotten a date. And it had cost him. Dearly.

Thankfully, his minor breakdown at the Pearce house hadn't cost him his job, and if the worst happened, he'd have a place to live temporarily. Taking a room from Michael didn't feel a whole lot different than his room with Seamus, because of the uneven power dynamic, but something about Michael made Josiah want to trust him. Josiah wasn't quite sure yet if he did trust Michael, but he wanted to. A lot.

So he cleaned and tried not to think about what was waiting for him when he went home—no, back to Seamus's house. For all that the place had been his "home" these last two years, its four walls were no longer *home*. It was a house and a room. A room that had never truly been Josiah's. Everything had always belonged to Seamus, from the room to the furniture to Josiah's own body. Even his own damned paycheck had been under Seamus's control.

No more. He'd go to the bank tomorrow and change that. Do whatever he needed so he had his own money going forward. He wouldn't live on the streets again. Never again.

He finally quit cleaning a little after five and collapsed onto the sofa near Elmer. Elmer was watching a local news broadcast and hadn't said much to Josiah in the past hour, not since he last needed to use the bottle for personal business. Josiah eyeballed the card table he'd set up nearby with a two-hundred-piece puzzle on it that they'd begun yesterday, mostly to exercise Elmer's dexterity and coordination.

They hadn't made much progress.

The cleaning supplies were all neatly stored away underneath the kitchen sink when Michael returned home from the second half of his day. Michael, who exuded warmth and safety and kindness, and whose presence made Josiah feel less like a clueless mess. More in control of his life and surroundings. But it was a false sense of control, because Josiah wasn't in control. Hadn't been for pretty much his entire life and probably never would be.

All he could do was fake it one day to the next.

"Staying for supper?" Michael asked from the kitchen. Josiah got a brief glimpse of him pulling something out of the freezer before Michael moved out of his line of sight.

"I can't, but thank you," Josiah replied. Since he wasn't here over the weekend, he gathered up his book and cloth bag he brought snacks in. Even though his clients almost always said to help himself to their food, keeping his own was a habit he couldn't seem to break.

"See you Monday," Elmer said.

"See you then. Good night, Elmer. Michael."

"Night!" Michael shouted back from the kitchen.

Normally, Josiah would leave proud of himself for his first full week at a new job, with a new patient. Tonight, he walked out with dread in his gut, his feet leaden and not wanting to carry him forward. Yes, he'd done well with Elmer and he liked the man very much. Michael, too. His melancholy wasn't about them; it was about leaving.

Seamus's car was in the driveway, which was a bit unusual, but Josiah had left a roast in the slow cooker, so Seamus would have had dinner ready to eat. Josiah got out on stiff legs and trod up the stone path to the porch. Up its three wide steps and across to the front door. Grabbed the knob and turned.

It was locked.

Startled, because Seamus didn't usually lock the front door until after dark, Josiah found his house key. It went into the knob but nothing turned. "What the hell?" He tried his key in the dead bolt and it didn't work, either. Icy panic filled his stomach. Why the hell had Seamus changed the locks? Almost everything Josiah owned was in that house.

He hoped.

Real terror flooded his veins as he circled the house to the backyard. They didn't have any sort of town trash service, so Seamus stored their trash in the garage out back and made a dump run about once a month. The garage door was locked, too, which it never was, and he couldn't see if the cans were overflowing in the dim interior. Hands shaking and heart trying to break through his ribs, Josiah approached the rear door of the house. The kitchen door.

With no real hope of it working, Josiah tried his key. Useless. The door's single curtain was closed, and the narrow set of steps didn't extend far enough for him to look in through any of the other kitchen windows. Josiah was too short, the house's foundation too high so he couldn't see shit. He banged his fist against the back door. "Seamus! Let me in!"

Several agonizing moments of silence passed. Threatening to call the police dangled on the tip of his tongue for a split second before he remembered his place. Seamus was the fucking sheriff and Josiah's name wasn't on the mortgage. He hadn't signed any official lease giving him rights to access this property. Technically, he was trespassing.

"Seamus, please! What's going on?"

Determined to be a nuisance until he got answers—or at least his fucking phone charger and some clothes—Josiah called Seamus. Seamus shocked the hell out of him by answering the call, but his terse, "I'm busy, call back," and hang-up stunned Josiah into momentary paralysis.

Seamus's car was here, so he had to be home. Had to have heard Josiah banging and yelling. What was he playing at? He called again but it went right to voice mail, which was unusual. As the sheriff, Seamus's phone was almost always on in case of emergencies. But what if he wasn't actually home? The house seemed dark, and he hadn't heard Seamus's phone's ringtone. It wasn't a huge house.

Frustration began overtaking some of his fear and he stabbed out a text:

If you're home let me in. Now.

No response.

Josiah circled the house and sat in his car, so mixed-up he didn't know what else to do besides wait. A tiny part of him wanted to call 911 and report a break-in at the house just to see what Seamus would do, but the rest of him was terrified of accidentally getting himself arrested. He'd spent the night in jail twice as a teen, and it was not an experience he ever wanted to repeat, thank you very much. That same fear kept him from testing any of the windows and simply breaking in to get his stuff. He also mentally flogged himself for not seeing this coming. For not seeing this coming as Seamus became crueler and more distant with him. For letting himself become one small mistake from homelessness again.

But I have a place to go. Michael will help.

Josiah loathed being dependent on others for his own security. Loathed it. But he'd fallen into the same trap again, and now all he really had to his name was a hardcover novel, his cell phone, and his car. He did have his car, the title in his name. If nothing else, Josiah had a roof and four walls to call home.

The sun went down and no lights came on in the house. Since Josiah couldn't imagine Seamus hiding out in the dark simply to avoid a confrontation with him, Seamus had to be out somewhere. But where and with who? His stomach rumbled with hunger, and he tried not to think about the pot roast either overcooking in the kitchen, or possibly being eaten elsewhere with someone not him. Both possibilities infuriated him, but that anger never rose completely above his fear.

Josiah ate a granola bar from his bag of snacks, and half regretted doing so when he realized he had nothing to drink to wash the sweetness down.

Around eight thirty an SUV pulled in behind his car. The engine didn't shut off. Heart galloping, Josiah watched in his rearview mirror as Seamus got out of the passenger side and walked right past his car. Straight to the front porch. Without thinking, Josiah leaped out of his car and made it to the porch before Seamus had the door unlocked.

"Why did you lock me out?" Josiah asked, fully aware he'd practically shouted the words when he rarely ever raised his voice to anyone.

"Because you don't live here anymore," Seamus replied, his voice as bland as if delivering ingredients in a cake recipe. "I don't want you in my house."

"You don't...your house..." For as much as Josiah had suspected this as the truth, it still punched him right in the stomach, and he gasped for breath. "You're...kicking me out? What did I do?"

"You met your expiration date, kid."

Lights flashed and the SUV was gone, leaving Josiah completely alone on a dusty, dark street with a man he hadn't trusted in a long time. Angry, bitter tears burned hot behind Josiah's eyes. "Can I at least get my things?"

"Nah. I'll just haul it all to the dump next week. I mean, some random squatter abandoned it in my house. I can do what I want with it."

Josiah gaped at him, completely at a loss for words. Almost everything he owned was in that house, including the very few sentimental items he'd managed to keep from his old lives. Pictures of his parents. A napkin from the first place Andy took him out to dinner that wasn't fast food. His laptop and clothes and toothbrush and his nursing diploma.

His entire life was nothing but garbage to Seamus.

"Please," Josiah said. "Five minutes. For the important stuff. Then I'll leave you alone."

Seamus leaned against his front door, arms crossed, so smug Josiah wanted to slap him. No neighbors were in earshot or eyesight of the house, and the isolation only amped up Josiah's anxiety. "You can have two minutes for a blow job. Five minutes for one last fuck."

His already aching ribs gave a scream, and Josiah took two steps backward, his hip hitting the porch rail. "No. I have unequivocally revoked your access to my body. From now until the end of time, Seamus Mc-Bride. No more."

"Then I guess your shit's going to the dump next week. Don't come back, Jo-jo. Not unless you're willing to trade that sweet ass for your crap."

Unwilling to cry any more tears in front of the man, Josiah turned and stalked back to his car. Flung himself into the driver's seat and gunned the engine. Maybe all his earthly possessions would be on fire an hour from now, but Josiah didn't care. Not in this moment, because he was free. Finally free of the hell Seamus had lured him into. Free of insults and fists and sex he didn't want. Free of everything that had tormented him for the last two years of his life—except his own memories.

He'd always carry his memories with him, using the best to bolster him when his present life felt untenable. Mental reminders of how good things could be at times.

It looked like the physical reminders of those memories were going to end up in the trash pile.

Josiah wiped a few stray tears off his cheeks as he drove, not even sure where he was going until he parked in Elmer's yard behind the familiar vintage pickup. Lights shone downstairs, a comforting glow against the dark sky, and Josiah didn't even think as he rang the doorbell, over and over.

The door swung open and Michael's perturbed expression shifted directly into alarm. "Fuck, Josiah, what's wrong?"

"He kicked me out." Josiah's entire body wobbled, and he flinched when Michael reached for him. "He kicked me out with nothing and I didn't know where else to go. I'm sorry."

"Who what? The sheriff kicked you out? Of your place?"

"Yes." Shame heated his face, and Josiah resisted the urge to run back to his car and hide. "He wouldn't let me get anything. He said… I don't have anything. My clothes, my fucking toothbrush. I never wanted to be here again. Fuck."

"Okay, we'll figure this out. Come on inside. You're safe here, I promise."

"That Josiah?" Elmer called from inside. "What's goin' on, boys?"

The genuine concern in Elmer's voice helped Josiah go inside the house, into a familiar living room, with two familiar faces that expressed identical levels of curiosity and apprehension. "I'm so sorry to disturb you this late," Josiah said to Elmer.

"S'okay, son. Come on in. Whatever's goin' on, we'll fix it."

"I'm not sure you can."

"The sheriff kicked him out of their place," Michael said. "Won't let Josiah in to get his stuff."

Elmer scowled. "That ain't right on any level. You late with rent or something?"

"No." Josiah couldn't make himself repeat the hurtful things Seamus had hurled in his direction. "I never had an official lease with Seamus. Sheriff McBride. Legally, he can kick me out whenever he wants, and

I guess he wanted to tonight. I didn't do anything, I swear."

"I believe you," Michael replied. "But there's gotta be some law that lets you get your stuff from that house, lease or not."

"I don't know." He put his palms on the back of the sofa for balance, a little woozy from lack of food or water for the last few hours. "I'm so sorry to bring this to you guys, because I'm just an employee, but this was the first place I could think of that was safe. I've been here for two years but still don't know many people."

"This is a safe place. What do you need right now? Water? Soda? Whiskey? A sandwich?"

Josiah's lips twitched, wanting to smile but he didn't have the energy. "Juice or something would be great. It's just... I've been homeless before and I swore I never would be again, and now this happens."

"You aren't homeless, Josiah." Michael stood next to him, a solid, supportive presence without getting too far into Josiah's personal space. "I said earlier you can rent the trailer outside. Not sure when it was aired out last, but it's a roof and four walls. And we'll get your stuff."

He pinched the bridge of his nose, hating how close he was to sobbing. Michael went into the kitchen and returned a moment later with a glass of orange juice. Josiah sipped it, grateful for the liquid and time to think things through. Elmer watched him with quiet sympathy, while his sharp eyes seemed to contemplate something. Michael hovered nearby, attentive but not overbearing. The two men made Josiah feel safe in a way he hadn't in a long time.

"You're both being so generous," Josiah said after he'd drunk about half the juice. It helped his roiling stomach calm a bit, but he still craved a real meal. "I don't want to keep putting you out. I can drive to that motel near Daisy for the night, and maybe we can talk about the trailer tomorrow."

"You will not," Elmer said in a tone that dared him to argue. The voice of a stubborn man whose mind was made up. "Tonight you'll either sleep in the trailer or upstairs in the guest room. No need to waste money on a motel, especially not after this shock."

"Are you sure?"

"Don't say anything I'm not sure of. We've got the space—you just need to say yes."

Josiah didn't have any real pride left to defend by saying no, so he nodded. "Okay. Thank you. I, um, don't have anything to make a deposit on the trailer rent."

"Shush, we'll worry about that tomorrow. Trailer's got water and electricity. Michael can show you the thermostat so it isn't too chilly."

"I appreciate it. Truly."

Josiah left his juice glass on the side table and followed Michael out of the house. He stopped by his car to grab his few belongings—the bag of snacks and his book—then met Michael by the trailer door. The thing was small but pleasantly cozy. A tad cold but they got the heater going enough to knock the chill off.

"This is more than I expected," Josiah said after inspecting the tiny bedroom. "But I sincerely appreciate the room. Even if it's only for a few nights."

"You're welcome. I can't lie and say I know what you're going through, exactly, but I can sympathize with someone else blowing up your life. Not giving you a choice in the matter. Happened to me a few weeks ago. I wasn't sure how I'd get through it. So I came home."

"I don't have a home to go back to."

"Okay. But you know what you do have? Friends. Dad and I got your back, Josiah. We'll get your stuff."

"How?"

Michael's mouth twisted into a smile both secretive and sinister. "Doesn't matter. But we will. Promise."

Scared and alone and not entirely sure this was a good idea, Josiah decided to believe in Michael's promise. The older man hadn't lied to him yet. Hadn't done anything to make Josiah doubt his word or his intentions. But he'd believed the same things about Seamus once upon a time—a hero swooping in with a place to stay and lots of attention for an affection-starved man.

But Michael wasn't Seamus. Josiah saw that in Michael's eyes and smile. Kind eyes and a gentle smile that held no ulterior motive. No malice that would pop up without warning. While Michael did not have his complete trust yet, he did have some. Josiah latched on to that and said, "I believe you."

"I'm glad. Come inside for breakfast around nine?"

"I can do that. See you in the morning."

"Yeah. See you then."

Michael tipped an imaginary hat at him, then left the trailer. Josiah gazed around, a little overwhelmed by everything that had happened in the last few hours. He locked the door, grateful to have even the flimsiest of barriers between himself and other people right now. On the rare occasion Josiah had slept in his "own room" Seamus never let him lock the door. Even if he had tried, Seamus had a key.

A glass of water from the tap did little to help his persistent hunger, but Josiah was too mentally exhausted to care. He collapsed on top of the trailer's double bed, pressed his face into a slightly stale pillow, and tried to block out all his negative thoughts for just a little while.

Long enough to sleep without dreaming.

He woke with the sun and lay there for a bit, not used to spending a whole night in bed alone. Unmolested. Still hungry, he found a snack-size pack of sandwich cookies and ate those with a big glass of water. Washed his face and finger-combed his hair, since showering made no sense. He'd just have to put his same clothes back on anyway.

Michael had said to come in at nine for breakfast, but the small space in the trailer and his overall nerves had Josiah pacing too much. He unlocked the trailer door and stepped out into the bright early October sunshine. And he nearly tripped over a cardboard box. Several boxes, and a familiar suitcase. A piece of folded paper was taped to one box. Confused by what this was, Josiah plucked up the paper with trembling fingers and unfolded it.

Got your stuff. See you at 9.—M

"My stuff?" he asked the paper.

When he found the nerve to pry open the top of the closest box, Josiah's legs gave out. His diploma was right on top. His ass hit the bottom trailer step and he started to cry.

Chapter Nine

Michael couldn't let it go.

Maybe it wasn't his job to protect Josiah, who was an employee and quasi friend, but everything inside Michael insisted he do something to fix this. Finding Josiah on his front porch at nine o'clock at night, his eyes full of desperate terror, had set off something brand-new inside Michael. A protective instinct he'd never felt before, not even for Kenny. He'd needed to do something.

Installing Josiah in the fifth wheel had been a start, but not enough to calm the boiling rage deep in his belly. Rage at how devastated Josiah had been tonight. Rage at McBride for pulling a shitty stunt for no apparent reason and hurting Josiah in the process. Rage over Josiah losing everything he owned, just like Michael had lost most of what he owned.

So he'd paced the living room for a while. Dad had stayed quiet, watching whatever show was on television on a Friday night and not commenting on Michael's mood. Not until Dad muted the TV and said, "You ain't gonna let this lie, are you?"

Michael stopped near the alcove to the kitchen. "How can I? Kenny stole my money, kidnapped my dog, gave him away, and left my ass in the lurch, and I couldn't do anything about it. I'll be damned if I'll sit on my hands and watch that happen to another person." Maybe he'd been too weak to fix his own personal crises before, but Michael could stand up for Josiah now.

He *had* to.

"How you gonna fix it?"

"I don't know." Driving over to the sheriff's house and demanding Josiah's things seemed idiotic and, frankly, kind of dangerous. But he couldn't just let Josiah be treated like this. The guy was too kind, too caring, and Michael liked him too damned much to do nothing.

"Give me the phone."

Michael blinked. "What?"

"The phone." Dad could reach it on the table nearby if he stretched far enough, but something in his expression said he expected Michael to do as asked. To let his father sort this out. He couldn't say no to that look.

So Michael picked up the handset and gave it to Dad. "Who are you calling?"

"An old friend with influence." Dad punched in the number, then put the phone to his ear. "Wayne? It's Elmer Pearce. I got a situation and need a favor."

And that was how, twenty minutes later, Michael found himself in the bed of Wayne Woods's pickup truck along with Brand, Hugo, and their dog Brutus— Wayne and Jackson were in the cab—on their way to Seamus McBride's house. Five men and a dog to rescue the possessions of a young nurse they all knew and liked, and Michael had no idea why Jackson was along for this particular errand. But he was glad for the extra support.

The sheriff's car was in the driveway when they arrived, and Wayne left the truck engine idling, the lights trained on the porch. He led the charge forward, and Michael kept close, ready to do whatever he was asked. Brutus stood next to Brand's hip, ears forward, tail straight out, waiting for a command from his human.

Wayne rang the bell. Several times.

The front door swung open. McBride had a beer in one hand and stared at Wayne first, obviously confused, before realizing how many people were on his porch. "What the hell's this, Woods?" McBride asked.

Wayne tilted his head in Michael's direction, which gave Michael the opening to say, "We're here for Josiah Sheridan's personal belongings."

"Don't know what you mean. He moved out tonight."

"Sure he did. That's why he ended up on my doorstep with nothing but his car saying you kicked him out. We're not here for a fight, Sheriff. Just his stuff." Finding courage in his own words, Michael shouldered his way past McBride and into the house. It was basically a double-wide trailer dropped on a patch of land, and it was easy to navigate.

McBride grabbed Michael's shoulder. Brand whistled and Brutus let out a vicious bark but didn't lunge. McBride backed off.

"Where's his room?" Michael asked.

After leveling him with a deadly glare, McBride said, "First door on the left. Take his shit. I don't care."

Jackson and Hugo followed Michael down the short hallway to the bedroom. It was very plain, almost impersonal, and the side table had a layer of dust on it that made Michael silently question how often Josiah actually used this room—and what exactly was his relationship with McBride?

Didn't matter in this moment. Hugo found a suitcase in the closet and began throwing clothes into it. Under the bed, Michael unearthed some faded packing boxes and set those up for whatever else they found in the room that seemed personal. Clothes, books, a few things from the night table's drawer. A box of mementos Michael didn't look through too closely.

The lack of anything in the bathroom across the hall told Michael everything he needed to know about this "roommate" situation. He stalked one door down and into the master bedroom. He glared around its shabby decor and outdated furnishings a beat before going into the attached bathroom. Two toothbrushes. Two hairbrushes. Different kinds of shampoo and soap in the tub.

Roommates my gay ass.

Michael didn't know the details of whatever arrangement Josiah had with McBride, and right now he didn't care. He knew the broad strokes and it pissed him off to think McBride could just punt someone as kind and caring as Josiah to the curb with no warning and without his own personal belongings. Furious now, he got a box and threw every damned thing he could find in that bathroom into it: toothpaste, towels, a crossword puzzle book, room spray, razors, whatever.

In that moment, all he saw was the tiniest bit of retribution for someone he considered a friend. All he saw was Rosco and everything else Kenny had taken from him. Maybe a half-used bottle of shampoo wouldn't fix anything wrong in Michael's life, but taking it for Josiah felt good. It felt fair.

And because Michael was feeling exceptionally petty tonight, he took the batteries out of the remote for the bedroom's wall-mounted flat-screen television. The remote for the streaming system, too. He couldn't begin to guess which clothes in this bedroom might belong to Josiah, other than the stack of scrubs he found in one drawer, so he took all the underwear he saw and a handful of socks. Whatever. If Michael got arrested tomorrow for theft, he'd deal with it.

Tonight, he was trying to help a friend because he hadn't been able to help himself.

By the time he returned to the living room with his box, Hugo and Jackson were there with a suitcase and two other boxes. McBride leaned against a far wall, still sipping at his beer, while Wayne and Brand stood at flanking positions, Brutus still close by Brand's hip.

"Anything in here or the kitchen that's Josiah's?" Michael asked. "I don't wanna have to come back a second time."

"Slow cooker on the counter, but it's a piece of shit," McBride replied. "Just like Jo-jo. Take it. Then get the fuck out of my house."

"Before you do what? Call yourself to have me arrested?"

"Don't tempt me. Only reason I'm holding back is because I don't wanna spend my day off tomorrow cleaning out his shit. I got better things to do."

Michael glanced at Jackson, who stalked right past McBride without a care in the world. He returned from the kitchen a moment later with a slow cooker in his hands, which he held with two kitchen towels. The thing still had food in it.

"You find anything that's important to Josiah," Michael said in the growliest tone he could manage, "you call me and I'll come get it. Clear? Sheriff?"

McBride blinked at him. "Get out. You want that piece of trash, you can have him."

Brand stepped in front of Michael before he could charge McBride. "We'll be leaving in just a few minutes," Brand said.

Michael pulled on all his restraint and remained behind Brand while Jackson, Wayne, and Hugo took the suitcase and boxes out to their pickup. McBride kept a steady, challenging gaze on him, and Michael returned it, unwilling to back down. Not when the true nature of McBride's relationship with Josiah—and his betrayal—were becoming clearer and clearer.

And he had a feeling the only reason McBride wasn't putting up a bigger fight was because of Brutus and his firm attention on their enemy.

Once everything was loaded up, Wayne let out a sharp whistle. Brutus padded outside, followed by Brand. Michael held McBride's stare as long as he dared, part of him wanting to goad the man into a fight. But this wasn't about him. This entire exercise was about getting Josiah's stuff back, and they'd done that. Most if not all. Time to make their retreat and regroup for any future battles.

Michael left the house last, hoping he made a goddamn point by doing so. He was silently furious with McBride over his treatment of Josiah, while also insanely grateful to the four men who'd come with him tonight to rescue Josiah's belongings.

They got back to Dad's house a little after ten. The trailer was dark and silent, so their quintet quietly put the boxes and suitcase outside. After shaking every-

one's hand and thanking them for their help tonight—
Michael even ruffled Brutus's ears—he went inside
the house. Dad was asleep, snoring quietly in his bed.
So peaceful.

Michael found a piece of paper in the kitchen's junk
drawer. It was too late to wake Josiah and explain what
had happened tonight, so Michael wrote a succinct
note. The simplest thing he could come up with, while
also reminding Josiah he was still welcome in their
home for breakfast.

Got your stuff. See you at 9.—M

He taped it to the top box, then stood outside the
trailer for a long time, staring at the door, wanting to
knock but not willing to disturb Josiah if he was asleep.
And he must be if he hadn't responded to the noise of
Wayne's truck coming and going, the boxes being left
behind, et cetera. Or the poor guy had no idea what
all the activity was about and was hiding in the rear
of the trailer.

The latter made Michael's heart hurt, because he
didn't need details to know Josiah's life with McBride
had been…dramatic. Probably traumatic. And that
pissed him off.

But Josiah's life wasn't Michael's to fix, so he went
upstairs to his own bedroom and didn't sleep up there
either. Not for a long time. As soon as he finally dozed
off, his phone alarm buzzed at eight, and he dragged
his exhausted ass out of bed and into the shower. Fatigue sloughed off and he dried, dressed, and then
looked out his bedroom window. It oversaw the trailer.

The boxes and suitcase were gone.

Confident it was because Josiah was awake and not because McBride had driven over to reclaim the stuff, Michael went downstairs. Dad was already awake and watching TV with the volume low, and Michael realized he'd forgotten to close the curtains last night so Dad could sleep longer. Dad just tossed him a wave, though, on Michael's way into the kitchen. He hadn't really thought breakfast through when he invited Josiah, but he had stuff for French toast, so after getting Dad a glass of juice Michael started making a good cinnamon custard for the bread.

The bread was soaking and almost ready to fry up when the doorbell rang. Michael wiped his hands on a towel and strode across the living room. Dad had that familiar *I want to get up and answer the damned door* look on his face, but he was still weeks away from that particular activity. The tenacity was great to see, though.

Josiah stood on the porch, his face the perfect mix of surprise and confusion, and he thrust the note at him. "You got my stuff from Seamus?"

Michael took the crumpled piece of paper. "Well, not just me. I had a little help."

"Why?"

"Because it was your stuff. He had no right to keep it from you. And we probably didn't get it all but we tried our best."

"Who's we?"

No one last night had said to keep their involvement secret. "Me, Wayne and Brand Woods, Hugo Turner, Jackson Sumner, and Brutus. It was a last-minute group effort."

Josiah's eyebrows crept up into his hairline. And

then he let out a sound that was somewhere between a laugh and a sob. "You took Brutus? Seamus hates dogs."

"Well, I don't trust people who hate dogs."

"That's probably a good life motto." He shoved his hands into his pockets and angled his head down. "Thank you. For getting what you did. It's more than I ever expected to get back from him. You didn't have to."

"You're welcome. And maybe I didn't have to in terms of our professional relationship, but I had to do it for myself. I don't expect anything from you in return. This was me trying to earn back some karma points from the universe."

Josiah's lips parted and Michael saw the question *for what* forming there. But Josiah closed his mouth and nodded, instead. "Thank you. For whatever reason you did it, thank you."

"You're welcome. We're, um, having French toast for breakfast. Please, come inside?"

The way Michael phrased the final few words as a question seemed to battle against some of Josiah's defenses, because he physically relaxed. "I'd like that, thank you. It probably sounds pathetic, but I'm not used to having friends in my corner. It's been a while. I'm kind of awkward in social settings, and Seamus only ever occasionally brought his poker buddies over, but I didn't care for them."

"Well, you've got some friends now. You're great with Dad, and you obviously made an impression on the Woods family a few months ago. Come on in and relax a while. You aren't working today."

"Okay." Josiah entered the house like someone walking in for the first time, seeming to really take it in. The size, the decor, the placement of things.

Dad waved from his bed, his own smile bright and cheerful. "Morning, young man. Guess you had a night."

"It was something. I'm so grateful for the trailer, Elmer, I mean it. We'll figure out rent."

"Don't worry about that right now. Let's all just enjoy a nice Saturday morning brunch cooked up by my son."

Michael smiled and took that as his cue to head back into the kitchen. Once the skillet was nice and hot, he began adding the custard-soaked bread slices to it. It wouldn't be a full brunch, since he didn't really have other sides to offer his guest. On a whim, he cored and sliced up two apples just for the extra food.

Dad had found an old Western movie by the time Michael brought in the tray of hot French toast, syrup, butter, and apple slices. He put it on the coffee table, then went and got plates for everyone. The coffee was brewed, and Josiah took over that duty, pouring mugs for himself and Michael. They briefly danced around each other in the kitchen in a way that wasn't forced. It was almost practiced. Easy.

And it kind of felt right.

Once Josiah had his plate, Michael prepared one for Dad and himself, and he took over the spot in a folding metal chair beside Dad's bed, both of their plates on the rolling table. He assisted when Dad needed it without babying him, and while also eating bites of his own meal. The entire production was both strange and easy. As if their trio had done this a thousand times in the past, despite it being the first.

Michael wasn't sure what it meant other than he was

comfortable with Josiah here, in his home, as part of his family. And as much as he liked it, it also kind of unnerved him.

Once the meal was over, the dishes done, and he and Josiah both on their second cups of coffee, Michael asked, "Did we miss anything important at McBride's house? I assume you went through the stuff we collected for you."

"I went through them very fast, yes," Josiah replied. "You got the important stuff, so thank you. I'm not put out by the loss of a few shirts or a bottle of aftershave." His eyes narrowed. "Besides, I was never fond of that smell."

"Okay, good. And feel free to use the washer and dryer in the basement for your laundry. I mean, it's kind of your only option, since we don't have a coin-op in town, and I doubt you want to spend an hour scrubbing stuff by hand in a metal bucket."

He laughed. "No, I don't. I've done it and I'd rather not. Actually, I should head to the store this afternoon and get some stuff. Snacks and food. A lot of what I'd bring for my own lunch was leftovers of the meals I'd cook for me and Seamus." His voice went distant, his expression the same.

Michael glanced at Dad, whose own face was difficult to decipher. Somehow a mix of sad, angry, and determined. But who were those emotions directed at? Hopefully, the anger was directed right at Seamus McBride, where it belonged.

"Get whatever," Michael said. "And if you feel like cooking something that your little fridge can't hold, you can store it here in the house. Not a big deal at all."

Josiah's eyebrows jumped. "Really?"

"Sure. I remember trying to keep shit in a minifridge in college, and after we packed in the beer, there wasn't a lot of room left for real food. Especially if the ice monster took over."

"Ice monster?"

"Yeah, you know how sometimes in those fridges the freezer part just ices over and crowds out everything else? My college roommate and I used to call that sucker the ice monster. We'd have to let the fridge he brought defrost in the dorm showers every other month. Lost a lot of Hot Pockets to that monster."

"I bet." Josiah laughed again. "I will beware of the ice monster. But I don't plan on stocking any beer, so I should be okay on space to start. I appreciate the offer and since old habits die hard, I will probably still be making slow cooker meals. And sharing them with you guys. You're not technically my roommates, since we're under different roofs, and I will possibly be exchanging work for part of the rent, but I like to share food. Feeding people makes me happy."

"And this boy loves to be fed," Dad joked, breaking the seriousness of the conversation with his peal of laughter, and jacked his thumb at Michael. "You share what you can. Not like he can cook all that good. Except maybe French toast."

Michael made an exaggerated eye roll. "I can cook fine in a pinch, I'm just not used to it. Kenny usually—" He stopped, not used to bringing up his ex around, well, anyone in his life here. "I didn't really cook much, but my delivery app game was on point. Not many options for that around here."

"You young'uns and your apps. Can't just go do things, you gotta have an app for it all."

"If it helps," Josiah said to Dad, "I've never used a delivery app, either. I still only use my cell for basic things like phone calls, Solitaire and checking out ebooks from the county library system."

"Nothin' wrong with the basics, son. Only reason I got one of those monthly flip phones is because I got a flat once out in the middle of the county, didn't have my spare tire, and I ended up walking five miles to the nearest neighbor. About wore out my boots and my legs that day."

As Dad and Josiah began debating the merits of cell phones, Michael leaned back and listened. It was familial in a nice way, while also familial in a way that made him jealous. The pair obviously got along well and were at ease enough to tease each other. So different from the politeness that coated every interaction Michael had with his dad. But neither one of them was ready to really discuss the issues between them. Or what had happened the day before Michael left Weston for nearly two decades.

Part of Michael wanted to discuss it. Dad's stroke had scared him. The idea of his father dying before they cleared the air hurt his heart. Addressing that air and all the drama in it? It scared him on a very different level. The level of a son who still wanted a reason to love his dad.

"Michael?"

He startled, nearly spilling coffee on his hand. "What?"

Josiah's calm smile soothed the feathers ruffled by Michael's stray thoughts. "I asked your dad if you'd like me to leave the slow cooker here in the house, so I can prepare evening meals for you both. It's no trouble."

"Oh." Michael looked at Dad, who gave him a slight nod, on board with the idea. "That's fine, but we'll obviously contribute to the groceries for meals you want to share with us. Help with meals is great, but we don't expect you to cook for us. That's not part of the conditions of renting the trailer."

"I just want to earn my keep."

"Like I said, we'll negotiate all that. Trailer rent against your pay for helping Dad, any meals you help with, we'll figure it out. It hasn't even been a full day for you, Josiah. We don't have to know it all right away."

Josiah held his gaze for a long moment that seemed to stretch out and out…until Josiah blinked. "Thank you. And thank you again for brunch. And my stuff. I suppose my impulse to keep all those moving boxes was a good one."

"It made things a bit easier. We didn't have to tear through McBride's house looking for his stash of plastic grocery bags to haul everything out in."

"Under the kitchen sink." Josiah cleared his throat. "Um, if you both don't mind, I need to finish going through those boxes and organizing things. Plus a grocery list for later. Toiletries and stuff, too."

"Sure, that's fine. If you need help with anything, let me know. Dad will be fine on his own for half an hour."

Something odd flickered in his eyes. "Of course. You're, um, obviously free to stop by at any time. I'm sure I'll see you both soon."

Michael didn't say anything while Josiah took his coffee mug into the kitchen, then left quietly out the front door. He wanted to go after Josiah and ask him questions, ask more about what his life had been like with McBride, but he didn't want to stress Josiah out more by being nosy—or make Dad suspicious about Josiah's sexuality. Michael was only guessing himself, based on what he'd seen at McBride's house.

"I don't know much outside of ranching and metalwork and junk," Dad said, "but I do know when things aren't right. And things aren't right between Josiah and the sheriff." Michael looked over, working hard to keep his surprise off his face. "You keep an eye on Josiah, hear me? He's a good boy."

"I agree, Dad," Michael replied. "I'll do my best."

"Good lad. Now, go find something else to do and let me watch my movie."

"You've probably already seen it five times."

"So?"

Dad's perfectly deadpan response made Michael laugh as he stood and took his coffee mug into the kitchen for a refill.

Chapter Ten

Josiah stared at the piece of scrap paper he'd scrounged from a drawer in the trailer's compact kitchen and tapped his pen against it, unsure if he had everything he needed on his list. Michael and his friends had managed to collect the bulk of what belonged to Josiah, including clothes and personal things from his bedroom. Things like his toothbrush and deodorant could be replaced easily—someone had grabbed both toothbrushes but Josiah needed to get a new one anyway—and he was forever grateful to Michael for not bringing up the giant elephant in the room.

The fact that Michael and his friends probably hadn't known which toothbrush was Josiah's because it was in the same holder as Seamus's. That their toiletries shared the master bathroom, rather than Josiah's being in the guest bathroom. Michael understood that Josiah hadn't simply been Seamus's roommate, and he was trying to be discreet about the information. Josiah owed him for that.

He finished putting his things away, stored the flattened boxes and suitcase under the trailer's bed, and then took a quick shower since he now had clean clothes to wear. The tiny bathroom didn't have the enema attachment Seamus liked him to use, which was comforting in its own way. No expectations, only a shower. Refreshed by the simple act, Josiah headed to Weston's only general store for supplies.

The place stocked the bare basics of everything from food to clothing to the hardware farmers usually needed last minute to mend a fence or fix a tractor belt. Not a lot of variety but it did its job, saving folks from a much longer drive out to the nearest big-box store. He gathered up his list of items, including food for a few meals next week. What little he had in his account barely paid for the bill, but he wasn't completely broke. He'd figure out his finances on Monday. Make sure whatever pay he received from the Pearces was his alone.

No one in the store bothered him, and the young lady who rang him up only gave him a curious smile. After being in town for about two years, he was known by face, but he was also an outsider. Not born to Weston or any of its tiny neighboring towns.

"You're Josiah something, right?" the clerk asked as she bagged his stuff. "You're taking care of Elmer Pearce right now."

"I am." He glanced around but no other shoppers were nearby. "You are?"

"Sorry, Leanne Miller. My parents own Woods Ranch, where Michael Pearce is working now. I talked to my parents the other day and they told me all what's happening around the ranch. Staff changes and stuff like that. Between working and the kids, it's hard to keep up with everything."

"Right. Nice to meet you, Leanne." Josiah tried to modulate his voice so his anxiety didn't bleed through.

"I don't know your family well, but it seems like Michael is content working there."

"As content as you can be with a sore ass every night." She handed over another plastic bag of stuff.

As much as Josiah knew she meant a sore ass from riding a horse for hours a day, he couldn't stop a brief flashback to his last night with Seamus. "Right. It's honest work, though, and I think I can safely guess that Michael is grateful for it."

"Yeah, I heard he had some sort of falling-out with his gay lover down in Austin before his dad's stroke." Leanne glanced over her shoulder, then hushed her voice. "I mean, I've got a gay brother who's married, and now apparently one who's bisexual and with a guy, but I don't get that stuff."

Totally done with this conversation, Josiah grabbed his last bag off the counter and dropped it into his cart. "People love who they love," was all he could manage before quick-stepping it out of the small grocery store. He honestly didn't care what she thought about him and his abrupt departure. His default mode when people brought up anything gay-related was to ignore or deflect, mostly out of self-preservation. Whenever Seamus hosted poker nights, he went right along with every homophobic joke his pals made, and that had always hurt, considering their arrangement.

Today was no different, even while a tiny, unacknowledged part of him hated that instinct. He wanted to scream "I'm gay!" at the top of his voice and be done with it.

Survival kept his mouth shut.

After loading up his groceries and returning his cart, Josiah hit the road—in the wrong direction. Habit had him going toward Seamus's house, and he had to turn around in a church parking lot to go the other way to the Pearce property. That was going to take some getting used to, but in a good way. He could go to sleep tonight, alone, and not worry about any sort of pain.

He hoped.

Michael's car was still parked behind Elmer's truck, which didn't really surprise him, since Elmer shouldn't be left alone for very long. Not until his mobility increased dramatically, especially in his hand and arm. Josiah parked closer to the trailer and began unloading his haul. It really wasn't that much, but as he tried to put his cold things in the small fridge, he realized it wouldn't all fit. He'd bought a whole chicken for a slow cooker recipe, but it was too late today to try it.

He'd planned to share the meal with Michael and Elmer, so maybe it was okay to ask if he could put the bird in their fridge. Hadn't Michael said it was?

Once everything else was in its proper place, Josiah grabbed the chicken and walked over to the house. Rang the bell with a slightly trembling finger, because they'd already done so much for him in the last twenty-four hours. Even storing a chicken in the fridge felt like too big of an ask, but his only other option was wasting the meat. Raw or cooked, it had to be refrigerated somewhere.

Michael pushed open the screen door with his familiar, patient smile on his face. "Hey, what's up? You can't miss my dad already."

"I, um, was hoping to take you up on your offer to put something your refrigerator," Josiah said, hating the tremor in his voice. He wasn't used to asking for things. Hadn't been for a long time. "My chicken won't fit in mine."

Michael's lips twitched like Josiah had said something funny, but Josiah was only being honest. "Sure you can. Come on in. You know where the fridge is."

"Thank you." The only reason he wasn't more nervous about going into the house after asking a favor was because Elmer was awake, his attention split between the TV and what they were talking about. Sometimes being alone with Seamus was so stressful he'd wanted to vomit.

Josiah put the chicken on an empty bottom shelf, glad he wasn't taking up much space in the large appliance. He turned and nearly yelped because Michael was standing a few feet away, still smiling but so damned tall and broad and just *there*.

"Do you want to stay for dinner?" Michael asked. "I have no idea what I'm going to make, but you can stay. I'd offer the food that was still in your slow cooker when we grabbed it last night, but I honestly didn't trust that McBride hadn't tampered with it in some way, so I tossed it."

Josiah didn't blame him. Seamus really was that petty. "No, that's okay, really. I have stuff." Lunch meat and white bread wasn't fancy but it was stuff. And it took up less space than frozen dinners. He hadn't forgotten Michael's story about the college ice monster, so he'd only gotten a few frozen breakfast sandwiches for now.

"That's cool. Another time?"

"Sure. I, um, the chicken is for a meal I planned to make Monday while I'm here with Elmer. It'll be enough for multiple people and meals."

"Awesome. I really appreciate it, because I wasn't joking when I said I'm really basic when it comes to cooking. I just generally don't do it. When I got here, I read a bunch of recipe blogs just to remember the basics and get ideas for something other than frozen dinners."

"Well, I don't mind helping. It's part of the deal, right?"

Michael tilted his head to the side. "The rent and work deal? You don't owe us cooking at all, Josiah. I asked Dad what he usually rents the trailer for, and you'll still be getting a good paycheck from us every week. We absolutely appreciate the food and cooking, but it's never been a requirement of you staying here."

Josiah nodded, grateful for the reassurance while also not completely trusting it. He wasn't used to generosity without conditions, and that wouldn't change for a long damned time. "Thank you. You and your father have been very generous this past week. You agreed to hire a daytime nurse, not all this extra drama."

"Everyone deserves a safe place to land. Come on, I'll walk you to your trailer." A statement, not a question. Michael was going with him to the trailer. They'd be alone.

With a new flash of fear locking his jaw tight, all Josiah could do was nod and walk out of the house. He barely waved good-night to Elmer. His brain was full of what would happen when he and Michael were alone inside the trailer. Of so many times when Josiah wanted to say no and he couldn't, because he didn't have any power in the relationship. When saying yes meant one more night in a warm bed under a roof, instead of cold on the street.

By the time Josiah unlocked the trailer's door, his

entire body had slight tremors running through it. He went directly inside, then wasn't sure what to do next. He knew the script with Seamus, but Michael was a new quantity. Josiah stopped in the middle of the small kitchen area and waited to be told what to do. Where to go. It took him a long time to realize that he was alone inside the trailer.

Michael stood on the outside steps, frowning now, but not angry, with the closed trailer door between them. "Have a good night?" Michael asked, voice muffled.

"I'm sorry. I think I'm out of practice at being a good host." Even though he preferred Michael outside, he pushed the door open. "Come in, if you want."

Each step Michael took inside the trailer made Josiah's insides clench tighter, and he kept taking steps backward. Michael seemed to notice and stopped by the stove. "I genuinely want to make sure you're okay with the trailer. I mean, a fifth wheel is a big step down from a room in a nice house with a full-size kitchen and bathroom. And it was a last-minute option."

"The trailer is great." Was this the moment when he offered up something for Michael's generosity? When he bent over or went to his knees? Michael's signals were so off that he truly wasn't sure. "Do you want me to thank you now or, um, later?"

Michael's eyebrows furrowed. "You've said thank you more than once. I might have hit my own rough patch recently but I have also been blessed in many ways, so I'm cool with helping when I can. And Dad trusts you, which is great after that whole thing with Hugo, his stepbrother and the missing coins."

"I would never steal from a client. That's not why I became a nurse."

"I believe you. Just saying where we're coming from." Michael took a long look around the living area of the trailer. "This place could really use a fresh coat of paint or something, huh?"

"I can do that."

"Dude, I wasn't asking you to do manual labor on our property, just musing out loud. Are you sure you're okay? You've been kind of tense since brunch."

"I'm just used to routines and, uh, things have really been shaken up since yesterday." Josiah swallowed hard against a rise of acid in his stomach, desperate to get this over with. "I need you to tell me what to do next. Should we go in the bedroom?"

"The bedroom? Why, is something broken we need to get fixed?"

"What?"

"What what? What's wrong with the bedroom? I mean, you're the tenant and I'm the landlord, so if something is broken I'll fix it."

Josiah stared at Michael, buried under the entire conversation, and he didn't know how to dig his way out except to be honest. "If you want sex, Michael, just say so and we'll do it. I can't take this roundabout thing you're doing. I need people to be direct. It's how I've survived most of my life."

Michael's face went slack and he gaped at Josiah for a long time, his jaw working, but no words came out. Then he took several long strides backward until he hit a wall and couldn't go any farther. "What the fuck? I don't want sex from you. Not a single thing since I hired you to take care of Dad has been about sex, and that includes renting you this trailer." His eyes narrowed. "But that was obviously your arrangement with McBride. Sex for a place to stay?"

The word *yes* stuck in the back of Josiah's throat. He stared at the floor instead of saying anything, his peripheral vision still on Michael just in case. Small stains in the carpet came into sharp focus as he waited for Michael's condemnation or ridicule.

"I'm not judging you," Michael said. "I do not have any pedestal from which to judge another person's life choices. I just need to know you hear me right now. Josiah?"

Despite Michael's words, Josiah couldn't bring himself to look Michael in the eyes, his embarrassment too damned strong. He did look up as high as Michael's throat, positive his face was going to burst into flames any second. "I hear you."

"Good. Thank you. And since you're listening, I am saying now that I will never, ever ask for sex from you in exchange for anything. I'm gay and very open about that, but that's where it stops for me. I get with guys who are interested in me. Or at least who say they are."

That last sentence got more of Josiah's attention, and his mind flashed to a brief mention of someone named Kenny.

"You are an employee and a tenant," Michael continued firmly. "Not a commodity. And when I say this I mean it—if you ever have issues with Sheriff McBride again, come to me. I'll help you. Do you believe me?"

"I want to." He'd meant to just say yes, so they could end this humiliating conversation but something about Michael made Josiah want to always be honest. "I'm sorry."

"Don't apologize. I gotta say after this conversation I'm even more glad you're here now instead of back at McBride's place."

"Why?"

"Because you're a human being not a body. I…" Michael cleared his throat hard. "I was with someone for a long time who I thought loved me for who I was. But in the end, he loved me for my bank account. No one should be loved for what someone else can take from us."

Those words finally gave Josiah the courage to meet Michael's eyes. Eyes both sad and determined, and something deep inside of Josiah responded to that. Responded to what seemed like compassion and understanding when he genuinely hadn't expected either. At the easiest, he'd expected judgment; at the worst, he'd expected to be bent over the nearest solid object and used. But all Michael seemed to be offering was… commiseration?

Maybe even friendship?

"Thank you," Josiah said. He couldn't find any other words and hoped they were enough.

Michael's entire body ached soul-deep for everything Josiah hadn't admitted to, but his silence in the last few minutes had said more than enough. So many truths in what he hadn't spoken out loud, and Michael wanted to charge right over to McBride's house and slam the asshole into the wall. He wanted to avenge all the hurts in Josiah's past, and instinct told him there were a lot. Probably more than he wanted to know about.

Somehow, he stayed still and calm, because his first priority was keeping Josiah comfortable and reducing that glimmer of fear in his eyes. Fear that knew what a fast fist felt like. Or worse. And the "or worse" infuriated Michael in a way he didn't understand.

"I don't know your story and I'm not asking for it tonight," Michael said. "But you are safe here on our land, and you have allies in me and my father, and the men I work with. I won't tell them anything about this, because it isn't my business unless it ends up on our doorstep. I just hope you can take comfort in knowing that as long as you are here, your body is yours. You are my dad's caretaker and a tenant and that's it."

Josiah's eyes gleamed, and if he started to cry Michael wasn't sure he'd stay calm. But Josiah blinked a few times, then shook his hands out. "Thank you, Michael. I want to believe you. I'm just, um…"

"It's okay. That's why I'm way over here. And if you feel better about it, buy a second lock for the inside of the trailer to keep me out. It won't hurt my feelings. I'm not a predator. This is your home. I want you to feel safe here. Do you believe me?"

"I want to."

Honest. "Okay, then I'm going to go. I really just wanted a chance to talk to you tonight, without Dad around, but I see I misjudged things a bit. You settle in and I'm sure we'll talk tomorrow. Lock up behind me, okay?"

"Sure. Right."

Michael didn't want to leave. He hated the wounded look still haunting Josiah's eyes, but something in him said this was the best thing to do. To give Josiah space and prove Michael wasn't some manipulative bastard who only wanted Josiah for sexual favors. Josiah had obviously been trading his body for safety and shelter for a long time. For so long that he'd expected the same deal from Michael.

A deal he'd obviously fallen into with the county sheriff. A deal that pissed Michael off, especially when the sheriff had been so fast to dump Josiah on his ass without his own goddamn belongings. He'd have a hard time holding his temper the next time he saw McBride in public, but Michael wasn't a headstrong teenager anymore who spouted off when he was pissed. He was a grown man who could think rationally and calculate any move he might make.

First, he needed Josiah to relax and find the sense of safety he'd obviously been missing for a long time.

Dad was awake when Michael let himself back inside. "He settlin' in?"

"Slowly, yeah. Part of me wants to start locking the front gate like we did when we had cattle. Especially while I'm at work."

"If you think that'll help the boy, fine. It's gonna need to be greased up, though. Haven't shut it in a long time. Got outta the habit after you left."

Michael flinched, remembering why they'd gone back to locking it after selling the herd. "Yeah. I'm going to see what I can scrounge up for dinner. I invited Josiah in but he'll probably stay in the trailer."

"Fine, fine."

He didn't see Josiah again for the rest of the night.

Dad had been a regular churchgoer before Michael left, and he obviously couldn't go yet, not until he was stronger, so it didn't completely surprise Michael when Pastor Lorne rang the bell a little after lunchtime on Sunday. Michael wasn't much for religion, so he excused himself outside while the pastor did whatever he'd come to do. Visit, probably read a few Bible verses.

No thank you.

He glanced at the trailer, a little surprised to see Josiah sitting on the steps, eyes closed, face tilted to the sunshine. No earbuds in, so no chance of Michael scaring him. Plus, he had to have heard the pastor drive up, so he wasn't asleep. They did have another bright, sunny autumn day, so Michael stepped down off the porch and said, "Gorgeous weather."

"Yes, it is." Josiah blinked his eyes open. "I'm not fond of being outside when it's cold or raining, but I love the sun."

That didn't surprise Michael one bit after his admission of having been homeless at some point. "I enjoy all the time I can get outdoors, which is probably why I've acclimated to the ranch so quickly. My old life didn't allow for more than a few vacations here and there, or an evening on the balcony with a glass of wine."

"Can you tell me more about your old life? All I've heard from whispered gossip is you worked with computers?"

"Software design." Michael's old life was still pretty raw, but Josiah had trusted him with some difficult secrets yesterday. He didn't mind sharing a bit and getting to know his new friend. "I went to college for it and have an aptitude for numbers and coding. Software just makes sense to me. After I graduated, I got a good offer from a company in Silicon Valley, but I love Texas. I was born here and didn't want to leave. So I joined a small start-up in Austin. Met a guy named Kenny Wilde there."

He closed his eyes briefly, trying to block out the

memory of Kenny's handsome, smiling face on Michael's first day. Michael opened his eyes and took a few steps closer, keeping a respectful distance between them. "Kenny and I hit it off, and we were working with two other guys at the time, but we all couldn't agree on an app. And remember, this was twenty years ago, so smartphones were just really taking off, and everyone was saying 'There's an app for that.'

"So after one particularly late night that included sushi and a lot of wine, Kenny and I started lamenting our dating lives. We talked about how hard it was for people, especially those of us who were workaholics, to get out and meet people. Why not meet on our phones? Our two partners didn't like the idea, so Kenny and I decided we'd develop it on our own. It took us about two years, because we were also doing small jobs that paid, and we worked on the side.

"At one point, my landlord decided to sell his house, so I was losing the room I rented. Kenny was losing his roommate, so I moved in with him. We started dating and falling in love so slowly, because we were both completely oblivious we even had feelings. Not until our app was complete and took off. We were twenty-three and had actual money. As phones got more sophisticated and new models kept coming out, we kept up. And the real money started coming in."

"Are you rich?" Josiah blurted out, then immediately covered his mouth with his hand. "I'm sorry, that was really rude."

"It's okay. Am I rich? Yes and no. As our personal and business relationship grew, we broke off from the original team and formed our own firm. I agreed to let Kenny handle the financial aspect as CFO, while I remained director of development. We had a small staff and a nice office. We began to buy things for ourselves as a couple, including a beautiful three-story McMansion out in Barton Hills. We worked and even got married, and for a long time, I thought we were happy."

"But you weren't?"

"I was, actually." Michael scuffed the heel of his boot in the dirt, hands stuffed in his jeans pockets. "We had a dog and a big house. We threw lavish parties, invited all kinds of people, especially in our industry, and we even had the mayor of Austin over once."

"Wow." Josiah's eyes kept growing wider the more he learned, and he held on to every single one of Michael's words. "So you left all that behind to come here and stay with your father?"

"Yes, and not because I'm some sort of truly noble, selfless person. I would have come, but before I probably would have arranged help 24/7 and then gone home. Back to my life. My father and I had a major falling-out the summer before my final year of college, and I honestly never intended to come back here."

"But you did. And you stayed. I assume you working at Woods Ranch is part of the *no* of not being rich anymore? Wait." He squinted. "You said Kenny was the CFO."

"Yes."

Josiah seemed to put the puzzle pieces together on his own and paint a clear picture so Michael didn't have to explain. "He stole your money?"

"Yup." A fresh wave of pain blazed through his chest. "He left me for another guy, took all my share of the profits, even took our dog in the divorce. All he left me of any value was the house, which I'm trying to sell as soon as possible."

"But…" Josiah stood slowly, seeming to favor his ribs a little, and crossed his arms. "Can he just do that? You helped build that company from the bottom."

"Trust me, I spent a lot of time with lawyers trying to untangle the financial web Kenny had woven, but he was smart. He knew how to shift things when I wasn't looking, and he had everything in place before he dumped me. What little was left in our shared account was chump change compared what he took."

"What about stocks? You didn't have any stock in your own company?"

"I was told I did." Shame flooded his belly. "After we lost our steers and quit ranching, Dad got into buying and welding junk into art. So he spent a lot of money buying things. Cash got tight. The only way I made it to college was scholarships and work-study, and I was living on ramen and peanut butter sandwiches for a long time, even after I graduated. Once the money started rolling in on the app, I didn't know how to handle my money, but I trusted Kenny." He snorted. "Biggest mistake of my life. When the app went public ten years ago, I didn't even make sure Kenny got stocks in my name. All I cared about was watching our bank account get bigger and bigger. Well, his bank account now."

"I'm so sorry someone you thought you could trust betrayed you."

He held Josiah's sad gaze. "You know what that's like."

"Yeah. Thank you, Michael. For being honest and telling me things that are obviously still very painful."

"You're welcome." The impulse to reach out and hug Josiah hit Michael all at once. He wasn't used to opening up with employees, especially about things this personal. To stop himself, he shoved his hands deeper into his pockets and rocked back on his heels. After all he suspected Josiah had been through, the guy would probably not appreciate being touched. "And if you ever want to talk about anything, my door is always open."

"How long do you think you'll stay here in Weston?" Josiah expertly changed the subject without acknowledging his comment.

Michael could take a hint. "I'm not sure. Right now, I'm playing things by ear. I'm still on probation at the ranch, but I have a feeling they'd hire me on. If my house sells quickly, I'll have the money to hire Dad round-the-clock help and start over somewhere else. Maybe come up with a new app or something. I don't know what I'm going to do yet."

"But your end goal is to leave Weston?" A hint of something kind of like betrayal coated Josiah's words. He had to tread carefully with his response so he didn't hurt Josiah's feelings in any way.

"It was my end goal when I first moved back here, yes. Am I open to staying? Possibly. I enjoy my work at the ranch and the guys there. I like working for a family ranch again, like we used to have."

"Maybe this is your midlife crisis moment. A chance to try something new. You can still do computer stuff remotely."

If Michael didn't know better, he'd think Josiah was lobbying him to stay. And he was doing a damned good job. Behind his glasses, Josiah's eyes seemed to gleam in the afternoon light.

"I can still do a lot of things," Michael said. "Including ask if you're feeling up to heading over to the Roost with me for a beer."

Josiah's lips parted, and it took him several seconds to reply. "Can I get a rain check on that? I'm still a little off after what happened Friday night, and if Seamus isn't on a call, there's a good chance he'll be there on a Sunday afternoon."

Damn, he hadn't even considered running into McBride when he made that impulsive invitation for a beer. "Of course. Rain check. Whenever you want."

"Thanks. I think I'm going to go inside and read for a while. I'll see you in the morning." Josiah turned, yanked open the trailer door, and was gone in less than ten seconds.

Michael stared at the door, unsure if he'd driven Josiah away by asking him out for a beer, completely platonically, or if Josiah really needed space to read and process everything that had happened this weekend. And he truly hoped one day Josiah would come to Michael to talk. About anything.

In the end, he took Josiah at his word and went back inside the house.

Josiah was quiet the next morning when Michael let him in, and he went directly into the kitchen with a small bag of groceries. Probably for whatever dish he'd mentioned cooking today for everyone's dinner. Dad was still asleep, and Josiah knew how to handle breakfast so Michael grabbed his lunch bag from the small table by the front door and left for work. As much as Michael wanted to see how Josiah was doing, after not seeing him for the rest of yesterday, he also didn't want to push the younger man.

He'd been pushed around enough.

As soon as he parked, Brand and Hugo emerged from the barn and headed straight for him. Michael had texted Brand on Saturday to let him know Josiah was settling into the trailer and stressed, but nothing else. Everything else Josiah had admitted to him was between them.

Michael climbed out of the cab with his lunch. "Hey, guys, thanks again for Friday night."

"Happy to help," Brand replied. "Our dads go way back so yours calling mine was the right move."

"How does Josiah seem?" Hugo asked. "I texted him once to ask but all he said back was he was fine."

"He's adjusting," Michael replied, choosing his words carefully. "Getting kicked out for no reason and then denied your stuff can screw with anyone's mind. I'll tell him you asked after him."

"Thanks."

"No problem. Is it just us three today?" He'd had such a busy weekend that Michael couldn't remember today's schedule and who was on it.

"Alan's on, too—he's just running behind," Brand replied. "Me and him are going out to make sure the last of the regular herd are ready for slaughter, then we're back in the barn. You and Hugo are out with the organic herd running the fence line."

"Got it, thanks." Michael was a tad surprised Brand had put himself on barn duty, which varied from polishing saddles to feeding the horses, but he'd always seemed like a hands-on boss. Having grown up here on the ranch, Brand knew how much work it took to keep this sort of business running.

As he saddled up his horse for the day, he couldn't

help wondering if Josiah knew how to ride. Or if he had any interest at all in learning. If he did, maybe Michael could get permission to bring him out here on a weekend—as long as Michael could find someone else to sit with Dad for a few hours. He could almost imagine Josiah on a horse, face tilted up to the sunshine, enjoying the freedom of wandering the vast acres of the ranch.

Freedom from all the things weighing on his heart and soul. Freedom Michael himself had begun to rediscover by being here. A freedom he hoped they both got to feel for a long time to come.

Chapter Eleven

"Press against my palm as hard as you can," Josiah said. Elmer did as asked with his right hand. They'd begun their first daily physical therapy session after breakfast, which was legs and feet, and now that lunch was done and had settled a bit, Josiah was working Elmer's arms and hands. The workouts not only kept blood flowing while Elmer was bedbound, but also strengthened his weaker right side.

Elmer huffed. "I'm pushing, I'm pushing. When do you think I can get up from this damned bed?"

"Okay, relax your hand. Thank you." He grabbed the bottle of lotion from the table near Elmer and squirted some on his own palm. Past clients always seemed to like hand massages, and Elmer was no different—even if he had huffed about it the first time. They were incredibly relaxing. "You're doing well with your leg strength. Maybe by the end of the week we can try getting you sitting on the edge of the bed. Possibly even on the bedside commode."

"Hate those things." Elmer eyeballed the commode, which they'd put in the far corner of the living room until needed. "But I guess it's better than the damned bedpan."

"Most patients prefer them to the bedpan, yes." Josiah rubbed the lotion into the center of Elmer's hand, gently pressing against the muscles and tendons and sensitive skin. "And I'll be doing most of the lifting, I just want to be sure you can put both feet on the floor and brace them."

"Lifting? I'm bigger than you, son."

"Trust me, I've had a lot of practice and know how to stand and lift. Once you and I have it figured out, I'll show Michael for the weekends when I'm not here."

"Joy." But a half smile tickled the corners of his mouth. Josiah imagined it wasn't easy for a grown man to let his equally grown son give him a bedpan and clean him up after, but Michael had done a great job this past weekend. Elmer was clean, his sheets were clean, and Elmer was in good spirits today.

Josiah moved on to massage Elmer's left hand. "I know you're probably tired of me thanking you for the trailer, but you have no idea how much I appreciate it. There aren't exactly a lot of housing options around here, especially on short notice."

"It's no trouble at all. Place has been empty for a few months, and I'd rather see it used than rot away in the yard. Besides, I don't guess you've got family in the area who'd take you in, since you said you were from Tulsa." Elmer was fishing and not very subtly.

"No, I'm very much alone." While he'd admitted to growing up in Tulsa and going to school there, he hadn't told Elmer much else about his past, and he was grateful that Elmer didn't push. He poked gently a little, probably out of natural curiosity, but didn't push.

"Except you ain't alone, son. You've got friends here, and I don't know why that idiot sheriff kicked you out like that, but you're welcome to stay for as long as you need."

Josiah's mind jumped back to a few months ago, when Elmer's coin collection went missing and Seamus had arrested Hugo for it. "You aren't worried Sheriff McBride kicked me out because I stole from him? Or lied or did something worse?"

Elmer studied him for a while, not answering until Josiah had finished massaging his left hand. "No, I don't think I am. I like to think I can judge a person's character, and I was wrong when I asked Hugo to leave. I should have trusted him, because I liked the boy a lot. He reminded me a bit of Michael when he was younger. But I listened to McBride instead, and I regret that. If you could have seen your own face when you showed back up Friday night? You'd have believed you, too."

"Thank you."

"Plus, my son and I are trusting you in this house five days a week, and with me stuck in this bed, there's nothing stopping you from robbing me blind. But neither of us thinks you will. Don't think Michael would have hired you if he thought otherwise. So whatever the reason for McBride kicking you out, it don't affect our relationship."

Josiah blinked hard, so sick of crying over this. "I'm glad. I enjoy it here. The job isn't for everyone, but I love what I do."

"Even if I can be a grouchy old coot sometimes?"

"Even then."

Elmer chuckled. "Come on, then, let's finish up this exercise crap. *Bonanza* is about to come on."

"Yes, sir."

Josiah worked on Elmer's arms and shoulders as the

theme song for the old Western show came blaring over the television. He tried to watch it with Elmer sometimes, but it didn't always hold his attention. It had a set cast of characters, but you didn't see them every episode. Some of the episodes seemed like they were about completely different people with the sheriff making a cameo at the end.

Oh well. Elmer loved it, and that's what mattered most.

After Josiah declared the session over, Elmer groaned his appreciation and focused wholly on the TV. Josiah put the lotion away, checked the catheter bag for fullness, then went to wash his hands in the kitchen. The chicken and potatoes in the slow cooker had been going for about an hour, but the herbs already scented the room with a lovely fragrance of thyme and rosemary. A whole chicken would give them plenty of meat for sandwiches for the rest of the week.

As he dried his hands on a kitchen towel, a weird feeling hit him in the gut. Josiah used to do this exact same thing for Seamus: slow-cook a chicken or roast on Sunday, so he'd have plenty of lunch leftovers for the rest of the week. Maybe today was Monday, but it was the same damned habit. Anger burbled up inside him—anger directed not just at himself and his stupid habits, but also at Seamus for being an abusive asshole, and at the world at large for taking his parents and Andy away from him.

The anger urged him to pick up the slow cooker and toss it out the backdoor, to get rid of it and that stupid habit.

But he loved his slow cooker. It had been the first adult equipment he'd bought during nursing school, so he'd always have something to eat, and he didn't care he'd found it at a thrift store for five bucks. It had carried him through the last six years of his life, and he wouldn't let Seamus's assholery steal it from him. Seamus had already stolen enough.

Josiah checked his phone, stupidly hoping for a text from Seamus. Anything to explain his bizarre behavior. Sure, Seamus had been emotionally distant this past week, but he'd never truly been emotionally available, either. He'd still demanded sex regularly. Shoved hard and squeezed too tight. Josiah's ribs were still sore from the other night when Seamus demanded he leave the room after sex, then shoved Josiah to the floor before he could leave on his own. Josiah had bounced off the corner of the dresser and lost his breath.

He should have known they were creeping toward the end of things; he just hadn't expected it to end quite like it had.

Thank God for the Pearces, or Josiah probably would have slept in his car Friday night, and who knows where on Saturday? But Michael had welcomed him into his home, given him a place to stay, and gotten his stuff back, and all he expected in return was for Josiah to pay rent. It didn't seem real, and Josiah still didn't completely trust it, not even after Michael declined his offer of sex, but he wanted to. To trust Michael.

Because Josiah liked it here. He was comfortable with these two men—which was exactly why he needed to be careful. Everyone he cared about was either taken from him, or they sent him away. As much as he liked Michael—probably more than he should—he had to protect himself first.

He wasn't sure his heart could survive any more breaks before it shattered completely.

The rest of the week took on a familiar, comforting pattern for Michael that was almost too domestic. He greeted Josiah in the morning before work, did his job out at Woods Ranch, and came home to a hot supper waiting, either new or heated leftovers. Every night, Michael invited Josiah to eat supper with them, but Josiah refused and took his plate out to the trailer. He really wished Josiah would join them one night.

But was that a good idea? Josiah was an employee, but didn't that technically stop at five thirty when his shift was over? Didn't seem to matter to Josiah, who left as soon after that time as possible, unless Michael was running a few minutes behind. He tried not to be, though, because Michael enjoyed the few minutes they managed to chat in the morning and evening.

Sometimes after dinner, he'd catch Josiah sitting on the trailer stoop, often reading but other times staring out at the horizon. Michael had invited him to sit up on the porch where they had more comfortable wicker chairs, but Josiah preferred keeping his distance when he was off the clock. He didn't take it personally. The poor guy was only a week past being kicked out by McBride, and everyone handled trauma differently.

Still, he wished Josiah would talk to him about something more personal than Dad's daily urinary output.

On the plus side, Dad had graduated to sitting up on the edge of his bed for about five minutes at a time, which Josiah said was great progress. And he wanted Michael to help Dad with that over the weekend, too, which Michael promptly agreed to do. Dad groused at Michael more when he had to do caregiving things for him, but Michael was his son. Josiah was a nurse being paid to wipe Dad's ass.

"Do you have any plans for the weekend?" Michael asked Josiah while the younger man fixed himself a plate from his latest slow cooker meal. They'd have enough leftovers for tomorrow, and then Michael could easily cobble something together for Sunday with what they had in the fridge.

"Um, not really." Josiah carefully replaced the slow cooker's lid and balanced the gravy-covered spoon on the stove's spoon rest. "I suppose I'll hang around and read."

"Really? You should go do something. Get out of the house for a few hours. Maybe drive out to Littleton and see a movie." They had the only working drive-in theater in a dozen counties, and Michael remembered so many trips there as a child.

"I don't know." His cheeks darkened. "I'm not used to making my own plans."

"Oh. Right. Sorry."

"It's okay. Most grown men can do what they want, within reason. I just…got out of the habit with Seamus. I did what he wanted."

Michael dug his thumbnail into his palm to keep his annoyance at bay. "Well, the good news is he's out of the picture, and you're free to live your life as you see fit. Do what you want. Go get a burger at the Roost. Go to a movie or a museum, or just walk around the town park. You don't need anyone's permission anymore."

"I know I don't. I just…" He glanced through the kitchen doorway. "I don't want to run into him."

Never in his life had Michael wanted to hug someone more. To reassure them that they'd be all right, even if they crossed paths with the bogeyman. McBride was the county sheriff and wouldn't do anything cruel or violent in public. God knew what the asshole was capable of behind closed doors.

"I don't blame you," Michael said gently. "And I know it'll take time, but this is a pretty big county with several towns. You can't become a hermit on the off chance you might see him across the street or in a crowded restaurant. Don't let McBride take your independence away just when you got it back."

Josiah studied him for several long seconds, his face giving away nothing for a change, when Michael could usually read him easily. "I'll keep that in mind. Thanks."

"Anytime. And even if all you want to do is walk half a mile up and down the road, I'll walk with you."

"What about your dad?"

"He'll be okay for an hour, and I'll have my cell on me in case the stubborn old goat tries to get up and falls."

"Can we take a walk tonight?"

Michael blinked hard, surprised by the fast invitation. "Definitely. And if we're going to take a walk after dinner, why don't you stay and eat with us?"

"I can't. I, um, I have to change out of my scrubs anyway. I'd feel weird taking a walk wearing these."

"Totally get it." If Josiah still wanted to eat his evening meals alone, Michael would respect that wish. "Just knock on the door when you're ready to walk."

"I will." Josiah's sweet smile lit Michael up inside in a new way. "Thank you, Michael."

"Not a problem."

After Josiah left, Michael fixed plates for himself and Dad, and they ate together while watching a rerun of *Mister Ed*. The show was kind of ridiculous now, but as a child Michael had been enthralled by the idea of a talking horse. He used to spend hours a day in their barn with the horses, trying to coax them into conversations—until Dad caught him, told him the trick of putting peanut butter in the horse's mouth, and the magic was gone.

Parents were good at breaking their kids' imagination, either on purpose or by accident. Michael hadn't always been sure which one the horse incident had been on his father's part, only that Dad hadn't wanted Michael going off on some flight of fancy, not while the ranch was struggling.

Another old show came on after, but Michael didn't pay attention. He cleaned up their plates and the kitchen, then put on a pair of sneakers instead of his boots. The evening was chilly enough for him to grab a sweatshirt to slip on over his work polo. And then he waited. It was almost dusk before Josiah walked up onto the porch. Michael didn't want to seem too eager for their walk, so he let Josiah ring the bell before he opened the door.

He didn't often see Josiah in regular clothes. Now he wore jeans and a buttoned-up denim coat and had a black knit cap over his hair. "Hey, ready to go?"

"Yep, let me just grab one thing out of my truck as we leave. Dad, you okay for an hour?"

Dad waved them both off. "I'll call you if I shit the bed."

Josiah laughed. "Hey, you're on Michael's watch now."

"Gee, thanks," Michael deadpanned, amused at the teasing. "Come on." From his truck he retrieved a flashlight, since the sun was setting and there weren't streetlights for miles. The yard lights from their property would provide a decent glow from a long distance, but Michael wanted to be prepared.

They walked through the main gate side by side, about a foot of distance between them, shoes crunching on the mix of dirt and gravel. Michael had plans to oil and fix the gate this weekend, and he set himself a mental reminder. Josiah turned right, and Michael followed, allowing him to set the pace and direction. The road was paved but not lined, and the surface had definitely seen better days. The gravel shoulder was no wider than his hand before it met dirt and grass. They crossed the street to walk against traffic—if any came—and Michael situated them so Josiah was on the grass, Michael closer to any passing cars.

The crisp night air bit into his cheeks in a pleasant way, and Michael gazed around the land as they walked. So familiar to his younger self, and yet so different to the man he was today. Foreign and yet also not.

"Do you see that?" Michael asked, pointing to a slight glow on the horizon. "It's Woods Ranch. They're our closest neighbors."

"That seems so far away."

"It's not so bad as the crow flies. Or as the horse gallops."

"I never realized how isolated we are out here, not until you really look around at night and see the lack of other lights. I mean, at Seamus's house we didn't have any neighbors within eyesight, but at night we could see their lights in all directions. I didn't feel quite so alone."

Michael glanced at Josiah's profile. He looked straight ahead, jaw set, but his eyes gleamed in the starlight, maybe a little too wet. So many questions dangled on the tip of Michael's tongue, but this walk was the first solo time they'd had all week. He didn't want to push too hard and make Josiah shut down.

"I felt alone surrounded by people," Michael said. "Especially at the parties Kenny threw at our house. Dozens of people, all laughing and drinking and congratulating me for my latest development, but it was like they were talking to someone who wasn't even there. All the money in the world and no real friends."

"Sounds awful." His tone was flat, though, almost... sarcastic?

Michael stopped walking, defensiveness overtaking his common sense, and his voice rose. "So what? Because I had money I'm not allowed to have problems?"

"What?" Josiah turned so fast he nearly tripped over his own feet. He shook his head, mouth flapping open several times. "No, that's not what I meant. I'm sorry, I was only half paying attention and that was rude." His entire body seemed to hunch a bit, as if expecting a loud (possibly violent) rebuke for not listening.

He hated having put that fear in Josiah, but it irritated him when folks assumed having money solved all his problems and life should be a breeze. He reined that irritation out of his voice, though, wanting to give Josiah the benefit of the doubt. "Then what did you mean?"

"I meant the lonely part even when you're surrounded by people." Josiah seemed to relax a fraction, as if sensing Michael wasn't going to scream or attack. Michael silently berated himself for causing that sort of reaction from Josiah in the first place. "I've never been in a situation like that, where I'm at fancy parties with food and people and music. It sounds like a fairy tale compared to my life, only knowing a handful of people at a time, and I always lose them. I guess we both know what it's like to be lonely. My comment wasn't about the money at all, I promise."

"Okay. Thanks for that." He never thought Josiah was the kind of person to judge someone for their wealth, and he was right. "And I'm sorry I snapped. I wasn't trying to downplay your feelings of isolation at McBride's. Just trying to tell you I get it."

"I know. Like I said, I wasn't paying attention like I should have. I let my mind wander." Josiah took his glasses off, rubbed both eyes with the fingers of his free hand, then put them back on. The brief glimpse without glasses showed a much younger, more vulnerable face than with them. "Sorry."

"It's okay, Josiah." Michael looked up at the dark sky littered with thousands of twinkling lights of all sizes. Stars that had long since burned out before their light even made it to Earth, but no less beautiful for having arrived. "My favorite place in our—my—old house was the upstairs balcony, and not because we had a great view of our neighbor's pool."

Josiah smiled. "Why then?"

"Because I could see the sky. I mean, we were in the city so the light pollution kept me from seeing a lot of stars, but for our first anniversary of moving into the house, Kenny bought me a telescope. I used to tell him about the stars out here. They were one of my best memories of Weston. The telescope helped me see more stars. To remember that even when the people around me didn't see me, the stars still did because at least for my lifetime, their light is constant."

"That's...wow." He blinked hard several times, eyes glistening and not from the stars. "I think that's one of the most profound things I've ever heard someone say about the stars."

"I'm sure Galileo said something even more poetic."

"I doubt it, because that was personal to you, Michael. The stars mean something to you. You feel seen by them, while I don't feel seen by anything."

Michael's fingers twitched and he barely resisted the impulse to take Josiah's hand. "I see you."

Josiah blinked hard, and Michael could have kicked himself for letting those honest words slip out. He'd known Josiah for two weeks, and in that short time Josiah had gone through at least one major trauma with McBride. The last thing he needed was Michael panting after him, no matter how much Josiah's sweet, boy-next-door looks and demeanor appealed to him.

He braced for Josiah to walk away in a huff, maybe look disgusted at practically being hit on by an older man on a dark country road. Hell, Michael would deserve it if Josiah told him to go to hell and quit tomorrow.

Instead, Josiah shook his head. "I can't even see myself anymore. But thanks for saying it."

"Then let me help you see yourself. You are a kind person with a huge heart, and even if you don't see those things, other people do. Not just me. We see the way you shine even if you don't."

"I appreciate what you're saying, but I'm scared to let anyone else see me. Probably for a long time."

Josiah's expression wasn't sad or resigned, merely

tired and confused, like someone waking up after a long, deep sleep and still orienting themselves to the world. Still figuring out what being alive was all about.

It made something hopeful flutter behind Michael's breastbone. "But not forever?"

"I can't think about forever. Only what's happening right now. And right now? We both just got out of bad rela—situations."

Michael hadn't missed the word slip, and it made him hate McBride even more for how badly he'd hurt Josiah's feelings.

"I don't want to rush into something," Josiah continued, "and risk losing your friendship. I like you, Michael. You've been amazing and patient and kind. It's been a long time since I've had someone like you, someone I know in my heart I can rely on. Can we please be friends and just keep getting to know each other?"

"Of course we can be friends. We *are* friends. And you're right. I still need to lick my wounds over Kenny, and you need to get past what McBride did to you. And as your friend, my offer to listen is open-ended."

"I know. Thank you. You're a fantastic friend." Josiah flashed him a sad smile. "I, uh, think I'm ready to go back." He stepped around Michael and started walking back to the farmhouse.

Michael watched him go, giving Josiah the space he was clearly asking for. He was grateful Josiah felt comfortable enough with him to share everything he had, and to verbalize what he needed from Michael going forward. Friendship was all he'd expected during this new adjustment period, so he would accept and give it back in return. Josiah deserved all the peace and happiness in the world.

Michael gave the stars another long look, made a silent wish for his friend to receive those two important things, and then followed Josiah home.

Chapter Twelve

Josiah stood in front of the trailer's door peering out the small window, his attention on the Pearce house. Only two lights seemed to blaze: one in the living room and one upstairs in Michael's bedroom. He'd stood there for half an hour or so, his walk and conversation with Michael tumbling around his brain without stopping. Part of his heart pulled in the direction of the house and Michael, while the rest of it kept his feet firmly rooted in place.

He'd enjoyed their walk more than he could put into words. Not only the comfort of Michael's company, but also the blanket of stars above that meant the world to him but in a vastly different way than for Michael. For Michael, the stars made him feel seen and not so alone in the universe. For Josiah, they made him feel infinitely small and unnoticeable, and that's what he wanted to be from now on.

Unnoticeable to everyone except his patients. No more friends or loved ones. Just work and as much anonymity as possible. Compared to the rest of the planet, Josiah was just a speck, no more than dust to eventually be blown away. But now he was beginning to see the stars as Michael did, and he wasn't sure if he was happy or angry.

Being unnoticeable gave him comfort. Being seen… Well, maybe it depended on who saw him. He didn't want Seamus to see him ever again. He didn't mind if Michael saw him, though. Elmer, either, but Elmer was his patient and friend, and he amused Josiah with his stories and grumpiness and determination to walk again. Josiah didn't even mind if Hugo saw him, because Hugo was a friend, too. Not dangerous.

No, the important one was Michael, and that terrified him on the deep down level of a man who craved affection. Who remembered how it felt to be in love and who wanted to feel it again one day. But Josiah's heart was still too bruised by Seamus's betrayal. Maybe neither of them had ever said "I love you" to the other, but Josiah's affection for the man had been real in the beginning. Then fear had overtaken affection, and survival had overtaken fear.

Josiah wasn't sure he'd survive his affection being metastasized like that again. Keeping his distance from Michael, just being his friend, was the safest route forward.

He spent the weekend mostly in his trailer reading, doing his best to avoid Michael, who couldn't stray too far from the main house anyway. He took a few long walks around the barn and yard and a bit into the old fields, unwilling to walk the road alone even in daylight. Michael's comment that he could drive into town or go do something elsewhere stuck in the back of his mind, but why waste gas money when he was content right here?

Content behind a metal front gate that Michael cleaned

of rust, greased and got working again. He knocked on Josiah's door Sunday afternoon with a key. "We used to keep the front gate locked all the time but I guess Dad got out of the habit," Michael said. "I'm gonna start keeping it locked while I'm at work."

"Okay." Josiah added it to his meager key ring, which only had his car key and the trailer key. "What if someone stops by with a package or something?"

"There's a bell you can definitely hear from inside the house. Dad put the sign in the barn somewhere, so finding it is my next mission. I don't suppose you want to help me dig around in old tools, dust, and spiders?"

Despite his dislike of spiders, Josiah had yet to get a good look inside the big barn, and he was curious. Glances in from the driveway only gave him a small view of a riding lawn mower and what looked like a wooden door of some sort. "Um, I guess so."

"Cool."

"One sec." Josiah put on his sneakers, then joined Michael outside. The day was slightly overcast but no call for rain. Just clouds and the occasional gust of wind.

The barn was two stories, and he imagined the top was the hayloft, like in most barns Josiah had seen around these parts. The upper hayloft door still had a wood post and pulley attached above it, likely for hauling up bales of hay in the old days. As they went inside, he could see the way the place had once been divided into stalls up front, likely for horses. Various pieces of equipment lined the walls, and many of the stall doors were missing. A lot of the stalls were filled with what Josiah would generously call junk: twisted hunks of metal, plastic five-gallon buckets, parts of old bicycles, and any manner of detritus he couldn't describe without examining it further.

A lot of it was covered in a thin layer of brown dust, with the occasional streak that suggested someone had touched it somewhat recently. Likely Elmer in the weeks before his stroke, since Michael hadn't been in town, and he couldn't imagine anyone else skulking around the barn.

"Does your dad ever sell any of his stuff?" Josiah asked. "This stuff, or his finished art?"

"Sometimes." Michael toed at a stack of rusty rotary saw blades sitting in the dirt outside a stall. "We've had pickers stop by over the years because they see the stuff along the front fence. Sometimes Dad will sell from the barn, but it's tough because he's got an idea for everything. Always has. But he will occasionally sell his finished art if he believes the person buying it truly appreciates it."

"Sounds like a real artist. Only selling to those who love it."

"Yeah. He even agreed to set up a small booth at the Founder's Day Picnic this year. Said he made things all summer to sell to the locals."

"Wow, really? That's amazing."

"Yeah. Not sure who convinced him it was a good idea, but apparently he said yes." Michael poked his head into a stall and shone a flashlight around. This one was full of cobwebs, what looked like stacks of blankets or grain sacks, and not much more. "His workshop is farther in the back, so if he's got a stash of finished things for the picnic, it will be back there."

He followed Michael deeper into the barn, which was lit by a scattering of exposed bulbs on the ceiling. The atmosphere was incredibly creepy in a slasher film kind of way, but Michael's calm, stoic presence kept Josiah's imagination at bay. "So did Elmer do this collecting and art making and selling when you still lived here?"

"Not the selling, but the other stuff. He's collected junk my whole life, and he told me about selling the other night while we were watching some random antique show on TV. I was impressed he got rid of anything and that he was doing the picnic. Said if anyone stopped by interested in buying stuff to make sure I went through him before making any sales."

Josiah laughed, then sneezed twice in a row thanks to the grime. "Sounds like him. We're looking for a sign, right?"

"Yep. I asked Dad where he thought he put it, but all he could remember was one of the stalls."

"That doesn't really narrow things down."

"Nope. Especially if he buried it under more junk. If nothing else, I'm sure I can find a piece of plywood or something to paint on. We'll just lean it against the fence near the bell."

We?

Michael poked around in a few more stalls but seemed as reluctant to really dig as Josiah was. Not that Josiah was afraid of a little dirt, but the stale, slightly musty air was getting to his lungs. His eyes stung a bit and his nose was watering. Finally, they passed all the stalls and moved into a more open area with a ceiling that went straight up through the second floor to the actual A-frame roof. A ladder on the wall went up the hayloft. The rest of the space was full of different kinds of equipment, some covered in tarps so Josiah couldn't identify them. But he did recognize a blowtorch and welder's mask resting on an uncovered table. All around them were more piles of things and what looked like partially finished projects.

"Is welding in here a good idea?" Josiah asked. "I don't know anything about it except that it takes flames and shoots sparks."

"Dad usually welds up by the front barn doors. I dragged this back here about a week and a half ago, since I knew he wouldn't be using it for a while. Didn't want anyone to see it from the road and get big ideas about stealing it."

"Got it." He gazed around the cavernous space, grateful it was a tad easier to breathe in here. A few windows dotted each wall and they looked clean enough to have been opened recently. "Is this where you kept the cattle?"

"Naw, Dad said he tore that barn down about fifteen years ago after a bad summer storm rolled through. He thought it was a tornado, but it was just superhigh winds. Hit it and ripped off the roof. Since he didn't have cattle, he got a bid for someone to tear it down and haul off the lumber." Michael's gaze went briefly distant. "There was some nice old lumber in that barn. Our family built it by hand with their neighbors back in the eighteen-eighties. The Pearces and the Woodses were two of the first families to settle out here and build the town of Weston."

"It's amazing to have those kinds of roots."

"You don't have any roots in Tulsa?"

"No." Instead of annoyance at the personal question, Josiah felt only melancholy. "No, my parents...drifted a lot around Oklahoma. Job to job, city to city. I tagged along, went to school when I could." Much easier than admitting he and his parents were homeless for the better part of ten years. "We were in Tulsa the longest, so that always felt the most like home. But no, no roots or emotional attachment to the place."

"I'm sorry to hear that."

"Don't be." Josiah wandered to a long worktable that had various metal sculptures on it. The first looked like a horse made out of cutlery, screws, nuts, and other metal things he didn't recognize. But it was definitely a horse. "This is really good."

"It is." Michael came up beside him, distractingly close. "Mostly he does larger lawn sculptures or cuts silhouettes out of sheet metal. This small stuff is pretty new."

"I love it."

"I'm sure he'd give it to you if you ask."

"Oh no." He put the horse down and took a step back. "I'd never presume. Just admiring it, that's all. I'm impressed with artists of any caliber." One of his favorite things to do was watch Andy graffiti the underside of an overpass, or the corner of an abandoned building. Leaving his own artwork behind on the world in swirls and loops and colors that represented the future he longed for but would never experience.

"Josiah?"

"What?" He blinked up at Michael, whose hand was paused a foot from Josiah's arm. "Sorry, I spaced out."

"You looked a little upset just now. Was it something I said?"

"No, it was something I said. Don't worry about it."

Michael's soft scowl said he was definitely going to

worry about it. "Well, feel free to poke around. I'll look for something to make a bell sign on."

"Okay."

While Michael scoured the workshop for what he needed, Josiah inspected the pieces on the table. Something that looked like the body of an insect but without legs. Horseshoes welded together but not into anything in particular yet. An abstract tower thing that could be a base or simply a finished sculpture. Josiah stroked the joints with his fingertips, admiring the deft hand that had created the welds, and the mind that had led those hands toward a finished piece. A piece that lived only in Elmer's mind for now but would one day be complete.

"Here we go." Michael approached with a triumphant smile on his face, as well as a piece of plywood about three feet tall and two feet wide, plus a can of black spray paint. "I'd make the sign in here, but the fumes might make us both pass out."

"Good call. It's already a little stuffy." He'd seen enough of the barn for now, so he followed Michael back out to the front yard.

Michael leaned the board against the side of the barn and sprayed Ring Bell for Service with an arrow pointing up. It seemed a bit silly, but it wasn't his gate. They situated it against the main fence, to the left of the gate latch. Josiah had noticed the old, iron bell on a post right by the gate, but he'd never paid attention to the rope tied to it. Michael pulled the rope, and the bell let out a sharp clang.

Josiah flinched. "Yeah, we'll definitely hear that from the house."

"Yes, we will. It's a simple padlock on a hasp." They

went through and Michael shut the gate. Flipped the hasp over onto the staple, put the padlock through the staple's loop, and snapped it shut. Unlocked it again with his key. "We can lock it at night, too, if that makes you more comfortable."

"During the day is fine." *At night, I know you're here.*

Not that he'd ever say that out loud to Michael. The man should not make him feel so at ease but he did. Michael had only ever been his friend. He didn't flirt, he never made a pass at him. He was safe. And so freaking handsome he took Josiah's breath away some days, especially decked out in his cowboy boots, hat, and flannel jacket.

A real Texas cowboy, even if reluctantly so.

"Do you expect some kind of trouble?" Josiah asked. Not that such a simple lock couldn't be ripped off by a determined man and his pickup truck, but the precaution seemed a touch, well, overprotective. Probably because of his dad and his medical condition. Nothing to do with Josiah and Seamus at all.

"I don't expect it, no, but I'd rather be prepared in case trouble comes knocking. And before you ask, no, I wasn't a Boy Scout. Just practical from a young age. Plus…" Michael ran his hand along the top bar of the metal gate. "We didn't lock it once and we lost something very precious we'll never get back."

With Michael's back to him, Josiah couldn't see his face but could hear the grief in his voice. "There's nothing wrong with a little precaution. I know I appreciate it."

Michael rested his upper arms on the top of the gate and leaned forward, gazing out over the vast land on the opposite side of the road. Josiah mimicked his pose as best he could, but he was about six inches shorter than Michael, so his chin basically met the top of the bar. They faced south, and the sun was slowly setting on their right, casting a gorgeous golden glow across the acres of waving grass and scrub bushes.

"I never thought I'd be anything but restless here when I came back," Michael said, his voice near a whisper. As if the moment was too important for loud words. "Guess I don't know myself as well as I thought I did."

"I doubt most of us know ourselves as well as we think." Josiah kept his gaze straight ahead, but something still seemed to pass between them. A silent, unseen connection over having found some sense of peace on this land, while the rest of the world spun out of control around them. Spinning in wildly different directions, but they'd both lost something precious this past month. They were mourning. They were rebuilding.

Most of all, they'd each found someone who understood. And if all they ever were was friends, Josiah could live with that.

The annual Founder's Day Picnic was held the last weekend in October, rather than on one specific day of the month. Michael fondly remembered the local holiday for its familial atmosphere and all the games planned for the kids, complete with prizes. Unlike the county fair, which was open to any resident of any town in the county, this celebration was for the citizens of Weston and their families.

The Baptist church had a large pavilion with two dozen picnic tables, and two large charcoal grills just outside, and they hosted it every year. Every family brought at least one covered dish, while the town council (all three members of it) coordinated with the churches to provide utensils, cups, plates, and napkins. The Roost always donated burgers for the grills. And while the day was mostly one big community picnic, often with live music from the Catholic church's performance choir, which had actually won a few regional awards, the picnic was now also a bit of a stand-in for trick or treating these last five years, thanks to the local Protestant church. This was news to Michael—Halloween was the devil's night or some such nonsense, so all the kids under twelve were invited to participate in a candy hunt on the church lawn. The whole thing sounded silly to Michael, but this wasn't his town.

Except it was kind of becoming his town a little bit.

In the two weeks leading up to the picnic, Michael threw himself into work on the ranch and once his probation period was over, Wayne and Brand officially offered him the job. Michael agreed on a six-month term to start. He wasn't having any luck selling his house, and besides, he was content with Dad and Josiah. Way more content with Dad than he'd expected when Michael first moved back. They still hadn't talked about Mom or their fight, but the awkward silences from those first few days were gone.

And Josiah? Once Michael got his attraction to the adorable young nurse under control, Josiah was becoming his closest friend. Sure, Michael joked and chatted with the guys at the ranch, but he looked forward to coming home in the evening and seeing what was for dinner. Josiah still frequently ate alone in the trailer, but he occasionally stayed. Or he came back in the evening to watch TV with them. Dad loved it, as if Josiah was the second son he'd never had, and Michael enjoyed watching the pair bond.

Dad's physical therapy was also progressing rapidly, and Josiah had a good report each night. His right arm was strengthening faster than his leg, giving Dad a lot more independence. He could feed himself and, while he still needed help getting onto the portable toilet, he could clean up after himself. After procuring a wheelchair for him, Michael proudly showed Dad the wooden ramp he'd commissioned from a carpenter in Daisy. It fit perfectly over the porch stairs without being too steep, and was wide enough that one person could still walk up the steps on the right side.

Dad coughed a lot when he saw it and rubbed at his eyes, before offering the most sincere "thank you" Michael had ever gotten from the man.

The ramp allowed them to take Dad out to the barn for the first time since his stroke. The ground was hard packed enough that the wheels rolled right over it. Michael pushed, his chest tight with joy at the wide smile on Dad's face. He was out in the sunshine again, free of the confines of the house, thanks to his Pearce stubbornness—and Josiah's constant support.

"Who left this place such a mess?" Dad grumped as they passed the stalls on their way to the workshop.

"You did, you old hoarder," Michael replied. "I should've had someone from the scrapyard come down here while you were stuck in bed."

"I might be stuck in this chair a while longer yet, but I'd have tanned your hide if you'd done that."

Michael laughed. He'd joked privately with Dad about selling his junk several times over the last month, but Josiah didn't seem in on the joke. His face was pinched and upset, and Michael could have kicked himself—not specifically for his own words but for what Dad said about tanning his hide. While Michael had gotten the occasional whack on the behind with Dad's open palm, usually for mouthing off, Dad wouldn't do that.

"We're teasing each other," Michael whispered to Josiah. "It's fine."

"'Course we're joshin' around," Dad said. "Must be all the sunshine and fresh air but I can't remember being in a better mood in a dog's age. Can't wait to see my ornaments again."

"Ornaments?" Josiah asked.

"Pet name for his finished projects," Michael replied. "Even if said project is a six-foot-tall statue made out of old stovepipes and motorcycle engines."

"Well, I look forward to seeing the master at work one day. Welding fascinates me but I've never been brave enough to try it."

"Takes a deft eye and a practiced hand," Dad said proudly. Michael pushed him into the workshop and right over to the table holding his partly finished ornaments. "Look at these beauties just waiting to be done. Can't say as they'll be ready for the picnic, though. Ah, well, maybe next year."

"Can't you still do the booth, though? Maybe take some of your equipment and a few ornaments? Even if you can't show the kids how to weld, you can tell them what you do and what that thing does." Josiah pointed at the welding torch.

"Ayup, could probably do that. Could definitely do with some conversation, that's for damned sure. Only folks I've seen besides you two lately is Pastor Lorne and Wayne when he brought over that damned good roast dinner from Rose the other night."

Even though Michael had assured Rose Woods that their little trio was eating just fine thanks to Josiah, she'd still sent her husband over the other Sunday evening with a full pot roast supper, including apple pie for dessert. They'd eaten the leftovers all week for lunch, giving Josiah a small break from cooking for them.

"Yeah, I bet it'll be nice to get out for a while," Michael said. Sometimes he missed the parties Kenny used to throw. Designing software had been an extremely isolating career for him, and he'd enjoyed the social aspect of being Kenny's partner in business and romantically. At his heart, he enjoyed being around people. He also enjoyed his solitude and smaller social situations, like a beer at the Roost with Brand, Rem, and Hugo once in a while. By now everyone in Weston knew he was back and why, so the picnic would be an interesting exercise in battling gossip and intrusive questions.

"Are you going to the picnic?" he asked Josiah.

"Hadn't really thought about it," Josiah replied. He'd wandered to the other side of the table and was once again admiring the metal horse. "I'll go if you need me to be there for you, Elmer, of course."

"Nah, it's your day off, son," Dad replied. "Michael and I can handle things if you wanna go and enjoy yourself."

Josiah's mouth twisted unhappily, and Michael didn't have to ask why. McBride would be at the picnic in some capacity, and Josiah was likely calculating the odds of running into the man that day. McBride was unlikely to do or say anything in such a public setting, but just seeing the man could be traumatizing for Josiah, if he'd experienced even a fraction of what Michael suspected was true about the pair's former relationship.

"Come with us as a friend," Michael said. "We all live here, so we might as well all go together."

Relief softened Josiah's expression. "Okay."

"Awesome. And since you're the kitchen wizard, you can tell me what I'm making for the potluck, because I have no idea what to pick. Especially something that can be made in big quantities."

He chuckled, a soft, melodic sound Michael didn't hear often enough. "I can do that. Some kind of cold salad is your best bet, anyway, since the weather will be nice, but not the usual suspects, like potato or macaroni."

"I bow to your expertise. Tell me what you need and I'll buy the groceries this week."

"Deal."

They shared a fond smile over Dad's head, and in Josiah's smile he saw a bit more hope peeking through. Hope for Dad's continued recovery; hope for Josiah's own mental recovery from his time with McBride; hope that things would finally bend in their favor and turn out all right.

Hope for a brighter, happier future for all of them.

Chapter Thirteen

Elmer took full advantage of the new freedom of his wheelchair, despite the chillier weather of late October, and Josiah loved seeing the elderly man come alive in the sunshine. After physical therapy, both morning and afternoon, Josiah allowed Elmer to spend an hour in his workshop. Mostly Elmer told Josiah where to move this or that, or he explained how a particular tool worked, because he wasn't strong enough yet to use the tools himself. Elmer grumped a lot about it, but every time Josiah reminded him that pushing too hard could set him back, Elmer gave in.

They did a bit of cleaning, too. Josiah hauled a big plastic trash barrel out of a stall, shoved a sturdy garbage bag into it, and set it up by Elmer wherever he was working for bits of trash as he found them. Scraps he'd saved for an idea, but that maybe, now that he'd had one health scare, he might not actually get to use as planned. Scraps that were no good to anyone except his imagination.

Actual trash went into the bin, too, like water-damaged car magazines, torn boxes of nails that could be consolidated into a glass jar with others of the same size, and plastic baggies with contents long melted or disintegrated due to air exposure. The place slowly decluttered on the surface, but there was a lot of work yet left to do for it to be anywhere close to organized—at least in Josiah's mind. Elmer seemed to know exactly where everything was supposed to go in the chaos.

They talked about the booth Elmer would set up for Saturday's picnic. The Baptist church provided a single folding table per person/company who wanted to set up and talk about their products. The other four churches would set up with tracts to talk about their particular religions—not that everyone in Weston hadn't already chosen one or none at that point—as well as places like hunting clubs or the Loyal Order of Whatever type of places. Probably a Boy Scouts table. Woods Ranch, according to Michael, would have information on their organic beef, plus a penned-in young bull from their spring group of calves for kids to pet.

Michael had reserved a table for Elmer and promised to print out some flyers with information on welding, metal art, and recycling to hand out. For as miles apart as Michael and Elmer had seemed on Josiah's first day, the pair had come together more in the last month-plus, and he loved to see it—except on the rare occasion they dipped into certain parts of the past. The one part they always avoided around him was Michael's mother.

Josiah knew very little about Carol Pearce, other than she'd died when Michael was in high school. Her and Elmer's wedding photo still adorned the living room's mantel, plus a picture of her holding an infant Michael that Elmer had once requested Josiah bring down from his bedroom, but those were the only obvious traces of the woman. He could ask but he also didn't want to push. She was a ghost for a reason, and he didn't want to stir up the past if it caused both men pain.

Thursday afternoon, Elmer was going through each drawer of a huge standing toolbox, picking out bits of trash, admiring other things, and basically moving items around as an alternative to being inside watching TV. Josiah didn't mind. He perched on a sawhorse beside Elmer and asked the occasional question about what something was, what it did, and if Elmer really needed to keep it. At one point, Josiah found an old shoebox that seemed sturdy enough, and Elmer began a small "give away" pile, mostly of small wrenches, screwdrivers, and sockets.

It surprised Josiah a bit that an artist was willing to part with his stuff, and he questioned Elmer on it.

"Can't take it with me, son," Elmer replied. "And I know Michael don't wanna bother with it after I'm gone. Can't see saddling him with more than necessary."

"You don't think Michael will want to keep the ranch?"

"What ranch? We ain't been a ranch since we sold the last horse to that fellow down in Littleton. It's just a lot of land that's not doin' anyone any good. Should've sold it a long time ago."

"But you didn't for a reason."

Elmer spun a small hex key between his fingers, his profile giving away nothing to Josiah. "Guess I kept hoping Michael would come home one day and want the place."

"He did come home."

"Temporarily. He's made it clear he's here until I'm

better and he sells his house in Austin. Then he's outta here again."

Josiah's skin prickled with unease. Michael hadn't made that clear to Josiah at all. Had Michael waffled about leaving in front of Josiah to make Josiah feel better? To get closer to him, all the while planning to leave, after all? Josiah didn't need Michael's emotional charity, he needed honesty from his friend.

"Michael seems content here," Josiah hedged, keeping his other thoughts to himself. "He likes working at Woods Ranch. I've seen him staring out over the land, as if he's imagining what it could be beyond empty fields."

"You sure he ain't just remembering what it used to be?"

"No, I'm not." It was probably his own wishful thinking, hoping that at the end of things, Michael would stay. Those hopes and doubts were exactly why he'd kept Michael in the friendship zone these last few weeks, and kept his own feelings for the man buried deep down beneath his survival instincts.

Elmer tossed the hex key into the donate box. "Had a lot of dreams for this place when I took over after my father died. Wanted to keep his dream alive and pass it on like he passed his dream on to me. But Michael wanted something else. Can't even say it was our fight—I saw it from a young age. He worked his ass off here but his heart wasn't in ranching."

Josiah bit his bottom lip so he didn't ask about the fight. A fight Michael had only brushed up against without revealing any actual details. Whatever had been said between father and son had driven a two-decade wedge between them and created a rift. A rift only briefly bridged because of Elmer's stroke. Despite their differences and the separation of time, Josiah still saw paternal love in Elmer's face and heard it in his voice when he talked about Michael. Was pride keeping Elmer from seeking forgiveness and permanently mending that rift? Was pride doing the same to Michael?

It's not my place to interfere.

Didn't stop him from wanting to, though, if only because he truly cared about both men and their happiness.

"Nope," Elmer continued. He tossed a scrap of cardboard into the trash. "I'll be the last Pearce to have worked this land. Once I'm gone and my ashes are scattered out under my wife's favorite tree, Michael can do what he wants. Keep it or sell it, won't matter to me. He'll have a hell of an auction with all my stuff, believe you me."

Between the things in the barn, the antiques in the house, and all of Elmer's art, Josiah didn't doubt there was money to be made with an estate auction, but he hated to think about such a hypothetical future. Elmer was larger than life, even from his hospital bed, and Josiah couldn't imagine a world without him and his jigsaw puzzles in it.

"Money is nice," Josiah said softly, "but I'd bet every dollar I have that Michael would rather have you around than that cash in his pocket. Even if he can't say so himself."

Elmer met his gaze then, his deep-set eyes surrounded by wrinkles and laugh lines and other etchings of time and experience. He didn't speak for a long time, then shrugged. "Even so." He tossed another hex key into the donate box. "Can't leave too much of a mess behind. No sir."

Unsure if he'd been of any use to Elmer this afternoon, Josiah let the subject drop and returned to helping Elmer sort his toolbox.

Josiah woke Saturday morning with squirrels chasing each other around in his stomach, and he lay in bed for a while, staring up at the trailer's ceiling, willing his racing nerves to calm down. He wasn't nervous about the picnic itself. He'd attended the last two years (always with Seamus), and he knew most folks in town. Most of his day would be spent assisting Elmer at his welding booth, so he wouldn't have to walk around and mingle. Their food contributions for the picnic were ready and waiting in the fridge.

No, his mild panic was over possibly seeing Seamus again for the first time since being kicked out of his house. They'd had no contact of any sort, not a phone call, text, or passing by each other on the rare occasion Josiah wandered into town for groceries. In most ways, Josiah was glad for it; he never wanted to see Seamus again if he could help it.

In other ways, it made him nervous. Seamus wasn't the type to easily forgive a grudge, and Josiah still didn't know why he'd been kicked out. He was still waiting for that other invisible shoe to drop and scare the piss out of him.

Speaking of piss, his aching bladder roused him from bed. He did his business and took a quick shower in the cramped space, then forced down a piece of toast with peanut butter on it. No coffee, because he was jittery enough this morning. When he left the trailer, Michael was already outside loading Elmer's requested equipment into the bed of his pickup. His warm smile and cheerful "Good morning" did nothing to quell the squirrels still doing battle in Josiah's stomach. But he did feel a touch safer, knowing Michael would be around all day.

Despite sharing a beer on the porch last night, Josiah hadn't brought up Thursday night's conversation with Elmer about the future of the Pearce land. It wasn't his place to interfere in the relationship between father and son, and Josiah didn't want to influence Michael's decision about his future. Michael had to do what was best for himself, and if what was best took him away from Weston again, then so be it.

It would hurt, but Josiah would survive. He always did. He bent and occasionally broke, but he'd yet to be completely destroyed by the actions of others. He'd survive this misplaced crush on Michael Pearce.

Elmer was sitting on the side of his bed and keeping his balance well. His progress with standing for several seconds and easily transferring from bed to wheelchair to toilet pleased Josiah like crazy. He had a lot of work left before he could take the stairs up to his actual bedroom, but tomorrow's plan was to convert the downstairs den into a bedroom for Elmer. His queen mattress was too big for the space already somewhat crowded with a desk, two bookcases, and various storage boxes full of stuff that wasn't Josiah's business.

Michael had located a new twin-sized mattress and bed frame at a thrift store forty minutes from town, and he was driving out tomorrow to pick it up. Once they were sure the room was set, Josiah would call about having the hospital bed picked up and removed from the house. It would open up the living room again, and also give Elmer more space to maneuver around in the wheelchair. Giving him the independence of a private bedroom again would help his mental state, too, and that was just as important to recovery as the physical.

"Morning," Josiah said. "You have breakfast yet?"

"Yeah, had oatmeal earlier," Elmer replied. "Barely slept all night, so I was up early. Michael, too. You?"

"I didn't sleep much either. Had some toast. I don't want to eat too much with all the good food that'll be at the picnic."

"A man after my own stomach. Say, uh…" Elmer frowned and tilted his head to one side. "They gonna have a handicap port-a-pot at this shindig? Don't see us both fittin' into a regular one if I gotta go."

"I'm not sure, but I called the pastor and he gave us permission to use the church's bathroom if you have to go." Thankfully, the Baptist church had a ramp, and Elmer was unlikely to be the day's only guest in need of handicapped facilities.

"Good thinking, son."

They did Elmer's morning exercises while they waited for Michael. Once everyone was ready to go, they got Elmer into the passenger seat of Josiah's car— it was easier to get him in and out of it—and stowed the wheelchair in the pickup. Josiah packed the two cold salads in a cooler bag for the trip, and he put that in his car's back seat. After double-checking that he had enough bottles of water and Elmer's medications, Josiah and Elmer hit the road with Michael following behind.

The Founder's Day Picnic location was easy to find, and not just because it was the first church on this way into town. A huge banner hung across Main Street, welcoming locals to the celebration, as well as marking it the one-hundred-fifty-seventh anniversary of breaking ground on the first official building, which was the big brick building on the corner of Main and Filbert (their only stoplight intersection) that housed the post office and bank. Streamers and balloons hung off light poles, mailboxes, and other surfaces in a more over-the-top way than even the July Fourth celebration.

A burly man in a yellow vest directed them into a field by the church, where they could park. Michael pulled in right beside them. They weren't too far from where the booths were ready to be constructed. Some folks went all out with banners and borders, while others just put out a tablecloth and their stuff. They were somewhere in the middle, with a bright red tablecloth and a cardboard sign on an easel Michael had borrowed from the high school art room.

Pushing Elmer over the grass wasn't the easiest thing in the world, especially with a big cooler strapped to his shoulder, but Josiah managed. At least he wasn't hauling equipment like Michael. After conferring with an organizer, Josiah left Elmer behind his designated table and dropped off the cold salads with the ladies in charge of the picnic buffet. After a bit of deliberation, Josiah had put together green chili hominy and vinegar-based slaw, hoping his own spin on the flavors set his apart if someone else did a similar dish.

Not that he was all that vain about his cooking, but nobody wanted to look like a copycat. Especially when half the people in town would be gossiping about the food for at least a week after.

They were four tables away from the Woods Ranch display, which was on the end of the row. A good thing, too, since they had erected a pen of rope and steel poles to protect the young cow they'd brought along to show off. Josiah caught Hugo's eye and waved; Hugo waved back. Townsfolk milled around, already browsing the booths as they were being set up. Quite a few came over simply to see how Elmer was doing, since the only people who'd seen him in the last month-plus were the few who'd bothered to stop by and visit.

A small stage had been erected at the north end of the pavilion, and at ten on the dot, the mayor stepped up to the microphone and welcomed everyone to the Founder's Day Picnic. His voice boomed across the field, thanks to several speakers on all sides of the pavilion—a weeklong Revival Camp was held there every summer so the place was wired to be heard—and the crowd listened while he droned on about the first settlers in this area, the founding of the town itself, blah, blah.

Same story, different year, but the little kids seemed to eat it up. Or they were just excited the festivities had begun and they'd be able to eat soon. The long tables set up for food were covered with dozens of dishes, and the scent wafting over helped ease Josiah's stomach away from angry squirrels and closer to hungry hippos.

Elmer's booth proved popular with the young and preteen kids, boys and girls, probably because of the propane tank and torch. He'd brought one finished ornament, several in progress, and a small tray of various parts as examples of the raw materials he sculpted with. Josiah hung close without crowding him, proud of how engaged Elmer was with the kids, while also aware of his fatigue levels. He didn't want Elmer too exhausted to enjoy lunch.

The scent of grilling burgers and other meat made Josiah's mouth water, and he found himself consistently checking the time on his phone, counting down the time to eat. At eleven-fifty, he glanced up from his phone and right into the last face he wanted to see today: Seamus McBride's.

Seamus stood about twenty feet away in full uniform, with a male stranger by his side. About Josiah's age, the stranger had jet-black hair and the kind of sharp gaze that reminded Josiah of a hawk. They weren't touching, but there was an air of possessiveness about the stranger that raised Josiah's hackles. Not that he had any claim on Seamus now or ever, but it still weirded him out. Seamus watched him, his expression kind of bland, before blinking and looking away.

Instead of fear, Josiah only felt a brief splash of surprise and curiosity. Nothing else, not even revulsion. The further he got from his previous relationship with Seamus, the freer Josiah felt to move through the world. No longer constrained by the limitations Seamus had wrapped around his life, the rules he'd set, or the demands he'd made of his mind, body, and heart.

As the pair moved away, the stranger looked over his shoulder, right at Josiah. His eyes narrowed in some sort of disapproval, or even challenge—Josiah wasn't sure. It unnerved him, but Josiah was no threat to this guy; he was welcome to Seamus and his coldness, fluctuating moods and rash decisions.

Josiah's skin prickled and he looked down the row of booths to the Woods Ranch area. Michael was watching him with an intent expression, and even from the long distance, his face seemed to ask if Josiah was okay.

He'd seen it. Josiah smiled and nodded. He really was all right.

And for the first time in a long time, he was confident he'd stay that way.

Michael was enjoying himself at the ranch booth a lot more than he expected he would, because kids were not his thing. He didn't want them, he didn't particularly like being around them, and he was already not much of a social butterfly. Code didn't talk back to you. But the kids who came around to pet and feed Minnie Moo the cow were sweet, funny, and they asked a lot of questions.

Brand and Wayne took point at the table, talking to adults about the ranch, the organic beef, and even the wind farm they'd erected in the south pasture two years ago. A lot of it was simple socialization, some of it business, all of it some level of entertaining. Michael got a few questions about Dad's recovery, and he thanked folks for their thoughtfulness. No one specifically asked Michael how long he was in town for, but the day was young.

At exactly noon, someone rang an old-fashioned dinner bell, signaling the beginning of the potluck. Some of the younger kids cheered and charged the buffet, only to be corralled by some of the adults, either their parents or Sunday school teachers—Michael didn't know or care. His stomach grumbled for food.

Brand waved him off, so Michael met Dad and Josiah behind their table. Dad's cheeks had a rosy, healthy glow, and his eyes shone with more joy than Michael had seen since coming home. Dad loved his art, loved talking about his art, and he was in his element surrounded by young people asking him about it.

Their trio joined the line and after a quick discussion, Dad held his and Josiah's plates, so Josiah could serve them both, and Michael managed his own plate. Little note cards stood next to every pot, pan, or platter, naming the dish and the person or family who'd brought it. By the time they got to their own bowls, the food was halfway gone. Michael caught Josiah's eye and winked. Josiah blushed.

Michael basked in the simple familiarity of Josiah helping Dad pick out his food and scoop it onto the foam plate. Their trio joked and talked like they'd been a family for years, rather than six weeks, and Michael wanted to be doing this for months. Maybe even years.

He didn't dare imagine forever.

Josiah found them a spot at the end of a picnic table so Dad could roll right up to it. Once their plates were settled, Josiah went to get everyone drinks. Michael sat on one side of Dad. Josiah's plate was opposite him. He'd much rather have Josiah beside him, but this wasn't a date. It was a potluck lunch with most of the town of Weston, plus an assortment of former residents and out-of-town family members.

Michael didn't pretend to know half the people there, and it didn't matter. The two most important people in his life were eating with him.

Hugo and Brand joined them before the table filled up, both of their plates overflowing. They sat on Josiah's side of the table. Every time Michael interacted with the pair socially, he found himself battling strong jolts of jealousy at how in tune and in love the pair was. Even during his best, happiest days with Kenny, Kenny had never looked at Michael like that. Michael wasn't sure if he'd ever looked at Kenny like that, either.

But neither of them had truly been in the relationship for the other person, not really. They'd been in it for their business, their app, their fortune, and their popularity. The best thing that had ever come out of their relationship for Michael had been Rosco, and he'd lost his dog in the "divorce." He wanted the kind of love Brand and Hugo had, the kind Wayne and Rose had, even the kind his own parents had before Mom died.

For all the stress they'd endured after they quit ranching, his parents had loved each other. He'd seen his father's love in how hard he'd grieved. And in the anger he'd shown during that final, fateful fight between Michael and his father.

Someone tapped the back of his hand. Michael snapped his head up and looked right into Josiah's curious dark eyes. Josiah quirked a questioning eyebrow. Michael was not dragging Josiah down that particular train track of thought today, especially not surrounded by several hundred people. So he waggled his own eyebrows to show he was fine, then took a big bite out of his burger.

"Hey, Josiah, do you ride?" Hugo asked out of the blue. "I've been meaning to ask but never think to when I see you."

Josiah stared at him stupidly for several seconds. "Um, ride a horse? No, I never have. Why?"

"No real reason. I figured if you did, you were probably having withdrawals, because once a horse person, always a horse person. But if you've never ridden I'd be happy to teach you. Or Michael could teach you one weekend when he isn't working."

"I'd love to teach you," Michael blurted.

"Really?" Josiah sat with his fork poised halfway to his mouth, a piece of potato salad threatening to fall off the tines. "You never mentioned it before."

"It never really occurred to me until Hugo said something. I think you'd look good on a horse." Michael realized how that sounded and cleared his throat, not missing the look Hugo tossed at Brand. "I mean you seem graceful, the type who'd ride well." Shit, he was not doing himself any favors. He shoved half a dinner roll into his mouth to stop the idiotic statements.

"I'm not sure. Um, we can't leave Elmer alone on a weekend day."

"Pshaw, son," Dad said. "I can sit by myself for two hours so you can learn to ride a horse. Ain't nothing more freeing in the world than galloping around these parts on horseback. It'd do my old body some good knowing another young'un was out there enjoying himself."

Josiah glanced at Dad, then Hugo, then finally at Michael. "Okay. Maybe next weekend?"

"Sounds like a plan," Michael replied, working to keep his joy down to moderate levels so he didn't give away how much he loved the plan. Josiah really would look gorgeous up on a horse, wind whipping through his hair as they rode across the valleys and plains of the Woods property. "As long as Brand doesn't mind us using their horses."

"No skin off my nose," Brand replied. "The more people who learn to love and appreciate horses the better, and I know my dad would agree."

"Thank you." The statement poked at that small thing niggling at the back of Michael's mind. The thing that wanted to do more with Dad's land than let it sit there and grow grass as tall as his hip year after year. Thoughts that had swirled in his brain all morning while he worked the ranch booth. Hugo had been great with a shy, eight-year-old boy who'd been terrified of the young cow, coaxing him forward and giving him some hay to feed the big animal. Slowly but surely, the boy had reached out and petted the cow's side.

His smile had been blinding.

Most of the kids in Weston and surrounding towns had grown up around horses, cows, and other farm animals, but that didn't mean they were comfortable around them. And things had been different in the city, where Michael had spent half his life. Seeing those animals was for the State Fair or other special occasions, not daily life.

But what if…?

Kids also seemed to get a kick out of Dad's welding, which was a useful skill to know in general and could lead to a good career. Over the last six weeks working at the ranch, he'd heard at least half-a-dozen stories from Hugo about the tourists who'd come on vacation at Clean Slate Ranch. City slickers who couldn't mount a horse without steps, who sprayed air freshener in the barn, and who thought camping meant an air-conditioned, luxury RV. The idea of those sorts of visitors to Woods Ranch amused the hell out of Michael.

Not that Wayne Woods would ever allow such a thing. They were a working ranch that relied on their cattle to feed their family and pay their employees, and their horses were working animals, not gentle mares for trail rides. But what if the Weston area had something similar to draw folks out of Amarillo and other larger towns for a day of exploration? Horse rides and welding demos and…well, other stuff.

Dad had the land. Michael enjoyed his work at the ranch, but being a cowboy wasn't a forever career for him. It was his job now, his identity right now. But would it still be his identity a year from now?

Not that he could do anything with this nebulous fantasy idea right now. Most of his paycheck from the ranch went toward paying Josiah, buying groceries, and paying whatever bills Dad's own Social Security benefits didn't cover. He didn't have any cash to spend on a pipe dream that might actually be a terrible idea.

A terrible idea that could keep him in Weston for a long while yet, allow him to be his own boss again, and let him get closer to Josiah.

Across the table, Josiah laughed at something Hugo had said, the joyful sound ringing clear as bell. Michael smiled at his mirth, glad to see Josiah so happy and relaxed and enjoying himself. He looked at Dad, whose attention had been snagged by another elderly man who'd stopped by the table to chat. Over their shoulders, though, Michael saw him.

McBride stood two tables away, a plate in his hand, watching them. Probably watching Josiah, with an odd look on his face. Something akin to jealousy but that couldn't be right; McBride had kicked Josiah out, so he had no reason to be jealous of Josiah being happy without him.

As if sensing his disapproval, McBride turned his head slightly and met Michael's gaze. Michael stared back, expression calm, even though his insides blazed with still-smoldering anger toward the man. They held eye contact for a long time, Michael silently daring him to say something, do anything to disturb Josiah's new-found joy.

McBride blinked first and walked away.

Chapter Fourteen

All three residents of the Pearce property were exhausted by the time they returned home that evening, no one more so than Elmer. He'd nodded off in Josiah's car before they pulled into the driveway, and while Josiah hated waking him, he and Michael couldn't exactly carry him into the house. Elmer was as tall as Michael and while he'd lost some weight since his stroke, he was still a big man.

Elmer grumbled a bit but didn't complain openly while Josiah took him inside the house and straight to the bathroom to wash up for bed. It was only seven thirty, but even Josiah was ready to face-plant in the trailer as soon as possible. After more than eight hours in the bright sunshine, all he wanted was sleep.

Michael hadn't followed them inside, so he was probably unloading Elmer's ornaments and equipment from the pickup, instead of leaving it out all night. Even with the gate locked, he was careful about not leaving important things lying around the property. Probably a personality quirk about clutter, especially when he couldn't do much about all the metal art strewn around the place.

Elmer drifted off before Josiah returned to his room

with a glass of water, in case he got thirsty during the night. Josiah smoothed out the top of the blanket, overjoyed by the half smile on Elmer's sleeping face, confident he'd had an amazing day at the picnic. He embraced a bubble of familial pride for the older man, whom he'd come to think of as a father figure. Elmer definitely treated him more like a son now than an employee, and Josiah wasn't always sure how to feel about that.

Yes, Elmer promised Josiah had a place to live for as long as he needed it, but would that same paternal affection exist for Josiah when he was no longer their employee? Was Josiah getting too attached to something he'd lose in a month or so, when Elmer was more independent? Elmer might never regain the strength to ascend the stairs to the second floor, but Josiah was confident that one day he'd be able to move around the downstairs without the wheelchair.

Josiah wanted that for Elmer. He much preferred when his employment ended because his patient recovered, rather than because they passed away. Both reasons had their own built-in grief, though, especially when Josiah grew close to his patient and their family— if family was even in the picture.

He'd never had a family member in the picture the way Michael was now, all involved and attentive and so damned appealing to Josiah in every possible way. He'd never wanted a family member the way he wanted Michael, but reaching for him was pointless unless Michael planned to stay. Josiah wouldn't be left behind again.

The front door opened and shut with a familiar squeal. With Elmer settled, Josiah went into the living room. No Michael, but he followed the sound of glass clanking to the kitchen. Michael had pulled a six-pack of longnecks from the fridge and a bottle opener from a drawer, and he seemed to be contemplating both.

"Hey," Michael said with a familiar, warm smile that made Josiah grin right back. "I was thinking about taking the truck out into the back field to stargaze for a bit. Relax and unwind. It's a clear night."

"Okay." That sounded stupidly peaceful, but he wasn't going to invite—

"Wanna come with me? Share a few beers?"

Stargazing and drinking with Michael on a gorgeous autumn night? Yes, please. Also, danger alert! His endorphins from the great day still buzzed in his bloodstream, though, and Josiah couldn't say no. "Sure, why not? Elmer's fast asleep."

"Awesome."

Unsure if this was a good idea or not, Josiah grabbed his light jacket, because the temperature had dipped a bit since the sun set, and followed Michael to the pickup. Got into the cab with the beer and bottle opener. Michael's presence filled the truck's cab, everything from his body's bulk to his cologne wrapping around Josiah's senses like a warm blanket. So comforting and safe.

Michael didn't drive them far, maybe a hundred yards from the house. Close enough the yard lights were still clearly visible, as were the very distant lights of Woods Ranch across the horizon. They got out, and Josiah wasn't too surprised to see a faded quilt in the truck bed. Michael pulled down the tailgate and helped Josiah up, then climbed in himself. Spread the quilt over the slightly dirty, dusty bed.

Josiah settled on one side with the six-pack between

them, his stomach quivering with nerves. How many times growing up had Michael parked like this with someone he was interested in? Josiah had never really dated, not in the traditional way most people did, and while this wasn't a date, the teenage him who'd survived on the streets for too many years pretended it was. Just for a little while.

Michael popped the cap on a beer and handed it to Josiah. Beer wasn't his favorite, but this was a pale American brand that wasn't too strong, so Josiah sipped at his while Michael opened his own.

"It was a great day," Michael said after taking a long pull from his bottle.

"Yes, it was." Josiah rested his elbow on the wheel well and tried to relax as much as possible with the object of his inappropriate crush leaning back on one hand in a casual (and sexy) pose. "Your dad was in his element, I think. I've never seen him so conversational and, well, alive, I guess."

"He really is a people person, even though he likes to deny it. The whole grouchy recluse is a part he plays to keep folks from getting too close."

"I get that. Sometimes it's easier to keep walls up than risk getting hurt."

"I think all three of us have a lot of practice with that." Michael's intent gaze met his and seemed to look right into his heart. "It's not easy putting yourself out there when you've been betrayed too many times by people who were supposed to love you. Take care of you."

"Yeah." He took another, longer drink from his beer. The yeasty liquid swirled in Josiah's mostly empty stomach, but he'd been too stuffed from lunch to eat anything when they got home. Now he kind of regretted it, because the alcohol was already loosening his tongue. He also wanted to confide in Michael, to show he trusted the older man, and maybe earn some of that trust in return. "You know Seamus and I weren't just roommates."

"I know."

"It did start out that way, though. Just roommates." Josiah pulled more courage—and beer—from the bottle. "I'd been working in Amarillo, and my patient's neighbor had an uncle in Daisy who lived alone and was going to need help recovering from surgery, so he recommended me. When I drove out for an interview, we talked about the commute from Amarillo, and he'd heard that the new county sheriff had just moved into the area and had a room to rent. It was cheaper than my rent in the city, and I'd save a ton in gas and mileage."

"What was he like when you met him?"

Josiah didn't need to clarify the "him" was Seamus. "Charming, actually. He didn't flirt or make a pass. He was kind and polite. Said he worked a lot so I'd have run of the house during most days. I could use the TV and kitchen and even the exercise bike in his bedroom if I wanted. For a few months, everything was perfectly platonic."

"But then things changed."

"Yeah." He picked at the damp paper label on his bottle, finding it both easy to confide in Michael and also insanely embarrassing at how he'd been duped. Lured into being nothing more than a toy for Seamus to use when he saw fit. "It's hard to pinpoint exactly when things changed, because it was a gradual process. But I guess most controlling, emotionally abusive relationships are. You don't see what's happening because you're right in the middle of it." It had taken Josiah many sleepless nights to understand he couldn't have stopped what happened to him; he hadn't known anything truly bad was going on until things completely hit the fan.

Until the first time Seamus demanded sex and Josiah said no. Things had gotten bad after that, until he learned things were better when he said yes.

Always yes.

"I think I get that to a point," Michael said. "Not seeing the bad even when it's right in front of you. You get so used to your own distorted view of the world that you can't see anything better beyond it."

"Pretty much. And then, when you see how far down the rabbit hole you've fallen, you're too deep and too ashamed to ask for help getting out." He gently nudged Michael's shoulder with his. "It takes five guys and a pickup truck to get you the help you need."

"Don't forget an overprotective German shepherd."

"Can never forget Brutus. I'm sorry you lost your dog."

Michael flinched and tilted his face up to the stars. "Thanks. Is it sad that I miss him more than I miss Kenny?"

"No. Dogs are more loyal than people." And since he'd brought up the subject— "Have you thought about adopting another dog?"

"Sometimes. We've definitely got the land for it. Plenty of room for a few dogs to run around, chase field mice, and have a good old time."

"But?"

Michael shrugged and sipped his beer again, but when he looked at Josiah, those same "I don't know if

I'm staying" questions lingered in his eyes. He grabbed a second beer, popped the cap, and drank without replying. Josiah knew, though. Adopting a new dog was too big of a commitment. Too much, too soon.

"Elmer is convinced that when he dies, you're going to sell the land off and leave town for good," Josiah said, and good God, he needed to stop drinking beer on an empty stomach. Too much sun and a little bit of alcohol had fried his brain-to-mouth censor. "Is that your plan?"

"My dad isn't dying anytime soon, and I don't know what my plan is." Michael scowled at him. "You guys really talked about that stuff? Him dying?"

"A little, yeah. It isn't unusual when someone his age has a health crisis to start thinking ahead to what family will be left to deal with when they pass. He doesn't think you'll want to deal with the barn or the ranch, and I probably shouldn't be telling you this." Josiah put his empty bottle down. "Shit."

"Hey, I won't tell Dad you broke his confidence, and I appreciate getting his perspective. You're, uh, kind of a lightweight, huh?"

Josiah snorted. "Little bit. If beer looks bad on me, you should see me after one tequila shot. Actually, strike that. No hard liquor around you, ever."

"Why not?"

"Because alcohol fucks with my head, and I need to stay focused around you."

"Why?"

"Because you are everything Seamus wasn't, and you also sign my checks. Two very huge reasons to stay in my lane and out of yours." Josiah shook himself all over, not liking the slightly floaty feeling from that single stupid beer, and scooted a bit closer to the wheel well. Away from Michael, with his sweet smile and appealing scents of cologne and sweat. "If you did inherit this place, what would you do with it?"

Michael quirked an eyebrow at him but seemed to take the hint that they were done talking about Josiah for now. "I've been thinking a lot about that today, believe it or not."

It both did and did not surprise Josiah, and he wanted—no, needed to know more. If there was an actual chance Michael wasn't going to become another person who left him behind. "And?"

"I think if I was going to do something to change this property I wouldn't wait until after Dad passed, because I think I'd miss an opportunity to make up for lost time with him." The bald emotion in Michael's voice snared Josiah's attention and didn't let go. "We both made some huge mistakes, and we both threw a lot of blame around years ago. But I don't want to leave in six months and not come back again until he has another crisis."

"So what do you want?"

"To make a difference again." Michael finished the rest of his second beer, then released an amusing belch. "Sorry."

"It's fine." Josiah latched on to Michael's words. "You don't think you make a difference?"

"Right now? Here? Not the same difference I made a month ago when I was wiping my grown father's ass. Now all I really do is cook his meals and make sure he can get from his bed to his wheelchair to the can without face-planting."

He was definitely selling himself short in his contributions to Elmer's recovery, and it hurt Josiah's heart to hear Michael so down on himself. It was such a far cry from the confident, if slightly heartbroken, man he'd first met. "So how did you make a difference back in Austin?"

"In my personal life? I'm not sure I did." Josiah didn't object when Michael popped the cap off a third beer, but he did make a mental note to confiscate the truck keys soon. They weren't too far away from the house to walk back. "But my app made a difference in people's lives. They made connections, sometimes romances, sometimes disasters, but I helped people reach each other. All I do here is rustle cattle and try hard not to flirt with you."

Josiah's chest warmed pleasantly at that blunt admission. "You brought personal interactions to others with your app."

"Yep."

"You don't think you do that just by being here? Your dad enjoys your company. I enjoy your company. Your coworkers seem to love you. You made a huge difference for me when Seamus kicked me out."

"Dad would have taken you in even if I hadn't been here."

"What about getting my stuff from Seamus?"

"Dad made that call to Wayne. Would've happened either way."

Josiah frowned, frustrated by this grumpy, semi-drunk version of Michael who seemed intent on putting himself down. Maybe it was time to redirect the conversation again. "So what would you do to change this ranch? You got off topic."

"I'm not really sure. Small-time ranching is pretty impossible to get into nowadays with the way the big corporations own most of the livestock and land, so no sense in revisiting that old dream. But I think I'd like to see animals out here again. Maybe be a place where city kids can learn about farm life. Learn to milk a cow, eat a freshly laid egg, ride a horse. Small stuff we take for granted because it's all around us. Maybe even work in tandem with the Grove Point CSA."

For someone who said he'd only been toying with ideas, Michael sounded like someone with very real thoughts on what he wanted to do with his family's property. "So an educational center?"

"Sort of but interactive and not stuffy. But we're so far from most places, and Amarillo isn't exactly a megacity like Austin."

"True, but not all rural communities have farms with livestock for kids to experience. A lot of the times they're just trying to get by with what they have, never mind go explore new things."

"But again, that kind of shit requires money to get started, and I wouldn't want to charge anything. Not really." Michael tapped one finger against the neck of his bottle. "It's all just a bunch of pipe dreams anyway. Can't see Dad going for a bunch of tourists and teenagers wandering around the property. Too many strangers, too much danger."

"Your dad enjoyed himself today surrounded by people."

"They weren't on this land, though." That mysterious pain flashed in Michael's expressive eyes again, and Josiah couldn't help wondering what had happened here for both men to lock the gate. For father and son to spend years keeping the world out.

It had something to do with Michael's mother—he was sure of it.

He hated that sad look on Michael's face and found another conversational redirect. "Is it weird that I'm surprised Seamus didn't say a word to me today?"

"No, because I'm a little surprised, too. But also glad, because I'd have hated to punch him in the face and get arrested for assaulting a law officer."

Josiah chuckled. "I'm glad about that, too. That guy with him gave me the creeps, though."

"Same. Fortunately, his personal life is no longer your business, and yours is no longer his. As long as he remembers that and keeps his distance, I won't have to hand him his ass for hurting you."

"I doubt you'll ever need to bother. I've known men like Seamus McBride before. He took what he wanted, and when he was done, he tossed me aside. I didn't leave him, so he has no reason to come at me again."

"Other than jealousy over seeing you happy without him?"

Josiah shook his head and pulled his second beer from the carrier, but didn't open it. He stared at the damp label so he didn't have to look at Michael. "Seamus is a practical guy. I've never known him to be ruled by his emotions. He needed a roommate, he got one. He needed someone for regular sex, and he got that, too. He needed someone desperate enough for attention and a place to live that I'd jump when he told me to, and bring him coffee at all hours of the night, even if I was fast asleep. Then he lost interest and I got the boot."

"A harsh fucking boot."

"It was, but again, it was his call. For as scared as I was of him for the first week or so after, worried he'd change his mind and demand I go back to that existence, I think he's moved on."

"What about the guy with him today? Do you think he's in the same situation you were?"

Do you think he's in physical danger? went unasked.

"I don't know," Josiah said. "I've never seen him before, and today he almost seemed possessive of Seamus. It was bizarre."

"Could he be an ex back in the picture?"

"No idea. Seamus never talked about his past or previous partners, male or female. Although sometimes I got the odd sense he was hiding here."

Michael reached out and popped the cap off Josiah's beer. "Hiding from what?"

He shrugged and sipped the warming beer. "Dunno. People finding out he's gay? Your guess is as good as mine, and it's too nice a night to keep talking about Seamus. Let's keep celebrating a great day. Do you know any constellations?"

"Not really. Dad knows some but I never cared enough to learn. I just like looking at the light and finding my own patterns. Sort of like cloud watching and looking for shapes in them." Michael stretched out on his back, bottle resting on his stomach, his free hand pillowed behind his head. Josiah looked up at the stars so he didn't stare at Michael's long, muscled body.

"You know, when you invited me to stargaze, I thought you might have something to teach me," Josiah teased.

"Surprise. I just wanted to spend time with you, away from other people. Talk and stuff."

"And stuff?" Josiah wasn't sure he was ready for "and stuff," but Michael painted a very tempting picture lying that way, smiling up at the sky. After another long pull of beer, Josiah put his bottle next to his empty and lay down next to Michael. The position gave him a much better view of the blanket of stars above them.

As he stared up, he began to understand Michael's view on the stars a bit more. The way their light made Michael feel seen even when he was alone. How they themselves were like the stars—specks of individual light in a sea of billions, both the same as every other one, and also completely different from each other. No one light identical but each serving the same function.

"The stars see you, Josiah," Michael whispered, as if hearing his own internal thoughts. He spoke softly, almost reverently, and Josiah didn't object when Michael rested one hand over Josiah's. A gentle pressure without taking or demanding. Simply making contact.

"I feel seen by them." He let his head loll to the side; Michael was staring right at him. "And by you."

Michael's entire body seemed to thrum with energy, a live wire ready to snap, but it didn't scare Josiah. Michael moved slowly, pulling his hand away from Josiah's so he could sit up on one elbow. Stare down at Josiah with so much tenderness Josiah's heart wept with joy and relief. He was absolutely safe here with this man; Josiah knew it in his bones. And in that moment, he wanted nothing more than for Michael to kiss him.

Michael stroked his thumb across Josiah's left cheekbone in a featherlight touch that warmed Josiah's blood in a pleasant way. With tender caresses, Michael touched his face and neck with only his fingertips, while his gaze seemed to study him, mapping his cheeks and chin and the small mole on his jaw. Josiah didn't think he was all that interesting, but Michael? Looming over him like he wanted to devour Josiah? He was gorgeous, with his dark eyes and square jaw and light dusting of evening scruff. Scruff Josiah resisted running his own fingers over. He couldn't make himself touch, only experience.

"May I?" Michael whispered so softly Josiah saw the words more than he heard them.

In an equally quiet, breathy voice, Josiah said, "Yes."

Michael sifted his fingers through Josiah's hair, and Josiah leaned into the tender gesture of being petted. So thoughtful and kind, making no demands on him or his body, melting Josiah's hesitation with each passing moment. When Michael finally leaned in, Josiah didn't tense. He remained relaxed, curious as Michael brushed his warm lips over Josiah's, barely hard enough to feel or catch the taste of the man.

Needing to know more now that he'd had a sip, Josiah arched up and captured Michael's mouth with his. Michael moaned softly and parted his lips just enough for Josiah to catch the delicate, intoxicating taste of beer and man. They kissed like that for a while, their lips questing and tasting, without deepening it. Then Michael's body slid closer and pressed against his side, and the erection that brushed Josiah's hip sent a jolt of reality through him.

He pulled back and sat up too fast, nearly clipping Michael's chin with the top of his head. His own body thrummed with arousal and desire, but Josiah couldn't indulge. Not now, not with this man, and he had reasons for that.

Boss. Paycheck. Wrong.

Right. "I'm sorry," Josiah said. "I shouldn't have allowed that."

"I'm not sorry." Michael twisted around so he was

facing Josiah, legs crossed, hands in his lap. "I didn't plan it when I asked you out here tonight, but I can't say I wasn't wondering what kissing you would be like."

The part of him that craved genuine intimacy and affection couldn't help asking, "What was it like?"

"Sweet. Intoxicating. Craveable."

"I thought it was pretty good, too." Josiah saw the intent in Michael's expression and the moment he started to move in. He reached out and put a staying hand on Michael's shoulder. "We can't. I know I'm giving you mixed signals, and I'm sorry about that. I do like you, Michael, but I work for you, and I need this job."

"I'm not going to—"

"I know you wouldn't kick me out if things don't work out between us. You've said it and I believe you. This is about me and my headspace right now. Most of my adult life, I have traded my body for a place to live and I finally have a semblance of independence. I can't give that up."

Not right now, no matter how much I want you.

"That's fair," Michael said after a few seconds of watching him with an indecipherable expression. For all the beer he'd consumed, he seemed incredibly sober now. "I don't want to pressure you. I will be blunt and say I like you. I'm attracted to you, and I would love to take you out on a date. But I also hear you and what you're saying. Friends?"

"Definitely." He held his beer out.

Michael tapped the neck of his against Josiah's with a grin. "Good. You wanna stargaze in silence for a little longer? I promise no more kissing."

"Sure."

Josiah stretched back out with Michael by his side,

the stars a blanket of twinkling light above. He'd enjoyed his long, sensual kiss with Michael, but it couldn't happen again—no matter how much his body craved another kiss, another touch, maybe even a real, full-body hug. Those were dreams for another time and place, not for here and now. Not for him.

For here and now, he had friendship and the stars. And for here and now, those two things would have to sustain him. Period.

Chapter Fifteen

"Did you notice I swapped out your sandwich filling for a can of Dog's food?"

Michael nodded around his mouthful. "Uh-huh."

"Big fan of liver giblets and gravy?"

"Sure." He swallowed and reached for his can of cola, gaze fixed on the break room wall without seeing it, mind still full of his weekend with Dad and Josiah. Especially with Josiah.

"Michael, buddy, are you here?" Jackson snapped his fingers in front of Michael's face, and that shook him out of it.

"What?" He looked at his sandwich. Still roast beef from last night's Sunday supper. "What did you say about my liver?"

"You were a million miles away just now. Everything okay?"

"Yeah, things are great." And they were, not counting being turned down by Josiah on Saturday night. Michael hadn't been completely surprised by it, given Josiah's employment status and his prior relationship (such as it was) with McBride, but it still hurt his pride a little.

He hadn't shown it yesterday, though, when he and

Josiah teamed up to get Dad's new bedroom ready. Michael had picked up the twin bed right when the thrift store opened at eleven. He and Josiah had assembled it with no hint of awkwardness between them, only a familiar camaraderie, and Dad hadn't seemed to sense anything had changed. Dad had been thrilled to see his new room, decorated with some of the framed photos and personal items from his upstairs bedroom.

A photo of Mom sat on the small table they'd used as a nightstand. One of the windows faced out over the front yard and so many of Dad's favorite sculptures. He'd get some morning sunlight now that they were moving into the winter months. After existing in the living room for almost seven weeks, Dad finally had a space of his own again, and Michael had been proud to give him that.

"You sure things are great?" Jackson asked. "Tell me to butt out, because you know I will, but you've been really distant today."

"I've just got stuff on my mind, that's all. But things really are great. It was a good weekend." He told Jackson more about the picnic and then assembling Dad's room, leaving out his stargazing with Josiah, because that was private. As much as he wanted to confide in someone, he wasn't sure Jackson was a close enough friend yet to tell about his feelings for Josiah.

Brand came into the break room just as Michael was tossing away his sandwich wrapper. "Hey, Michael, do you have an hour to go over the new website?"

"Sure, no problem." His afternoon schedule included mucking three horse stalls, so he didn't mind pushing that off for a little while. He grabbed his mostly empty cola and followed Brand out of the barn, across the yard to the bunkhouse/office. Brutus was spread out on the small porch, and his tail thumped against the wood floorboards when he spotted his human. Brand reached down to rub the top of his head as he passed.

The simple sight made Michael's heart pang him for his own dog. He'd finally found out via a mutual acquaintance that Kenny had given Rosco to a neighbor Michael knew and trusted to care for Rosco, but the separation was still raw. It probably always would be. Right now, Michael found a bit of solace in spending time with Brutus and Dog.

Michael had uploaded the new Woods Ranch website a few days ago as a beta, giving Brand and his family time to explore and test the new features, one of which was an interactive blog where customers and vendors could post feedback and recipes for their beef. Brand had loved that idea, because it hit a demographic of younger foodies who leaned toward natural and organic eating, and he hoped it would help get their beef into more grocery stores and other sales outlets around the state.

Slow expansion was key, Brand often said. "Give the customer a product to believe in and no reason to doubt you."

So far, so good.

They fussed with the site for a while. Some of the changes Michael could make right there, but others he wrote down to fix when he got home. Hopefully, the new site would go live by the weekend.

"This is really great work," Brand said from his spot behind the desk. Michael circled around to sit in one of the wooden chairs opposite. "I knew hiring you was a good idea."

Michael laughed. "Glad it's all working out, boss. And I wanted to tell you that I can be more flexible with my hours now that Dad's getting more independent. Doesn't just have to be nine-to-five, weekdays anymore."

"Yeah? Josiah okay with that?"

"Sure." They'd briefly discussed it last week as a trio. Dad still needed help getting in and out of the wheelchair and with preparing his meals, but he didn't need a babysitter (his word) all the time anymore. "The set hours worked for Josiah when he was living with McBride, but now that he's away from that and close to the house, he says he can work odd hours and weekends if I need him to."

"That's good for him, getting that flexibility back." Brand picked up a coffee mug, stared into it, then put it back down. "He seemed really happy and relaxed at the picnic Saturday."

"He was." Michael didn't want to lie to his boss/ friend, but he also didn't want to spread Josiah's personal business all over the place. Not that Brand couldn't have made his own conclusions about Josiah and McBride's prior relationship based on the night they'd rescued Josiah's stuff. "Josiah's happy living on our property. He can breathe there."

"Good. He deserves that."

"Yeah, he does."

"Can you breathe?"

"What?"

"Just an observation from a friend." Brand leaned back in his chair, hands resting over his stomach. "You seem happier, too, since Josiah came to live with you."

"He doesn't live with me, he's renting our trailer."

"Uh-huh. You can tell me to mind my own business,

but I think Hugo is rubbing off on me, so I'll just say this—if something makes you happy, hang on to it. It's usually worth fighting for."

Michael quirked an eyebrow. "Hugo's rubbing off, huh?"

"You know what I mean, and way to deflect my point. I tried to push Hugo away because I was scared of what loving him meant for me and for this business, and we almost lost this amazing thing we have."

"I'm not pushing Josiah away. He's doing that." Michael grunted, not liking the hint of bitterness in his voice. "But I understand why. He's not ready, and we agreed to be friends. I'll be his friend."

"He's lucky to have you."

"Well, I am a pretty terrific friend."

Brand burst out laughing. "And so modest."

"Of course." He picked at a tiny rip in his faded, work-roughened jeans. "It's not fair to Josiah to pursue anything, anyway, not when I don't know my future plans. I don't know if I'll still be here in six months, or if life and opportunity will take me someplace else. I couldn't start something, and then ask him to come with me."

"Why not? Couples move for employment all the time. It's not like Weston is his home, or as if he's got an office here. In-home nursing is in demand pretty much everywhere."

"True." Michael hadn't even considered the idea of Josiah going with him if Michael left Weston for another big city. Probably not Austin again. Too many negative memories now. "Everything is hypothetical anyway. I could stay. I could go. Nothing will happen until I sell that damned house."

"You do realize that if I got a vote, I'd vote for you to stay put. You're not only an asset here at the ranch, but I consider you a friend, Michael. And maybe you took this job because it was the best paying one you could find around here, but you're good at it. Any ranch in the state would be lucky to have you."

"Thank you." For all he'd been a reluctant cowboy, Michael did enjoy his job. "Thank you for taking a chance on a rusty city boy. I do love this job, and part of me wants to stick around Weston, but I am the first to admit I love being my own boss. A lot more than I like being someone else's employee."

Brand snorted. "I hear you. For all I grumbled about inheriting the ranch after Colt left, I do love being in charge. It's stressful, sure, because if something fails, it's on me. But when something goes right? It's a special kind of pride over the accomplishment. So, you got any ideas on being your own boss again?"

"Less ideas and more like nebulous musings. Dad obviously doesn't have the acreage he used to, but we still have a decent bit of land. He had a lot of fun talking to kids about his art this weekend, and I can see him teaching a whole new generation about turning rusty junk into something special. Giving kids a place to get out into the open country and just be kids."

"I didn't know you liked kids that much."

Michael shrugged. "I don't dislike them. Never imagined being a dad myself. There's just something real about life out here in our small towns. Austin always felt like an illusion to me. Glass and pavement don't have anything on dirt and manure."

"You'd rather have manure than a coffee shop on every other corner?"

"Yes." The answer came without hesitation. The more time Michael spent here in his old hometown, the more comfortable he was. The more distanced he felt from the city life he'd once valued and fought for. He wanted to stay. But stay and do what?

"I'd love to hear more about this," Brand said, "but we're both on the clock. How about I take you out to the Roost for a beer or two after work? I want to pick your brain."

"Yeah, sure, let me text Josiah and make sure he's okay to chill with Dad for a while longer tonight."

"Do that. If he isn't, let me know and we can re-schedule."

Josiah would be fine with it. He'd yet to balk at any request Michael made, and he often suspected it was less about the extra pay and more about spending time in the Pearce house. Being part of their family. "I will. Thanks, Brand."

"Anytime. Now go. Those stalls won't muck them-selves."

With a mock salute to his boss, Michael stood and left the office, buoyed by the conversation and curious what ideas of his own Brand might bring to the table tonight.

"No, no, maybe over there?"

Josiah bit back a weary sigh as he began to shift the heavy tool chest for the fourth time in about fif-teen minutes. He and Elmer had been in the work-shop since supper concluded, completing a task they'd begun that afternoon. Elmer was still determined to clean up the space and get rid of excess garbage, but his donate pile had turned into a "save for next year's picnic" pile. More than just talking about welding and his art, Elmer wanted to demonstrate what he did, and he'd "need spare parts for the kids to waste."

The wood floor had scratch lines all over from him dragging the tool chest around, and he could kind of track his path around the space. Josiah didn't mind the work. Despite the dust that made him sneeze every ten minutes or so, he liked the workshop, and he loved listening to Elmer talk about it. Anything that kept his patient active and engaged, rather than sitting on his butt watching TV, was a win in his book.

"How about here?" Josiah smacked the top of the metal toolbox.

Elmer squinted. "That'll do for now."

"Oh good. What next?"

"I think I need that bookcase."

"What bookcase?"

"The one in the horse stall over there." He waved vaguely down the long corridor that led to the front of the barn. "If we bring it out, I can organize some of that scrap copper and aluminum on it. Can't use it if I can't see it."

And by "we," he meant Josiah would bring it out. Josiah had no idea which stall had a bookcase in it, so he went searching while Elmer fiddled around with a bucket of random, rusty tool parts. It took a bit of searching to uncover the four-shelf bookcase—how on earth had Elmer remembered the thing was there when it was buried under grain sacks and horse blankets?— and then a lot of huffing and puffing to get the damned thing out of the stall. By the time he wrangled it back into the workshop, Elmer's face was pinched.

"Hey, are you doing okay?" Josiah asked.

"Yeah, just, uh…" He scowled. "I need to go inside and use the can."

"Oh, no problem. It's getting late and a little cold, so why don't we call it a night? I'll take you in."

"Fine, fine."

Elmer was getting better at handling the wheelchair around the living room, despite still having some grip weakness in his right hand, so Josiah pushed him out of the barn and toward the house.

"You forgot to turn off the damn lights," Elmer said just as Josiah began to push him up the porch ramp.

"It's okay. Let's get you settled first, and then I'll go back and turn them off."

Elmer grunted, and Josiah did just that. Once Elmer was situated in the bathroom, Josiah mostly shut the door to give him privacy, then went back outside. The cold night air nipped at his cheeks as he strode across the yard to the big, open barn doors. It never stopped surprising him that Elmer didn't want the barn doors shut at night, but the property had two bright outdoor lights that probably dissuaded potential thieves from sneaking around.

He stepped inside the barn and reached to the right where four switches controlled the lights from the front all the way to the rear workshop. He slipped the farthest two switches down, casting the back of the barn in darkness. On the dirt floor ahead, a splotch of green caught his attention and Josiah paused. Probably a rag or something that they dropped—only he hadn't messed with any cleaning rags tonight. He took four long strides toward the fabric and picked it up, curious.

His curiosity shifted into surprise as he shook out a T-shirt with white block lettering that said Kiss Me

I'm Irish. Andy had given him a shirt like that a long time ago as a joke, something he'd picked up at a swap meet for cheap. One of the only meaningful things Josiah had kept from that period of his life, and he'd left it behind at Seamus's house. Well, technically Michael and his friends had left it behind, but Josiah had never bothered to ask anyone to fetch it, assuming Seamus had tossed out anything that his five saviors hadn't claimed.

With shaking fingers, Josiah checked the left side seam for a familiar—there. The small tear the shirt had come with and Josiah had never bothered stitching back up. Fear turned his stomach to ice. Had Seamus brought this shirt here and left it as…what? A warning? To rattle him? What the hell?

Someone had been inside the barn in the last few minutes, because he knew in his bones the shirt hadn't been on the ground when he took Elmer into the house. Shirt clutched in his left hand, Josiah slid his right into his back pocket. Fingers brushed his cell phone. He turned. Something dark zoomed at him.

Pain exploded in his face, and he fell.

Chapter Sixteen

A beer with Brand at the Roost turned into three beers, a platter of loaded nachos, and a lot of personal commiseration about failed relationships. Not so much Michael commiserating, because he really only had Kenny to grump about, and he didn't have much new to talk about that night. A lot of the grumping was coming from Brand, which surprised Michael. He would have assumed Brand talked about this stuff with Hugo, but sometimes past relationships could be tricky to discuss with current partners.

Michael definitely learned more about Brand than he expected, particularly about his high school girlfriends. He understood why someone struggling with being bisexual in a small community would choose to date only women. Michael had faced something similar as a teenager, but he'd also never pretended to be interested in dating women; he just hadn't dated, period.

As amusing as it was to watch Brand down nearly a full pitcher of beer by himself and ramble about some girl named Ginny, his first high school love whose family moved away after their junior year, it was getting late, and Michael had told Josiah he'd be home by eight at the latest. Michael installed Brand at the bar with a mug of coffee near Ramie's station. Ramie promised to keep an eye on him. After settling the bill and collecting a to-go cup of coffee for himself, Michael headed home.

He texted Josiah he was on his way before leaving the parking lot. His car seemed to take forever to warm up and belch out hot air to combat the unexpectedly cold night. He only had the fleece jacket he'd worn to work, instead of a sturdier winter coat—something he needed to buy now that he was facing winter farther north. It would be November tomorrow.

He idled at the gate so he could unlock it. Michael had gotten four keys made: one for Josiah, one to keep in the house, one for Michael's key ring, and another to keep in a hidden spot on this side of the gate in case someone needed to get in from the outside during an emergency. It was kind of a pain to turn off his car, unlock, and turn it back on again. Maybe when he went out to buy a winter coat, he'd get some sort of carabiner that easily attached and detached to the rest of his keys.

Lights blazed in the downstairs of the house as usual, so Dad and Josiah were likely inside watching TV. After relocking the gate, Michael parked next to Josiah's car and went inside with his coffee. He stopped short, a little surprised to find the living room empty and the television off. The kitchen light was off, too.

"Hello?" Michael called out.

"Michael!" Dad's shout from the downstairs bathroom spurred him forward, confused by what was happening.

"Dad?" The bathroom door was mostly shut. Michael pushed but it hit something that gave a metallic clang. "Dad, what's going on?"

"Damned chair. Hold on." Dad grunted and the door

opened wide enough for Michael to slip inside. He stared, shocked to see Dad sitting on the bathroom floor, his back against the tub, face red, and glaring right at him. "About damned time."

"What happened? Why are you on the floor?"

"Couldn't get my weak ass back in the wheelchair, that's why. Help me up."

"Where's Josiah?"

"Dunno. I've been calling for him. Get me up."

Okay, he'd figure out where Josiah was in a minute. Dad first. Michael pushed the wheelchair to the side, locked the wheels, got into the correct position, and then stood the way Josiah had shown him to best help someone off the floor. Off the cold floor. "Okay, Dad, on three."

"Yeah, yeah."

"One, two, three."

Dad's increased strength in both legs and Michael's workout every day at the ranch gave them the exact leverage they needed to haul Dad up and into the wheelchair. Dad landed with a grunt. Michael got his feet situated on the footrests and unlocked the wheels. "Okay, you okay? Did you hurt yourself when you fell?"

"Just bruised my pride is all," Dad said. "Where's Josiah at?"

"I don't know. I didn't see him in the living room." He hadn't noticed any lights on in the trailer when he drove up. "Did he leave you in here?"

"Ayup, boy forgot to turn the barn lights off, and I had to squeeze one out, so he left me to do my business while he went back outside."

All that made sense. He pushed Dad out of the bathroom, which took a bit of maneuvering because of the size of the room and where Dad had fallen, but he got them both out and into the living room. "Josiah!" Michael's voice seemed to echo through the otherwise empty house.

"It's not like that boy to disappear," Dad said.

"No, it's not." Josiah had always struck him as the type who disliked even taking a bathroom break while he was on the clock. No way had he forgotten he'd left Dad on the toilet, gone back to the trailer, and fallen asleep. Something wasn't right. "Dad, I want you to stay here and by the phone, okay?"

"Why?"

"Because something's wrong, so stay put." Michael checked that he had his cell and keys. Then he lifted Dad's shotgun from its rack above the front door. To most people, it was simply decoration, but Dad kept it in good repair and fired it regularly. He also kept shells in a small box under the couch, which Michael found and loaded into the shotgun.

Dad watched him silently, his face a mix of confusion and worry, but he didn't remark on the gun. Michael locked the front door behind him when he left, the cold night air biting his cheeks. Adrenaline rolled through him, leaving a bitter taste in his mouth. He descended the porch steps, the shotgun by his side, muzzle pointed at the ground. Hopefully, he was overreacting but everything about Josiah's disappearance left him uneasy.

He went to the trailer first and knocked. No response. "Josiah?"

His cell rang. Michael yanked it out of his pocket with his left hand, hoping to see Josiah's name on the screen. Instead, it said Dad.

"What?" Michael snapped.

"Have you called him yet?" Dad asked.

Michael nearly banged his head off the trailer door at the complete *duh* behind the question. "No, why didn't you call him?"

"I don't have his number memorized. Might have it on that notepad he left on the side table, though, dunno."

"It's fine. I'll do it." Michael ended the call, found Josiah's contact, and called him.

Chimes echoed from somewhere in the yard. Michael turned in a slow circle, observing his surroundings. Two parked cars. Dad's pickup. The barn and its open doors, the interior bathed in blackness just beyond the reach of the outdoor lights. The ringtone seemed to be coming from that direction. Michael ended the call, put his cell back in his pocket, and lifted the shotgun to his hip. Josiah could have easily dropped his phone at some point while wheeling Dad out of the barn, but everything in Michael screamed with alarm.

Something was very wrong.

He approached the barn slowly, every sense on high alert, straining to hear anything, to see any shadow that moved. The yard was eerily silent, the loudest sound the beat of Michael's own racing heart. The interior of the barn brightened slightly the closer he got and as his eyes adjusted to the lights and shadows in front of him. The shape didn't make sense at first, because why would a sneaker be in the middle of the aisle between stalls?

"Fuck." Michael smacked at the light switches as he bolted, managing to turn on half the bulbs along the stalls, and he stopped short beside the sneaker. A sneaker connected to a leg and a hip and a torso.

Josiah lay sprawled on his back, his left arm bent

above his head, his right across his chest. His glasses were in the dirt nearby. The sheer wrongness of him like that took a back seat to Michael's shock and fear at the blood on Josiah's forehead and left cheek. And the fact that he was unconscious.

"Christ, Josiah." He dropped to his knees, careful to keep the shotgun pointed away, and instinctively pressed his fingers to Josiah's neck. His skin was chilly but his pulse was strong. Michael yanked his own fleece off and tucked it awkwardly around Josiah's chest. The cut on his forehead still oozed blood but it wasn't gushing. "Josiah, can you hear me? Hey?"

Nothing.

Unwilling to panic while he was the only able-bodied person on the property, Michael called 911. Told the lady who answered his address. "I found my tenant unconscious in the barn. He has a head wound, but I don't know what happened or how long he's been out. At least ten minutes, I think, and it's cold out here."

The woman promised to send paramedics and alert local authorities. That done, Michael called the house. Dad answered after half a ring, and Michael did his best to describe what was happening. "You sit tight, okay?" Michael said. "I'm going to wait out here for the ambulance."

"You think he tripped over something and hit his head?"

"I have no idea." He scanned the area around them. "There really isn't anything he could have tripped on. I'm sure he'll tell me when he wakes up. For now, don't panic. Just… I don't know what, but don't panic."

"Doesn't sound like I'm the one panicking, son. Josiah's a strong boy—he'll be fine."

"Yeah." He hung up, then gave Josiah's shoulder a squeeze and shake. "Come on, man, wake up for me." When a firmer shake didn't work, Michael cast around for something else to cover Josiah with. Michael was half-frozen himself without his fleece, and he wasn't sprawled out on the cold ground. The horse blankets in one of the stalls were dusty, but they were warm, and he piled two on top of Josiah.

Maybe he kicked up a bit of dirt doing that, because Josiah coughed and muttered without opening his eyes. His nose twitched and his lips parted.

"Hey, there you are. It's Michael. Wake up for me, Josiah. Come back to me, please."

"Guh." More muttering that Michael couldn't decipher. Josiah's eyes began moving behind his lids.

Michael cupped his right cheek, hoping to ground him with his touch. "Come on, baby, I'm right here. Open those pretty brown eyes for me. Please."

It took some work, but Josiah finally, blessedly, blinked his eyes open. They swam with confusion and pain, and both hurt Michael's heart to see. "Mich—Michael?"

"Yeah, it's me. You're in the barn. You hit your head somehow. Do you remember?"

"My head?" His arms moved beneath the heavy horse blankets. "Hurts."

"I bet. You've got a cut and it's bleeding a little. Baby, what happened?"

"The lights." Josiah frowned, grimaced. Closed his

eyes for a few seconds. "There was a shirt. A green shirt. Shouldn't've been here."

"A shirt?" Michael looked around their immediate area but didn't see any clothes, much less a green shirt.

"It was mine. Picked it up. From Seamus."

Just the sound of that prick's name irritated Michael on a cellular level. "You found McBride's shirt in the barn?"

"No, mine. Left it there. You didn't know to get it. Picked it up." Josiah's eyes widened with alarm. "Someone hit me. With something. I turned. Wham. Lights out. Ouch."

Josiah was only partially making sense, and Michael wasn't sure if it was the head wound, the cold, or a combination of both. "Okay, listen, we're going to get you up and into the house. It's freezing out here, and you need to get off the ground."

"M'kay. Wanna sleep."

"Oh no, no sleeping right now. You might have a concussion, and an ambulance is on its way. You need to get your head looked at."

He grunted. "I'm a nurse."

"A wounded nurse who is in no condition to diagnose or treat himself." Michael leaned down and traced his thumb across Josiah's cool cheekbone. "Please. I need to know you're okay."

Any remnant of fight Josiah had in him disappeared. "Okay."

Michael tucked his glasses into his jeans pocket before pulling the dusty horse blankets off Josiah. Josiah sat up with a loud, pained groan of displeasure, and he sat there, awkwardly hunched over, while Michael tied the fleece around his shoulders. It wouldn't do much, but they'd be indoors soon enough. Getting Josiah to his feet took a bit more effort, and Josiah swayed into him. Michael wrapped an arm around his waist, the other holding the shotgun, and he took as much of Josiah's weight as necessary while they began a slow trek to the house.

A distant siren's wail met his ears at the same time as Dad unlocked the front door. He took the shotgun and rolled out of the way. Michael led Josiah straight to the couch and helped him lie down on his back. Covered him with the throw blanket, then grabbed two extra quilts from the steamer trunk tucked beneath one of the living room windows. The trunk had belonged to Michael's great-great-grandfather and traveled across the Atlantic from Wales many generations ago. The quilts were pretty ancient, too, but they were warm.

Dad wheeled out of the kitchen with a dish towel and settled by Josiah's head. Gently dabbed at the blood on his face without asking questions. The paternal way he tended to Josiah sent a jolt of jealousy through Michael that he shoved away. Josiah needed looking after and comfort right now; it didn't matter who gave it to him.

The siren came closer, got louder. Michael grabbed a light coat off the hooks by the door and jogged down to the gate to unlock it and allow the ambulance onto the property. He wasn't surprised to see a county sheriff's car following them. His temper did explode, however, when McBride and not a deputy climbed out of the driver's door. Ignoring the focus of his anger for the moment, Michael told the two paramedics to go inside the house—that's where their patient was. Then he turned the full force of his ire onto McBride. "What are you doing here?"

McBride blinked at him, his expression annoyingly blank. "Call came through about a possible assault here. I was on duty and am responding to the alert. Is your father all right?"

"Dad's fine. Someone hit Josiah in the barn."

"What?" His head swiveled first toward the open barn doors and the lights still on inside, then to the house. "What happened? How badly is he hurt?"

As if you don't know, you bastard?

Michael kept his temper and suspicions in check. After all, who else had any motive to hurt Josiah? "Someone came up behind him in the barn and hit him in the head. He isn't sure with what or who did it. I found him unconscious on the ground less than ten minutes ago, and I took him inside to get warm."

"Who the hell would do that?"

Not exactly a professional response from the county sheriff, and the genuine surprise on McBride's face cracked some of Michael's belief that McBride had done this. "I don't know, but I guess that's your job to investigate, huh?"

"Yes, it is. Can you show me where you found him?"

Michael led McBride into the barn and the scuffed spot on the hard earth where Josiah had been. The horse blankets were in a pile by a stall wall. McBride shone a flashlight around, mostly at the floor and at the stalls, but he didn't seem to come up with anything. Michael didn't bring up the mysterious shirt, curious if that's what McBride was looking for, making sure evidence was gone.

"I don't suppose you have any sort of security cameras on the property?" McBride asked.

"No, we don't." Michael had floated the idea after Mom died but nothing had ever come of it. There were plenty of inexpensive options nowadays, though, so it might be time to add it to his list of future home improvements. He hated thinking Weston was no longer the safe place it had been for the last two decades, but Brand nearly being killed by a drunk asshole a few months ago had already tarnished that shine.

"Other than a bit of blood in the dirt, I don't see anything helpful. If it's all right, I'd like to speak with Josiah now."

"Yeah, fine, just don't stress him out."

The bite in his tone got McBride's undivided attention, but the sheriff simply raised an eyebrow at him, then silently followed Michael to the house. The couch faced away from the front door. One of the paramedics was placing steri-strips on Josiah's forehead cut, so Josiah didn't notice their extra guest right away. When he did, his head jerked and he nearly took tweezers to the eye.

Michael stayed close to McBride, hoping his presence kept Josiah calm while facing down his ex. Especially after such a trauma.

"I know you probably just want to rest," McBride said in a gentle tone that didn't match his generally gruff exterior, "but I need to ask you a few questions about what happened tonight. While it's fresh."

"Fine," Josiah replied, as grumpy as McBride was calming.

"First, are you all right?"

"Do I look all right? Someone attacked me, Seamus."

"I'm sorry, that was an insensitive question. Can you please tell me about your evening? Take your time and be thoughtful." McBride produced a small notepad and pen.

Josiah waited until the paramedic was finished applying the bandages before he spoke. And he looked at Michael, instead of McBride. "Elmer and I were out in the barn working. He needed to come inside to use the bathroom, so I brought him in, but I forgot to turn off the barn lights. Once Elmer was situated, I went back outside to turn off the lights, since it was getting late and chilly and we weren't going back out tonight. I started hitting the switches and I thought—"

He stopped, his dark gaze flickering. Michael was surprised when Josiah looked away, at McBride this time. "I thought I saw something down the barn, maybe a raccoon moving, so I took a few steps closer. Didn't see anything, so I turned around. Something was sailing right at my face. I just remember a bright flash of pain, hitting something, and then Michael waking me up."

Michael studied Josiah's expression, curious why he'd left out the T-shirt. Had he been testing McBride for some reason? As if expecting him to know Josiah had left out a pertinent detail?

"You didn't see the person who assaulted you?" McBride asked.

"No. It happened too fast. All I saw was whatever hit me."

"Did the object come directly at your face, or was it swung?"

"What does it matter?" Michael asked, confused by the question and annoyed by the way Josiah's face was starting to pinch with pain. He needed to rest not suffer through the third degree from his ex.

McBride tossed him an impatient look he probably got a lot of mileage out of with teenagers speeding or drunks sleeping it off, but the look was lost on Michael. "The direction of the blow can help identify the weapon used. Some solid objects are more likely to be swung, rather than come straight at you." He gave a very pointed look to the shotgun Dad still held on his lap.

Michael fought to keep his temper both in check and off his face. Exploding on McBride would not help Josiah tonight. Josiah was getting stressed out, and Michael needed to fix this somehow. He glanced at Dad, whose own face displayed his annoyance at the entire production.

"I don't remember," Josiah said. "I really don't. It might have come right at me, but again, it happened so fast."

"All right, thank you." McBride pulled a business card out of his jacket pocket, probably out of habit, and started to hand it to Josiah. Michael didn't recognize the two paramedics, but he was pretty sure everyone in the room knew Josiah and McBride had once been roommates. McBride gave the card to Michael. "If any of you think of anything else, please call me."

"Sure," Michael said. He walked McBride to the door and waited on the porch until the man and his cruiser disappeared down the road. Making sure his enemy was off the property. Even if McBride had nothing to do with Josiah's assault tonight, Michael still did not like or trust the guy.

As Michael went back inside, he found Josiah and the paramedic who'd bandaged his eye in the middle of an argument over treatment.

"I'll sign whatever you need me to sign," Josiah snapped, "but I'm not going to the hospital. I understand I was unconscious, and I know the signs of concussions to watch for."

Neither paramedic seemed happy with the decision, but they gave Josiah the refusal to transport papers to sign, collected their equipment, suggested Michael wake Josiah every few hours as a precaution, and finally left. Once the ambulance pulled onto the road, Michael jogged out to the gate, shoved it shut, and snapped the lock into place. Even though it had been locked when whoever it was got in and hurt Josiah, Michael wasn't taking any extra chances with the lives and safety of the two other men in his house.

Michael locked the front door and snapped the dead bolt into place, adrenaline still up and his suspicion going haywire. He was vaguely aware of Dad speaking softly with Josiah as Michael went through the entire downstairs, making sure windows and the rear kitchen door were all locked up tight for the night. Flashes of Dad doing the exact same thing every night for weeks after Mom died assailed Michael for a long, grief-stricken moment.

He stood in the middle of the kitchen and let his body shake as he worked through the terror he'd felt tonight. Terror that had built from the moment he found Dad on the bathroom floor until right now. Josiah could have been killed, and Michael would have lost someone else he cared about to violence on this land.

But he hadn't. Josiah was shaken and bruised, but he was alive. Michael splashed some water on his face from the kitchen sink, scrubbed his skin dry with a towel, and then joined Dad and Josiah in the living room. They still had their heads together, but when Josiah saw him, he smiled. A real, if exhausted, smile.

As stressed as he still was, Michael smiled back.

Waking up on the cold dirt floor of the barn with a raging headache and the sound of Michael's terrified voice had quickly jumped into the top five of Josiah's least favorite memories ever. For several awful seconds, Josiah had no idea what was going on, why he was in pain, or why he was so freaking cold. His glasses were gone, blurring the world around him in a dizzying way, and he'd panicked until it all came back in a rush: barn, lights, ka-blam to the face!

Michael's stoic presence was the only thing that kept Josiah focused in those first five minutes after waking. Michael's voice coaxed him to tell what happened. Michael's firm but gentle touch helped Josiah sit up and ultimately walk back to the house when every step made his head want to explode.

He hadn't truly started to warm up until after Jules and Larry arrived with their gear. Josiah knew them from a few other calls over the years for his patients, and he liked them both a lot. Jules had carefully cleaned and bandaged his cut, and it had taken every last ounce of Josiah's self-restraint not to freak out when Michael led Seamus into the house. Seamus was the very last person Josiah had wanted to see that night. The shirt Josiah had found in the barn had come from Seamus's house, it had to have.

Michael was the only person he'd told about the shirt, and he'd silently thanked Michael for not mentioning it while Josiah told Seamus about the barn. Josiah couldn't articulate why he'd left the shirt out. Maybe to see if he'd get a reaction out of Seamus, which he hadn't. Seamus had been…oddly warm. As if he actually cared that Josiah had been hurt and wanted to find the person who'd done it for personal reasons, rather than professional.

It confused the hell out of Josiah.

He'd been insanely grateful when their three guests left. Elmer had rolled right over to the couch and asked if he could get Josiah anything. "Aspirin? Water? A shot of whiskey to soothe the soul?"

Josiah shook his head, which was an epically bad idea, because bright lights winked behind his eyes. "I just want to sleep for a while."

"Paramedic said to keep you awake and check on you every few hours."

"I know, but that doesn't mean I have to be happy about it."

"So it's true what they say, eh? Doctors and nurses make the worst patients."

"Yes, we do." Michael buzzing around downstairs wasn't lost on Josiah, and he felt awful for sending his friend into what he could only describe as a slight panic. A similar sort of stress bracketed Elmer's age-lined eyes, and Josiah couldn't help feeling as if he was outside of something huge shared by father and son.

He didn't ask, though. It wasn't his business.

Michael returned from the kitchen, his expression a bit more schooled than before, but he definitely looked like he could use a stiff drink. "You gonna raise the deflector shields, too, Captain?" Josiah asked.

Michael stared at him for several long seconds before cracking a half smile. "Someone sneaked onto this property and hurt you. I don't like that. No one's breaking into this house while I'm here, and I'm going to buy an alarm system tomorrow."

Elmer grunted but didn't otherwise respond.

"Do I get one for the trailer?" Josiah asked.

He must have been too tired for his teasing to come across, because Michael tossed him a serious stare and said, "Absolutely. I'll buy fucking motion sensors for the perimeter fence if I have to."

"Don't jump into the deep end right off," Elmer said. "You have any reason to think someone was after Josiah specifically, and it wasn't just some homeless drunk who wanted to steal from us, or spend a cold night in the barn and was scared to get caught?"

Josiah tried to meet Michael's eyes, but Michael wouldn't look at him. They were both keeping the T-shirt from Elmer, and it probably wasn't fair. At the same time, Josiah could have imagined that shirt, since he had been bashed in the head and Michael hadn't found it anywhere near where Josiah was attacked. It wasn't as if a raccoon had come along and stolen away with it.

"I don't know what happened out there or why," Michael replied tersely. "I just don't want it to happen again. That fucking barn is cursed."

Elmer pressed his lips together. "I think we've all had enough excitement for tonight. Josiah, you're welcome to my bed if you don't feel like sleeping alone in the trailer tonight. Especially after all this shit."

"No way. The couch isn't good for your leg or hip," Josiah replied. "I'll be fine right here where I am. Besides, your couch is pretty lumpy so it'll be harder for me to fall asleep. Since I'm not supposed to sleep."

"I'll help you get ready for bed, Dad."

Michael and Elmer disappeared down the short hall that led to the downstairs bedroom, leaving Josiah completely alone for the first time since being bashed over the head. He closed his eyes and tried to focus on those few moments between turning around and getting hit in the head. Tried to see past the solid object coming at him, to the shape of the person wielding that unknown weapon.

The more he reimagined it, the more he was pretty sure the weapon had come straight at him, but that didn't tell him much. Anything with a semiwide, flat surface could have done it, from the butt of a rifle to a two-by-four. The barn wasn't exactly lacking for weapons. But more than the what, he wanted to know who and why? And had that shirt actually been there, or was his mushy brain making it up after the fact?

"Hey, no sleeping yet." Michael's comforting voice startled him into trying to sit up.

Way wrong move. Pain flashed behind Josiah's eyes. "Fuck, you scared me."

"Sorry, pal." He parked his butt on the edge of the couch near Josiah's legs, face serious. "Why didn't you tell McBride about the shirt?"

"I'm not really sure. Part of me thinks I imagined it, because you didn't see it."

"And the other part?"

"I think I was hoping to trick Seamus into giving something away, that maybe he had something to do with it. But he didn't."

"How can you be so sure?"

"I know him." Beyond living together for two years, there had once been a genuine emotional bond between himself and Seamus. For a while, Josiah had adored their private relationship, even though being denied in public had hurt. Seamus had been great at playing straight, but beyond that he wasn't a great actor. "He didn't do it, Michael. He doesn't know anything about it."

"So how did your old T-shirt end up in the barn?"

"I don't know. Maybe that's why I'm second-guessing if I saw it at all." He didn't like having this conversation flat on his back with his head slightly propped on a pillow, but sitting up felt like way too much trouble.

"Maybe things will be clearer in the morning. Why don't you let me help you upstairs? You can sleep in my room. The sheets are clean. I'll take Dad's bed. That way I can keep an eye on you tonight."

Everything about Michael's tone, posture, and expression told Josiah not to argue, that this was happening. Protective Michael warmed Josiah deep inside on a cellular and emotional level, and instead of fighting it, he gave in. He was too sore and exhausted to battle what his body and mind wanted. "Okay."

"Excellent."

Michael put the shotgun on the bracket above the

door, double-checked the locks, and began turning off several of the downstairs lights. He left one side lamp blazing in the corner of the living room, giving the space a gentle glow and leaving few shadowy places for an attacker to lurk.

Not that Josiah planned on coming back downstairs until well after sunrise tomorrow.

Sitting up took more effort than he expected, and at one point, Michael got behind him and acted a bit like a human lever. Once he was upright, Josiah closed his eyes until a wave of nausea passed. He really should have taken some aspirin or ibuprofen for his headache, but at this point all he wanted was to lie down in a bed.

Michael did most of the work on their ascent of the stairs, and Josiah had no shame in leaning heavily on him. Getting his feet to move took more effort than he imagined, but he did manage it. Josiah had been upstairs a handful of times, usually to get something for Elmer from his room, once to use the upstairs bathroom while Elmer had the downstairs occupied. But he'd never been inside, never even peeked inside of Michael's room.

It both did and did not surprise Josiah. He'd stepped back in time by about twenty years, judging by the band posters on the walls, the matching teal and maroon patterns on the curtains and bedspread, and the collection of young adult books on a shelf over the desk. The room also smelled pleasantly of Michael's cologne and deodorant, and those scents wrapped themselves around Josiah like a warm hug.

He allowed Michael to ease him onto the bed, and he didn't protest when Michael took off Josiah's sneakers, socks, and jeans. Nothing about this was sexual, and Josiah trusted him not to cop a feel or do anything disrespectful while Josiah was in so much pain.

"Do you need to take a leak before you get comfortable?" Michael asked.

"Might as well." Once he got into bed, he wasn't getting out for a while, and no way was he going to piss in a bottle. They made a quick trip to the bathroom, and Josiah let out a satisfied groan when he finally slipped under the covers and stretched out on his back. His pain level had reached a dull throb, and once he was horizontal again, it spread down from his head to his shoulders in a weird way, but at least he felt less like his skull was going to explode.

Michael tucked the covers up around his chin, sitting on the side of the bed beside Josiah's hip in a reassuring, comforting way Josiah hadn't experienced since he was a small child. The tenderness made his eyes burn with gratitude and a hint of grief. "Get a little rest," Michael whispered. "I'll check on you in two hours."

"M'kay."

Michael stood, reached into his back pocket, and put something on the side table. "Your glasses. One of the lenses has a small crack but they aren't broken."

"Oh good. They're my only pair. Can't take care of Elmer without my eyes."

"Don't worry about Dad tomorrow. I'm going to call Brand and take the day off. Maybe Wednesday, too, depending on how you feel."

"Not gonna argue tonight."

"Good. I'd hate to fight with a disadvantaged opponent."

Josiah had enough energy to stick his tongue out at Michael, and then he was done. He closed his eyes, took comfort in Michael's familiar scent and nearby presence, and allowed himself to sleep.

Chapter Seventeen

Michael spent the next six hours in a state of constant agitation, sprinkled with small moments of peace whenever he checked on Josiah, and Josiah woke without much prodding. Concussion checks weren't fun for anyone, but Michael couldn't sleep anyway, so he didn't mind the task. He needed to know Josiah was okay. Josiah could have very easily not been okay tonight, and Michael still couldn't shake the last of the overwhelming terror he'd felt at finding him bloody in the barn.

Was that how Dad felt when he found Mom in the barn twenty-plus years ago? Like his entire world had just stopped and he didn't know how to restart it again? The pain of the loss had been much worse for Dad after so many years of marriage, but that kind of pain had still knifed Michael in the chest tonight. He'd nearly lost something precious before he'd ever truly had it.

After his third check on Josiah at four thirty, Michael finally yawned. Fatigue started to settle over him, and he sat on Dad's bed. Scrubbed both hands over his face and through his tangled hair. Those beers with Brand seemed like a lifetime ago. When he called Brand around eleven to explain why he was calling out tomorrow, Brand had been both shocked and outraged that anyone would attack Josiah.

He also promised anything they asked for, from meals to help with Dad, and that Michael could take off however long he needed. The ranch would manage. "Focus on your family, man," Brand had said.

Michael flopped onto his back and the slightly musty scent of the bedspread filled his nose, teasing at an upcoming sneeze. Dad used to make his bed every morning, and the morning of his stroke had been no exception. Michael hadn't seen the point in changing out the sheets while Dad was stuck downstairs for the foreseeable future, and he honestly didn't care in that moment. He closed his eyes and let his mind drift in the gray thoughtlessness of exhaustion for a while.

A high-pitched whine broke his peace, and Michael jackknifed upright, legs still dangling over the edge of the bed. His brain swam from the sudden position change, and he struggled to understand the sound that had woken him. He heard it again and nearly pitched onto his face in his haste to stand and dash out of the room. Straight across the hall to his room, where light from the window showed Josiah tangled up the bedcovers, his face twisted and sweaty, and breathing hard through his mouth.

Michael didn't even think. He turned on the bedside lamp and put his hands on Josiah's shaking shoulders. "Wake up, baby, come on. You're safe."

Josiah yelped and rolled to the side, away from Michael, but Michael held firm until Josiah's wide, terrified eyes finally met his. Seemed to see him and understand where he was. Josiah panted a few times and licked his lips as his senses returned. "Fuck me, that was a bad dream."

"You're okay now." Michael released his shoulders and eased on the bed beside him, one hand still resting on Josiah's chest. His adrenaline was racing again, and he worked to keep his own panic off his face. "You with me?"

"Yeah. Ugh. Didn't mean to wake you."

"You didn't. Not really. I'm glad you were close by when the nightmare started."

"Me, too. I have a hard time waking up from them sometimes."

Michael helped him untangle the bedcovers from his legs, glad Josiah was allowing him to stick close and be a comfort, instead of pretending he was fine and sending Michael away. Josiah had been scared by his dream and wasn't ashamed to admit it. "Do you remember what the nightmare was about?"

"Sort of. It started out about tonight. In the barn. But then it wasn't me being attacked, it was someone else I used to care about."

"Family?"

"Kind of family, yeah." Josiah sat up a bit against the headboard, expression still somewhat spooked, but his eyes were clear. Steady. "His name was Andy. After my parents died, I was on my own for a while. I'd dropped out of high school at sixteen because we were living on the streets and school was pointless when I could make more money washing dishes under the table. They died a week after I turned seventeen."

Michael could empathize with the pain of losing a parent but not two at once. "How did they die? If you don't mind me asking."

"Some drunk asshole lost control of his brand-new luxury SUV and drove it into our tent. I wasn't home at the time, or I probably would have been crushed with them."

"Christ, Josiah. Did the asshole serve time?"

"Two years for manslaughter." Josiah released a bark of bitter laughter. "I guess the judge wasn't very harsh because my parents were just two more homeless people the city didn't have to deal with. For about a year I alternated between sleeping in shelters and on the street, depending on the weather, but shelters were... scarier than the street. Especially for a gay teenager. And then I met Andy."

Josiah smiled, a genuinely happy smile, but he didn't elaborate. He seemed to get caught up inside a more joyful time of his life, and Michael waited, unwilling to break his brief moment of peace.

"André Gustovo Colicchio, but he preferred Andy because it sounded less Italian," Josiah continued, a fond smile quirking his pink lips. "He was about eight years older than me, which at seventeen, going on eighteen, sounds bad, but it wasn't remotely sexual at first. I thought it was, because when he found me hiding under some cardboard in the pouring rain and offered me a bed for the night, I assumed what he wanted from me."

Michael growled without realizing.

"All he did was let me sleep on his futon, so relax. He let me take a shower, gave me breakfast and clean clothes, and he offered to buy me a bus ticket out of Tulsa. Anywhere I wanted to go."

"Did you take him up on that?"

"Not at first. Andy was kind but very, very sad. He actually let me stay for a week, and I spent every night waiting for him to join me, or demand something from me. But he didn't. He fed me and bought me clean clothes, and we talked. A lot. I told him about my dream of being a nurse, and he told me about inheriting money from an uncle who'd recently passed and had been in the oil business. He didn't know what to spend his money on, so he bought things for strangers.

"We became really close friends, and since he didn't work, we did stuff together. Traveled, went to football games, museums, he even took me to Six Flags Over Texas for my eighteenth birthday. He helped me get my GED so I could take the classes I needed to become a certified nursing assistant, and he paid for that, too. And not once did he ask for sex or anything other than being his friend. His companion. I was the one who initiated a physical relationship."

Michael sorted all this new information around in his head. The idea that someone had taken Josiah in with no ulterior motive and showered him with money was...weird. Suspicious. No one did that out of the goodness of their heart. And Josiah had already been taken in and taken advantage of by Seamus McBride, so what if this Andy person had been the one to groom Josiah into being that sort of submissive person? To accept what others gave him and then believe it was Josiah's decision to add sex into the mix?

"I can hear you thinking doubts," Josiah said. "The older man taking advantage of the young homeless teen, but I promise it wasn't like that with Andy. With Seamus? Yes. I didn't find out Andy's whole story until I earned my certification. He took me out to dinner to celebrate, and when we got home that night he gave me a copy of his new, amended will."

Michael's upper body jerked with surprise. "His will?"

"Yeah." His dark eyes sparkled with grief. "Apparently, a few weeks before we met, Andy had been diagnosed with cancer. It was his fourth battle in twelve years, and he didn't want to fight anymore. He just wanted to live his life, maybe make a difference, and if possible, fall in love before he died. That night, he told me he'd done all three of those things by meeting me. He was the only person besides my parents who'd ever said they loved me. And I loved him back."

Michael didn't know how to respond to that, especially at zero dark thirty and on a severe lack of sleep, so he stayed quiet and allowed Josiah to finish this tragic story.

"I promised to take care of him," Josiah said, voice hoarse, cheeks flushed, and he spoke to his lap rather than Michael. A single tear dripped down the side of Josiah's nose. It took all of Michael's self-control not to reach out and wipe it away. "But Andy didn't want that. So he left. I went to work one day, came home, and he wasn't there. His phone was disconnected. I checked the online obituaries for nine days until his name appeared."

"How did he die?" Michael asked when Josiah didn't speak.

"Hypothermia. The police and medical examiner said he just sat down in an alley in January, went to sleep and never woke up. He left me, too, and I would have stayed with him until the end." Another tear followed the first.

The second tear shredded Michael's restraint. He circled the bed so he had room to climb on next to Josiah and tuck the trembling man close to his chest. He wrapped his arms around Josiah and hugged him as tight as he dared, hoping to take some of the grief and replace it with support and affection. Josiah sagged against him, not hugging back, but he also wasn't pulling away. He existed, as if he'd lost the energy to do anything else.

Michael hadn't expected to hear so much of Josiah's personal life story when he came in to wake him, but he was incredibly grateful that Josiah had finally opened up to him. Shared some incredibly personal experiences and heartbreak. Michael hated that he was hurting but there was no demon to fight right now, no enemy to defeat other than a few ghosts that still lingered in Josiah's mind. All he could do was hold Josiah and hope he was doing something to help his friend chase those ghosts away.

Josiah didn't cry after the first few tears slipped out without permission. He'd mourned Andy's death a long time ago, but like any kind of grief, sometimes it bubbled up and out with no warning, especially when his guard was down. And his guard came down way too easily around Michael Pearce. Michael's very presence made it safe to be vulnerable and express his emotions in ways he'd hadn't allowed himself for years.

Michael made him believe he could fall in love again; he might have been a little bit in love already.

He leaned against Michael's broad chest and existed in the older man's body heat, scent, and the steady thump of his heart beneath Josiah's ear. For the first time since that wonderful first kiss in the bed of Elmer's pickup, Josiah knew he was safe. Protected. Wanted. "Stay," he whispered.

Fingers lightly stroked his shoulder and down his back. "Are you sure?"

"Yes. I like the way you hold me."

"I'll hold you for as long as you need. Promise."

Michael hadn't changed out of his jeans and flannel shirt, and while he left his jeans on—Josiah appreciated that more than he could say, even though it had to be uncomfortable—he did take off the flannel to reveal a white sleeveless tee. He climbed under the covers and scooted up close to Josiah, arranging them so Josiah leaned against his chest, using Michael like a human pillow. His head still hurt but he didn't care anymore.

This was right.

He closed his eyes and slept.

Michael woke with sunlight streaming in the window and a slender body plastered against his. Josiah had shifted at some point so his cheek rested in the crook of Michael's shoulder and one arm was slung across Michael's waist. It was almost too hot under the covers, but he wasn't going to move or complain. He was too damned content.

Until his phone alarm began to blare across the hall where he'd left it. He'd set the alarm Sunday night and forgotten to turn it off last night after he called out of work.

Josiah snuffled and turned his face into Michael's arm, only to come awake with a grimace and pained groan. "Fuck, I thought last night was some kind of fever dream."

Michael ruffled Josiah's hair with his free hand.

"Sorry. This is a nice thing to wake up to, though. I could get used to it."

Instead of tensing or moving away, Josiah rested his palm over Michael's heart. "It is nice. Thank you. For everything last night, especially listening while I babbled about Andy."

"That wasn't babbling, and I was very happy to listen. I'll always listen."

"I'm glad, but we're also both still listening to your alarm, and it's kind of annoying."

Michael released his first bark of genuine laughter in what felt like weeks. "I'm going, I'm going. I'll check on Dad, too. You rest as long as you need. I took the day off so I could be here for both of you. The only thing you need to get up for is the bathroom. You want food or a drink? I'll get it. Phone charger? It's yours."

Josiah flashed him an adorable smile that was both amused and exasperated. "I got my head bashed in, not my legs. Once you get Elmer settled, come back up and help me downstairs. I'd rather hang with you guys than lie around up here by myself."

"Absolutely can do. Be back in a little while."

Since he planned to take a shower later, Michael slipped yesterday's flannel shirt back on. It still smelled faintly of horse, but whatever. He worked with them for a living and *he* kind of smelled like horse. Josiah hadn't complained, and Michael relived the awesomeness of sleeping with Josiah in his arms on the short walk downstairs.

Dad was awake in bed with a book on his lap. "How's Josiah?"

"He smiled," Michael said.

It was all he needed to say, because Dad smiled,

too. They both understood the importance of that first smile after a trauma.

"So what do you want first?" Michael asked. "Shower or breakfast?"

"Shower, I think. You get me on the chair and I'll do the rest."

"Good man."

Once Dad was situated on the shower chair in the downstairs bathroom with the detachable showerhead in his hand, Michael went back upstairs to help Josiah. Instead of going out to the trailer, Michael found a set of clean sweats for Josiah to change into, and then he spent some time making sure all the dried blood was out of Josiah's hair. Josiah used a wet washcloth on his face and neck, determined himself clean enough for now, and let Michael help him down the stairs.

Dad was done by then, so Michael got him dried and dressed while Josiah chilled on the couch with his feet up. It was still a bit strange to have Josiah around while Michael took care of Dad, but like all the evening and weekend meals they'd shared recently, it also felt perfectly natural. Familiar and right. Like family.

While Dad and Josiah debated what to watch on TV, Michael fixed them all a simple breakfast of boxed-mix pancakes and sausage patties. Josiah only ate a single dry pancake and sipped juice, which was fine. If he got hungry later, Michael would gladly fix him a snack. He hadn't been so eager to wait on someone hand and foot since the last time Kenny crashed from the flu.

In the bright light of day, Michael went back outside to the barn with a flashlight and inspected every inch of space within eight feet of the barn doors, inside and out. Part of the yard was the hard-packed earth that also made up the driveway, a lot of it was drying grass with no discernible footprints. No sign of a green T-shirt anywhere, either. He wanted to walk the entire perimeter fence line, but that was stupid and pointless. Most of the fence around the farthest pastures was simple wood stakes and barbed wire, not electrified for more than two decades.

For as much as the locked front gate made Michael feel better, anyone with gloves and protection could get through the fencing. Maybe he'd look into the electric system and see how much it would cost to get it up and running again. Michael wasn't losing anyone else he loved to random acts of violence.

McBride returned around ten thirty with no new leads. Michael walked him around the barn again, not daring to hope McBride might spot something Michael's untrained eye hadn't caught. He didn't. They did end up walking the fence line, but there were no cut wires or patches of disturbed earth. Whoever had attacked Josiah could have as easily climbed over the front gate as slipped through a rear part of the fencing.

When he was finished his inspection, Michael walked him back to his cruiser. "How did Josiah fare last night?" McBride asked.

Since it wasn't his place to comment on Josiah's nightmares, Michael simply said, "He got through it. Didn't mention remembering anything new, though."

"Okay. I don't wanna bother him and add to his stress, so if he does remember, make sure he calls me. Despite our differences recently, I do wanna find who did this to him."

Differences. Is he fucking serious?

Michael kept a lid on his temper. "I will. I'd like to

find who did this and shove my size-thirteen boot right up their ass, after I stomp their face into the gravel with it."

"Trust me, Pearce, I'd turn the other way if it happened." For the first time, Michael saw what he could only identify as stress brackets around McBride's eyes. Was the son of a bitch actually upset by what happened to Josiah? Did that mean he had a heart after all? Even if the heart was shriveled up and cruel?

McBride worried the brim of his hat. "I'm not from around here, but I heard through the gossip vine what happened to your mother way back when. I'm real sorry the sheriff at the time didn't give your family justice."

Michael bristled. "We aren't talking about that. We've got a common goal here in getting justice for Josiah, but that's where it stops. We aren't friends and never will be. Not after how you treated him and then tossed him away."

His eyes narrowed briefly. "That's fair. I'll keep this professional from now on."

"Good."

McBride got into his car and left, and Michael took great pleasure in locking the front gate after him— even if locking it now felt more symbolic than for real safety. A car couldn't roll up on the property but a person could sneak in unnoticed.

That afternoon, a retired electrician friend who owed Dad a favor came over and took a look at the electric fence system. He'd have to order a few replacement parts and check all the relay boxes along the line, but he could have it back online in a few days. Michael didn't have a lot of extra cash to pay him, so he bartered for the parts and labor by promising to help patch a hole in his barn roof. Good deal all around.

After that, Michael drove to the nearest superstore and bought DIY home security systems for the house and trailer. The trailer was easy since it only had one door, but the house took a little longer. Even though no one had broken into either building, having them ready to arm if they wanted them made Michael feel a bit safer in his own home.

Josiah moved around that day more than Michael would have liked, but Josiah was the nurse and knew what he could handle. He also wasn't the type to sit on his ass all day, which was why the house had always been perfectly clean since Josiah started working for them. Meals made, dishes done, bathroom sparkling, rugs vacuumed or beaten clean with a broom handle.

The left side of his forehead and eye were bruised in various shades of blue and purple. The swelling wasn't too bad, thanks to frequent ice packs and Tylenol. He did have a long, narrow bruise on his pecs, which suggested he'd crashed into the side of a stall after being hit and before hitting the ground. Michael hated those bruises with a furious passion, even while their existence was proof of life. Josiah had been hurt and scared, but he was also alive and mending. And still very much a treasured part of Michael's life.

Ramie Edwards surprised the hell out of him by showing up at five o'clock with takeout from Weston's only diner. "Don't tell my boss," she said as she handed the plastic bag of foam cartons to Michael by the front gate. "Brand called and asked me to drop off dinner, and I didn't think you guys would want greasy burgers and wings from the Roost."

"This is amazing, thank you," Michael replied, flabbergasted by the thoughtful gesture. "I'll be sure to thank Brand, too. I was just going to raid the fridge for leftovers."

"Well, I think this'll be better. How's Josiah?"

"Shaken but resting. Do you want to come in and say hello?"

"Nah, we aren't really friends, and he needs his rest. I'll see you both around, okay?"

"Of course. Thanks again."

Dad and Josiah were both floored by the thoughtfulness of the food Ramie brought, and their trio squabbled a bit over who got which meal: chicken-fried steak, baked ziti, or meat loaf and gravy. The food was good, the company the best, and they ate on TV trays while watching sitcom reruns.

Michael insisted Josiah spend one more night in the house, and Josiah acquiesced quickly. He escorted Josiah to the trailer for clothes and toiletries, not caring if he seemed paranoid and overprotective. Josiah showered and changed in the downstairs bathroom, then retired upstairs to Michael's room at eight, pale and exhausted. Michael wanted to stay with him, to hold him until he fell asleep.

He watched TV with Dad and played a game on his phone instead.

"That boy's lucky to have you," Dad said during a commercial break.

Michael paused his game. "He's a friend who didn't deserve what happened to him."

"No, he didn't, but that ain't it. I might be old but I ain't blind or dumb. You've taken a shine to him, and I expect he's got a shine for you, too. I see how you two look at each other when you think I'm not paying attention."

"Josiah is a great guy who deserves a great guy. Someone better than me."

Dad let out a loud, wet raspberry. "Not many people better than you. Don't let what that piece of crap Kenny did kill your confidence, Michael. That confidence got you the hell out of this town and into that big mansion you used to live in."

"Confidence also lost me my relationship, my dog, and my creation."

"Don't confuse confidence with arrogance. Arrogance is what gets folks in trouble. Confidence gets what you want. Worked for that boy in that movie with the rock-eating giant you loved as a kid and wouldn't stop watching."

Michael stared, unsure what… Oh. "*The NeverEnding Story* is your life lesson here?"

"Be confident. Got him through those laser-eyed statues."

He remembered the scene and how scared he'd been for the movie's lead as a child. The boy in the movie had needed confidence in his own abilities and in his self-worth in order to make it past a pair of deadly gatekeepers. And he'd done it. Was this huge bump in Michael's own personal and professional lives his own battle with the sphinxes? His own test to see if he believed enough in himself to find his worth and be a hero?

He was nobody's hero.

"Look, Michael, I'm gonna ask this plain because I think you and Josiah owe it to yourselves to be honest. Do you got feelings for him?"

"Yes." Their shared kisses the other night slammed into his brain and wouldn't go away. "I like him a lot, but I can't promise him anything. Not if I'm staying or going or where I even want to be in a year."

"No one can really promise anything except that we try our best. I promised your mom a lot of things that I never delivered on. The wedding vows, sure. To have and hold, sickness and health, 'til death did us part. I promised to protect her and I didn't. Someone took that outta my hands. Other people will always be a threat to our promises, except the promise to love. I never once stopped loving your mom and I never will."

Michael blinked hard against warm wetness in his eyes. Their last conversation about Mom had been an ugly screaming match of blame and anger; this was calm and kind and almost reverent. The kind of conversation they should have had long before now, so they could both let go of ghosts from their shared past and move forward.

To find a path toward mutual forgiveness.

"We both loved her," Michael said softly. "She was my mother. But I never gave true consideration to how much you loved her as your wife and life partner. I was too selfish and focused on my own grief and blame."

"I deserved a lot of it."

"But not all of it." He angled to face Dad more fully, elbows resting on his knees. "If last night taught me anything, it's that we can't always protect the people we love. Sometimes they get hurt and it's not our fault. I'm finally starting to understand that." He truly was. Coming home and getting to know his dad again, really know him and interact with him, was driving those points home.

Maybe he'd spent the better part of two decades clinging to blame and anger, but those two things had faded immensely over the years, leaving behind only the thinnest veil, as fragile as a spider's web. An illusion of holding him back when all he had to do was step through, dust off, and keep on going. He could forgive and live his life without those old hurts holding him back.

"So does this mean you're gonna ask Josiah out on a proper date?" Dad asked.

Michael chuckled. "I don't know. We actually did talk about our feelings a few days ago. He's not in the headspace to date right now. And I couldn't say if I was going to stay or leave in a few months, so we aren't really doing anything except being friends."

"Friends, huh?"

"Yes, friends. But, uh, say I had an idea about what else I might stick around here for besides Josiah. Something to bring this land back to life again. You want to hear about it?"

Dad perked up. "Definitely."

"Okay, great." Michael sipped from his glass of lemonade to wet his parched throat, then started talking.

Chapter Eighteen

Despite all of Josiah's weak arguments against it, Michael took off Wednesday as well, to look after him and Elmer. Being waited on and sort of pampered was a new experience for Josiah, and the comfort it provided warred with his self-reliance, which chafed at being handled with kid gloves. Elmer quietly told him to just go with it and enjoy.

He hadn't had any more nightmares about the attack, and his confidence returned with each day between him and that terrifying moment in the barn. Michael took Elmer out there Wednesday morning to get some work done, but Josiah couldn't make himself leave the relative safety of the front porch, where he sat with hot chocolate and watched the occasional car whiz by on the road.

The quiet chill of North Texas winter was slowly settling in all around them. Summers were hot and dry but winter did occasionally bring a dusting of snow. Thanksgiving was in a couple of weeks. Josiah had vague childhood memories of quiet dinners with his parents, and then the one holiday season he'd spent with Andy. Seamus had celebrated by accepting invitations to multiple dinners at different times of the day, and coming home with plates of leftovers for Josiah to forage from.

God forbid he bring Josiah along even just as his roommate.

He did not miss living in the closet so no one suspected his arrangement with Seamus was anything more than platonic. He didn't have to pretend anything around Elmer and Michael. All he had to do was keep his feelings for Michael tucked away and protected from scrutiny so he didn't get his heart broken again when Michael decided to leave. For all the ideas he'd fed to Josiah the other night under the stars, Michael hadn't brought any of it up again in front of Josiah.

Michael went back to work the next day and, while Josiah was still a bit sore in the face, he could handle Elmer's needs just fine, thank you. He did miss having Michael around, though, and Michael's frequent texts throughout the day were more sweet than annoying. Elmer, bless him, didn't ask Josiah to take him out to the barn. One day Josiah would face that fear, but not quite yet. Not until he had a bit more distance between himself and his attack.

Michael worked Friday and picked up part of Alan's Saturday morning shift to make up for lost hours. Josiah and Elmer were finishing up lunch when Michael got home—with a bag of groceries in hand. Josiah usually did the shopping, so that was new, and Michael didn't want any help unloading what he'd bought. Elmer ignored the whole thing and kept working on his puzzle. Josiah's curiosity, however, stayed piqued all afternoon.

Around four someone honked at the gate, and Michael went outside to let them in. Josiah nearly dropped his tablet when Wayne and Rose Woods came inside the house with Michael in tow.

"Ain't you a sight for sore, bored eyes, Rose," Elmer said. "You could've left the ball and chain home, though. You know you've been sweet on me these last few years."

Rose laughed, the lines around her eyes deepening from her genuine smile. "You old dog, you know my heart belongs to this old cattleman." She patted Wayne on the forearm. "How are you getting along, Elmer?"

"Can't complain too much. Getting around a lot better than before." He waved a hand at his wheelchair. "Still got a ways to go yet."

"Well, I expect you'll get there soon enough." Rose's kind, patient smile turned to Josiah. "How are you feeling?"

"I'm doing much better, ma'am, thank you." Josiah's face was still a mess of healing bruises, some of which were now a sickly green shade, but the bulk of the pain was gone. He'd have a small scar on his forehead but such was life. "How has your family been?"

"We're all doing just fine, thanks for asking. My boys are hard at work at the ranch, and my girls are happy as can be with their little ones. I'm actually watching Leanne's kids tomorrow so her and John can spend the day in Littleton doing some ministry work with their church."

Josiah managed to keep his polite smile firmly intact. "I hope you have a great time with your grandkids."

"Always do."

"Can I get either of you something to drink?" Michael asked. "I can make coffee."

"We're not stayin' long," Wayne said, adding to the conversation his wife had previously dominated. Josiah expected Wayne dominated when it came to ranch matters, but Rose was the driving force of their social interactions. The roles simply seemed to fit their personalities. "We actually stopped by to see if Elmer was feeling up for dinner at our house tonight."

"Yeah?" Elmer said. "What's she cooking?"

Rose laughed. "I've had chicken marinating half the day, and Wayne is gonna fire up the grill when we get home."

"Don't have to ask me twice." Elmer winked at Josiah. "Miss Rose over there could give my lovely Carol a run for her money when it came to grilled chicken. But she didn't have my wife's secret ingredient. Only I know that one."

"I'll get it out of you yet, Elmer."

"I think dinner at the Woods house sounds like a fine idea," Michael said. "You haven't been out much lately, Dad."

Josiah wanted to mention Elmer had been out a week ago for the picnic but socialization was good for recovery. Elmer needed to be around friends his own age, instead of always hanging out with his grown son and daytime nurse.

"Good, then let's get your coat on and go," Wayne said. "That chicken won't cook itself and I'm starving."

With plenty of people to help get Elmer settled in the back seat of Wayne's pickup, wheelchair in the bed, Josiah stayed on the couch and watched what he could from his view out a front window. It didn't hit him right away that this was the first time he'd be completely alone with Michael in this house until Michael came back inside and dead-bolted the door.

"Well, that was a nice surprise," Michael said, his tone a touch too innocent.

Had they all planned this to give him and Michael time alone together? Did it have something to do with the groceries Michael brought home? The chances were good, but Josiah had no fear of Michael, so he embraced his curiosity and played along. "Yeah, a great surprise. I'm sure Elmer will enjoy himself."

"Absolutely. Are you getting hungry? I can start something for dinner."

"Um, sure, that'd be great." He wasn't hungry yet, having eaten a late lunch because he'd fallen asleep and napped until Michael got home from work, but Michael sounded eager to cook for him. And Josiah wanted to see what Michael had up his sleeve.

At first, he didn't hear much from the kitchen other than the sounds of water running or something being chopped. The floorboards creaked as Michael moved around, occasionally passing by the archway between the living room and kitchen with things in his hands, probably setting the eat-in kitchen table to the left of the arch. Their trio had eaten in there a few times but they mostly preferred trays in front of the TV.

A little after five, something began sizzling, and the fragrant aromas of garlic, herbs, and roasting meat delighted Josiah's nose. Josiah tried to pay attention to the book he was reading and ignore the activities in the kitchen, but now his stomach growled and he practically drooled for whatever Michael was preparing.

Around five thirty, Michael strode directly to the couch and held out his hand. "Dinner is prepared. Ready?"

"Sure." Josiah took Michael's hand, accepting the

gentle tug to his feet. Michael didn't let go as he led Josiah into the dining area, and the sight took his breath away. Two lit taper candles in silver holders bookended the old, rectangular table. Two settings were directly across from each other, loaded with food, as well as a glass of water and a wine goblet holding something red. A basket of dinner rolls held court between the plates, along with a small plate of butter.

"Wow," Josiah said, unsure what else to say as he took in the food. "This looks amazing. You cooked all this?"

"Yup." Michael pulled out a chair. "Please, sit."

He did, loving this chivalrous side of Michael; not that he ever doubted Michael had one. His plate had a perfectly seared steak half reclined on a cloud of mashed potatoes, a stack of bright green string beans with bits of bacon in them, all surrounded by a glossy brown gravy. "I feel like I just fell into a fancy steak house. You didn't have to do this."

"I wanted to. I'm not a gourmet chef, but I do know how to search online recipes for special occasions. I haven't had a reason to bust one out until now."

"Why now?"

Michael sat across from him, his expression as adorably shy as Josiah had ever seen on the guy. "Our first date?"

"We're dating now?"

"Only if you want to consider this our first date. Or our second, if the stargazing last weekend counts as the first. I'm game for either, or neither if you don't want to." Michael leaned forward, hands flat on the table. "But I learned something very important this week, and it's how much I care about you. I needed to show you that somehow. But if this is too much and you don't feel the same, then no hard feelings. We can go eat by the TV like normal and pretend I didn't make us a fancy steak dinner."

"I don't want to eat like normal." Josiah couldn't stop the words even if he'd wanted to, and he didn't. They'd both come so close to losing a potentially great thing before it ever started, and Michael had been wonderfully supportive this week. Present without smothering, sweet without pressuring. And to top it all off with a home-cooked meal that looked and smelled amazing?

What was a boy to do?

Josiah picked up his wineglass. "To our first date."

Michael beamed as he picked his up, too. "Our first date." He gently clinked the rim of his glass to Josiah's.

The wine was bitter with just a hint of sweetness to balance it out. Red wine wasn't Josiah's favorite thing, but after he tried the steak, he knew he'd be having at least two glasses. The food was amazing, the steak a perfect medium rare, the potatoes nice and creamy.

"This is beyond fantastic," Josiah said. "I don't think I've had a better meal at a restaurant." Not that he had much restaurant experience beyond diners and simple mom-and-pop places along the highway. Eating out of the garbage cans of the fancier places definitely didn't count. He shoved that maudlin thought away and focused on the perfect bites he kept putting in his mouth. Even the dinner rolls were flaky, moist, and everything he'd ever wanted in a piece of bread.

He did manage two glasses of wine and most of his plate of food before his stomach rebelled and said no more. Michael had done the same, his cheeks rosy from the wine, and he grinned like a fool over his very successful meal.

"I feel like I should leave you a tip," Josiah teased.

"You can tip the chef by giving him a kiss later."

"I think I can manage that. The chef definitely earned at least one kiss for his efforts."

"Yeah? How do I earn two?"

"Did you make dessert?"

Michael's eyes went comically wide. "Uh…"

"I'm joking." Josiah reached over and briefly squeezed Michael's wrist. "I couldn't eat another bite for the rest of the evening. I am well and truly stuffed full of meat." Michael's eyebrows started wiggling with humor; Josiah laughed when he realized what he'd said. "Down, boy. Why don't you find us a movie or something to watch, and I'll do the dishes."

"You don't have to."

"I want to. You deserve a bit of a rest as reward for that meal."

"Can't argue with that." Michael topped off their wineglasses with the last from the open bottle, then strolled into the living room.

Josiah watched him go, appreciating the sight of Michael's ass in those faded jeans, and got to work. Michael was the kind of cook who cleaned as he went, so there wasn't a lot for Josiah to do besides their plates, the pan he'd cooked the steak in, and two pots. Some green beans were left, so he put those in a plastic container and slipped it into the fridge. A second bottle of wine was chilling, this one sweeter and fruitier.

With a grin, Josiah opened it and took it with him into the living room. Put the bottle on the side table, then sat next to Michael, who'd perched dead center on the couch. Josiah sat close without crowding him, glad he had his wineglass as a prop, because he wanted to reach over and kiss Michael. To crawl onto his lap and know he was safe, that Michael wouldn't do anything Josiah did not invite.

His nerves kept him firmly in place—nerves slowly being beaten back by the warm buzz of alcohol. "So dinner and a movie, huh? That's pretty classic for a first date."

Michael gently tapped his knee against Josiah's. "Not so classic, considering we technically slept together before we started dating."

"True." Didn't count in Josiah's book, though. Monday night had been all about comfort, and they'd only shared a bed that one time. When they actually slept together, there would way fewer clothes involved. "So no dessert but you bought two bottles of wine?"

"We can throw it in the freezer for two hours and make a sorbet of sorts. That can be dessert with a touch of alcohol."

"It's fine." Josiah sipped his red wine. "You know, you're kind of easy to wind up. Is that from so many years hosting swanky parties with protocols and fancy toast points and caterers who wear cummerbunds?"

"Pretty much. Although Kenny usually hired a party planner to manage the caterer and servers, so I only had to make my ten-minute appearance, pretend I liked all those people, and then I could go back to my office and hide."

"I've heard you talk about your life in Austin and not liking to be sociable, but you were amazing last weekend at the picnic. You weren't hiding from people— you were engaged, especially with the kids. Maybe you were just in the wrong environment before. Around stuffy people who didn't really see you or understand you."

"Maybe I was. I let my resentment and anger at my dad keep me away, stuck in a world I never really embraced. I thought being rich was the key to being happy, but if I really look back, I was just as unhappy in Austin as I was here."

"What about being here now? Are you still unhappy?"

"No." Michael ran his fingertip around the rim of his wineglass in an oddly mesmerizing way. "Dad and I had a really good talk the other night, about a lot of things. Neither one of us actually said 'I forgive you' for the fight we had, but I think we reached an understanding about it. I get him more than I used to, and I think he gets me. We feel like father and son again, and it's been a long time."

"Since your mom died?"

"Yeah."

Josiah wanted to gulp his wine before venturing here, but if Michael answered him, he didn't want to be sloshed when he got this story. "Michael, you can tell me to fuck off, but can I ask what happened between you and your dad? I've heard it was a falling-out because of your mother's death, but no one's ever told me how she died."

Michael leaned forward, elbows resting on his knees, the wineglass dangling in the fingers of his right hand. He swirled the wine as he stared down at it, his jaw tight and occasionally twitching as his mind worked through something. Josiah stayed quiet, unsure if he'd crossed a line. He didn't regret asking, though. If Michael truly wanted to date him, to get to know him, then Josiah needed to get to know Michael, too.

"Mom's death is one of those small-town secrets that people who were around for it know," Michael finally said, "but we don't talk about it."

That statement told Josiah one thing for sure: Carol Pearce hadn't died of natural causes.

Josiah put his wineglass down, took Michael's from him and did the same. Then he took Michael's hands in his and squeezed, urging Michael to look at him. Michael angled his way but his eyes stayed down, his mouth a flat line.

"Dad found her in the barn," Michael said, his hoarse voice barely above a whisper. "I was having trouble passing my driver's test, so Dad took me out after dinner to practice driving. We were only gone for about two hours, because it was Tuesday, and we had a lineup of favorite sitcoms we watched as a family on Tuesday night. It was our must-see-TV night. But when we got home, Mom wasn't in the house. We checked every room, then went outside and started calling her name."

The naked emotions in Michael's voice punched Josiah right in his heart, and his throat tightened with grief for what was still unsaid. Josiah hated putting Michael through this pain, but it was also the big secret that had kept Michael and Elmer at odds for so many years.

Michael looked up, his dark eyes swimming with misery and glistening with tears. "It took a little while for the county sheriff and state police to piece it all together, but a vagrant named Silas Dufresne had snuck into the barn to rip us off, steal tools and whatever else he could pawn. Mom must have heard something and surprised him, because he hit her in the head with a crowbar and ran." He blinked hard, leaving his lashes wet, and Josiah wanted to weep. "By the time Dad found her, she was already gone."

"Michael, I am so sorry. So freaking sorry."

"Thanks."

"But they caught the guy?"

"Yeah. Dumbass hitched to Amarillo and tried to pawn a socket set with Dad's name on it. The cops had just circulated a memo with our stolen items, so they were able to pick him up. Got twenty years for murder two. But even that sentence didn't fix the huge rift between me and Dad. I blamed him because Mom had asked him for weeks to fix the front gate. He blamed me for not passing that stupid driving test the first time, sure if we'd been home Mom wouldn't have been killed. I definitely inherited my temper from him, so the anger and resentment just festered until we both exploded. Every bad thing I ever thought about my father, every jab I could take about him losing the herd and selling the horses, I blasted at him like machine-gun fire until our relationship was torn to shreds." Michael sighed deeply. "I did the same thing with Kenny."

Josiah's hands jerked and he released Michael's. "What do you mean?" He'd seen hints of Michael's temper peek through over the last two months, but this was the first he'd heard of Michael having any sort of altercation with his ex.

"We had a pretty huge fight about a year ago. As much as I want to pretend everything was always great between us, and that him cheating on me had come out of the blue, it didn't. Not really. After our first app took off, we were under a lot of pressure to come up with the next big thing. We had money, but it was never enough for Kenny. Never enough money, never a big enough party, never enough blog articles written about us. The more pressure he put on me, the more I resented him and our success, and I let it bottle up. I started drinking heavily, pretty much all day long, for weeks. I was that metaphorical champagne bottle that keeps getting shaken, and at some point, you can't keep it in and you explode. I exploded.

"I got ripping drunk, destroyed my office and then passed out on a raft in the middle of our pool. I was honestly lucky I didn't fall off and drown. Kenny was pissed when he found me. He shoved me into rehab for fourteen days, and when I got out, everything was different. I didn't see it then, but that was the beginning of the end of us. It just took another half a year for me to figure it out."

Michael drew Josiah's hands into his lap and held them there, his expression more naked than Josiah had ever seen before. "I'm really good at ruining the relationships I have with people, Josiah, but I'm not the guy who passed out in a fancy pool anymore. I'm definitely not the angry teenager who couldn't pass his driving test or see his father was grieving as badly as he was. I drove back into Weston in September with a clean slate, a new man, and I think that man could be very good at being in a relationship with you. If you'll take a chance on me."

Whoa. Their conversation had gone from first date to serious relationship in less than thirty minutes. Josiah stared at their joined hands, his mind whirring with all the information he'd been given tonight. Michael had been incredibly honest with him, peeling back painful layers and showing Josiah bits of his worst self. His worst impulses and the things that still haunted the far recesses of his conscious mind.

Some of those impulses worried him, thanks to the bullshit he'd put up with from Seamus. But Seamus and Michael were nothing alike, not in temperament or their personal lives. Seamus was angry, resentful, and so deep in the closet he'd probably forgotten what the light looked like. Meanwhile, Michael was self-aware, maybe a little lost in terms of his future, and very much comfortable with who he was as a gay man in a small town.

Michael was someone Josiah could see himself with years down the road, happy and in love, and as equal partners. "Do you think we could put the *r*-word away for a while," Josiah asked, "and just do the dating thing first? Maybe do the relationship thing down the road?"

"Of course." Michael raised Josiah's right hand and kissed the knuckles in a sweet, promising gesture. "I want to do this right. If you ever feel like I'm pressuring you, tell me to back off and I will. If you think I'm moving too slow, well, you take the lead and I'll follow. This can be something really great. I believe that. And I'm pretty sure Dad is rooting for us, too."

"Of course, he is. Was Elmer in on dinner at the Woods house so you and I could have some privacy tonight?"

"Yeah, that was all Dad. He told me this morning before I left for work, so I swung by the store for groceries on the way home."

"He's a devious old man, gotta give him that."

"He just wants us both to be happy, and he's very much Team Dating. So am I, actually. You?"

Josiah chuckled. "I'm on board with it. And since we've agreed to the dating thing, there's something I've wanted to do since dinner. My way of thanking the chef for a fantastic meal."

"Something besides doing the dishes?"

"Oh yes, something much more personal that I've missed this past week."

A too-innocent smile quirked his lips. "Oh? Stargazing?"

Tired of words, Josiah leaned in and kissed Michael, a firm press of heat and softness accompanied by the bitter taste of wine. Michael moaned softly and parted his lips, his tongue flicking out to caress the seam of Josiah's mouth. Exploring without deepening or demanding.

Movie forgotten, real world just a dream now, Josiah existed in that kiss for a long, long time.

Chapter Nineteen

Kissing Josiah as frequently as possible became a new kind of wonderful game for Michael over the next two weeks. Quick pecks in the morning when they passed each other in the front door. Longer kisses stolen in the kitchen while putting their dinner plates together (Josiah no longer ate alone in his trailer). Making out in the trailer on weekends when they had more time alone together. They kissed and hugged and touched above the waist, and as much as Michael longed to go further, he wasn't going to push.

McBride had no leads on who'd attacked Josiah. As his bruises faded, Josiah's confidence and sense of safety returned. He still slept and kept his clothes in the trailer, but he spent most of his time at the house, either working or simply existing with Michael and Dad.

Dad could do most things for himself now, but he still struggled with weakness in his leg. A recent doctor's appointment had left him slightly dispirited, because he might never walk again without assistance. His long-term goal was to eventually be able to use a walker; for right now he still needed help getting in and out of the wheelchair. It gave Michael more freedom to work different shifts at the ranch, but Josiah seemed troubled.

Michael brought it up the Saturday before Thanksgiving. He and Josiah had gone grocery shopping together after collaborating for the next week's dinners, including their small holiday celebration at home. Their trio had been invited to the Woods house, but Dad hadn't wanted to crash what was going to be a huge family gathering, featuring their prodigal son from California and his husband.

Josiah was thrilled to cook his very first Thanksgiving dinner for them. Even a pared down one with only a few side dishes and one frozen pumpkin pie. "Even though I did spend one Thanksgiving with Andy," he had said, "he insisted we go out to a Chinese buffet instead of cooking. He did pack away about five plates of food, though, so he definitely got his money's worth."

"What did you eat?" Michael had asked.

"I may have made myself sick glutting on Crab Rangoon. Anything with cream cheese in it is a guilty pleasure for me."

Michael had made a mental note of that.

Dad was working on another two-thousand-piece puzzle when they got home with groceries, and he waved without looking up. He was pretty close to completing this one, and when he got into the final stretch, he hated to break his concentration. They went past him and directly into the kitchen.

Seeing Dad with the puzzle made Michael smile over his memory of their conversation last week while Josiah was at his own postconcussion checkup. Dad had finished his latest puzzle and sent Michael upstairs to hunt for another one for him to assemble, insisting there was one in Dad's bedroom closet. All Michael had found was the unopened 3D puzzle he'd sent to Dad last year, so he'd taken that downstairs.

Dad had given the puzzle an exaggerated grimace. "Don't wanna do that one."

"It's the only unfinished puzzle left in the house, Dad. Unless you want me to call Josiah and have him pick up a few on his way home." They had three more coming in the mail that week but Dad got fidgety when he didn't have one in progress at any given time. Plus, it was great for his dexterity after the stroke.

"No, don't bother him, this one'll do for now. Just don't see the point in these. A puzzle's a picture, not a building model."

Michael studied the picture of the 3D puzzle he'd chosen because the building had reminded him of the church in Weston where Mom and Dad had gotten married and attended service for years. "Sorry, I didn't know that."

"No reason you should. Not like we ever talked much after you left. The gesture was nice, though, and I thanked you for it in the last birthday card I sent."

"But that was last year. I sent you the 3D puzzle this past Christmas."

Dad frowned at him. "I sent you a birthday card this spring."

"I never got it."

"Oh." So much regret and understanding had never been rolled so tightly into two little letters. "When I didn't hear back, I guess I figured you were finally done with me. Then you showed up in the hospital, real as rain. Couldn't believe it. Didn't wanna believe it was more than pity, but you stayed."

"I stayed."

"And now you're thinking about turning this old land into something again."

"Definitely thinking." Michael had held up the church puzzle. "Want to try something brand-new with me, old man? See how we do together?"

Dad had grinned so brightly that Michael had known without them saying it—things between them were truly, finally forgiven. The finished puzzle proudly held court on a shelf near the fireplace, carefully varnished to protect it against age and time.

Michael began taking groceries out of his and Josiah's bags and lining them up on the counter for Josiah to put away. Josiah had slowly taken over the kitchen and rearranged a few things in the cupboards, which was fine with Michael since Josiah did the bulk of the cooking. Dad couldn't reach the upper cabinets anyway so his opinion didn't matter. The only thing Josiah hadn't changed—beyond taking everything out once to give it a good scrub—was the fridge. Eggs were where Michael always remembered them being, same with fruit in the left crisper drawer and vegetables in the right.

"Do not touch the stuff on this shelf," Josiah said, pointing into the fridge. "That's stuff I need for Thanksgiving, and I don't want to have to go back to the store last minute. Especially not one so far away."

"Off-limits, got it." Michael pulled an apple they'd gotten for snacking and took a big bite, so glad they'd managed to find the last of the Honeycrisp for the season. They were his favorite apples. "Is it too soon to leave the turkey in the fridge?"

Josiah quirked an eyebrow. "It's a twenty-pound turkey and I want to brine it Wednesday, so yes, we need to start defrosting it."

"Cool. I've never done this, either, you know. Mom always cooked our Thanksgiving meal. My first few years with Kenny, we either bought a meal from a restaurant or went out, and after that everything was catered. I really love the idea of cooking with you. I guess Dad can assist if he wants."

"How benevolent of you." Josiah rolled his eyes but was grinning. Dad basically stayed out of the kitchen now unless they were having a rare dinner at the table. "I'm sure if Elmer wants to help, he'll find a way to help."

"Yes, he will." That was the perfect segue into the topic Michael wanted to broach tonight. He took a step closer to Josiah and lowered his voice. "Dad's regaining a lot of his independence."

"He is." He put a box of instant stuffing mix into a top cupboard. "I'm really proud of him."

"I bet it worries you a little, too."

"Why would it worry me?" Josiah turned to face him, his repaired glasses perched too low on his nose, and he stabbed them back up. "I love seeing my patients heal and regain their previous independence. Your dad deserves his life back."

"I know, and I agree with you. I didn't mean to imply otherwise. I am so grateful for Dad's recovery, and so much of that is you, Josiah. I guess I don't want you to feel beholden to our original agreement if there's another job out there with a patient who..."

"Who what? Needs me more?"

"Well, yeah, kind of. Dad loves you, and I adore you, but there isn't a lot for you to do, and I don't want you getting bored. Or to think I'm taking advantage of you or your time."

Josiah crossed his arms and took a full step backward. "Are you asking me to leave?"

"No, God no. I love having you here, and not specifically Nurse You who takes care of Dad, but just you, Josiah Sheridan, the guy I'm dating." Dating was relative at the moment, since they hadn't actually gone out anywhere in the last two weeks. There weren't very many places for them to go nearby. One gay bar existed but it was a forty-minute drive, and Michael preferred their time spent alone anyway. Even "dates" as simple as sharing beers in the cab of Dad's pickup, because it was too chilly to sit outside while stargazing, were amazing and fun.

"You see? This is why I turned you down the first time. Me working for you and dating you is getting complicated, and I didn't want this to be complicated. I've had too many complicated relationships in the past, and I need one thing to be simple."

"It doesn't have to be complicated."

"No? How do you un-complicate it? I quit?"

"I don't want you to quit." Michael took a chance on getting into Josiah's personal space and resting his hands on Josiah's hips. He waited until Josiah looked up at him. "I just think maybe you've outgrown this particular position. You are better than sitting around most of the day with nothing to do except PT twice a day. PT you could help him with in the morning and evening, before and after a shift somewhere else."

"Then tell me what you want me to do, Michael. You're my boss, so this is your decision."

"That's the thing. I don't want to be your boss anymore. I just want to be your boyfriend."

Josiah's eyebrows went up. "Boyfriend, huh?"

"Yes, boyfriend. Part of your salary is your rent on the trailer, plus a check for the rest. What if in exchange for your rent, you continue to do Dad's physical therapy twice a day, but you also have the freedom to take on another paying client outside this house. You are still welcome in the house at any time, for any meal or just to hang out. That won't change. Would you feel comfortable with that?"

"I'm not sure." He chewed on his thumbnail, head tilted down. "I love being here, in this house with you and your dad. But you're right. Sometimes I don't feel like I'm doing enough to earn my check. I am thrilled with how far Elmer has come and how little he really does need me every day. And if I'm being honest, if you were a regular client I wasn't dating and didn't basically live with, I would have brought it up myself and probably sooner."

"So you *are* dissatisfied with the job as it is now."

"Yes. I don't think Elmer needs full-time care anymore. I'm nervous about him being home alone after what happened to me, but it happened to *me*. Not to him. Maybe next week, once the holidays are over, I can look into some other work in my field. Someone else whose life I can improve by taking care of them."

"And I am all in with that. I want you to do what makes you happy. Please, don't ever feel obligated to do something because you think it's what I want you to do. I spent too many years doing that with Kenny, and it left me basically broke and homeless." While the homeless part had fixed itself the moment Michael came home to Weston, he was still subsisting off his ranch paychecks. He'd had one offer on the Austin house so far below asking he'd laughed until he ended up with a hiccup fit.

"You know I understand making others happy at my own expense." Josiah rested his own hands on Michael's forearms in a familiar hold. "Your support means everything."

"You've got my support. You mean so much to me." More than Michael had words to express, and he hoped he put some of those emotions into his smile.

"Same." Josiah took a single step forward, leaving only a few inches of air between their bodies. "Do you mind if I, um, stay a bit later tonight? Maybe after Elmer goes to bed?"

Michael's pulse raced. "Yeah?"

"Yes. We haven't had any real privacy in a few weeks, and I would really like some time with you. Upstairs? With some time to just be together?"

"We can definitely arrange that. And I promise no pressure. As much time as I spend imagining what it will be like to make love to you, I want it to happen when we're both ready." *Especially you.* Josiah had given up too much of his body, his autonomy, and his self-respect already. Michael wouldn't be another person who took from or used him.

"I'm getting there, and I need you to know I trust you. I'm a big fan of sex, and I've had some pretty great sex. I've also had some pretty awful sex, and those are my most recent experiences. The fact that I know you'll be patient with me and won't push is actually a huge turn-on."

"Yeah? I will go tortoise slow if it turns you on. I will

go frame-by-frame forward if it turns you on. Although some touching would be good, too."

"There will be touching." Josiah slid his hands up Michael's arms and rested them on his shoulders. They were so damned close now. "I promise lots of touching very soon."

"I'm down with touching. Can we start dinner now so we can get to the touching?"

Josiah chuckled. "Even if we start dinner now, Elmer probably won't go to bed for a few more hours."

"I know, but at least cooking will distract me and make time move faster." Michael leaned down and kissed him. "I'm so glad to be here with you."

"So am I."

"Good. Now let's get cookin', good lookin'."

On shared barks of laughter, they did exactly that.

Josiah did his best to behave during their simple dinner of spaghetti and frozen meatballs, but the entire exercise of dinner and a movie—something pretty typical for their trio now—was seriously testing his restraint. Michael proved more ticklish than Josiah expected, a secret he unlocked while they boiled pasta, heated sauce, and browned meatballs. Poking him in the ribs got a lot of laughter that buoyed Josiah's mood and reinforced his decision to spend some alone time in Michael's bedroom tonight.

He and Michael sat close together on the couch during the movie. Elmer's new spot was the love seat opposite them, and he was getting better at pulling himself over to the wheelchair without help, because they were basically at the same height. Halfway through the movie, Michael made popcorn, and Josiah had too much fun stealing the buttery kernels out of Michael's fingers. If he noticed any of it, Elmer didn't say a word.

Elmer did, however, excuse himself to bed as soon as the credits rolled with an exaggerated yawn and arm stretch. "Might read for a bit but I'll probably just go to sleep. Josiah, you gonna join us for breakfast?"

"Probably, yes," Josiah replied. They had a new tradition of eating a late breakfast, not-quite-brunch on Sunday morning, and Josiah wouldn't miss it. He wasn't sure if he'd be there because he woke up in Michael's bed, or because he'd walked across the yard from the trailer. They'd know soon. Even if things didn't progress to full-on naked sexy times tonight, Josiah did miss sleeping in the same bed as Michael.

He missed sharing his bed with someone he had strong, positive feelings for and felt perfectly safe with.

"Good enough," Elmer said. "Michael? About five minutes?"

"I'll be there," Michael replied.

Elmer wheeled his way to the downstairs bathroom first. Josiah leaned more into Michael's chest for a few wonderful minutes, until the bathroom door opened. Michael stood and followed Elmer to his bedroom, leaving Josiah alone with his anticipation of what might happen when Michael returned. His stomach erupted with nervous wiggles. The fun kind of nervous, though, not the scary kind.

Michael returned an interminable amount of time later (probably only a few minutes, but whatever) and stood in front of Josiah, hands deep in his jeans pockets. He almost looked nervous, and it was incredibly adorable. "Do you want something to drink? Beer? Wine? Water?"

"I'm okay." He stood so Michael wasn't towering over him. The position change increased his courage to say what he wanted. "I'd actually really like for you to take me upstairs to your room."

"Yeah?" A new kind of hunger overtook Michael's smile, and it doubled Josiah's nervous wiggles.

"Definitely."

Michael took his hand and pulled Josiah toward the stairs so quickly Josiah let out a soft, startled yelp. He gave in to Michael's handling, though, enjoying the alpha side of Michael's personality that was coming out the more comfortable they got with each other. The more they folded each other into their separate lives and began to grow a united one.

They'd shared some of the darkest secrets from their pasts and were working to create something unique between them emotionally and spiritually—something Josiah really wanted to see progress further on the physical level.

He allowed Michael to lead him upstairs and into his bedroom. Shutting the door didn't bother him, and neither did the way Michael pulled him into a firm hug and tender kiss. A kiss that asked silent questions as Michael's mouth quested over his, giving without taking, promising without demanding. Josiah used that kiss and the courage it provided to take a few steps to the side, bringing Michael with him, until his legs hit the side of the bed.

Bed. Hot man. Closed door. Yes, please.

For all his hesitations and uncertainty earlier in the day, Josiah wanted this. Even if he and Michael weren't a forever thing, they were definitely a "right now" thing Josiah wanted more than anything else in the world. To be held and comforted by this man. To make love to this man and be loved in return, even for only one night.

It won't be just one night, though. It won't.

"Please," Josiah whispered between kisses. "Please, Michael."

"Whatever you want, baby. Just ask."

"I want you."

"You've got me any way you want me." Michael kissed the tip of his nose, then pressed their foreheads together. Josiah closed his eyes and leaned into the pressure and warmth. "I want to know what every inch of your skin tastes like."

Josiah couldn't stop a soft moan of pure need. He rubbed his palms up and down Michael's chest, curious what he looked like beyond the layers of flannel and cotton, desperate for fewer layers between them. He was also nervous to be skin-to-skin with another man again, even one he admired, trusted, and genuinely wanted to be with. To be with now, three months from now, maybe even forever, even though *forever* was a terrifying concept when sometimes *tomorrow* was too big to ponder.

All that mattered was right now. And right now, he wanted Michael.

"I want to taste you, too," Josiah whispered. "I'm tired of being scared. I'm tired of pretending I don't have feelings for you, Michael. I don't know what will happen tomorrow, and I don't care. For the first time in a long time, all I can think about is right now. Here. With you."

Michael released a long, warm breath that gusted across Josiah's lips. "I have feelings for you, too, and I think you know that. I want to make love with you, too, and I have for a while, but you need to promise me something. Promise if I do anything you don't like, you will speak up. We'll talk and change things up. Whatever it takes so everything we do is perfect."

"Promise." He pressed a kiss to Michael's mouth. "I'm not sure exactly how far I want to go tonight, but do you, um, have stuff?"

"I do. Might have to check the dates, though, because it's stuff I brought with me from Austin."

"Really? You and Kenny never went bare?"

"No. He was always really fussy about anal sex and the mess and not wanting me to get his come all over the sheets after. I didn't care one way or another, but looking back, I'm glad we always used condoms, considering he cheated on me so much our last few years together."

"I'm glad you were safe." The idea of Kenny running around on Michael—his dear, sweet, supportive Michael—and then having sex with him bare infuriated Josiah. Kenny could have exposed him to all manner of things. Maybe fussiness wasn't such a bad—wait. "He didn't want *you* getting *his* come on the sheets?"

"Yeah." Michael's tender smile never wavered. "I'm a switch, but Kenny wasn't a fan of bottoming. He tried a few times for me but it just wasn't something that got him off, so we stuck to the other way. How about you?"

"Me?" Josiah's brain was still stuck on Michael liking to bottom, when everything about the cowboy screamed alpha top. The mental image of Michael bending over and letting someone fuck him heated Josiah's blood in a fantastic way and sent happy signals right to his dick.

"Yes, you." Michael brushed a thumb across his cheekbone. "What do you prefer?"

"I, um… I'm not sure?"

He gently drew Josiah down to sit beside him on the bed, that smile still firmly in place. Dark eyes gazed at him with curiosity and not an ounce of judgment. "Tell me why you aren't sure."

"Because the majority of my experiences with sex were transactional, rather than emotional. When I was homeless, I did what I had to do. When I was with Andy, things were really good. I know he saw me as a person, but he was very much an exclusive top, so I never got to explore that with him. Then I was too busy mourning him and working, establishing myself, to date. I wasn't into casual like a lot of guys. And then Seamus, well, I don't have to tell you what our roles were."

"So you've never topped?"

"No." He expected to be embarrassed admitting to not having tried something most gay men had explored by the age of twenty-eight, but he wasn't. Because Michael wasn't judging him, he was asking questions and learning. Collecting information so their first time together was wonderful, instead of peppered with regrets. Josiah didn't want to regret his time with Michael, not a single second of it.

"Do you want to?" Michael lightly squeezed his hip. "Because I would love to feel you inside me, Josiah. Very much."

"Yeah?"

"Absolutely. And again, we don't have to do it tonight if you aren't ready."

Josiah was getting more ready by the minute. A huge part of his hesitation to advance his physical relationship with Michael was what Michael would expect from him. He'd assumed Michael would want to top, and Josiah had spent too many nights trying to sleep while his backside ached and Seamus snored away, to go there without a lot of mental and physical prep. And now Michael was flipping what Josiah had assumed to be true, and while his brain was still stumbling a little, his dick was very much on board with this turn of events.

"How about we see where things go," Josiah said. "Is that okay?"

"That sounds perfect. And to get things started, may I take my shirt off?"

"Please."

Michael turned the simple act of unbuttoning his flannel shirt into the sexiest kind of striptease, taking one button at a time, top to bottom, allowing the red-and-black material to reveal the smoothness of the white tee underneath. A white tee that stretched over his abs and dipped into the waist of his jeans. Michael rarely tucked his flannels in so the tucked-in undershirt was oddly sexy.

The flannel shirt hit the floor, showing off his muscled arms and shoulders. Not the bodybuilder type of muscles found on gym rats and fitness magazine cover models, but the kind created by hard work shoveling and roping and doing manual labor five days a week. Michael tugged the undershirt out of his jeans and added it to the pile on the floor. His torso was the same golden brown as his arms, with a smattering of dark brown hair on his abs and down his belly. The rest disappeared behind his belt and jeans, and Josiah resisted the urge to lean over and inhale. To touch and lick and explore the body on display for him.

And why the hell was he resisting what Michael offered so freely?

Josiah ran his palms over Michael's bare arms, up to his shoulders, and then down his pecs to his lower belly. Light caresses that left no mark behind on the skin but imprinted his touch and warmth on Josiah's senses. He stroked Michael's back and arms again, loving the way Michael's eyes went half-lidded, his whole body relaxing by degrees under the impromptu massage.

"Feels amazing," Michael whispered. "Want to touch you, too."

"Okay." Josiah snagged the back of his shirt collar and tugged, hoping to be as sexy as Michael was in removing his clothes. Only the shirt got stuck around his head, didn't lift enough in the front, and his glasses snagged in the material. Michael had to rescue him and his glasses from the shirt, and they both ended up laughing over the entire production. Josiah slid his glasses back on. "That's not how I'd planned things going."

Michael brushed his nose against Josiah's, then kissed the tip. "I think it went perfectly. I love that we can laugh while being intimate. It speaks to our level of comfort with each other, I think."

"It does." He couldn't remember ever laughing in bed with Seamus, and he was not going to bring his ex into bed with them now. Tonight was he and Michael, no one else. Not Seamus, not Kenny, not Andy or anyone else. Just them.

Josiah scooted toward the middle of the bed and pulled Michael on top of him, the position similar to how they'd kissed that first time under the stars. Michael rested one thigh between Josiah's legs, a delightful pressure against his hard dick, Michael's own erection firm against Josiah's hip. Michael nuzzled his cheek before plundering his mouth, licking inside, exploring every possible inch with lips and tongue, leaving Josiah dizzy with desire.

They kissed and rutted together, and Josiah barely noticed when Michael slotted his entire body between Josiah's legs. Their jeans-covered cocks rubbed in a simulation of sex that was everything he wanted and not quite enough. He reached between them and thumbed at his own fly button. The lack of space made the zipper difficult, until Michael sat up and helped. He tugged Josiah's jeans off, followed by his socks, leaving him in his boxer briefs.

Michael watched him, cheeks flushed, chest heaving slightly, one hand fiddling with his own fly.

"Go ahead," Josiah said.

In mere moments, they were both stripped down to just their underwear, and then Michael was back on top of him. The heat of his erection thrust against Josiah's, over and over, driving him higher. He could definitely get off like this and go to sleep a happy man, but he wanted something more. Something primal that had settled inside him tonight—the urgent desire to be inside Michael. To share this one special thing with him and try something he'd yet to explore.

To fully embrace who he was deep inside, within the safe place provided by the man in his arms.

"Get your stuff," Josiah said. "Please?"

"Fuck, yes." Michael scrambled off the bed and to

his dresser. Yanked open a squeaky drawer. Pulled out a box of condoms and bottle of lube, which he brought back to the bed. "It's been a hot minute, so you'll have to prep me a little."

"Of course." He never wanted to do anything that hurt Michael, not even by accident, and especially not in bed.

Michael peeled off his underwear, showing off his straining cock. While he was kneeling on the bed, Josiah took the opportunity to reach out and clasp it at the root. To stroke him base to tip, enjoying the way he gasped and moaned. The way his balls got tighter at Josiah's handling and the little pearls of fluid oozed from the slit. "Do you prefer to get off before or after?"

"After," Michael panted. "Sometimes I can during but it's been a while."

"Okay. Um, position?" Josiah preferred being on top so he had more control over the sex, but that hadn't happened often with He Who Shall Not Be In Bed With Them.

"Whatever you want, baby, but doggie might be easier for your first time."

"Okay." Even though he wouldn't be able to look Michael in the eyes, the position gave Josiah more control. They could explore other things later, as long as Josiah didn't get laughed right out of the bedroom for his lack of technique or finesse.

Prepping Michael with the lube was actually pretty fun. Michael knelt on his hands and knees facing the headboard, ass tilted into the air, while Josiah carefully worked a slick finger inside him. Michael wiggled his hips, encouraging him, head angled to the side so Josiah could see his ever-present smile. The tight heat around his finger made Josiah impossibly harder as he imagined that pressure around his dick. Soon he'd know.

"Two," Michael said.

Too soon, Michael was fucking himself on two of Josiah's fingers, and the sight of that puckered muscle stretching to take him made Josiah a little bit crazy. Desperate to get his dick in there before he erupted in his briefs. "You ready?"

"Yeah. Can't wait to feel you in me."

"Me too." Josiah tugged his underwear off and tossed them, not caring where they landed. His trembling fingers had a minor struggle with the condom, but he eventually got the damned thing on his dick. Spread on more lube. Notched the tip of his cock to Michael's glistening entrance. "Are you sure?"

"Never been more sure in my life." Michael reached behind him to squeeze Josiah's hip, a firm hold that also pulled him forward while Michael pressed back. The intense pressure against his glans made Josiah cry out with absolute pleasure. Michael encouraged him with light thrusts that slowly, almost painfully slowly, pulled Josiah inside him.

"Oh fuck," Josiah said as his cock disappeared in Michael's body. The heat and glide was almost too much sensation, too overwhelming a thing. Too much and not enough, and when Michael clenched around him, Josiah stopped thinking and allowed his body to take charge. To snap his hips, burying himself deep in Michael's body. To grab Michael by the hips and thrust, in and out, skin slapping skin. Instinct drove him, an encompassing need to climax, to claim, to experience this brand-new thing for as long as possible.

"Fuuuuuck," Michael drawled, his hole squeezing impossibly tight. So tight Josiah stopped moving. Michael shuddered and panted, and it took Josiah a moment to realize why: Michael had come. One hand was still braced on the bed while the other milked the last of his release, until he let go and grabbed the headboard. The position angled his hips down, pushing him deeper onto Josiah's dick.

He kissed the back of Michael's neck. "Want me to pull out?"

"Hell no. Come in me, baby."

Trusting Michael to know his body, Josiah rushed toward his own climax. It didn't take long before his balls drew up and his release shot out his dick. Pretty lights winked behind his shut eyelids as Josiah thrust through it, savoring the sensations buffeting his body for as long as possible. Coveting every motion and sound until his dick began to soften. He reluctantly pulled out and dumped the condom over the side of the bed.

Michael flipped onto his back and collapsed, the perfect picture of a satiated man. Josiah took his glasses off and tossed them onto the foot of the bed. Snuggled up to Michael, half-draped over his body, one leg between his in a possessive way. He kissed Michael for a long time as his body came down from its endorphin high, explosive energy replaced by satisfied fatigue.

"How do you feel?" Michael asked.

"Amazing. That was amazing." He nuzzled his face

into the side of Michael's neck. "Can we hold each other for a while?"

"For as long as you want, baby." Michael draped a possessive hand over Josiah's hip and squeezed. "That's a promise."

Chapter Twenty

Josiah woke with a start and flailed for several agonizing seconds, unsure where he was or why. The sunlight was brighter than in the trailer, the bed a lot softer, and he was surrounded by the combined scents of cologne and fabric softener. He was also alone in a large bed, dressed only in his underwear, his lack of glasses making it hard to take in the fuzzy room.

Then he got a deeper inhale of the cologne and it clicked: Michael's room. They'd had sex last night. But why was he alone the morning after?

He fumbled at the side table for his glasses and shoved them on, kind of missing the contacts he'd yet to replace because Michael had once said he thought his glasses were adorable. The room came into sharp focus. He was very much alone. Before he could start overthinking that, the door swung open and Michael stepped inside with a small tray. Michael's entire body lit up with the force of his smile. He slid the tray with two steaming mugs—Josiah's nose said coffee—and a plate with some sort of toast onto the dresser, then crawled onto the bed on his hands and knees. Planted a firm kiss on Josiah's very willing mouth.

"Morning," Michael said. "I wanted to get back here before you woke up."

"Well, you did bring food so I guess I can forgive you for me waking up alone on the morning after." He pretended to pout.

It worked perfectly. Michael tugged the covers down and manhandled Josiah onto his lap in a new position both strange and intimate. Josiah looped his arms around Michael's neck and relaxed into his hold, barely aware of being nearly naked while Michael wore sweatpants and a T-shirt.

"How are you this morning?" Michael asked.

"I feel great. I was a little discombobulated when I woke up, but I think that's because I slept like a rock. I don't usually sleep so heavily."

"Probably a combination of an endorphin crash and maybe feeling safe?"

"I definitely felt safe." He kissed the side of Michael's neck, and Michael's early morning scruff abraded his lips in a pleasant way. "Thank you for helping me experience something amazing last night. I am very glad we took that step."

"You are more than welcome. I'm grateful I was able to give you a safe place to explore something you wanted to try. And if you aren't completely sure how you felt about it, I am very much down with giving it a second try."

Josiah laughed at the perfectly innocent tone of Michael's voice. A cartoon halo practically glowed above his head. "I think a second try is very likely to happen in the near future, but I definitely need coffee first."

"Absolutely." Michael slid the tray onto the bed and

handed Josiah one of the mugs. "As you like it, Mr. Sheridan. Black with a teaspoon of sugar."

"Perfect." Josiah balanced the mug on his blanket-covered knee so he could study the toast. Instead of just white bread and butter, the toasted triangles had something brown sprinkled on top. "What is that?"

"Cinnamon toast. It was something Mom used to make for breakfast on special occasions, even though it's probably one of the simplest things in the world. Just toast with butter, cinnamon, and sugar on top."

"I love that. I don't have any specific food memories of my mother. Most of the life I remember with my parents was about survival." He picked up a piece of the toast and inhaled the warm, comforting scent of cinnamon. "Although Mom had a way of making cheap white bread and margarine feel like a gourmet meal."

"Because she loved you, and that love was in the buttered bread."

"Yeah."

They feasted on the simplest, loveliest of breakfasts, sipping bitter coffee in between bites of the sweet toast. Josiah had never eaten a better, more satisfying breakfast in his life, and he couldn't imagine a better person with which to share it. Michael fed him bites of toast, and Josiah took great delight in licking bits of crumb and butter from his fingertips. The finger licking seemed to amp Michael up, but before anything could get started his cell rang.

Michael grabbed his phone off the side table. "House number." He answered. "Hey, Dad. Yeah, I'll be down soon." He tossed the phone to the foot of the bed. "Dad's ready to get up, so I guess this is where I have to be an adult, put my hormones in a box, and go take care of him when all I want to do is smother you into the bed and never let you go."

"As wonderful as being smothered by you sounds, go take care of Elmer. I'll bring our dishes down to the kitchen." He glanced at the dregs of his coffee. "Um, are you going to tell him about us?"

"I'm not sure I'll have to, to be honest. But if he asks directly, do I have your permission to tell him? That we're together?"

Josiah worried his bottom lip with his teeth for less than three seconds. "Yes, you do. I don't see your dad being against us in theory, but I'm a touch worried what he'll think about us pursuing this while we're employer/employee. He's a little old-fashioned about some things."

"He can be, yes. I also think he's realized recently that it's more important to embrace what's in front of us rather than cling to what's old and familiar. To take the now instead of the comfortable. We both existed in our own anger for two decades, and it just ended up hurting both of us." Michael kissed him, his lips tasting of sugar and spice. "I love my dad, and I want him to accept all of me. Not just me being gay, which he's known for half my life, but who I choose to date. Who I choose to fall in love with."

The weight of those final three words punched Josiah right in the solar plexus, and he had trouble taking a full breath. They crushed him beneath their significance, and he wasn't sure how to surface again so he could breathe right. For all Josiah wanted to admit some variation of the statement, he couldn't find the words, so he went with what his brain could manage in that moment. "He will. Accept all of you, I mean. All of us both."

"From your mouth to the universe's ears." Michael gave him one more kiss, then left the room.

Josiah took a quick shower, dressed, and then carried the tray of empty dishes downstairs. Elmer was settled on the love seat with the TV on, and he waved a polite hello as Josiah passed. He didn't seem surprised at all by Josiah walking down the stairs with a tray of coffee mugs in his hands, and that simple thing buoyed his confidence.

Michael was in front of the stove stirring something in a pan. A quick glance showed scrambled eggs. "Can you press down the toaster for me?" Michael asked.

"Sure." Josiah put his dishes in the sink, then pushed the button on two slices of wheat bread. "How did your dad seem this morning? He didn't say a word to me."

"He seemed fine. He's not usually a subtle person, so maybe he's waiting for us to say or do something first and, if you'll pardon the expression, come out to him."

"Could be." Josiah rested his chin on Michael's shoulder and watched him stir the eggs. It stretched his neck a tad but the slight discomfort was worth it to be close to Michael while he cooked a simple, healthy breakfast for his father. "I almost feel guilty for liking this as much as I do."

"Liking what specifically?"

"All of this. You bringing me coffee in bed. Making breakfast. Just being together as a couple instead of friends."

"I like all of that, too. Can you get the nondairy butter and a few strawberries out of the fridge?"

"Sure." Josiah fetched the two items as requested. Washed the berries and put them on a plate. When the toast popped, he put a light smear of butter on each piece. He finished just as Michael began to plate the eggs. Elmer fussed sometimes about the healthier alternatives they fixed for him—like whole wheat bread versus the plain white sandwich bread he'd grown up eating—but he maintained a healthy appetite at each meal.

Josiah poured a glass of juice and followed Michael into the living room. Elmer thanked them both for his breakfast and started eating while watching a black-and-white Western. Michael pulled Josiah down beside him on the couch and sipped at his second mug of coffee. The familiarity of it relaxed Josiah into leaning his shoulder against Michael's.

During a commercial break, Elmer asked, "What are you boys up to today?"

"Not really sure," Michael replied.

"Last night Wayne mentioned you wanting to ride their horses for fun, maybe teach Josiah how to ride, too. Be a good day for it. Sunny, not too cold."

Josiah opened his mouth to reply but nothing came out. That day at the Founder's Day Picnic when Hugo asked if he knew how to ride seemed like a lifetime ago, and somehow also yesterday. So much had happened since then, and he had to admit he did want to learn. He wanted to experience something that was part of Michael's everyday life. Elmer's too, although to a lesser degree now.

"What do you think?" Michael asked.

"I'd love to learn how to ride," Josiah replied. "I've

been around horses a few times but never actually on one. Do you think you'll be a good teacher?"

"Well, I'll never have a pupil win any ribbons in dressage or competition, but I can teach you how to stay in the saddle and guide the horse where you want them to go. Both very useful skills, even for in-home nurses."

"Excellent," Elmer said, as excited by the idea as someone who'd be doing the riding himself. "I'll give Wayne a call in a little while and tell him you both are coming over to ride. I'm sure he'll have some good horses ready for you."

"Sounds like a plan?" Josiah looked at Michael.

Michael grinned right back. "Sounds like a great plan. I'll even pack us a small picnic lunch we can eat in the middle of nowhere."

"You promise you'll lead us both home?"

"Promise."

And that's what happened about three hours later. Michael prepared them a lunch he wouldn't let Josiah peek at while he put it into a backpack with ice packs. Josiah fidgeted in his seat while Michael drove them over to Woods Ranch, a less familiar location for Josiah. They had acres of land that stretched far beyond the horizon line. Josiah couldn't imagine being responsible for so much property at once, but the Woods family had been there for several generations.

So much history was etched into every rock, every scrub tree, and every dry gulch. The history of a family with deep roots in one place—something Josiah had no experience with, and it left his mood a touch down when they arrived at the main house. He didn't have family members only a few miles away who came over regularly for Sunday supper. He didn't know what it was like to walk across a porch that multiple generations had walked across before.

Wayne met them at the entrance to the barn and shook their hands. "Brand and Alan are out with the herd," he said, "but I made sure we had a good riding mare for young Josiah there. I think Shirley Temple is a good horse for him."

A horse named Shirley Temple? "Don't tell me she's got a curled mane," Josiah deadpanned.

Wayne chuckled. "Nah, just got a sweet disposition. Don't take this wrong, but she's the horse we let the grandkids ride when they're in the mood. She's real good with the youngest ones."

"No offense taken. I am very definitely a novice here, so I welcome the help. The last thing I need is another concussion from falling off a horse."

Michael scowled, probably not liking the reminder of that night in the barn. Josiah didn't like remembering it either, but it had happened. They couldn't pretend it hadn't.

"I wouldn't worry about that," Wayne said. "Miss Shirley Temple isn't one to buck or bolt. You two enjoy yourselves. Just stick to the east pasture, so you don't stumble over the herd."

"Not a problem," Michael replied. "Thank you so much."

"You're quite welcome, young man."

Wayne ambled off. Josiah followed Michael into the massive barn. His nose itched from the combined odors of horse, hay, manure, and a dozen other things. Josiah had never been inside the barn before, and he took in the rows of horse stalls, most still with an occupant, that made up the first half of the barn. There was a tack room full of saddles, bridles, blankets, and other gear Josiah couldn't name.

Beyond that was a larger, open space. "It's for when the cows are close to giving birth," Michael said. "We bring them in, make sure they're monitored, and we have hands and a vet on call for the new calves. None due anytime soon, though, which is why it's empty."

"That makes sense. Didn't Woods Ranch feature a heifer giving birth at the county fair this year?"

"They did. Brand told me about that. It's another of those circle of life things I want more kids to experience firsthand, not just in books or online. Maybe one day, huh?"

"Hey." Josiah wrapped his hand around Michael's. "I believe you can accomplish anything you set your mind to. Whether it's turning your dad's land into a farm animal petting zoo, or inventing the next blockbuster social media site, you will make it happen. And I will be rooting for you to succeed."

"And just when I thought you couldn't be any more amazing. You are outamazing yourself."

"It's fun keeping you on your toes, Mr. Pearce."

"And you do it so well, Mr. Sheridan."

After a quick peek into the hayloft, because Josiah had never been in one before and probably never would again—the vertical wood-slat ladder made him a little dizzy—Michael walked Josiah through the process of taking out Shirley Temple. Then he brought out another horse named Mercutio for himself to ride. Josiah couldn't quite haul himself up into the saddle, so Michael brought out a small, two-step stool.

"It's how we all learned to mount as kids," Michael

said. "You have to work on the core strength as well as the right push-off from the ground. You'll get there."

"Hope so." He was a tad jealous of how easily Michael mounted Mercutio, but the man also did this for a living. He'd better be good at it.

Once they were both situated, Michael led them out. Josiah gently nudged Shirley Temple in the flanks like Michael told him, and the big horse lurched forward. Her gentle, plodding motion felt a bit like being in a small boat on the rolling ocean, and Josiah relaxed into the movement. Michael went east, over sprawling grasslands dotted with the occasional small tree or huge chunk of rock.

The breeze blew steadily around them, and Josiah was glad he'd worn his winter coat. For a long time, the only sound was the rustling of grass, the thump of hooves, and the creak of leather. They didn't talk; there was no need. This wasn't about conversation, it was about the experience they were sharing. Michael looked so gorgeous on his horse, straight-backed and square-shouldered, his hat casting shadows across his handsome face. Everything from the jeans to the boots to the denim jacket was the picture of an American cowboy.

My reluctant cowboy. Don't ever change, Michael.

Michael picked a spot near a mostly dry creek. The dirt channel was about four feet wide, with the smallest trickle of water dancing down its path. "It runs heavy after a good rain," Michael said. "We don't use it much this time of year, but come spring it's a good pasture for the herd."

"Gotcha."

Dismounting his horse was an even bigger challenge than getting up, but Michael gave him a hand down.

Without a stool, Josiah would definitely need a boost to get back up later.

For now, they spread a blanket over a patch of dry earth and settled in with sandwiches, apples, a bag of pretzels to share, and bottles of water. Not fancy food but that didn't matter. Again, it was all about the experience, and Josiah loved being here with Michael. Doing something as simple as eating a ham and cheese sandwich while their horses grazed nearby.

"Have you thought about keeping your own horses again?" Josiah asked.

"Sometimes. Even after Dad sold the herd, we did keep our horses for a few years longer. Mom couldn't seem to part with them. She loved riding. We both did. Sometimes we'd go out together, just to ride and feel the sun on our faces, the wind all around us. Having to sell them hurt a lot. I don't think she ever fully forgave Dad for that, even though we couldn't afford them anymore."

"Those sound like wonderful memories. Riding with your mother, I mean."

"I know what you meant, and they are. For as awful as her death was, it's a lot easier to remember all the good things than it used to be. Going home and facing your ghosts isn't for everyone, but it was definitely what I needed to do. To face them down and forgive Dad for the things I blamed him for, especially the things that weren't his fault."

"You got closure."

"I think I did." Michael clicked his tongue. Mercutio wandered over and took the apple core from Michael's palm. "I'm done passing blame and holding anger inside. I did that for half my life and I lost almost everything. It made me realize the things I truly needed were here the whole time."

Josiah squeezed his wrist. "I'm glad to be a small part of that journey."

"You are definitely not a small part." Michael hauled Josiah onto his lap and wrapped two strong arms around his waist. "You are a hugely important part. Never doubt that. Whether my Austin house sells today or in ten years, I'm here, now. Taking things one day at a time. And to answer your question from earlier, I like the idea of owning horses again. I can't afford it right now, and the barn is nowhere near ready to house a cat, much less a horse, but maybe one day."

"Cool. Because I can see myself really liking this whole horse riding thing. It's freeing in its own way."

"It is. Just wait until you learn how to gallop. There is nothing more freeing to me than galloping across the open countryside, with nothing around you except Mother Nature and all her glory." He nuzzled the side of Josiah's neck with his nose. "I didn't have that in Austin. Maybe that's why I disappeared for so long. I tried to be someone I'm not."

"A city boy?"

"Yep. A rich city boy. Don't get me wrong, the money was really nice. Not worrying about budgets and if fixing the car meant not paying the electric on time. I took for granted having more money than I needed, and I will never do that again. I'll never take anything I have for granted."

Josiah kissed him, a leisurely exploration that didn't deepen. Even though they were very much alone and the horses wouldn't care, Josiah wasn't into outdoor sex. Too many bugs and itchy things that could get into sensitive places.

They packed the food up and lazed around on the blanket for a while, pointing out shapes in the clouds above, until the sun started getting a bit too low on the horizon. Josiah needed a big boost from Michael to get back on Shirley Temple and thankfully, the big beast simply stood there while he struggled to right himself in the saddle.

Michael swung up like the professional he was, backpack and all, and they headed back to the barn. By the time they returned, the sun treated them to a brilliant color display as it set in the west, pulling the curtains on another day in the tiny town of Weston, Texas. When they finished untacking the horses, Brand appeared and invited them to Sunday supper. Josiah politely turned him down, eager to get home and check on Elmer. Today was the longest he'd been on his own in one stretch since the stroke.

Three vehicles were in the wide driveway, which wasn't altogether odd on a Sunday, since Pastor Lorne still stopped by to visit, but it seemed awfully late. And that wasn't the preacher's usual black sedan. The unfamiliar vehicle was a two-door sports car, similar to what Michael drove, and Josiah was pretty sure the brand was a hybrid.

"What the hell?" Michael said as he jerked the gearshift into park.

"Do you know who that is?" Josiah asked.

"Can't be."

Before Josiah could venture further, the front door opened and ejected a brown and white dog with a boxy head that reminded Josiah of a pit bull. The dog raced toward the car. Josiah reached for the lock button, panic spiking through him at the idea of a potentially dangerous animal coming right at them. Michael opened his door and scrambled out. Before Josiah could yell a warning, Michael dropped to his knees, opened his arms, and cried out when the dog barreled right into his chest.

Truly scared now, Josiah got out, too, and circled the car, ready to defend Michael with everything he had. Except the dog was licking Michael's face, Michael was hugging the dog, and crying, and it hit Josiah at all once: Rosco. This was Michael's dog.

And one glance at the front porch, where Elmer sat in his chair next to a smiling stranger, sent a blast of anger through Josiah's chest.

The infamous ex, Kenny, was here.

Chapter Twenty-One

Michael had driven home from Woods Ranch in such a delightfully positive mood he half expected rainbows and glitter to start shooting out of his ears. Between making love with Josiah last night—something he very much wanted to do again, and soon—and their amazing day at the ranch, nothing short of a nuclear detonation in the middle of town could spoil his happy.

Until he saw Kenny's car parked next to Dad's pickup. A chill had spread through his entire body, leaving his fingers trembling with anger and shock. There was absolutely no reason on earth for Kenny to have driven up from Austin, none. And yet there was his car, practically smirking at him with its rear lights and shiny bumper.

"What the hell?" Michael yanked the gear into Park and reached for the door handle, ready to storm the house and demand to know what the fuck was going on.

"Do you know who that is?"

He barely heard Josiah's question over the roar in his own head. "Can't be." And then the door opened and the most beautiful sight in the world had come racing toward him. Rosco was there. Rosco was barking and charging the car, and Michael hadn't been able to think. He'd somehow gotten out of the car and was hugging the life out of his boy. His beautiful pittie, who'd once been days away from being dumped in a kill shelter by his previous owner, until Kenny agreed to buy him from them.

Rosco had been a dream dog from day one. He never bit, he knew a few basic commands, and he was the biggest snuggle bug ever, spending days sleeping by Michael's feet and nights at the foot of their bed. Rosco licked his face and whined, his round body never stopping its wiggle-dance of joy, big paws stepping all over Michael's legs and junk, and he didn't care.

"Oh my God, boy, I've missed you." He held Rosco's face in his hands so he could look into those intelligent brown eyes. "You look good. So fucking good." Rosco licked his face again, and Michael had no shame in the few tears that spilled from his eyes.

"Is this Rosco?" Josiah asked. He stood near the car's fender, body illuminated by the headlights Michael hadn't turned off.

"Yeah, this is Rosco. Come here, he wouldn't hurt a hornet if it stung him."

Josiah came closer and offered a hand, which Rosco sniffed, then licked. "He's beautiful. I didn't realize he was a pit bull."

"Technically, he's a bit of a mutt, but he's got the face shape and body that most shelters automatically use to classify a dog as a pittie. We saved him from death row." Okay, so technically Kenny had saved him from being surrendered, and Michael had been leery at first, but Rosco had won Michael's heart that first day with his silly grunts and kisses.

And it struck Michael then that Rosco hadn't driven

himself to Weston. He looked up. Right at the porch where Kenny stood next to Dad, arms crossed, his posture oddly relaxed, considering the screaming match they'd had the last time Michael and Kenny had seen each other in person.

Michael stood and strode toward the house with as much authority as he could muster with Rosco weaving around his legs and trying to trip him. Josiah followed at a slight distance after turning off the car.

"What are you doing here?" Michael asked, working to keep his tone even when he wanted to snap and snarl. To protect his family from potential danger.

"It's almost Thanksgiving," Kenny replied with a bright, toothy smile, turning on his charm in a familiar way. "I wanted to surprise you."

"Why? Don't get me wrong, I'm fucking thrilled to see my dog, especially when you said you rehomed him." He scratched one of Rosco's ears. "But you and I don't have any more business together. You made that very clear when you cut me out of our company and stole my patents."

"That's old news, baby. I drove all this way with a barking dog in the car, and it's freezing up here. Can we go inside and talk?"

Michael looked at Dad, who shrugged. Kenny must have spun a great story to get Dad outside so he could unlock the gate and let Kenny onto the property. And as much as Michael wanted to go inside and slam the door in Kenny's face, he was curious why he'd made the long drive north. Plus, Rosco time. "Yeah, I guess we can talk."

He started forward but realized after three steps that Josiah was no longer beside him. Michael stopped and turned. Josiah's expression was perfectly neutral, but something flickered in his eyes. Something that looked a lot like doubt.

"I'm going back to my trailer," Josiah said. "You probably need privacy for this."

Michael's chest squeezed in an unhappy way. "You don't have to. I'm with *you*."

"I know. Go talk to him. Text me later if you want." Before Michael could form a response with his tangled tongue, Josiah turned and strode to the trailer. A trailer that, for Michael, was merely a formality at this point. Josiah belonged in the house with him, period. But if space was what Josiah needed, Michael would respect that.

Once Josiah was safely inside the trailer, Michael walked up onto the porch.

"That's one beautiful dog you got there," Dad said to Michael. "Friendliest thing I've ever met, even more than Jackson's Dog."

"Who's Jackson?" Kenny asked.

"Someone I work with," Michael replied, not ready to delve into that right now. That he'd failed to sell the house and had gone back to blue-collar labor to make ends meet and take care of his ailing father. He could imagine the way Kenny had probably sneered at the town as he drove through it on his way here. "Let's go inside."

He held open the door, and Dad wheeled directly down the hall to his room. Even though Michael's stomach gurgled softly for supper, he perched on the middle of the love seat, leaving the couch Kenny's only spot to sit. Rosco stood in front of Michael until Michael patted the cushion. Then Rosco jumped up.

Good to see Kenny hadn't slacked on his discipline. Rosco was allowed on furniture but only with permission. It had made it a lot easier to take him to friends' houses for visits.

"Why are you really here?" Michael asked. No pleasantries, no polite requests for something to drink.

"I told you, it's almost Thanksgiving, and I wanted to see you. You won't answer any of my texts."

"Gee, I wonder why?"

Kenny rested his ankle on his knee and leaned forward, hands in his lap, a familiar position he took whenever he wanted to charm someone into agreeing with him. "Look, baby, we both behaved badly this past year, and we were so good together for so long that I don't want us at odds forever. Can't we find a way to be friends again?"

"Why? Don't you have a bazillion friends back in Austin? What do you need me for? You made it very clear your only use for me was as an ATM, and once you got everything you wanted, you kicked my broke ass to the curb. Or am I remembering things wrong?"

"Water under the bridge, baby."

"Please stop calling me baby. I am not your baby anymore, and I am with someone else."

Kenny blinked hard, his confident veneer cracking the tiniest bit. "Really? You managed to find someone else in this tiny village of obscurity?"

"Yes, I did. He is kind and generous and doesn't give a shit about the money I do or don't have, because he can support himself just fine. Unlike someone else in this room."

He frowned. "I supported myself."

"Off my creativity and talent, not your own. You saw

a meal ticket early on, knew I was someone desperate for approval and acceptance, and I fell for it. Hook, line, sinker, and fucking boat. But I'm not that same gullible college graduate I once was. The only thing you have that I still want is right here, and you know it." Michael placed his hand on Rosco's neck. "That's why you brought him with you. To manipulate me into something."

"I brought him because you love him, and I wanted to be generous in the spirit of the holiday."

"Fine. Say I buy that for a hot second. You didn't drive all the way up here just to wish me a Happy Thanksgiving four days early. What do you really want?"

"Look, Michael, I made some bad decisions. I shouldn't have dumped you the way I did, and I shouldn't have manipulated the contracts to push you out of what you deserved. I am so sorry I did all that. I was selfish and egotistical to think I could do this without my number one guy. Without you."

Alarm bells dinged inside Michael's head. "Do what without me? You got away with millions, Kenny. Where's the money?"

For the first time in the last twenty minutes, Kenny melted into a picture of misery. "It's gone. I got taken in by a long con, okay? I lost everything. I've got my car, a few hundred in cash, and that's it."

Michael's initial impulse to gloat about Kenny being in the same position he'd left Michael in warred with his empathy. He knew exactly what it felt like to be almost broke with no immediate way to fix it. And Kenny didn't have the cushion of a parent to go home to and live with while he got back on his feet. Kenny's parents had been incredibly homophobic and unaccepting of him, having turned their back on him a long time ago. But Kenny had also lied, cheated, and manipulated Michael, and those things were not easily forgiven.

Not by a long shot.

"You lost everything in two months?" Michael asked. "Including the app I created?"

"Yes, okay? I met someone who promised me everything. He wanted to change the app so it appealed more to the younger generation, and I bought what he sold me. Then he took everything, and I am so sorry I did that to you, Michael. I never truly understood how much I hurt you until someone did it to me."

"You know, as much as I want to take some sort of perverse joy in seeing you like this, I don't. And again, I don't know why you're here and not crashing with one of your dozens of friends."

"Same reason you left town." Kenny's eyes glistened, and Michael was glad to have a dog on half his lap, because he hated seeing Kenny cry. "Some friends only love you for your money, and they disappear when the money does, too." He coughed. "I didn't have anywhere else to go."

Michael let out a long, disgruntled breath as he stroked Rosco's neck and back. Rosco began licking his front paw, a familiar gesture of contentment. "I'm sorry you're stuck, but I don't know what you expect me to do. The house hasn't sold. I live paycheck to paycheck right now so I don't have anything to loan you."

"Loan?"

"Yes, loan. Do you think after everything that's happened I'd just give you money if I had any to give? I can give you forty bucks for one night at the local motel, but that's about as far as my finances stretch right now."

"Motel? But you've got this big house. Surely there's a guest room Rosco and I can stay in."

"Rosco is more than welcome to stay here, since I'm pretty sure the motel has a no-pets policy, but if you came up here expecting to crash my life for the next week or whatever, that's not happening. I have a boyfriend, a job I really enjoy, and a life here in Weston. You are not part of those things, Kenny."

"If you and your boyfriend are solid, he shouldn't mind me staying over one night. We'll leave in the morning."

The "we'll leave" pissed Michael off, cementing his suspicion that the only reason Kenny had brought Rosco was as a bargaining chip. A way to guilt-trip Michael into acquiescing to his requests for a few extra hours with his dog. A dog who'd always liked Michael more than Kenny, because Michael had taken him to the dog parks and on long walks and cuddled him randomly throughout the day.

But more than throwing Rosco in his face, Michael silently fumed over the "if he and his boyfriend were solid" remark. Michael didn't have to prove his relationship to Kenny, and as proud as Michael was of Josiah, he didn't want to hand Kenny any more ammunition. Kenny was very much the type to throw the boss/employee thing right back in Michael's face.

"You should have called and saved yourself a hundred bucks in gas," Michael said. "Especially since it sounds like your funds are limited."

Kenny flat-out glared. He was used to getting his way and not to running face-first into obstacles he couldn't bulldoze through or sweet-talk his way out of. Michael never used to fight him, argue with him, or care too much about anything beyond the computer. No more. Now Michael cared about every aspect of his life and the relationships most important to him. Kenny was no longer on that list of relationships. The only way Michael could give Kenny money was to ensure Rosco was looked after and not dumped on another neighbor when things got too hard.

"How are you going to feed Rosco?" Michael asked. "You know he has a sensitive stomach and needs high protein food. You can't just feed him dollar store kibble."

"His food is in the car. He hasn't had dinner yet because I didn't know where we'd be eating. Actually, I haven't eaten dinner yet, either. How's that diner I passed in town?"

"It's good. Just avoid the soup of the day. It's the same soup every day."

"Why don't you come along and show me what's good?"

"How about instead, you check out the diner yourself. I'll stay here, feed Rosco, and then make something for me, Dad, and Josiah."

"Who's Josiah?"

Oh yeah, they hadn't been introduced in the yard earlier and that was Michael's mistake. No wonder Josiah had fled to the trailer. He'd probably felt insulted by the omission and Michael needed to make it up to him soon. "Josiah's the guy who was outside with me earlier. He's been Dad's daytime caregiver, and he rents the trailer from us."

He's also my boyfriend, I think I love him, and he's the best thing in my life.

"He rents from you and you feed him?" Kenny asked

in a sneering tone Michael had heard too many times when Kenny was complaining about his food to a restaurant server. It irritated him then and it irritated him now.

"He's family. Dad adores him, and he's a fantastic friend. He also cooks most nights during the week, and we never asked him to, so I can toss a few meals in his direction once in a while." That was a vast over-simplification of what Josiah meant to his family but, again, Kenny didn't need that kind of ammunition. He already had Rosco.

Kenny watched him silently for several long seconds. Then his eyes started to sparkle with familiar mischief. "Holy shit, you're boning the help. Is he this so-called boyfriend or just a piece on the side? You know, I knew you had a thing for our third pool boy, Travis. Were you sleeping with him, too?"

"Who? Fuck, no, I didn't screw around with any of our pool boys. Christ, I never cheated on you, Kenny, not once. I was too busy padding your bank account and taking your dick up my ass to have any time for fooling around."

"Interesting. You didn't deny boning the nurse."

"My personal life stopped being any of your business the first time you cheated on me. If you want to go into town for dinner, that's fine. Rosco and his food stay here. You can sleep in Dad's room upstairs for one night. That's it. If you choose to stay and keep playing up this Thanksgiving thing, you can go to the motel."

Kenny scowled. "Fine. I'll bring in his food and bowls."

"Fine."

Rosco barely twitched when Kenny went outside,

content and happy to be with Michael again, and Michael felt the same way. He loved his dog so much and didn't want to say goodbye tomorrow or ever again. But he had no real grounds to sue Kenny for custody of a dog. Even though their shared account had paid the vet bills and bought his food, Kenny had brought him into the relationship and both their lawyers agreed a judge would consider him Kenny's property.

Kenny returned with a cloth bag, left it by the door, and went back outside. A moment later, headlights flashed and an engine roared.

It only occurred to Michael then that he hadn't locked the front gate. No sense in doing it right now, since Kenny would be back in an hour or two, and they hadn't had a single odd incident in the couple of weeks since Josiah's attack. Instead of worrying, he filled Rosco's bowls with kibble and water, and then inspected the kitchen for dinner ideas while his beloved dog ate.

Most of his dinner ideas would take too long and he was hungry, so Michael pulled out the stuff to make BLT sandwiches for everyone. Bacon wasn't the best thing for Dad right now, but it cooked fast in a skillet, and they had plenty of lettuce and tomato. While the bacon began frying he called Josiah.

"Hey," Josiah said. "Are you okay?"

"I think so. This whole thing is fucking with my head, but Kenny went into Weston to eat at the diner, and I'm making BLTs for us. Rosco's here too, eating his dinner." Josiah was quiet for so long that Michael checked to make sure his cell hadn't dropped the call. "Hello?"

"I'm here. I, um, ate a frozen thing that was still in

my fridge, so you and Elmer enjoy the BLTs, okay? I'll see you in the morning."

"What? You don't have to hide in the trailer. Kenny is staying one night, because he's fucking broke, and that's it."

"You're letting him stay at the house overnight."

Not a question.

"Yes. One night. I get one more night with my dog before I lose him again tomorrow. I know the timing sucks for us as a couple, but I'd love for you to come over and at least be here while Dad and I eat."

"I don't belong there tonight, Michael. Enjoy your night with Rosco. He's a beautiful dog. I'll see you in the morning, okay?"

Michael wanted to argue and demand Josiah come back to the house, but Josiah had a stubborn streak that only got wider when challenged. He wasn't coming inside tonight, no matter what Michael said, and that hurt. It hurt, but he also understood Josiah keeping his distance. He had to be so confused about everything tonight and likely doubting his place in Michael's life. Michael had no doubt about Josiah's place and importance, and he vowed to show that to Josiah.

"Okay," Michael said. "See you in the morning for breakfast."

"See you then. 'Night."

"Good night, Josiah."

Deflated by the conversation, Michael sliced a tomato and pulled a few leaves of lettuce off the head of iceberg. Got four slices of bread ready to toast when the bacon was closer to finished. Once the bacon was draining on a paper towel, he went to get Dad.

"Heard someone drive off," Dad said. "Who left?"

"Kenny went to the diner for supper. I made BLTs for you and me."

"What about Josiah?"

"He wants to stay in the trailer tonight. Couldn't talk him out of it."

"But you're not taking Kenny back."

"Hell no." Michael pushed Dad into the kitchen so they could eat at the table for a change. Rosco stuck close the whole time, practically attached to Michael's hip. Once Dad was settled with a drink, Michael assembled his sandwich, added some pretzels, and served him. Toasted his own bread and made his dinner. He sneaked a tiny piece of bacon to Rosco.

The sandwich helped fill the weird pit in his stomach, and Michael contemplated making a second.

"So if your dog is here, I assume Kenny's coming back?" Dad asked.

"Yes." Michael snapped a pretzel in half. "I told him he could sleep in your room upstairs for one night. That's it." He summarized his conversation with Kenny.

"Figures he crawled back to you. Men like that are parasites. Take what they want regardless of how it hurts the other person. You were right to put your foot down and set him straight."

"Thanks. I just hate that I hurt Josiah's feelings without meaning to. But I don't want to go knock on his door and force myself on him when he clearly wants some distance." And it sucked even more after the amazing twenty-four hours they'd had together leading up to now. "I'll make it up to him somehow."

"I know you will. He's a good boy."

"He's amazing. He's everything Kenny wasn't and still isn't. And even if I hadn't met and fallen for Josiah, I still wouldn't have taken Kenny back. To borrow a tired cliché, he made his bed, and that bed can fucking eat him like Johnny Depp in *A Nightmare on Elm Street*."

Dad laughed. "Good to hear it. Figured as much, but I like hearing you say it, son. Granted, I didn't hear about all the crap that Kenny pulled on you until after the fact, but you are a good man. Dunno how much of that is my doing, your mom's doing, or your own doing, but I'm proud of you. Really proud."

Something burned behind Michael's eyes. "Thank you, Dad."

"You earned it. My only real regret is I didn't get to tell you sooner."

Michael opened his mouth to say something, but the sound of a car engine starting snared his attention. He looked toward the living room, as if he could see right through the wall and into the yard. No way Kenny was back. It hadn't been long enough and the car engine sound was moving away. Rosco loped toward the front door with a soft yip but didn't go crazy barking like he might have if someone was walking onto the porch.

Josiah.

He stood so fast his chair nearly went over backward. Michael ran to the front door and yanked it open. Taillights on the road disappeared fast, and an empty space stood where Josiah's car had been parked.

"What the hell?" He barely felt the cold air dancing around his ankles or the way Rosco's big head nudged at his thigh. Josiah had just driven away at suppertime on a Sunday night, the same night Michael's ex showed up begging for money. Josiah didn't know about the money part, though—he couldn't. And running away wasn't Josiah's style.

Michael yanked his cell out of his pocket and typed off a fast text:

Are you okay? Where are you going?

When ten solid minutes passed without a response, Michael allowed himself to panic.

Chapter Twenty-Two

From the moment Michael fell to his knees and embraced Rosco in the dirt, Josiah had felt a keen sense of loss. Michael obviously loved that dog. But inviting Kenny inside to talk had hurt in a way Josiah hadn't been able to voice, so he'd chosen flight over fight. He'd removed himself from the situation, hidden in the trailer alone, and lied about eating. He did have two frozen burritos in the minifridge that hadn't been engulfed by the ice monster, but his stomach was too tight to allow food inside.

Watching Kenny drive away without Rosco had given him the tiniest flash of hope—until Michael called and said Kenny was staying the night. Josiah had wanted to say no, that wasn't cool. If Kenny was staying anywhere it should be in the trailer. But Michael and Kenny had talked for a while, and while Josiah felt bad that Kenny was broke, Weston had a motel. The selfish part of Josiah didn't want Kenny anywhere near Michael overnight.

The part of Josiah that loved Michael and wanted him happy couldn't deny Michael one more night with his dog. The trade-off was worth it. Keeping his distance was the only thing that would let Josiah sleep tonight. He trusted Michael not to cheat, but part of Josiah still worried that with two big reminders of his previous life in Austin right here, Michael's heart and mind might start craving a life beyond Weston.

The life he used to have as a rich programmer who threw big parties and lived in a house with a pool. Josiah had needed to stay here alone with his big mood so he didn't say or do something to ruin this precious life he was creating with Michael.

Then his cell rang a second time with Seamus's ringtone. Josiah had stared at the phone's screen for a long time while leaning against the slim wall between the kitchen's seating area and the bathroom's folding door. Long enough he nearly let it go to voice mail, because he had nothing to say to Seamus. Nothing at all. But what if this was about Josiah's assault? So he'd answered with a terse, "Hello?"

"Jo-jo? Thank God you answered." Seamus's normally flat voice was, well, strained. Almost fragile and that put Josiah on instant alert.

"What's wrong? You sound weird."

"I, um, hate to call you for this, but they won't let me drive myself home, so I need a ride."

"Drive home from where? Are you drunk?"

"No, not drunk. I'm at the hospital."

Josiah's entire body jerked to attention, and he nearly dropped his phone. "The hospital? Why? Are you sick? Were you in an accident?" He hated the way he snapped to instant alert and wanted to know what was wrong with Seamus. Seamus was a selfish asshole who'd taken his bad moods out on Josiah for far too long, but he was also a human being. The part of Josiah who'd become a nurse so he could help people and families rebelled at anyone in pain, no matter the reason.

"I'm okay now," Seamus said. "Bumps, bruises, a few stitches. It's just, I hit my head so they won't let me drive myself home."

"Drive home…did you drive yourself to the ER? What happened to you?"

"I'll explain it later. I just really want to go home, and I can't call anyone I work with. I can't do that. Please, Josiah. Please, take me home."

"Okay." Josiah agreed before he could talk himself out of it. Seamus was in the middle of a crisis, and Josiah couldn't turn his back on the man, no matter how many times Seamus had hurt him in the past. He wasn't that person.

So Josiah left. He knew exactly which roads to take to the county hospital and he found a spot to park. His phone beeped twice with texts he ignored, his adrenaline already on overload, no idea what he might find when he walked into the ER. What he did not expect to find was Seamus in a waiting room chair with a bandage on his forehead, his left arm in a sling, and dressed in scrubs instead of his own clothes.

Seamus flashed him a familiar glare that cut off all of Josiah's questions. After signing whatever he needed to sign, Seamus limped his way out of the hospital and into the passenger front seat of Josiah's car—a very odd place for him to be, because Seamus had driven them everywhere when they'd "been together."

Neither of them spoke for the entire drive back to Seamus's house, but it wasn't the tense silences Josiah was used to. Seamus seemed unwilling to speak, and the fact that Josiah was waiting of his own accord gave

Josiah a tiny bit of power. Power he planned on using to his advantage so he could get some answers out of Seamus tonight.

Instead of going straight back to Seamus's place, Josiah pulled onto the shoulder about half a mile away and put the gear into Park. "What happened tonight?"

Seamus glared at him. "Take me home, Jo-jo."

Two months ago Josiah might have backed down out of sheer fright. Tonight, he grabbed hold of all his inner strength and stubbornness and held his ground. "Not until you tell me what happened to you."

"Fine." Seamus yanked the door open and got out, probably with the intent to walk the rest of the way to his house. Five steps along the shoulder, though, he stumbled and went to his knees with a pained shout.

"Damn it." Josiah scrambled to Seamus's side, concerned by how pale he was even in the yellow glow of the headlights. Seamus never showed weakness, so something was hugely wrong here. "Get back in the car, you stubborn ass."

"You giving me orders now, sweetheart?"

"Fuck, yes, I am. Come on." For as much as he disliked touching Seamus again, Josiah helped him stand and limp back to the car. He didn't have blood on his slacks or any obvious signs of a bandage, so Josiah's best guess was Seamus's ribs. Josiah had dealt with bruised ribs once, and they could make something as simple as breathing hurt like hell.

He got Seamus reinstalled in the passenger seat, barely feeling the cold air biting his cheeks. He still cranked the heat up on the short drive to Seamus's. Helped Seamus out and into the small house that had been home for two long years. Seamus sank into his recliner and let out a long, frustrated groan.

Unsure what to do, Josiah went into the kitchen and poured Seamus two fingers of whiskey. He nearly poured a glass for himself but wanted to keep as clear a head as possible right now. Seamus took the old-fashioned glass from him but didn't drink it. He stared at the brown liquid like it held the secrets of the universe. The living room was kind of a mess, with a broken picture on the floor, the shade knocked off a sideways lamp, and just a general look of disarray.

"You need to tell me what happened today," Josiah said. "Or I will call 911 and report an assault."

"I haven't laid a finger on you."

"I mean you, you dumbass. You didn't do this to yourself. Who did?"

When Seamus realized his cold glare wasn't going to make Josiah back down, his big body wilted deeper into the recliner. "Dale hit me with his car."

Josiah nearly smacked himself on the side of the head to dislodge whatever was in his ears, because no way had Seamus just said that. "Who's Dale and why would he hit you with his car? And if someone hit you with a car, why didn't you call 911 and report it? Did you hit your head that hard?"

"Dale is…he's the guy I was with before I moved here. He's *why* I moved here. To get away from him."

His memory flashed back to the Founder's Day Picnic and the black-haired guy who'd been with Seamus and glared at Josiah like Josiah had insulted him somehow. "How long has he been here?"

"Since the day I kicked you out. He demanded it so I did it." A tiny hint of fear flashed in Seamus's eyes.

"He said he'd hurt you if I didn't. You were safer away from me. I'm sorry things went down like that, and I'm sorry for the way I treated you sometimes. I have no moral leg to stand on here. They say that karma's a bitch, and man did she whale on me tonight."

"Dale abused you."

Seamus only nodded, shame flushing his bruised face.

Anger blossomed deep inside Josiah. "If you know what it's like to be abused, then why did you do what you did to me? The shoves, the slaps, the rough sex? Were you trying to punish him by punishing me?"

"I don't know, and that's the God's honest truth. I did like you, Jo-jo. A lot. Probably too much. Maybe I'm one of those men who doesn't have better angels on his shoulder. Maybe I just got the devil in me, and I'll never be any good to anyone. For what it's worth, which probably isn't much, I am truly sorry for everything I did to you. You never deserved any of it. I wish I could do something to make it right."

A single tear slid down Seamus's cheek, and it spoke to his sincerity with the apology. In all the time Josiah had known him, for the few times Seamus had ever apologized in the past for being too cruel, the man had never cried. Not once. It was almost more than Josiah could stand, watching a previously in-charge sheriff dissolve right in front of him, leaving behind a shivering shell of a man.

"I accept your apology," Josiah said. "You and I will never be friends, but we also don't have to keep living as enemies."

"Thank you."

"Okay, so why did Dale hit you with his car, and

why didn't you call the police on him? That's, like, attempted murder of a law officer, isn't it?"

"We got into a big fight. Don't even remember about what, just that we ended up shouting at each other. I was miserable with him, I missed you, and I just lost it. Told him to get the fuck out and stay out of my life, or I'd find a way to lock him up even if it meant planting evidence. It was an empty threat, but he believed me. I said I was taking a walk, and if he wasn't packed up and gone when I got back, he'd be sorry."

"So he ran you down?"

"Yep. I barely made it to the end of the driveway when I heard his car engine gunning. I figured he was leaving, so I kept walking. Then I woke up in the ditch and hurt all over. Was barely able to drive myself to the hospital."

"What did you tell them happened?"

"Said I crashed my motorcycle."

"You don't own a motorcycle."

"They didn't know that."

Josiah snorted and sat on the edge of the couch. "I still don't understand why you didn't report it. Why are you protecting him? How do you know he won't come back one night and kill you?" Then it hit him so hard Josiah's whole body swayed and his vision nearly blacked out. "Holy shit. He's the guy who attacked me in the barn. He had my shirt because he found it here."

"Yeah. I didn't know for sure at the time, because you didn't tell me about the shirt that night. I found it under our—my—bed covered in dirt a few days later. When I confronted Dale, he said he didn't like the way you'd looked at him at the picnic. Said he'd wanted to scare you into staying away from me."

"Fuck, Seamus, you should have told me. You should have fucking arrested him!"

"I know. But he said if I did that, he'd kill you. I kept my mouth shut to keep you safe."

"Am I supposed to thank you for that? I haven't felt safe in weeks."

"I'm sorry."

"Fuck, you're sorry. You need to report all of this. Dale needs to be arrested and charged for assaulting me then, and for assaulting you tonight. He should be in jail where he can't hurt anyone again."

"I can't. I'll lose everything."

"Because people will find out the county sheriff has been fucking around with men? Your pride is more important than the safety of the public? Because this guy sounds like a menace, and he will hurt someone else. You know he will, Seamus. You're not an idiot. Didn't you make some sort of solemn promise to protect the citizens when you pinned on that badge? You owe it to the people who voted for you because they believed you'd protect them. So do it. Because if you don't level up and make that call, I will."

Seamus let out a long, low growly noise that, in the past, would have made Josiah quail with fear and the anticipation of retaliation for whatever wrong thing he'd done. Tonight, Josiah stood and palmed his cell phone, squared his shoulders, and held Seamus's gaze. He didn't back down, not about this. Not ever again.

"I've got no proof it was Dale who hit me," Seamus said. "I didn't actually see his vehicle."

"Well, you weigh at least two-twenty, so unless Dale knows a miracle body mechanic who's open late on Sunday, there's going to be proof on his car. Dents for

sure, if not blood or hair. The longer you wait, the farther away he's going to get."

"When did you become a cop?"

"From bingeing true crime documentaries while
you were at work. Make the call."

Seamus stared at him for a moment more, obviously
at war with himself, before pulling out his phone. He
even showed Josiah the screen so he saw Seamus had
typed in 911, then hit the call button. Put the phone to
his ear. "Yeah, this is Sheriff Seamus McBride. I need
to report a hit-and-run."

Josiah stood and walked to the front window, content that Seamus was doing this. He half listened as
Seamus gave them the address and answered a few
other questions, and checked his own phone. Two texts
from Michael, both asking where he was and if he was
all right, and to please call him. He stepped outside and
called Michael back.

"Hey, are you okay?" Michael asked, his voice
slightly panicked. "Where did you go?"

On a regular day, Josiah might have been annoyed
at Michael questioning his choice to go out by himself, but today was far from regular. "Seamus called.
He needed a ride home from the hospital."

"He what? Why the hell did he call you?"

"It's a long story that I promise I will tell you all
about later. I'm going to stay with him until the authorities get here, and then I'll come home."

"Are you sure you're safe with him? I can come
wherever you are."

"I'm safe. He's not a threat to me anymore."

"Okay. I trust you. You trust me, too, right?"

"Of course."

"Okay, because I am not getting back with Kenny under any circumstances. Him staying the night is for convenience, and so I can be with Rosco for a little while. He is not staying here with me, even if he decides not to leave town right away."

His heart warmed with the declarations. Even though he loved Michael and believed Michael loved him back, a tiny part of Josiah had worried Michael would be taken in by his ex's woes and the temptation of his beloved dog. Everything Michael just said buried those small fears beneath trust and hope.

"I believe you. I'll text you when I'm on my way home. Hopefully it won't be long."

"I'll be here with hot cocoa at the ready."

"Perfect." Josiah kind of wanted to end the call with "I love you" but over the phone wasn't the way he wanted to say it for the first time. It could wait a bit longer. "See you soon."

"Yeah."

Josiah went back inside to wait for what he hoped would be state police. While they were still within the county, the sheriff couldn't really investigate his own assault. And when the cops learned about Dale assaulting Josiah, that investigation would likely be handed over, too. Best guesses, anyway, since he really didn't know how all that stuff worked. He was simply grateful to know his bogeyman had a name and would, he hoped, be behind bars soon.

He was more than ready for this nightmare to end and his life with Michael to truly, fully begin.

Michael wanted to scream, weep, and rage all at once while Josiah filled him in on everything over two mugs of steaming cocoa, which they drank at the trailer's table for privacy. Rosco napped at Michael's feet, oblivious to the emotional goings-on above, as content to be with Michael as Michael was to have him close by. Even if only for a little while.

He only had a few scraps of sympathy for Seamus McBride and his unfortunate past with this Dale guy. No one deserved to be abused, but instead of saying "I won't carry on this legacy of anger and physical retaliation," McBride had turned around and done the same thing to Josiah. He'd known who hurt Josiah for weeks and said nothing, until finally doing the right thing and telling someone.

Too bad it had taken being creamed by a car for McBride to see the light.

"I hope he doesn't expect us to be friends with him now," Michael said.

"No, he doesn't. I told him as much earlier. That we'd never be friends. But we don't have to be enemies anymore. I want to move forward, not stay stuck in the past."

"Me, too." He glanced down at Rosco. "Been thinking on that a bit tonight, actually. A way to unload more of my own past while getting something I really want out of it."

"Oh? Do I get a hint?"

"I want to run the offer by Kenny first, in the morning."

"Well, now I'm intrigued. Does this mean you're not going back to Austin?"

"Yes. There's nothing back there that I want or need. Everything I need to make me happy is on this land.

The most important person in that happiness is right here in the room with me."

"Rosco?"

"Dork." Michael chuckled as he reached for Josiah's hand and squeezed. "You. I love you, Josiah Sheridan, and I want us to keep building a life together. Here. With all its ups and downs. I may not be a rich man anymore, but you have my heart and that's the most expensive gift I can give. Please be gentle with it."

"I will." Josiah's voice cracked and his eyes gleamed. "I love you, too, Michael. And I want that life with you. Our life, with all the ups and downs that come with it."

"Good answer." They both leaned in and sealed the promise with a long, sensual kiss that left Michael a bit breathless.

Josiah rose, snared his wrist, and tugged Michael down the short length of the trailer to the bedroom. After making quick work of their clothes, they spent the rest of the night existing together and exploring each other until the first smudges of dawn's light peeked through the drawn blinds.

Michael lay naked with Josiah in his arms, stupidly happy after such a dramatic evening on all fronts, and basked in this beautiful thing he and Josiah had found with each other. Love, peace, and acceptance. Joy and friendship. A real relationship based on trust, understanding, and hope.

And he couldn't wait to see what tomorrow brought.

Epilogue

Josiah let out a loud groan of contentment and slight discomfort as he sank down onto the living room couch, his stomach almost too full of amazing food. He'd gotten up before dawn to get their massive twenty-pound turkey into the oven so it would be cooked in time for a midday Thanksgiving meal. Elmer had been instrumental in a lot of the prep work, like chopping vegetables for the dressing and various sides.

And Michael?

He'd amused the hell out of them both by parading around the kitchen in holiday pajamas and a Santa hat, basting the turkey whenever Josiah asked and mostly sneaking food from platters or bowls. Josiah loved the festive atmosphere in the house, and they'd even discussed bringing the fake tree down from the attic today and maybe decorating tomorrow. The chilly weather was here to stay, and Josiah looked forward to truly celebrating the season for the first time in a long, long time.

Dinner had been amazing, the turkey perfectly roasted. Michael had insisted on making brussels sprouts with bacon, and while Josiah had been dubious at first, he admitted to liking the final dish. They ended up with enough to feed at least ten people, so they'd be eating leftovers for a quite a while.

Jackson popped over for about thirty minutes to chat with Michael and go home with a plate of food for him and Dog. Dog got along great with Rosco, who was a happy new addition to their little family.

Kenny hadn't left Weston until Tuesday morning, because of the handful of legal things he and Michael needed to deal with first, but Michael had been beside himself with joy at the results of their long conversation. In exchange for giving Michael full, permanent ownership of Rosco, he and Kenny had come up with an equitable solution to the Austin house. Kenny could live there until it sold, maintain the property in lieu of rent, and then he'd get a portion of the final sale to start over with. The rest of the money Michael hoped to invest in repairing the Weston farmhouse, as well as preparing for possible future freelance IT work. Josiah had been initially leery of giving Kenny any money, but Michael assured him this was the best solution to keep Kenny out of their lives in the long term.

Plus, Michael glowed with love every time he petted Rosco, and Josiah was getting used to the dog warming their feet at the foot of the bed every night. Josiah had officially moved into the house, leaving the trailer without a tenant, but also leaving him and Michael incredibly happy with the new arrangement.

Josiah was also no longer Elmer's official caregiver. Elmer still couldn't manage the stairs and might always need a walker, but he was slowly gaining some independence from the wheelchair. Josiah had plans to submit a few applications next week to some local services who matched patients with caregivers. Time to start the next leg of his journey.

Michael flopped onto the couch next to him, the motion making Josiah's overly full stomach slosh unhappily. Rosco waited for the signal, then hopped up beside him on the free cushion to pout. Despite all the amazing food smells, Michael had limited him to only a few bites of turkey breast and mashed potatoes so they didn't upset his sensitive tummy.

No one in the house was much for football, so they found a good lineup of Christmas movies to stream and started with those, Josiah and Michael snuggled up on the couch, and Dad on the love seat, all of them sipping sparkling cider.

Best. Thanksgiving. Ever.

None of the drama that had happened this week could take the shine off Josiah's good mood today. Kenny was gone and, once the house sold, out of their lives for good. Dale Burns had been detained at the Texas-Oklahoma border and was sitting pretty in jail because he couldn't afford bail. Josiah had given his statements to the state police detectives investigating the case, both about his interactions with Seamus on Sunday, and Josiah's own attack in the barn.

Seamus had resigned as county sheriff, and while he hadn't moved out of town, he seemed to be keeping a very low profile. Josiah didn't exactly wish him all the best in the future, but he did hope the man found something that made him happy.

"Is it weird," Michael started to ask, "that no matter how many times I've seen this movie, I still want to yell out 'don't lick the frozen flagpole, Flick!'?"

Josiah laughed. "Not weird. It's probably an annual tradition we should keep alive. *A Christmas Story* followed by the shout of 'Don't lick the flagpole!' Maybe we should get T-shirts made for next year."

"Definitely." Michael wiggled his eyebrows in a suggestive way, and Josiah caught the double-entendre in the flagpole remark. "Maybe Santa will put them in our stockings this year."

"You are such a dork."

"Yes, I know. I also really love Christmas, so expect a lot of exterior lights to brighten up Dad's crazy sculpture hoard, plus all kinds of midcentury modern ornaments and decor. I swear, that attic is full of every decoration Mom ever bought."

"Never could manage to get rid of that stuff," Elmer said. "For a long while, I couldn't part with anything of hers. The idea hurt too much. Now I look at all those metallic ornaments and crazy-faced plastic Santas and I smile at them." He looked right at Michael. "I think of your momma and I smile."

"I smile, too," Michael replied. "I'm really glad we both smile again."

"Me too, son."

Josiah rested his head on Michael's shoulder, overjoyed that the pair had bridged the huge emotional gap that had been between them when Michael first came back to Weston. Michael still wasn't entirely sure about his future, but was going to continue working at Woods Ranch while he figured things out. Between the three of them, they could pay the bills and put food on the table, and they didn't need much more than that—because they loved each other.

And love, Josiah decided as he placed his hand over Michael's steadily beating heart, was the best reason in the world to smile.

* * * * *

Acknowledgments

All my thanks to the folks who read, loved and reviewed my Clean Slate Ranch series and made Woods Ranch a possibility. I have had so much fun creating the world of Woods Ranch and playing with characters both familiar and brand-new. Much love to my editor Alissa for all of your hard work, suggestions, and support in bringing this new series to life, as well as through all the recent tough times. Pet pictures are often the best medicine. Thanks to Carina Press for all you do and for continuing to bring my words to others.

About the Author

A.M. Arthur was born and raised in the same kind of small town that she likes to write about, a stone's throw from both beach resorts and generational farmland. She's been creating stories in her head since she was a child and scribbling them down nearly as long, in a losing battle to make the fictional voices stop. She credits an early fascination with male friendships (bromance hadn't been coined yet back then) with her later discovery of and subsequent love affair with m/m romance stories. A.M. Arthur's work is available from Carina Press, SMP Swerve, and Briggs-King Books. When not exorcising the voices in her head, she can be found in her kitchen, pretending she's an amateur chef and trying to not poison herself or others with her cuisine experiments. Contact her at am_arthur@yahoo.com with your cooking tips (or book comments).

Facebook Author Page:
https://www.facebook.com/A.M.Arthur.M.A

Facebook Reader Group:
https://www.facebook.com/groups/300209733646247/

Twitter: http://twitter.com/am_arthur

Newsletter:
https://vr2.verticalresponse.com/s/signupformynewsletter16492674416904

Website: https://amarthur.blogspot.com/

Hugo Turner's boots haven't touched Texas soil in almost a decade, and he's not sure they should now. Being in the state is complicated, but Hugo can't resist going back for a job working with his teenage crush. His best friend's hot older brother is now the ranch's foreman, so he'll be Hugo's boss. Inappropriate? Probably. Will it stop Hugo? Probably not.

Keep reading for an excerpt from
His Fresh Start Cowboy
by A.M. Arthur.

Chapter One

"That really sucks, man, I'm sorry to hear that."

Hugo Turner had just sat down at the long kitchen table with his dinner when that particular comment rose from the din of general conversation in the room. He'd chosen a spot in the middle so he could chat with his fellow Clean Slate Ranch horsemen, but now he looked up from his plate of meat loaf and mashed potatoes. The statement had come from Ernie and been said to Colt, both men older and more experienced than Hugo in, well, pretty much everything.

Except horses. Hugo had been around horses most of his life, and he loved working with them every day here at the ranch.

"What sucks?" Hugo asked, unable to help himself. He was the youngest horseman on the ranch, despite having just turned twenty-seven, and sometimes he struggled to really connect with his coworkers. Showing genuine interest in their lives was always a great in, right?

Colt sighed and poked at his own meat loaf. He was a handyman on the dude ranch/vacation spot, rather than a horseman. "Talked to my parents this afternoon. My father's having trouble getting new hands, and Brand is worried that their shift to organic, grass-fed beef is going to fail because they don't have enough people to run the operation."

"Oh, wow, that sucks." While Hugo had left the cattle ranching life a long time ago, he'd grown up on a ranch that failed when Hugo was ten. During his parents' messy divorce, they'd sold the last of their herd and some equipment to Wayne Woods. Small- and medium-sized ranchers were suffering all over the country because of corporate operations, and he was honestly impressed Woods Cattle Ranch was still in business. Especially with the neighboring towns of Weston and Daisy offering few prospects for new families moving to the area.

Families like the one Hugo hadn't gone home to see in years; friends he hadn't seen in years; teenage crushes he hadn't seen in years, except from a careful distance. When the entire Woods family came up to the ranch for Colt's wedding two years ago, avoiding them had turned into an art form for Hugo, helped along by his cowboy hat and allowing a bit of a beard to grow out. A beard he'd shaved off the day they left. He simply hadn't wanted to mix his new life up with his past in Texas. A past Colt didn't know about yet.

"Yeah," Colt said. "Dad and Brand are putting their heads together, but it's not an easy lifestyle, especially if you aren't born into it."

"I know." Off Colt's curious eyebrow quirk, Hugo scrambled to correct his comment. "I mean, I can imagine. I've, ah, heard stories."

After being hired at Clean Slate two and a half years ago, it had taken Hugo a few days to realize Colt Woods was the older brother of his high school best friend,

Remington "Rem" Woods. Colt had run away from home at eighteen, years before Rem and Hugo became friends, so Hugo hadn't had any clear memories of him. And when Hugo realized he and Colt had grown up in neighboring towns, he'd kept it to himself, not wanting to trot down that particular stretch of memory lane.

He'd left Texas for a reason, damn it.

"Your family thinking of selling out?" Ernie asked, then shoveled a fork of steamed green beans into his mouth.

"I hope not but it's a possibility," Colt replied. "Our family has worked that land for generations, and I'd hate to see them sell. It's why Brand is making some changes to their operations, hoping to hang on a while longer. Seems to be having good luck with the wind farm in the south pasture, but he's banking on the organic beef."

"It's a big thing in the larger cities. Not that I can taste the difference. A steak is a steak to me."

Several other guys at the table who were listening "hear, hear-ed" the comment. Hugo smiled and ate his food. This was very much a beef-consuming lot of horsemen, as were their weekly groups of guests. Every Sunday night, they held a welcome barbecue, and most dinners (for hands and guests) featured some sort of red meat.

As he ate, Hugo's mind whirred with all kinds of thoughts about the small Texas county he'd abandoned years ago, heading out on his own to seek…something. A different path, something that excited him more than a part-time job at the local grocery store. And that took him away from the humiliation that had been his first attempted kiss with another boy.

Far, far away from the walking wet dream that had been Brand Woods.

Hugo wasn't ashamed to admit—to himself but not out loud—that after realizing who Colt was, he'd done a social media search on Brand. Hugo had once fallen head over heels for Brand, a tall, well-built blond who was eight years older than him and about to leave for college the first time they'd met. The latest pictures of Brand showed him to be a near carbon copy of Colt, but while Hugo could admire Colt's aesthetic, he didn't excite Hugo the way Brand always had.

Only Brand had ever made Hugo want to roll over and beg. And only Brand had ever broken Hugo's heart.

He finished his dinner in a slight daze, born of old memories and hurts, and he put his plate and glass in the bus bin by rote. Headed out into the dark, late winter night on a familiar trek back to his cabin. Most of the hands lived in small, two-man cabins behind the ranch's main house, and a well-trodden path led him forward. Hugo's roommate, Winston, wasn't there, which was fine, because he wasn't in a chatty mood for a change. His first roommate, Slater, had been quiet to the extreme, avoiding all of Hugo's attempts at communication and friendship for months. But Slater had moved on from Clean Slate, and Winston had been his replacement, both as a horseman on the ranch and Hugo's roomie.

Normally, he adored Winston's ability to chat about anything. Tonight, he was grateful for the chance to sit on his bunk and think. Think about the people he missed and the potential next stop on his wanderlust journey to find what his heart truly desired. Because as much as he enjoyed his work here with the horses and guests, this wasn't his final destination. It was a way station on the path to where he was meant to be.

What if I'm meant to be back home?

It wasn't the first time in the last few years that he'd wondered such a thing. He loved discovering the States and learning new things, but so much of his heart was at home in Daisy, Texas, a one-stoplight town ten miles from Weston. He missed his mom and her comforting, if infrequent, hugs. Leaving her behind was one of his biggest regrets. They didn't speak often, but when they did she sounded happy. Seemed happy that he was far, far away from what had happened with Buck.

But Buck was cooling his heels in state prison for felony assault charges. His temper had finally gotten the better of him and landed him in a locked cage where he belonged. Hugo had contemplated going home this past Christmas, because he knew he'd be safe, but in the end had remained here as part of the ranch's skeleton crew.

He'd stayed away for years, and now he was actually contemplating going back to work and live there. He could catch up with Rem again. Hug his mother. Maybe give Woods Ranch the boost it sounded like it needed. Hugo knew ranching, and he was great on a horse. Maybe he could do something bigger than oversee camping trips and teaching city folk how to ride a horse.

Hugo had his phone out before he really thought about it, and he found the website for Woods Ranch. The background image was a picture of Brand, Rem and their father, all posing next to an impressively large steer. He studied Brand's face, still able to feel the pressure of Brand's lips on his the first and only time they'd kissed. Brand was still gorgeous after all these years—and according to Colt, single and seemingly uninterested in dating.

No, he couldn't let himself think too hard about that. He found the *Join Our Family* link and uploaded his résumé before he could stop himself. Brand would probably see his name and delete it, but Hugo had done it. No going back now. And it wasn't as if he had to accept the job on the off chance one was even offered.

Nah, he'd done it as a lark. He had friends here at Clean Slate—sort of, since the guys closest to his age all worked at the neighboring ghost town attraction—and a life he liked. Going back to Texas was idiotic.

Except the next day, Hugo checked his cell phone at lunchtime and found a message from Wayne Woods requesting a phone interview. Not from Brand but from his father. Hugo returned the man's call. Wayne actually remembered him as one of Rem's best friends in high school, and when Hugo talked about working with Colt and his own duties at the ranch, Wayne offered him a job on the spot. As soon as he could give notice and move back to Texas. Wayne even had a lead on a trailer Hugo could rent that neighbored the Woods property.

The entire thing happened so fast Hugo spent the rest of his lunch hour staring at the side of the guesthouse, unable to form a proper thought. His cheeks were half-frozen from the February chill but he didn't care. Had he really just accepted a job back in his home state? Had he committed to leaving a job he enjoyed and coworkers he liked for grueling long days under the hot Texas sun?

Would he really be around Brand again?

He was still staring blankly at the guesthouse wall when Colt approached, his brow creased. "Hey, dude, uh, can I ask you something?"

Hugo saw it coming but still nodded. "Sure."

"Were you ever gonna tell me you knew Rem? And me?"

Heat crept across Hugo's neck and cheeks, and he turned to face the older, taller man. "I never really saw the point in mentioning the past. I mean, we didn't really know each other at all. I did know Rem, though. And Brand and your sisters. But all that happened after you left."

Colt frowned at him while his left thumb twirled the gold band on his wedding finger. He'd married the love of his life not quite two years ago, and the pair somehow managed to make a long-distance relationship work, with Colt living here and his husband living an hour away in San Francisco. "You still could have said something when you realized who I was. Can't say as I remember a family named Turner from back then, though."

"Turner is my mom's maiden name. When my parents divorced, we both took it back, and even after she remarried, I kept it. Never did like my stepfather's name. Plus, we lived in Daisy."

"I vaguely recall my father buying cattle from a failing ranch in Daisy not long before I left. Was that you?"

"Yeah. Well, my parents. My mother inherited the ranch, but they went through a bad patch of hoof rot. Didn't treat it right. Money went south and so did their relationship. Everything got divvied up in the divorce."

"Sorry to hear that. It's a big kick in the head that we both ended up here, though, huh? What are the odds?"

"Pretty slim. But I've heard some of the other guys say there's something magical about Clean Slate. It brings people here when they're meant to be, for whatever reason. I, uh…" Hugo took a deep breath, held it, then released. "I applied to work at your family's ranch. Your father offered me a job."

Colt's eyes went comically wide. "You're shitting me. Really? I mean, he called me this morning and mentioned he'd gotten an application from a guy named Hugo Turner who worked here, and he asked me for a personal reference on your working habits. But he didn't mention he'd offered you the job."

"That's because it just happened. I honestly didn't expect anything to come out of it. I love it here. Arthur and Judson have been great, and I've learned a lot since I've worked here, but now I feel as if I have unfinished business back in Texas." No way was he going to admit part of that business included a never-ending crush on one of Colt's younger brothers. "I didn't leave on good terms with a lot of people. I kind of want to fix that."

"You don't have to leave the ranch to fix old hurts. When's your next week off?"

Hugo shook his head. All the hands got a week's vacation on a rotating basis throughout the year, but he'd never used his to go home. He rarely went much of anywhere, because everything he needed was at the ranch. Or so he'd thought. "I like this job a lot, Colt, but this isn't the end of the road for me. I'm only twenty-seven. I've got a lot of miles left to travel, and if those miles take me back home for a bit, I'm okay with that."

More than any other time since he'd left home, Hugo truly was okay with going back. With facing his past and all the ugly parts he'd tried to leave behind.

"Well, I can't say I won't miss you," Colt said. "You always were an easy mark on poker night."

Hugo laughed. Genuine laughter, because he did kind of suck at cards, and because Colt was just teasing him. The big, blond cowboy didn't have a mean bone in his body—much like his younger brother Brand. "You aren't wrong about that. I'll miss poker nights. And I'll miss our group visits in San Francisco to hang out with Slater and Derrick. I'll miss a lot of things, but the more I sit with it, the more this move feels right."

"Then go with your gut, pal. And hey, I'll see you next time Avery and I go home to visit my family. I'll bring you all the juiciest gossip."

"I'll hold you to that." Hugo wasn't much of a gossip himself, but he definitely wanted to know what was up with the friends he was leaving behind. "I guess I should find my courage and go tell Judson I'm resigning. Give him time to hire a replacement."

"I imagine it's easier for Judson to find new hires than it is for my father. Ranching is a bit more complicated than leading trail rides and camping trips for tourists. You sure you're up for that life?"

"Yes." Hugo stood a bit straighter. "I grew up on a ranch, and my stepfather still works for a local CSA. I got my first paid job there when I was fifteen, so I know hard work. I know cattle and horses. I've got a lot of metaphorical fences that need tending back in Texas, and I know I can't mend them in a week."

I can't mend myself in a week.

"I hear that," Colt said, his familiar, affable smile firmly in place. "I also won't spread your news all over the ranch. Promise."

"Thanks. I'll probably tell Shawn and Miles tonight.

Might as well rip the bandage off, right?" Hugo considered the pair of cooks to be his two best friends on the ranch. They were the closest people to his age, and he'd definitely miss seeing them in person. But the power of smartphones and the internet meant they could easily keep in touch.

"Yeah, putting it off never seems to accomplish much except hurt feelings." Colt checked his phone. "I gotta get back to work. Some of the south fencing needs repairs, and that'll probably take up the rest of my afternoon."

"I need to get back, too. I'm on this afternoon's trail ride with the guests. Thanks for the chat, Colt, I appreciate it."

"Not a problem. See you around."

Hugo watched Colt amble toward the big red barn to collect whatever tools he'd need for his fence mending, then walked around the back of the guesthouse to face the main house. Arthur Garrett, the owner of the ranch and adjacent horse rescue, lived there with Judson and Patrice, the woman who cooked for their guests and the hands. Judson was likely in his office, and there was no reason to put off giving his two weeks' notice.

He steeled his spine and strode toward the house.

"Good news, son."

Brand Woods looked up from the paperwork on his desk, startled by the sound of his father's voice coming from his office doorway. Usually, the old Woods family home's floors creaked loudly enough that you heard most anyone coming, going, or moving about above your head, but somehow Dad had gotten the drop on him.

Then again, they were close to the end of the month, and Brand was desperately trying to balance the books before sending things off to their accountant for tax season. He hated February with an unbridled passion, but he'd gotten a business degree for a reason and this was it. To help keep Woods Ranch in the black and running. They employed a lot of people in their county, not only as ranch hands, but also the grocery store, and their feed and hay suppliers. Only half of their current head of cattle were free-range, grass-fed, so the other half needed to eat just like the humans who raised them.

While the demand for organic, grass-fed beef had risen dramatically in recent years, the transition was still a gamble for a family who'd done things a certain way for multiple generations. But Brand was determined to make this transition work.

"What's the good news?" Brand asked, desperate for anything to make him smile today.

"I got us a new hire, and he's got experience with horses and cattle." Dad grinned in a weird way. "And he's someone you and Rem know."

"Oh?" Brand couldn't think of a single person in Weston or Daisy who didn't already work for them, or who'd tried and failed to make the cut. "Who?"

"Hugo Turner." Dad sat in the chair opposite Brand's desk. "Remember him? One of Rem's best friends from high school."

An uncomfortable ball of ice dropped into the middle of Brand's stomach, and he worked to keep his face as neutral as possible. He hadn't heard that name spoken out loud in years. His mind flashed with a memory of the jumpy, hyperaware, brown-haired teenager who'd seemed to be there whenever Brand turned around after Brand returned home from college. And flirting every chance he got—which was crazy distracting from someone Brand considered a kid but who was also cute in all the right (and wrong) ways.

He'd put up with it for two years, until the night things went sideways. The night Hugo kissed him and everything Brand thought he believed about himself changed in irreversible ways.

Brand coughed. "I didn't realize Hugo was back in town."

"He's technically not back yet. As fate would have it, he's been working with Colt out at Clean Slate these last few years. Heard through Colt we'd been having trouble finding qualified help, so he applied. When I saw the application, I called Colt for a reference, and it sounds like Hugo will be a good fit for our staff. Plus, he's familiar with the area and practically family."

"That's…wow." What were the odds Hugo would end up working the same dude ranch as Brand's big brother? Astronomical. What were the odds he'd end up working here alongside Brand, who'd spent years trying to hide the guy side of his bisexuality? Even more astronomical. And how on earth had Hugo hidden himself when their family was in California for Colt's wedding? Hugo hadn't said a word to any of them.

"So, um, when's he coming?" Brand asked.

"I don't have a specific date, but if his momma raised him right, he'll give at least two weeks to his current boss. I also gave him Elmer Pearce's number about that trailer he's always looking to rent. Should be a good fit."

Brand bit his tongue. Elmer Pearce was, well, eccentric, to say the least. The man owned several acres of property next to their ranch, and he'd filled the land with… Elmer called it art, but Brand called it mostly junk. He'd accumulated piles of metal, usually from properties that had been torn down in their county and neighboring ones, and while Elmer did make folk art out of some of it, a lot of it just sat in rusty piles. Pickers constantly tried to buy from Elmer, but the man rarely sold anything.

But the property did have a single-wide trailer not too far from Elmer's house, and more than one Woods Ranch employee had rented from Elmer over the last thirty years or so. Elmer always said the extra income gave him money to keep buying more stuff. Brand wasn't keen on continuing to feed the man's semi-hoarder habits, but their ranch needed hands, and Hugo would need a place to live.

"Sounds like it's all worked out, then," Brand said, a little annoyed that he'd been left out of the decision. Despite being named foreman about five years ago, sometimes he still felt like Dad was looking over his shoulder. Not quite trusting Brand to run the ranch as they'd agreed. "Wouldn't have minded a little heads-up about the new hire."

Dad waved a hand in the air. "You've got so much going on right now that I don't want to bother you with every little detail. I may have stepped back a bit but I can handle new hires no problem. You focus on keeping us afloat."

"I'm doing that, sir."

"Good man. Sage and her family are coming over for supper at six. Your mother's making pork chops."

"I'll have this finished up and be at the table on time."

"All right. See you in a few hours, then."

After Dad left the office, Brand leaned back in his chair and let out a long, frustrated breath. He loved his family, this ranch, and his job, but some days he wasn't sure his father completely trusted him to run the business. As if he was always looking over Brand's shoulder, because Brand had been the second son. Not the first choice.

His big brother, Colt, had run away from home when Brand was sixteen, and the job of taking over from their father had defaulted to Brand. At first, Brand had been furious, because he'd wanted to be a teacher, not a cattle rancher. He'd grown up expecting that task to fall to Colt. But Brand had enjoyed getting his business degree, and so far, it had helped keep their small-to-medium-sized cattle operation going in a time when small ranches were going out of business all over the Southwest.

Still, he couldn't help wonder if Dad would have been as hands-on if Colt was the foreman now, instead of Brand. Would Brand always be second best?

Only time would tell.

Brand tried to push those self-doubts out of his head and got back to work.

Don't miss His Fresh Start Cowboy,
available now wherever ebooks are sold.
www.CarinaPress.com